W9-ARJ-081

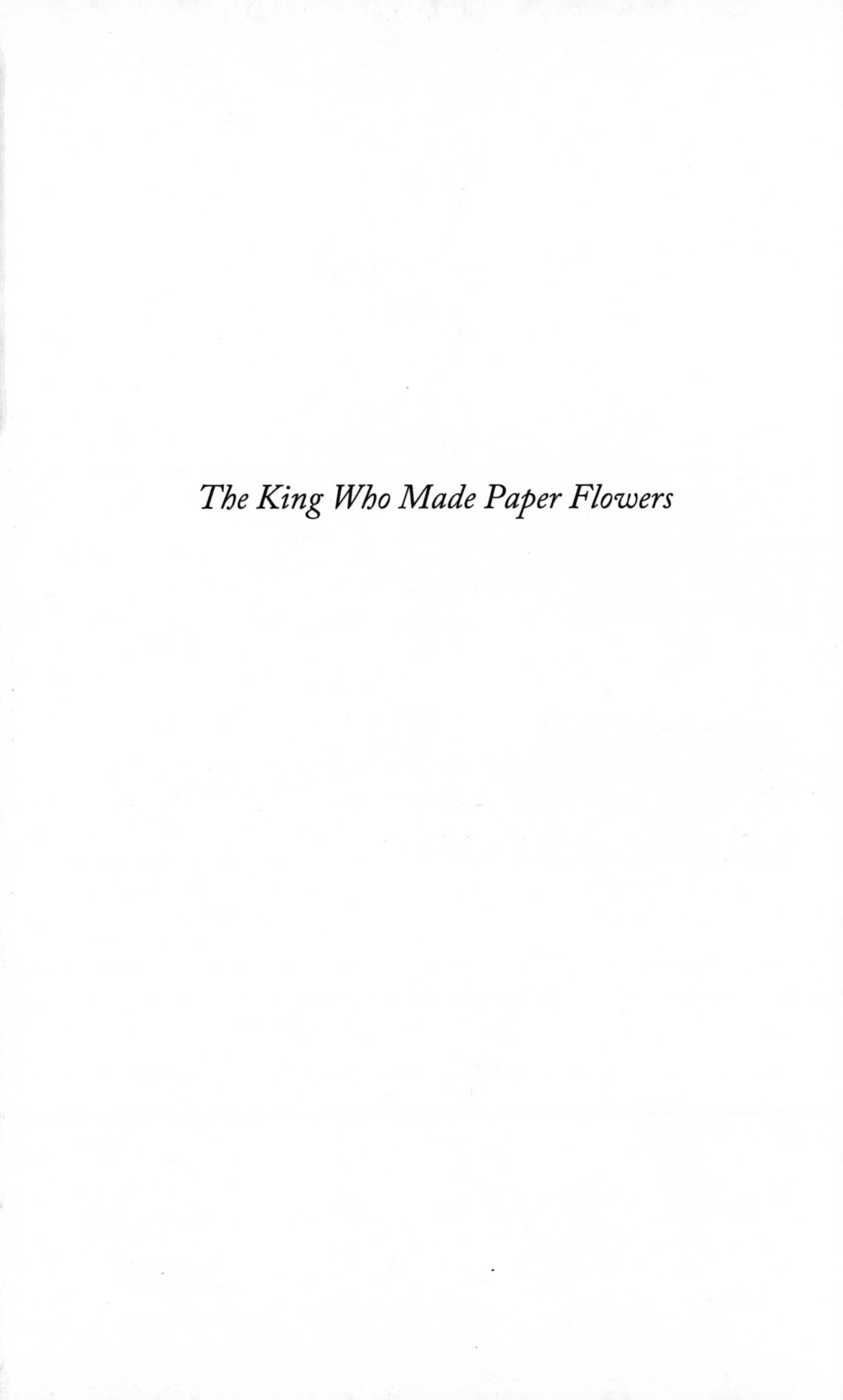

The King Who Made Paper Flowers

ALSO BY TERRY KAY

Song of the Vagabond Bird

The Seventh Mirror

The Greats of Cuttercane

Bogmeadow's Wish

The Book of Marie

The Valley of Light

Taking Lottie Home

Special Kay: The Wisdom of Terry Kay

The Kidnapping of Aaron Greene

The Runaway

Shadow Song

To Whom the Angel Spoke: A Story of the Christmas

To Dance with the White Dog

Dark Thirty

After Eli

The Year the Lights Came On

The King Who Made Paper Flowers

TERRY KAY

MERCER UNIVERSITY PRESS | *Macon, Georgia*
2016

MUP/ H913

Published by Mercer University Press
1501 Mercer University Drive
Macon, Georgia 31207

9 8 7 6 5 4 3 2 1

Books published by Mercer University Press are printed on acid-free paper that meets the requirements of the American National Standard for Information Sciences—Permanence of Paper for Printed Library Materials.

ISBN 978-0-88146-566-2
Cataloging-in-Publication Data is available from the Library of Congress

This Book is Dedicated to
Pat Conroy,
The Gifted and the Giver.
All the words of fiction I have written
Is because of him.

MERCER UNIVERSITY PRESS

Endowed by

TOM WATSON BROWN

and

THE WATSON-BROWN FOUNDATION, INC.

Acknowledgments

For their valuable advice and patience, I am sincerely grateful to attorney Robert (Bob) Brinson, of Rome (GA), and to the Honorable Susan Tate, Judge of the Probate Court for Athens-Clarke County (GA). To both I apologize for tampering with their suggestions regarding legal matters and conduct. It is far easier for a writer of fiction to manipulate than to be absolutely correct.

Appreciation goes also to Karen Thompson, my Savannah guide and a cherished friend from the golden days of journalism.

And to my wise and talented friend, Deidre deLaughter, I am again grateful for her keen eye in both content and line editing. Whatever blunders may be camouflaged among the forest of words (and surely someone will find something) are wholly of my own doing.

Author Notes

In the 1950s, a man named Jose Maria Lopez Lledin wandered the streets of Havana, Cuba. His history – debatable by the kindest of accounts – had him as an addled street person who was affectionately known as *El Cabarrelo de Paris,* or The Gentleman of Paris. He supposedly made quill pens for sale and gave flowers to ladies and offered discourse on topics from politics to poetry, religion to daily events. Occasionally arrested, public protests always freed him, for he was a popular and beloved man. When he died, a great crowd reportedly attended his burial. A bronze statue near the San Francisco Church in colonial Havana commemorates his life. People rub its beard for luck.

In *The King Who Made Paper Flowers,* I have modeled the character of Arthur Benjamin in part after Lledin, but only for his nature of being a charismatic figure who becomes heroic because of his contagious innocence. My Arthur is not addled. He is a man of uncommon understanding, offering wisdom and gifts of paper flowers and courage and the kindness of caring.

There's on-going debate among writers as to which comes first – story or characters. For me, it has always been characters (with one or two deliberate exceptions), because I had rather follow them than stumble along trying to lead them. When I began *The King Who Made Paper Flowers,* I had a suspicion it would be a dark and angry tale, yet, because he was a gentle and patient man, it was not the path Arthur Benjamin wanted to travel. I simply followed him.

This is an Us vs. Them story, a theme that has been addressed a few million times in everything from cave art to two-thumb texting. It's the powerful vs. the powerless, the haves vs. the have-nots. In the playing out of *The King Who Made Paper Flowers,* it's city government vs. a select group of street people having shelter in an abandoned warehouse owned by an eccentric older woman. In a nub, it's about people who care for one another. I believe such people stir our passions and keep us searching for a way to fit usefully into the scheme of things.

Last, it is important to make a declaration: this is fiction. I have not been overly concerned about details of location or history, though I have long been mesmerized by the uniqueness of Savannah. Still, I know very little about the city's political character. Not a sentence in the story has any hidden reference to mayors past and present, nor to any other officials. Residents tell me that Savannah – like all cities – has its seediness, its ugliness, its corruption, yet I have never seen any of it, for I have been there only for the visual pleasure of its setting and for the excitement of its great energy. For me, it is one of the marvels of America.

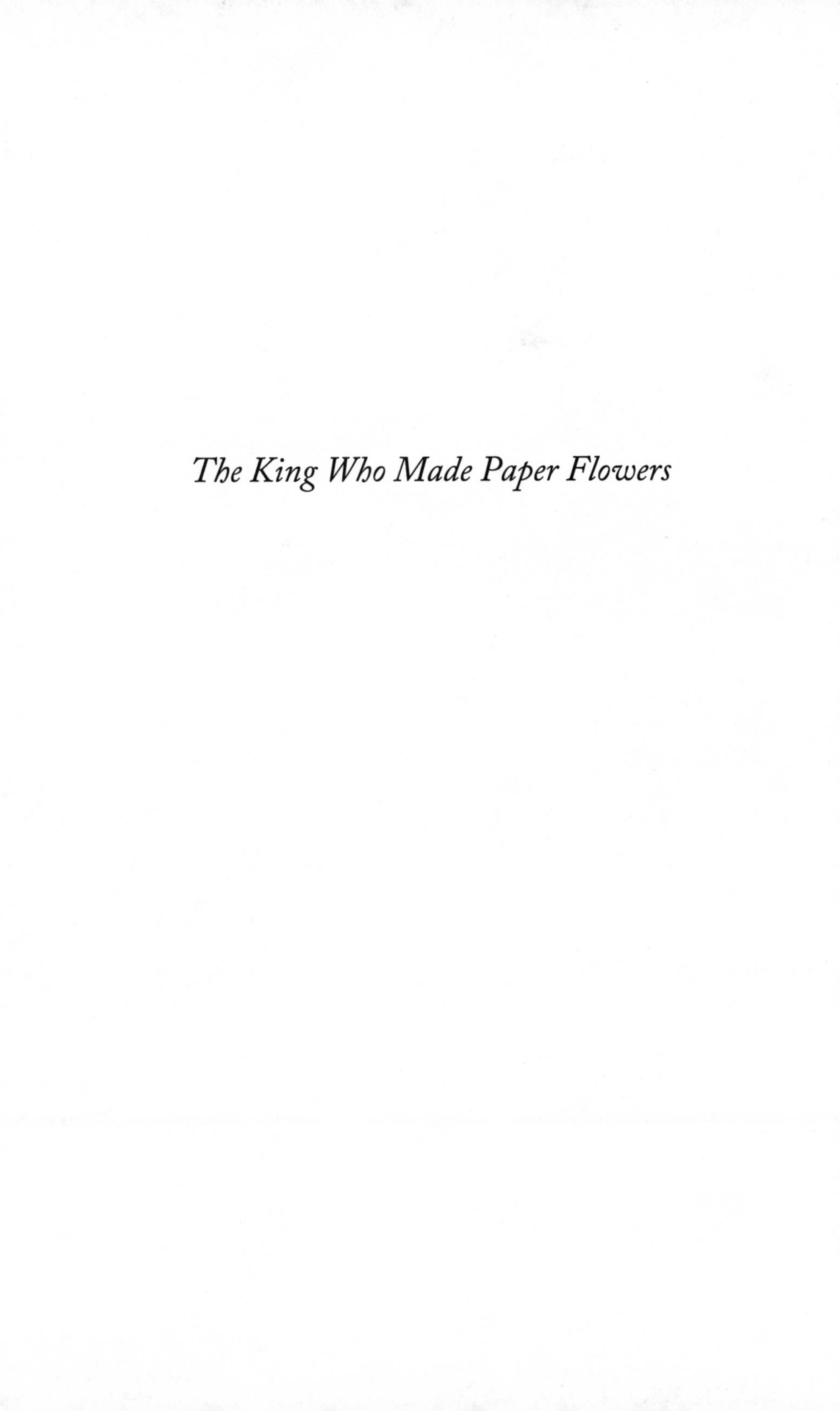

The King Who Made Paper Flowers

ONE

I begin this in shame, yet it is the beginning of it, and there is no pretty way of covering it up. The first time I saw Arthur, I became a thief. Not that I wanted to. It was circumstance. Me, being broke and Arthur having a wallet fat-full enough to be tempting.

And I had the advantage, descending from the Irish as I do and being a good enough street magician to earn loose change from tourists who are looking for a laugh and a memory to take home with them. Nimble tongue, nimble fingers. Arthur had no chance, God love him.

Still, it causes a tender ache when I think of it, a sadness really. Arthur stepping off the Greyhound, a helpless look about him, his face covered by a faint smile, like a person who has made smiling a habit even when the happiness behind it has long died. He wore a wrinkled brown suit, a dull white shirt, a dull maroon-colored tie, and an old-timey brown felt hat. He had a rolled-down paper bag in his hands, holding it like elderly ladies hold their dainty change purses. Dots of oily spots stained the bag, the telltale sign of greasy traveling food quick-bought at a quick stop.

I liked Arthur at that first seeing – before I knew his name, knew who he was, or who he would become. He had friendly eyes, the kind that make you take a second look. Soft eyes. Eyes like those of a child still young enough to be trusting. The fact that I would be taking from him within a minute or so of first seeing him, puzzles me even now. I had never stolen anything from anyone and I had no settled thought of robbing him. The only answer I have for it is this: it was meant to be, the Good Father's tricky little way of untying the knots of my life.

Truth is, I was at the bus station to gather my wits, having had the kind of day a one-armed man would have trying to shovel up the last pea on his plate with a butter knife, a day starting off-key and then losing all its melody by noontime.

Bus stations have always been like church for me on such days, in such moods. It started when I was a child, given to wanting and pestering. My mother, a wise and patient woman, would tell me in her cheerful voice that whatever I wanted was on order and would soon be arriving by Greyhound bus. She would then dispatch me to the station, which was a few blocks away on Oglethorpe Avenue, with instructions to wait for the delivery. My mother knew well about wanting things, having learned it the hard way from a vagabond husband who had promised her a life as grand as heaven's music, but had left her with little more than one-note echoes. My mother understood that if you gave it a little time, the want wilted into a melancholy of not having, and then the wish for it became so faint you'd think it had disappeared altogether.

Nothing I wanted ever arrived at the station, yet I became fascinated by the comings and goings of travelers and wondered, in a child's way of wondering, about each of them and about the people who were there to greet them or to see them off. There are many tears at bus stations. A little laughter, too. Yes. A little laughter, but many tears.

And so it is, when I am quarrelsome enough to cause a sigh, or a bellow of frustration, from those I hold dear, I take myself to the nearest bus station to watch the people, and the watching of them brings the blur of my mind back into focus and causes the sweet-sad melancholy of my soul to find its peace. It's the same as a chiropractor doing an adjustment to bones, I suppose.

I have never revealed this habit to friends, not even those cherished to me. They would not understand it. I'm not certain I do, either. My mother played her role in it, to be sure. Yet, her fibbing about imaginary gifts was not as profoundly distressing as a well-meaning psychologist might wish to make of it. She did other things far more remarkable to smooth the curvy and pockmarked road of childhood. Urging me to keep the music of the Irish in my hearing was one of them.

And maybe the memory of my mother has nothing to do with it.

Maybe it's the non-memory of my father.

He had a call of the road as internal as homing instincts of long-distance birds, my mother told me in her gentle excuse for his wanderlust. He, too, was an amateur magician and I suppose it is why I learned the tricks I know, hoping I would find one that would bring him home – wondering if he was off listening for the right incantation, the right *abracadabra*, or if he were hiding in the tip of a yard-twig from an oak tree that I used for a wand.

Maybe I am called to bus stations like a recovering alcoholic is called to a tavern door because of my father's genes doing their little jitterbug dance steps in the thick of my blood. Maybe I have always looked for him – thinking he would return as he left – on a Greyhound.

Or perhaps it's no more complicated than this: I like buses. Always have. A bus is my choice of transportation when the urge to see other places strikes me. I have a sense of companionship with those who are obeying the same urge.

There's something comforting about sharing a seat with someone who offers up his or her name in the kind of friendly come-on you get only from strangers. It's an exchange thing: name for name, story for story. Or, lie for lie. I have been many people on bus trips, lived many lives. My list of aliases is worthy of a wanted poster tacked to a bulletin board in a post office. I have been a singer Nashville-bound to make a recording, a priest assigned to a prison ministry, a baseball player headed for a tryout, a psychic, a poet, a painter. I do not invent these histories simply to be deceiving. I tell them for the adventure of being someone I am not, or could never be. I think of them as babbled dreams.

Talking about them shortens the distance between stops, makes the monotony of humming wheels and drift-by scenery less tiresome.

And I believe the traveler who sits beside me – the traveler who listens, who returns tale for tale – is likely playing the same game. Two harmless liars with a gullible audience of one – the way I imagine it to be in a Dublin pub. Yet, I have learned this about them – most of them, at least: when they are not telling their stories, they have a slight off-feeling expression, and it does not matter how exuberant they appear, they cannot put away whatever haunting it is that follows them. The grandest disguise on Earth is a smile. It is why clowns wear them.

I go to bus stations to see these people because I know them, because I am one of them. I stand near the opened bus door, posed as someone waiting for a guest, and I watch them exit. Always, I am struck by the same image: they have the look of miners coming up from a shift in a coal mine, even when they are clean-faced and smiling. Weary and listless is the look they wear, yet glad to be breathing fresh air.

It was what I sensed when I saw Arthur, though his smile carried something unusual about it. His smile carried innocence.

He stood at the foot of the bus steps for a moment, blocking the way, the mid-afternoon's heat resting like a blush on his face, and for a quiver of a moment I thought of Charlie Chaplin playing his tramp role. He had the look of a man-child who's been sent across country to meet with some never-seen relative, wondering if the relative would be there, and, if not, what would happen to him.

A lady behind him, carrying some heft and wearing an annoyed frown, gave him a little shoulder shove and Arthur stumbled forward awkwardly, tripped and fell. At my feet, he fell. And there was something telling in that accident. I did not know it then, but I do now: *All good kings bow before the feet of their subjects.*

I helped him to stand. Even picked up his stained paper food bag and handed it to him.

"I'm – sorry," he said in the kind of stutter that a person has over embarrassing moments.

"Not to worry," I told him, using my cheerful voice. "I've done the same many times myself – often without being pushed into it, if you know my meaning."

The smile stayed on his face. He took a handkerchief from the pocket of his coat and rubbed it across his forehead.

"It's a warmish kind of day," I said.

"It is," he replied.

And, then, as if following some stage direction lodged between two parenthetical marks, he removed his coat and tried to drape it over his arm. The gesture was clumsy. Two children rushed between us, squealing like monkeys at the sight of a young man dressed in a soldier's uniform. Arthur dropped the coat and his wallet fell out of the inside pocket. I leaned to pick it up, saw the cramped stack of bills wedged into the fold, and, God forgive me, I lifted them in an eye blink. Faster, even. Slid them into the front pocket of my trousers. Arthur never saw what happened. I closed the wallet and slipped it back inside his coat and handed the coat to him.

"Thank you," Arthur said graciously. "I think I've been riding so long I've lost my balance."

"That happens," I told him. "Yes, it does. Leaves you a little wobbly without your knowing it. Would you be staying over, or traveling on?"

His smile flashed happily. "Staying," he answered. He let his head swivel a bit, looking skyward as though the view held some indescribable beauty. "I've been trying to get back here a long time."

"Is that right?" I said, being polite, but wanting to sprint away and lose myself in the milling crowd.

"Came here once as a boy with my parents, many years ago," he replied, a hint of good memory warming his voice. "It was a good trip. It's stayed in my mind all this time."

"That's Savannah for you," I said, trying to be cheerful, yet still fidgety to be moving along. I added, "It's a fine place, it is, if you can bear the heat. Gets so humid in the summer it makes you wonder if you're not swimming rather than walking."

"I like it," Arthur said. He looked at me with satisfaction, and then introduced himself. "I'm Arthur Benjamin." He extended his hand.

"Hamby Cahill," I said. His grip was stronger than I had expected it to be. I could feel the weight of his money in my pocket. The taste of guilt was bile in my mouth.

"Cahill?" he replied. "That would make you Irish, wouldn't it?"

"It does, indeed," I answered. "Full blood."

"Well, Mr. Cahill, I count it a blessing to meet a true gentleman in my first minute in Savannah," he said warmly.

"Thank you," I replied. "Not many people think of me with such kindness."

Arthur made another smile, a little dip of his head. "Maybe you haven't met the right people," he said in a pleasant fashion.

I think I mimicked his head-dip and offered a return smile. My memory tells me I did. I know that I was backing away from him. I know the smile I offered was like a weight on my face. I believe I muttered, "Well, hope to see you around." And I think he said something in reply. I don't know what it was. I had already turned and was striding away.

In one of the parking areas on Factors Walk, near the Old Cotton Exchange Building, I counted the money taken from

Arthur Benjamin – seven one hundred dollar bills, five twenties, a ten, a five and two ones – but I knew I would never spent a penny of it for myself. I couldn't. Holding the money in my hands paralyzed something inside me, and as God and all my friends knew, I had a need for the bounty I was holding, owing as much as I did, dodging people like a shadow looking for a cloud.

Still, I knew I needed to put it away somewhere – in a church box or under a loose paving brick as an old pirate might have done. Anywhere. Carrying it was a curse, like the chilling things you read about in books telling stories of spirits hell-bent on vengeance. It wasn't blood money; that I would learn. Not exactly. Depends on what your blood is, I suppose.

It was late day, the sun spreading across rooftops in the silky haze of pre-night, when I heard the bellowing voice of a policeman I recognized as Billy Pottier. A rough fellow by nature, Billy was known by street people as a showoff, a man who loved the strut of being an officer of the law, loved the threat and the power of it, loved the figure he cut in his tailored uniform.

I'd had Arthur's wealth for three hours when Billy ordered me against a wall, legs spread, hands cupped behind my head, like a turncoat soldier facing a firing squad. He had his service weapon drawn and aimed; yet to my surprise, he did not frisk me. If he had, I would certainly have been in the lockup as the thief that I was.

It was Arthur who saved me.

I saw him step from behind the corner of a building as Billy was making his noise. He had a look of apprehension. His hands were trembling, yet the smile was still on his face.

Billy shouted over his shoulder, "This the man?"

Arthur moved closer. "I – I'm not sure," he said softly.

Billy muttered a curse that he spat from his tongue like a bitter taste. "Look again," he growled. "Closer. He's not going anywhere." He raised the barrel of his gun against my face. I could smell the gun oil of it. He snorted happily.

Arthur crept forward, taking the tentative steps of a man who is afraid of being tripped by unseen forces. He was holding a small suitcase.

"Looks like the man you described to me," Billy Pottier said in his bully manner. "And I know him. Chased his sorry ass off the street more times than I can count. Plays the con. Picking a man's pocket would be child's play. Nothing would please me more than to throw his worthless Irish ass in jail." He pushed his face close to mine, said in a hiss, "Do something stupid. I'm begging you."

For a long moment, Arthur studied my face. I am sure he saw terror. Had to. There was plenty of it washing over my body like a tide slapping at the shoreline before a hurricane roars in, spilling its fury.

And then Arthur lied. He said, "No. It's not him."

There are quick-flashing moments worth remembering in a man's life, but I'm hard-pressed to believe anything is more profound than being snatched from the slavery of a jail. It causes a rush of relief that's as seizing as a holy experience.

Only Billy Pottier seemed annoyed by it. He gave Arthur a lashing speech about wasting his time, then made a snide little remark to me before striding away: "I've got my eye on you, scumbag."

We stood for a moment, Arthur and I, watching Billy disappear, his head swiveling like a hawk in search of prey.

Finally, I summoned the energy to mumble to Arthur, "Thank you." I reached into my pocket and pulled out the money I had taken from him. "Here," I said, "it's all there. I didn't spend any of it."

Arthur looked at the money with a curious expression, like someone who has been asked a baffling question. "What's that?" he said.

"The money I took from you."

His smile made a little ripple across his face. He said, "No, no, it wasn't you."

"But it was," I protested.

"I don't think so," Arthur replied, his voice so calm it was unsettling to me. "No, I don't think so. I believe I'd know that." He wagged his head thoughtfully, turned and began to walk away. I followed after him, holding his money.

"Where are you going?" I asked.

"I thought I'd find a place for something to eat," he answered.

"How are you going to pay for it?" I said.

He paused in his walk, half-turned to face me. "I've got a little money," he said brightly. He lifted his hat from his head. "In the sweatband of my hat. It's an old habit my father taught me. Keep a few dollars hidden away for emergencies."

I saw a gathering of young boys – punk teenagers with dye-colored hair and enough tattoos to be in a circus sideshow – watching us with interest. I knew them. They would gladly knock a man in the head for stick candy.

"Don't do that," I whispered to Arthur.

"Do what?" he asked innocently.

"Don't show where you keep your money."

Arthur looked shocked. He fit his hat back onto his head. He said, "See, you've just taught me something valuable." His smile reappeared. "Have you eaten?"

"No," I said.

"Good. Let's find a fine establishment. At the bus station, perhaps. I'll buy you dinner."

"I know another place," I told him. "Better than the bus station. We can go there."

"That sounds nice," Arthur said.

TWO

I led Arthur to a nearby café misnamed Frank's Fine Dining. It had an up-front bar, where regulars gathered, and an eating area in the back where the hungry could order fried chicken and hamburgers and French fries and onion rings and canned vegetables seasoned with pig lard from the frying of breakfast bacon. The grease on the floor from the cooking was thick enough for figure skating, but when you live as I do – on the knife blade of circumstance – you become grateful for the fare offered by the Frank's of this world, and if you are a regular – knowing the name and personality of at least one waitress – there's always the chance for a few extra French fries or a slice of pie growing stale behind the counter.

I knew Holly Ellis, knew her in ways that would have displeased my dear, late mother.

"It's not much," I said to Arthur, "but it's cheap. Just ignore most of the people you see in here."

Arthur glowed. He said, "I like it. I believe I came here as a child with my parents. It seems familiar."

"You could have," I told him. "It's been around since Moses was a baby." My embellishment was meant in a fond way. Frank's Fine Dining was owned and managed by Frank Jeanetta, Jr., who had inherited the business from his father, Frank, Sr., in the early 60s. When people spoke of Old Savannah, Frank's was in the sentence.

Holly, who was tall and fair, having a ponytail that dangled to the V of her shoulders, made her way to the table Arthur and I had claimed. She leaned to me, said in a voice that carried some meanness to it, "I thought you'd forgot about me."

A rush of shame struck me. I know I blushed. "No, no, not at all," I said. "Busy. Just busy." I glanced at Arthur. He seemed pleased that I knew someone well enough to speak personally with them.

Holly curled her lip in a sneer and turned to Arthur. "And who's this?"

"A new friend," I answered. "His name is Arthur Benjamin."

"Well, God watch over him," she said in words flung like a spear toward me. Her eyes narrowed menacingly. "He'll need it if he stays around you."

"She's very pleasant," Arthur said in a kind and tender manner when Holly hurried away from the table after taking our order.

"She's flirting for a tip," I warned. "You have to know these girls. The thought of a good tip can have them doing handstands on a bar stool."

"And so we'll give her one," Arthur said. "A good one."

"Only if I do it," I told him. "I've still got –"

Arthur stopped my argument about having his money with a wave of his hand. "No reason to fret about such things," he said. "I've got enough to spend until it's gone, and then I'll start thinking about earning some more of it."

And that is how I learned about Arthur's history – by asking what he did to take home a wage. It was a sad story.

Arthur Benjamin had worked for forty-two years in a furniture store in Atlanta, a job he accepted out of college because he had accompanied the owner's daughter, Reba, to a Bar Mitzvah. That celebration led to marriage and the marriage led to discord and the discord to a short divorce after long suffering. At least, that was my take of it. He was kind in his description of Reba, yet I believed he was smoothing it over, the way a person forgives a hellion. In her eagerness to find joy with a podiatrist she had met at her tennis club, Reba made Arthur an offer that seemed pleasing enough to him – Arthur being easy-going and having the sort of soul that was so trusting it was dangerous: take some money and leave the city, and she'd not drag him through the courts. Arthur told me he took the money – not giving a sum, though I guessed I had most of it in my pocket – and bought his bus ticket to Savannah.

The rambling way he told the story, Arthur made it sound like a sweet adventure. There wasn't a hint of bitterness in any of it. Still, I knew he had skipped lightly over some facts that must have carried little jolts of pain and sadness with them. He said as much by the faintness of his smile, the kind I'd seen from my mother when my mother wanted to keep me from knowing the hurt she tucked around her chin at night when she pulled up the bedcovers. A shadow of a smile. A smile so soft it could have been made of feathers.

"So, you've come here to put all that behind you and to start over?" I said to him, wanting to bring an end to the story of Reba and what I imagined to be a niggardly settlement.

He did not answer for a moment. Instead, he rolled his lips together and furrowed his brow as though he had never thought about such a question. Then he replied: "That sounds right. Yes, I think so. Start over."

It was then that I learned to envy Arthur Benjamin.

He was a man without any noticeable concern, or fret, having left concern and fret in Atlanta with his history of Reba, and for a reason that brought a chill to my chest, I thought of Jesus and the story of the lilies of the field and how the lilies did not toil or spin. It was my mother's favorite Bible verse and I could hear her gently whispering it to me, like a secret she shared with no one else – my mother telling me there was as much magic in my mind as in my fingers. The way it all rushed through me – from chest to throat to mouth – I could taste the salt of tears.

I said to Arthur, "Bathroom call. I'll be back in a moment."

Arthur smiled. He seemed to be on a visit with a thought that was as lovely as lilies in a field.

I rushed to the bathroom and tried to wash the grime of disgrace off my face. I could feel the lump of Arthur's money in my pocket. The heat of it was against the top of my thigh, leaving a rash as telling as a social disease. On the way back to the table, I found Holly and gave her one of the twenty dollar bills I had taken from Arthur – more than enough to cover the check – and I warned her not to tell him what I'd done. "Just say it's on the house, a little welcome to Savannah. Play it up some."

Holly eyed the twenty suspiciously. "Where'd that come from?" she demanded.

The question slammed against me. I swallowed and lied: "From doing some magic."

"You must have pulled a kangaroo out of your rump," she sneered. Then: "What about the tip?"

"You got a twenty," I argued. "What's the check? Twelve? Fifteen? The change is the tip, and it's a far sight more than you'd get from the rest of this worthless group."

She looked at the money and I could tell she was making a calculation. Then she shrugged an agreement without words and hurried away to pick up an order from the counter.

I think Arthur believed her story about the complimentary meal. He thanked her profusely, said how good it was of Frank's Fine Dining to be so generous and friendly, adding it was a sure sign that his decision to come to Savannah was the right one.

"But, here, let me give you a tip," he said, taking two dollars from the sweatband of his hat.

I flashed a warning look to Holly.

"Oh, no," she said quickly. "It's all on the house. Everything."

"Then I must give you something else," Arthur told her. "Do you have some paper napkins?"

"Napkins?" Holly said.

"Yes."

"Sure."

"Could I have a few of them?"

"Napkins?"

"Yes. Two or three."

"Sure," she said, giving me a look that had worry buried in it. I knew what she was thinking: *A crazy. You've got a crazy man on your hands. Birds of a feather.* She dipped into her apron pocket and pulled out three white cocktail napkins and dropped them on the table in front of Arthur.

"Thank you," he told her.

"You're welcome," she replied. Then: "Got to catch a table in the back." She flew away.

"She's a nice young lady," Arthur observed. "I'm glad she's your friend." He added – philosophically, I thought: "People need to get along with one another."

I wanted to tell him my friendship with Holly had more to do with hormones than harmony, having long settled with her about such skittish topics as serious involvement. Holly had a reason, and a need, to rage about the miseries of her life – mostly brought on by the sort of men who offered charm and promises and electric touches, and then skipped off like some quick-footed tap dancer exiting stage left, leaving nothing but the fading rat-a-tat-tat of his steel-toe shoes. I know many such men would be counted among the lot of them if you believed the complaints of a few ladies who had cast their nets my way, only to discover I was good at ducking. With Holly, my role was to listen and to nod and to cluck my tongue and, occasionally, to pluck a quarter from behind her ear, doing it with the same "Ta-da!" I used on street corners with grinning tourists. Holly loved it. Holly wanted everything to be magic. For the listening and the nodding and the tongue-clucking and the quarter and the "Ta-da!" she would occasionally usher me into her bed in the cluttered little basement apartment she rented on Station Street, and there she would make love like an exorcism of demons.

Yet, as grand as the lovemaking was, I always left feeling uneasy on those nights. I knew magic was only illusion, and Holly needed something more lasting. It was why I kept returning to her, bearing my guilt like a weight of heavy chains locked to my body. In those moments, in the spilling sorrow of my apology, Holly was always tender and I knew it was her tenderness that made me fond of her.

I watched Arthur carefully fold and tear the napkins into what I judged to be two-inch squares, and then he stacked six of them neatly together and began to make accordion folds of the stack. He reached into his inside coat pocket and removed a package of pipe cleaners and pinched the accordion napkins together in the middle and tightly wound one end of a pipe cleaner around the middle, leaving a look like a bowtie. Bending over the table, close to the napkins, he gently pulled each thin sheet of the paper up toward the middle, over the wrapped-around pipe stem. And then he held it up. It had the look of a carnation full open to the sun, a white boutonniere worn by tuxedoed college gentlemen attending a dance with a lady of dazzling beauty.

"Well, fancy that," I said. "First time I ever saw anything like it."

I think Holly fell in love with Arthur when he presented the paper flower to her. Her eyes filmed over with moisture. She leaned to him, kissed him on the cheek. Arthur blushed.

"I'll keep it forever," Holly gushed. "When I die, I'll have it cremated with me."

"If you strike a match to it, it'll start the fire," I said in an ill-timed and regretful attempt at humor.

Holly shot a look of disgust at me.

"You do have to be careful," warned Arthur. "It'll come apart."

"Oh, I'll be extra careful," Holly promised.

"I'll make you another sometime," Arthur said. "Maybe a whole bouquet. Red roses if I get the right napkins."

Holly's eyes widened in amazement. "You can do that?"

"Dear lady, if you're patient and have enough paper, you can make the world," Arthur told her.

I tried to leave Arthur when we finally departed Frank's, but the guilt I had over his money – which he again refused to accept – and the lost way he looked standing there in the closing fist of night, it would have been the same as leaving a give-away baby to fend for itself.

I asked if he had a place to stay.

He raised his face and looked around, nodding. Again, it was as though I had asked a question he had never considered. "Oh," he answered, "I'll find something. Maybe stay over in the bus station for tonight. I left my other suitcase there, with the good people in the restaurant."

"I wouldn't do that," I said. "You never know what kind of low-life might show up. This town's full of them." I thought of myself.

"I'll be fine," he assured me. He put his suitcase on the ground, adjusted his tie and suit coat in a more presentable manner, then picked up his suitcase again.

"Why don't you go along with me," I said.

"Where to?" he asked.

"I know a place," I told him. "It's not much, but it'll be safe."

"Is it your home?"

His question was asked so innocently, I almost laughed. "You could say that," I replied, giving him my teasing voice with its ingredient of pretended merriment. "Temporarily, at least. I'm having a bit of a dilemma about which mansion I'll be buying with the bulk of my inheritance. I'm not one to rush into things. It's something my dear mother taught me when we were on the look for boarding schools up north. 'Take your time, Hamby,' she'd say. 'Nothing good ever comes of leaping at the first thing that seems to be calling your name.'"

I paused to study Arthur's face. He seemed engaged with my story, ridiculous as it was.

"It's nothing but a place," I said. "Some friends of mine stay there, too. You'll like them."

"I'm sure I will," Arthur replied.

THREE

I make this confession with some feeling of failure: I was, then, a street person of sorts, and I suppose I still am to those who consider the kind of life I have had as marching against the one-way parade of normal society.

Yet, then, in that time, I had no choice in it. After the death of my mother, I was forced to sell our belongings to pay what contribution I could for a decent burial and to settle accounts she had juggled like an artful circus performer working the center ring. I am still in awe of her. She divided pennies the way Jesus divided fish and bread. If anyone in our once-upon-a-time housing had the spectacular gift of magic, it was my mother. Compared to her, I was a fumbler who couldn't have pulled a rabbit from a hat with the help of a construction crane doing the heavy work.

On the first night of my life as a street person, with no ready money for lodging, I slept under the porch of the home I had lived in for all of my memory – a back-room apartment in a large house, our rent a trade-off of my mother's maid work for the owner, a quiet lady named Dale Stewart, a librarian who supplied throw-away books for my mother – and for me – to read. She was one of the kindest people I knew in Savannah. It was my suspicion then – and remains so – that she paid the bulk of my mother's internment in Laurel Grove Cemetery, but never let on about it. Her eyes were tear-glazed when she told me she had rented the apartment.

I thought of her – of Dale Stewart – on that first night of homelessness, huddled under the porch of the only home I had ever known. Above me, I could hear the walking about of the new tenants, their footfalls tapping out a Morse code of happiness at having found a place so well cared for. I wept most of the night – for my mother and for myself, and, I suppose, for the father I had not seen in many years.

After that it was a blur of places – the lush city parks that Savannah is famous for, the riverside, hidey-holes behind the covering of shrubbery growing close to churches, cemeteries of the sleeping dead, any place that looked safe enough or warm enough or cool enough for a few minutes of edgy rest. Along the way, I met myself in the faces and names of dozens of people who were living the same non-life. Down-on-luck people. Alcoholics. Addicts. Thieves. Runaways. Prostitutes. Some brilliant, some brain-damaged. Some as old as time, some little more than children newly weaned from the warm breasts of their mothers. You could have dropped all of them in a burlap sack and whirled them about until they were jammed into one another, making a single person, and when you dumped the sack, you would still have had the look of fear making a facemask. Down inside, lung-deep, gut-deep, they quivered. Even behind their laughing ways, or their snarling, they quivered. The good of them and the bad of them, they all quivered under the staring of passers-by.

What people do not understand about the homeless is this: you become homeless because of circumstance; you remain homeless because of habit. At least, it is true with many of my knowing – and the sound of it is a song of sorrow written by the helpless.

I could have taken real-job employment as friends – or used-to-be friends – urged in their good-meaning way. And I did. A few times. Once or twice the work was promising enough to leave me hopeful that I had found a turn-around worth bragging about. And then those jobs ended by cut-backs or closings, or by the behavior of scoundrels talking a mean talk with nothing to back them up. Each time, I returned to the streets with my tricks of magic – to make do, I said; to carry over to the next job – and each time, I found a little happiness from the look of awe on the faces of those who paused long enough to watch the tricks, and to offer oohs and applause and a few coins over what they had seen. Like most dreamers, I became seduced by the oohs and applause. It was a passable way to hobo a living, and if it got too lean, there was always a pick-up job dangling like fish bait from the want-ad section of the newspaper – if you didn't mind the taste of the bait or the pain from the hook you had to swallow, or the dish-washer wages you took home.

I thought of myself as being lucky.

It was not the same with others.

I keep in memory a man squatting under one of the moss-draped oaks near the river. He wore the filth of many days, his hair long and tangled, a wild-looking beard covering his face. A stench like rotting skin rose up from him. He was delicately picking something from his clothing and nibbling at it – bits of dropped food, I guessed, and when he looked up at me, his eyes told the story of a still-breathing dead man. I walked away quickly, wondering why the man had seemed familiar. Two days later I remembered seeing a gorilla in a traveling circus when I was still small enough to want the holding of my mother's hand. He was squatting in a steel cage, picking at himself, waiting for nothing more than the day to pass, too mind-numb to remember the distant forests of his freedom.

It is one of the curses of the Irish to keep hold of such mind paintings, hanging them on a wall in a corridor of the brain with just enough light washing over them to be seen in dark moments.

I have off-and-on wondered about the man under the oak, hoping he died with some peace, hoping his after-life was spent at a banquet table, dressed in fresh-washed clothing like angels wear, his skin as clean as the sky of his heavenly residence.

There were many such people as the man under the oak. Many.

Mind-numb. Living as they could, where they could.

But it was not to a park bench or an alleyway or a rooted-out space behind church shrubbery that I led Arthur.

I led him to the Castle.

It is what we called it, those of us who had been invited to share it. The Castle was on Beale Street, nearby the river. Its history was as uncertain as its future. Once it had been a holding place for cotton and other goods to be sent across the Atlantic on ships anchored in the Savannah River like large turtles, and then it had been abandoned because the size of it was judged to be too small and the distance to the river too far. Over time, it had been used for local storage and as a machine shop and as a fish market and as a factory for furniture made of cypress and cedar. If you closed your eyes and let your imagination go free, you could still smell the faint, ancient scent of fish and cedar.

None of us knew the truth of its ownership, only the threads of rumor woven together by the stitching tongues of derelicts and city officials – the two of them being much the same. The rumor started with Melinda McFadden.

Lady Melinda.

Lady.

Gossip had it that her family had resided in a very fine home in the city of New York, paid for by wealth her father had accumulated from timely, or perhaps shady, dealings in real estate. They had lived well, the McFaddens, or so said the story. Rockefeller-well. Well enough to have uniformed servants a bell-jingle away to attend whatever whim struck their fancy

Lady claimed the Castle was one of the McFadden holdings, insisting her father had purchased it on impulse, sight unseen, from an advertisement in a New York newspaper. At other times, she had her father winning it in a game of Joker's-wild poker played on St. Simons Island among cocky men of leisure and fortune. There were those who suspected both stories flew from Lady's mouth on the wings of imagination, that she was an imposter, a lunatic, a strange woman who appeared one day with a fancy travel trunk, asserting she was the rightful owner of the warehouse property on Beale Street, and since it had been deserted for years and no one seemed to object, she simply moved in.

It did not take long for people to wonder about her. "She's not right in the head," they judged. "All you have to do is take a hard look at her."

And God love her, she was certainly quaint enough to invite the opinion.

It did not matter to me. I liked Lady. She claimed her age to be in her early 60s, but the guessing – done with kindness – added ten years, or more. No one knew the truth of it. There were days when she had such energy and spirit it would put you in a mood to laugh and dance the day away without a care or worry to your name, and then there were days when she appeared comatose.

Whatever the spell that fell upon her, day to day, one thing never changed: she had a regal bearing. When she spoke, it was with the diction of a movie actress from the 1940s, though she did ramble about in her stories, sometimes making no sense at all. Her dress was that of faded dignity, the kind of dress found in antique stores on slender-waist mannequins telling tales of cocktail parties and cotillions. She wore her hair – a lovely steel grey – in a low, tight bun with knitting needles impaled in it at the back of her neck, and she had a tan wide-brimmed hat for out-of-doors use that balanced perfectly on the bun. A teal-colored ribbon tied under her chin held the hat on her head, giving her the look of Kathryn Hepburn in *The African Queen.* Her face was always dusted in powder, her lips painted in bright red. A faint dot of pink rouge rested on her cheeks. She carried a folding fan made of ivory with butterflies and dragons carved delicately into its handle. It is not overstatement to say she attracted attention on her daily stroll along River Street. I often walked with her, wearing the long-tailed tuxedo coat and silk top hat I had purchased in a

Salvation Army store for four dollars. Sometimes I would juggle tennis balls I had collected from the grassy surroundings of tennis courts. We were a sight, Lady and I – a queen and her court jester.

The Castle, bricked on the outside, was solid built of heavy timber and a rock foundation strong enough to stand against a hurricane. It was the size of a basketball gymnasium from an old grammar school, hot in summer, cold in winter. Over time, with repair and upgrade, it had been outfitted with two coal-burning stoves and a kitchen that could have been put there with thoughts of opening a restaurant – large gas oven and cook-top, and an aluminum sink deep enough for swimming. After she took occupancy, Lady had managed to acquire a refrigerator, a clothes washer and dryer, a microwave, two large fans, beds and dresser sets, a table and a few chairs, though the origin of each remained a mystery, the stories of them changing with each of her tellings. It was my belief she had had some money upon her arrival and had spent it mostly as a child engaged in playing house would have spent it. There was some evidence of her mindset in her collection of cheap, imitation tea sets – dozens of them – displayed in her room on the shelves of timbers balanced across cement blocks.

There were three enclosed rooms inside, previously used as offices for managers practicing a pecking order of importance – a large one, a medium-sized one and a small one. President. Vice-president. Working manager. Each had its own bathroom with a sink and shower tub. Lady did not change the pecking order. She occupied the large one with her travel trunk and tea sets. The other two were given over to those of us she called her Guests, saying the word with such meaning and tenderness and capital-G importance, it warmed your heart.

Her Guests included Gerty Ballew and Carrie Singletary: Lady's Ladies. And there were two men for balance – Leo Rosten and myself: Lady's Gentlemen. Five of us, total. Three ladies, two gentlemen, as we called ourselves at Lady's insistence. There were those in Savannah who would have questioned such lofty appointments.

Lady had chosen each of us without a given reason. She had simply walked up to us, one by one, and had handed us a key to the door of the Castle, saying, "You are now my guest," and each of us knew that having a key to a building of any sort, even one such as the Castle, was a gift from the Father, Himself. Being considered a lady or a gentleman was a soul-healing we all needed. Over time, I came to believe that Lady's acts of generosity might well have been more calculated than we realized. She needed care and she had somehow sensed in each of us the nature of a caregiver.

On the walk to the Castle, down several streets – me toting Arthur's large and heavy suitcase while Arthur held on to the smaller one – I told him a tidbit about each of us, giving each a sugar-coating that would have pleased the Pope. I did not want Arthur to wander wholly unaware into the unknown, peering around for the ghosts of questionable history that all of us carried.

Yet, my wish to put him at ease was a waste of words. Arthur was far more at ease than I. He listened, or seemed to listen, bobbing his head in nods that kept rhythm with his step and I wondered if he were merely being polite. I knew older people who were hard of hearing, who only pretended to understand what was being said. They, too, had a nodding way about them, giving them a look of dodging words being hurled their way. Yet, when I finished, he said, "They sound like very pleasant people, like your waitress friend."

"And, that they are," I replied, pumping some enthusiasm into my voice. "Like family to me." I wanted to say they were so normal they may bore him, but it would have been an exaggeration that bent truth to its breaking. The Guests of Lady Melinda were far from normal, me included.

I added, "Of course, they've all got their own little eccentricities, I suppose you could say, but nothing bad. Nothing at all, not when you get to know them."

"I'll be glad to meet them," Arthur assured me.

When we arrived at the Castle, we found Lady and Gerty and Leo in the large warehouse-type space we called the Great Room – Lady in a rocking chair reading the day's newspaper under the light of a bare bulb that dangled over her head from a floor lamp, Gerty reclining in a tilt-back lounge chair, sipping her nightly cup of tea, prepared from unknown ingredients that left a pleasant peppermint scent rising from her cup, and Leo sitting in one of the straight-back chairs taken from the throw-away of a palatial home on Ellison Street. The chair was pulled to a small table. He was playing solitaire, which was as much a nightly habit for him as Gerty's tea was for her. Carrie was not there.

A strange thing happened when I introduced Arthur to Lady. She gazed at him for a long moment, and then she stood and extended her hand to him. She said, "You have the bearing of my late husband." It was the first any of us had ever heard of a husband.

"And you, madam, have the bearing of royalty," Arthur replied softly. He offered a little bow, like the Japanese do when meeting or leaving someone.

"Oh, goodness," Lady sighed, "such gallantry." She waved her hand in a grand, theatrical gesture. "Welcome to our home."

Arthur lifted his head, did a slow, sweeping inspection of the Castle. "It's a wonderful place," he said. He repeated: "Wonderful." Said it with such gladness, I half-believed it myself.

"Meet our other guests," Lady said. She turned to me, her chin lifted high. "Hamby, you must do the honors."

Gerty and Leo followed Lady's example: they stood.

Leo was nearest to us and I made the first introduction to him. He narrowed his eyes suspiciously when I repeated Arthur's name. He said, "Benjamin?"

"That's right," Arthur replied.

Jewish?" Leo asked.

"Why, yes," Arthur answered.

"They don't like Jews in this town," Leo said bitterly.

Arthur smiled his patient smile.

"You'll see," warned Leo. He pushed his face toward Arthur. "You'll see," he repeated.

I led Arthur to Gerty and introduced her. Gerty gazed at him intently before saying in a voice so quiet it stayed in the distance between the two of them, "She never was married to nobody."

"I'm glad to meet you," Arthur said, keeping the soft gaze of his eyes on Gerty. "I can see why Hamby calls you beautiful."

A blink of surprise flashed on Gerty's face. The hard edge of her suspicion faded and her body seemed to lift at her shoulders, tugged up by Arthur's words.

I thought: *You're a smooth one, you old dog. Smooth as velvet.*

Then I felt another flush of shame.

Arthur was not being smooth. Not at all. Most likely, he did not know the meaning of it. He was being himself, being what the rest of us wished to be with our game playing and our clever little lies meant for pleasing.

"Sit with us," Lady said. She turned her gaze to Leo in a command that needed no words, and Leo quickly surrendered his own chair, moving it close to Lady's rocker.

"I've just made some tea," Gerty said. "Would you like a cup?"

"I would," Arthur told her. "It smells delicious."

Leo threw a glance my way. Gerty had never offered a cup of her tea to any stranger. Even sharing it with us – Lady, included –

could make her testy if her mood was dark-shrouded. Her offer to Arthur was as revealing as Lady's confession of having had a husband.

We sat in a pulled-close circle of chairs and I told the story of meeting Arthur. Most of it, at least. It seemed wise to omit the details of my regretful theft, though I knew Arthur would deny it. Lady insisted on civility in our conduct. It was one of her rules when she was lucid enough to have rules: we would behave with honor, and honor meant keeping a high regard for ourselves. The Castle was not a place for the low-life conduct she saw in the streets. As her guests, we would not partake of drugs, or drink excessively, or use foul language, or dress in throwaway rags. We would be the ladies and gentlemen she constantly told us we were.

"I thought we might ask him to stay the night with us," I said tentatively. "He just arrived from out of town, with no bed waiting to welcome him. There's the other single bed in our room. It'll be a little crowded, but it'll be comfortable enough – for the night, I mean."

For a moment there was no response, only a silence as fragile as the fine crystal the Irish make in Waterford.

"Of course, he will," Lady said, ending the pause. "We have more than enough room, and you shall be our guest." She let her eyes stay on Arthur. "You could be my late husband's brother," she added softly.

None of us were bold, or foolish, enough to inquire about Lady's late husband – if he had ever existed – and Arthur seemed to understand that we had uneasiness about it. He said, "Some of us go through life as a look-alike, I suppose. Never as exact as the real person, but close enough to give you memory of them. I just hope it's a good memory."

"It is," Lady purred. "He was a gentleman." A smile moved in the corners of her mouth. "And handsome." She turned to Gerty. "Wasn't he, Gerty?"

Gerty's eyes narrowed. "Looked like Clark Gable," she answered dryly.

"Oh, not that handsome, but close," Lady said.

The talk drifted about, like the breezes of spring playing tag. Lady was enthused about Arthur's career as a furniture salesman, offering an exhausting story about the furniture in the mansion of her childhood – all imported from Europe, all inspired by Louis the Sixteenth, though she sometimes referred to him as Louis the Sixth. As she talked, a blush of excitement made her face rosy through the dusting of powder, and she declared that on the following day she would be shopping for new furniture to make the Castle more livable. She wondered if Arthur would accompany her.

"It would be my pleasure," Arthur said.

Gerty rolled her eyes. Leo shook his head.

"Hamby, please make our new Guest comfortable," Lady instructed. "We want him rested. Tomorrow will be busy."

And the way she said guest – putting a capital G on it as she had done with us – I knew our small ensemble had increased by one.

At midnight, as everyone slept, I crawled my way in the dark to Arthur's bed and slipped two twenty dollar bills of the money I had lifted from him into the sweatband of his hat, which was on the floor beside his bed.

Only then did I have the peace of rest.

FOUR

When you spend nights on the street, your mind never turns off, not completely. A tiny part of your brain stays awake and little pinhead-size eyes – like those of insects – keep watch, seeing through your skull the way the beams of an X-ray machine seek out tumors. Dreams are made from what those eyes see. Floating dreams. Dreams so bizarre you would vow they are being performed by gods or by demons. The strangest dream is the one that jars you awake, telling you something unexpected is swirling about – something sending a shot of electricity through your muscles. It is why street people jerk when they are awakened.

It was how I awoke on the morning following my meeting of Arthur Benjamin.

With a jerk.

Knowing something was swirling about.

Arthur was not on his cot. His hat and coat were gone, though his suitcases were still where he had placed them.

It was early. The dull glow of pre-morning light, gray as fog, leaned against the high windows of the Castle. I could hear the easy breathing of Leo on the narrow bed near me and I knew he would sleep late. Leo was not a morning person.

I dressed and slipped out of the sleeping quarters into the Great Room of the Castle, thinking I would find Arthur resting in Gerty's lounge chair, having determined the bed was not to his liking.

He was not there.

And then I heard the faint sound of low-speaking voices outside, voices so soft-given they could have been from the wind rubbing against the door, making a plea for it to be opened.

The voices came from Arthur and Carrie.

I found them sitting on a stone bench the furniture maker had constructed in the semi-circle of a hedge of over-grown azaleas. Carrie was leaning close to Arthur, whispering something that caused her to laugh. They looked up with mild surprise when I approached.

"I see you've met," I said.

"Oh, yes," Carrie cooed. She gazed at Arthur. "I think I'm in love."

By the glow on her face, I thought she might have been making a confession, rather than a compliment.

Arthur smiled, reached to pat Carrie's hand. "Such a sweet young lady," he said to me.

I could give the back and forth of what was explained about their meeting, but truth be told, it had the sugary sound of a soap opera and it was too early in the day for such sweetness, especially without coffee. The only thing I wondered about was whether Carrie had let it slip about her past, or the rumor of her past. She was twenty-six. There was proof of it in the framed birth certificate she displayed, though I'd always wondered if the certificate was bogus, a clever forgery she needed as a daily assurance of her own existence. She looked no more than a teenager, had the face of an innocent always in awe of the world about her. It was a deceiving look. Street-talk had it that Carrie was a prostitute, or had been one before being rescued by Lady. It was a subject never discussed among us, though I had some suspicion that if the street-talk were true, she occasionally continued to practice her trade in order to help with economic necessities of the Castle, such as payments for utilities. Yet, in her heart she loved children and was a gifted caricaturist and a mesmerizing storyteller. Often we performed in the parks together, me with my few tricks of magic, she doing her drawings and telling stories that caused such brightness in the eyes of the young you would have thought they were the lodging places of stars.

As she told it, she had met Arthur at the door to the Castle as he was leaving for a short, pre-dawn stroll – which, I would learn, was his habit – and as she was returning from babysitting for a friend who worked a night shift as a chambermaid in one of the riverfront hotels. Or, so she said. There was a tired, pleased expression on her face, leaving me to wonder if the mention of a hotel was the only thing she had right in her story.

"I knew who she was at first sight," Arthur said. "From your description of her."

"I thought he was one of Leo's friends who'd fallen asleep and was just leaving the Castle," Carrie said.

"We've had a good talk," Arthur added. He looked at me. "And where were you headed?"

I lied, of course. I told him I was off to the bus station restaurant for a doughnut and coffee.

"Let's all go," Arthur said. He stood. "We'll get doughnuts for everyone. And coffee."

Carrie clapped her hands like a child learning of a party. "Let's do," she enthused.

And, so, we walked to the bus station and Arthur ordered a dozen doughnuts and six coffees, paying for them with money from the sweatband of his hat – one of the twenties I had placed there – and we returned to the Castle as the sun was making its first pass of light over the city.

Thinking about it now, I have a good memory of that morning, how Arthur's presence seemed to rise up with the sun and warm us with his innocence and gentle humor. It was as though he had no understanding of the hazard of our lives. If he knew we were nothing more than street people who had lucked upon a place to stay – as temporary as we all knew it could be – he did not mention it. In Arthur's view, we lived a fine life in a fine place, and before the doughnuts and coffee had been consumed, he and Lady had plotted the day's shopping for furniture. The way Arthur spoke of the possibilities, I had the feeling he was about to lead us on an adventure that would be as unpredictable as it was promising.

"If we're lucky, we could have everything we need for a party before nighttime," he said in his cheerful voice.

"Oh, maybe we should invite the governor," Lady added brightly.

"Seems to me he turned down our last invitation," Gerty said in Gerty's way of being Gerty.

"It'll be a good day," Arthur said gently. "I think it's in the air."

Curiously, I wanted to believe him, and I think Carrie had the same feeling. Not Gerty. A dark, bothering mood was coming over her, and not even Arthur could bring light to it. Leo also had doubts. I knew it by the way he gnawed at his lips and by the furrow of worry that lined his forehead. He had reason. He had been on many meaningless shopping assignments with Lady.

Still, I did try to pull the balloon of Arthur's dream down from the ceiling of his imagination. I said, "And how are we going to go about paying for everything?"

The smile that Arthur carried stayed calmly in his face. "Oh, I'm sure we'll manage. If you take your time you'd be surprised at the bargains you can find."

Lady, who had listened with closed eyes – as though mesmerized by a symphony in concert – said, "Of course we'll manage." She opened her eyes and looked at Leo. "Won't we, Leo?"

"We'll see, we'll see," Leo mumbled.

We spent the morning and early afternoon shopping, drawing stares of curiosity from tourists and the soft hiss of whispers from storekeepers. Arthur and Lady led the parade, with Carrie wedged between them like a giggly child in a Christmas shop. Gerty had stayed at the Castle, and I was happy for her decision. Leo lagged behind the pace and I lagged with him, keeping watch, knowing the temptations that would whisper to him from cluttered shelves.

Leo was proud that he carried the same name as the famous writer, Leo Rosten, whose book, *The Joys of Yiddish,* was always on a side table (a turned-over fruit crate, really) beside Leo's chair. It was the only show-off expression we ever saw from him. There was not a lot of joy in Leo's life, however.

He had been an accountant in Atlanta and had served time in Federal prison for embezzlement – a trumped-up charge by a bank manager as it turned out, but the accusation stayed with him after his release from prison. No one would hire him, in part, I suspect, because of the lingering suspicion coating his wiped-away record and also in part because of his disposition, which required some patience. Lady had assigned him the honor of managing her financial empire, which consisted of nothing more than the Castle as far as Leo could ascertain, and even that carried doubt with it. Still, he was considered our banker. We never worried about him embezzling from us, since there was nothing to embezzle. We worried, instead, about his kleptomania, which we accepted as his psychological retaliation against unlawful years behind bars, where he had learned as much from meanness as from pretended programs of rehabilitation. Yet, it was not a growling, dangerous meanness like you might find in a pit bull or a cornered German Shepherd. Leo's meanness was more of a yapping, like a French poodle with a nasty personality. Loud and sudden, then a retreat, and in his retreat he could become worrisomely depressed.

At night, Leo was a scavenger, going out with an empty knapsack and returning later with everything from throwaway clothing to odds and ends, mostly junk. Occasionally he would find small treasures left on street-sides by the well-to-do. We had useable goods from such discoveries – a radio, a waffle iron, some lamps. A large storage closet at one end of the Castle held his collections under lock and key, secured, he told us, for a giant yard sale when times turned truly bad. Sometimes, Leo would also cook for us, when the mood got in him. It was a craft learned in the prison kitchen and the taste of his preparations always needed the flavoring of imagination.

As Leo and I lingered in our walk-about, I could see Arthur and Lady and Carrie stopping often to examine a piece of furniture that, to me, seemed ready for the junkyard – armoires and pie safes, bookcases with sagging shelves, tables scarred from over-use, broken-down armchairs, folding screens used in dressing rooms, floor lamps with torn shades, framed paintings done by color-blind amateurs, easels old enough to have been used by Adam and Eve – the sort of hold-over furnishings that people would be ashamed to display in a yard sale. Occasionally, Arthur would kneel by an item and examine it as a jeweler would examine a rare stone and a faint smile would wave across his face and he would tap the item twice. I knew without explanation that whatever he tapped would be relocated to the Castle before the day had faded away.

"Remember this one," Arthur would say, directing the words to me. "It's a nice piece."

"Lovely," Lady would croon.

When the shopping was finished, Arthur and Lady and Carrie wandered away for a languid tour of the city, leaving Leo and me to do the haggling over price. Thankfully, the task was not as debatable as I thought it would be, being that the storekeepers wanted to be rid of us and, for the most part, the items we negotiated were near worthless to their trade. I could see snickering in some of their faces, the kind of covered-over smirk people have when they believe they've pulled a fast one.

There was the matter of money, of course. It was Arthur's suggestion that we purchase everything on a payment plan, the way his former father-in-law had conducted business for years in his Atlanta shop, and I suppose in his way of thinking it did make sense, yet he did not understand that none of us had a sterling reputation as credit risks.

"We'll work it out," I told him.

I decided to use the money I had lifted from his wallet. If he would not permit me to return it to him, I could at least make some good of it, and making good of it to pay for broken down furniture cost two hundred, twenty-three dollars and thirteen cents.

The only thing that caused concern for me was the look on Leo's face when I removed the money from my pocket, careful not to show the full amount of it. I could see the nervous twitch that fluttered involuntarily over his left eye whenever the urge to lift something from a store shelf overcame him.

He asked, "Where'd that come from?"

"I sold some stocks," I told him.

He snorted an evil little laugh. "And I'm the Pope's rabbi."

"Look," I said in a whisper, "don't say anything about this, and I'll buy you a new deck of cards."

"Don't need one," he countered. He pulled an unopened deck from his pocket.

"Okay, where'd you get it?" I demanded.

Leo smiled.

It took three hours and a wobbly wheelbarrow thrown into the bargain to move everything from the shops to the Castle.

I do not know how it got arranged. I invented a convincing tale of doing a magic show at a wedding reception and left to go directly to Frank's Fine Dining, where Holly greeted me sweetly, saying, "Why don't you stop by the apartment tonight?"

"Are you going to behave?" I asked in a tease.

"Not in the least," she answered in a better tease.

She was truthful, as it turned out. She had never been grander or more tender in her lovemaking. Her voice was a cooing whisper, holding no complaints about work or money or other men. The glow of her eyes could have been made from the tips of burning candles. Her skin was warm to the touch. She was quick and generous with kisses. The paper flower Arthur made for her was pinned to the lampshade beside her bed. She called it a love flower, vowed it contained enchantment, and I was not foolish enough to contradict her.

When I arrived back at the Castle in the dark purpling of morning, the furniture had been placed in the Great Room, the paintings displayed on easels. It resembled a room made for a stage play, blocked in by the eight folding screens Arthur had selected with his tapping approval. Inside the screens, in a space that seemed by my guess to be at least fifteen feet square, was the setting of a living room that had the appearance of having been there for years – old furniture with an old, comfortable look, a large and low coffee table serving as the center piece. On the table was a hollowed-out clay bust of Mozart that Lady had favored, offering a story of her father sponsoring a Mozart concert in Carnegie Hall.

It was a miracle. Truly a miracle. If the governor had been invited for cocktails, he might have been impressed.

I slipped soundlessly into the room I shared with Leo – and now Arthur – and found both asleep, both making the low, rhythmic snoring of men who have worked themselves into exhaustion. I found Arthur's hat on the floor beside his cot and checked its sweatband. It contained only two one-dollar bills, telling me had been on a spending spree with Lady and Carrie. I refilled it with twenty dollars and then slid into my own bed, closed my eyes and gave way to the thinking of how Arthur had wiggled his way into our lives. Like a ghost, almost. It had not yet been two complete days since he stepped off the Greyhound bus, and there he was, a few feet from me, sleeping the sleep of contentment, his presence spreading about us, filling the Castle. It was like the finding of a gift not expected, but wished for in secret, and I could sense my mother hovering over me, saying in her quiet, patient way that whatever I wanted had been put on order and soon would be arriving on the Greyhound bus. I wondered if Arthur was her doing.

A flush of sadness washed over me.

And then I thought of Holly.

Holly. Sweet Holly. Her perfume was still faint on my face.

FIVE

I dreamed not of Holly, as I had wished, but of Arthur. It was a bizarre thing, this dream – Arthur outfitted in the green of a Leprechaun's suit, strolling along in front of the St. Patrick's Day parade that barreled its way through Savannah each March, Carrie and Lady striding beside him in matching show-off gowns. Leo and I followed, me juggling tennis balls, Leo picking the pockets of passers-by. Gerty walked behind us, drinking tea from a small, china cup, crying out, *"Beware, beware, beware..."* I could hear the music of bands and the squeals of street-side watchers, and I could see Arthur taking money from his hat and tossing it into the air like confetti. And though I was laughing at the sight of it, there was an uneasy feeling that took roost across my shoulders even in the dream-state. I wanted to shrug it off, but knew it would not go away so easily. Bizarre dreams always have meaning.

And I was right.

It was I who overslept, not Leo, and it was Carrie who awoke me by pulling back the covers on my bed, with no shame at all that I might have been as naked as the day I was born. To Carrie, I was more brother than man, leaving me to wonder if, somewhere, there were brothers who anguished over her disappearance and if I had become a substitute for them.

She was wearing a dress colored as blue as sky on a bright day, dotted with little white flowers, looking for all the world like a young girl ready for school. She said, "Get up," and she smiled a smile as radiant as her dress.

"Why?" I asked, making a moan of it.

"You're missing breakfast."

"Food?"

"Food. We've got food."

"Doughnuts or bagels?"

"A real breakfast," Carrie said.

I sat up on my bed to sniff the air and there it was, the good, rich scent of eggs and bacon and coffee, and it put me in mind of the day Leo had lifted a dozen eggs and a wedge of cheese from a convenience store and had made omelets before we knew he had them. I asked, "Leo?"

"No. Arthur. He went out early and came back with groceries. Leo did the cooking."

"It's the best waking up I've had in a while," I said.

Carrie leaned close to me. "Where were you last night?" she asked.

"Caring for an ailing friend," I told her.

She leaned closer and inhaled in a slow, dramatic show. "She must have been grateful," she whispered. "It's a nice scent." She turned and skipped from the room.

I do not know if I have ever had a breakfast quite so fine as the one Arthur provided for us on that morning, even with Leo's limited cooking skills, and it was gladly consumed by everyone except Gerty. She was not in the Castle. Carrie told me in whisper that Gerty had left earlier to sit in Lafayette Square, her chosen place to converse with whatever dark spirits buzzed about her like gnats.

"She's got the look," Carrie said.

I asked if she had made any predictions of gloom.

"Nothing she said," Carrie replied, "but she couldn't take her eyes off Lady."

Carrie could tell I was bothered by what she said. "Hamby, it's just Gerty," she added. "Last week, she saw a ship burning in the river. Did it happen?"

I had forgot about Gerty's seeing of the burning ship.

"It's just Gerty," Carrie repeated. "You need to stop worrying so much."

I wanted to believe that she was right. Still, I had doubts.

Gerty was the first of Lady's guests. She was a runaway from a worthless man in Atlanta, a full-bodied, yet ethereally beautiful black woman in her forties, or maybe early fifties. As with Lady, no one knew her true age. No one asked. It was not a question worth risking the wrath Gerty could administer with the tongue lashing of her hair-trigger anger and the daring glare of her dark, laser eyes. Gerty, when soft-hearted, could weep at the sound of a cricket playing its leg fiddle, but when riled, she was an avenger, fearless and terrifying. Even in her minor agitations, she called the rest of us honkies, using the word like a fly-swatter would be used to swat at flies, yet it never offended any of us. The way Gerty said it, there was something endearing in it, like a good nickname.

She had been a seamstress, and her ownership of a foot-pump Singer sewing machine was a thing of pride as well as a foul memory of being enslaved to it from girlhood. It sat, mostly unused, in the room she shared with Carrie, kept, she said, because it had belonged to her mother. "Dead folks don't like you giving away what they give you before they was dead," was her explanation.

Gerty also claimed to have been born with a caul covering her face, giving her psychic powers to recognize on-coming gloom, and, God love her, there were times when I did not doubt she was so blessed, or cursed. Whenever she closed her eyes in the signal that a voice from some far-off place was whispering to her and she was seeing something that only the blind could see, I always found a sudden reason to be elsewhere. I am not a man who likes to keep company with gloom, though it has been my shadow most of my life.

In the time I had been in her company, Gerty had made a number of predictions that failed to materialize, but the failures never deterred her. "It'll happen, sooner or later," she would reveal in the low, whispery voice she used. "Sooner or later, mark my word."

And that was what kept me edgy being around her, even having a clear mind and knowing she was likely no more gifted as a soothsayer than Hobbler Bob, a crippled street fellow who never talked to anyone. Every person I know has a sense about things not yet happened. Mothers are that way. Especially mothers. A mother can be having a leisurely stroll with friends or be brain-deep in a business decision behind the mahogany desk of a giant corporation, and know suddenly that something is wrong with her child. It is like the leaping of light across reason. A chill seizes them and they turn away from everything holding their minds and they go to their child.

Gerty could cause such a chill.

And sometimes, she was right.

Three hours after our breakfast, Lady was in the hospital, having been struck by a car making a hasty turn at a corner, racing against the changed traffic light.

It was not a run-over, with crushed bones and bloodletting, only a brush of the front fender, sending Lady sprawling, causing a mild sprain of her ankle and a few bruises that would turn a crayon purple. Still, the commotion of it was high-pitch – the squealing of tires on the get-away car, the piercing scream of Carrie, the chorus of gasps from on-lookers nearby. One of the bystanders, reacting to Carrie's hysterics and the pitiful moan Lady gave off, called 911 from her cell phone, and before we could stand Lady up and steady her, an ambulance and two police cars were on the scene and Lady was placed in the ambulance and rushed to Memorial Hospital, sirens blaring. Gerty had come upon us on her return from Lafayette Square – no more than a minute after the accident – and she had bulled her way into the middle of things, issuing orders that scattered most of the crowd. The upshot of it was that she and Carrie went with Lady in the ambulance after a fuss with attendants, leaving me and Arthur and Leo to answer questions of the police. Gerty did not surrender to panic until the ambulance pulled away, and then I could hear her wails over the leaving sirens.

It might have been a put-aside incident, nothing for serious concern, except for one thing: the driver of the car – a woman from our quick seeing of it – did not stop. She sped away in a rush, like a bank robber looking for an open highway, and if it had not been for the vanity tag on her car, we might never have known who it was. The tag read LILMAR.

When I told the police about the tag, one of the officers writing notes in his notepad – a man whose nametag identified him as Sergeant Ted Castleberry – furrowed his brow and said, "What was it?"

I repeated the lettering on the tag – spelling it out, slow-like – and knew immediately that something had clicked with Sergeant Ted Castleberry.

"We'll look into it," he said, closing his notepad without writing down the information we had provided regarding the car. He added in a nasty voice, "My advice to the lot of you is to get off the street before we run you in for loitering."

It is a flaw of the Irish that they come quick to temper when offended, and, being Irish, I could not help myself. I said in a near-shout, "Loitering? Who's loitering? Here we are out for a morning stroll and a car near kills one of us, driving off without so much as a look-back, and you threaten us with a lock-up?"

The sergeant stepped close to me, shoved his face against my face. "Don't raise your voice to me, boy," he growled.

I could feel a hand on my arm, tugging me away. It was Arthur. He said in a calm, almost gentle, way, "It's all right, Hamby. We'll be on our way." He smiled politely. "I wonder, sir, if you'd answer a question for me."

Ted Castleberry, red-faced, snapped, "What question?"

Arthur did a little turn of his head toward the crowd that had gathered at the call of the sirens. "Did you get their names? The ones who might have seen what happened?"

Ted Castleberry let his eyes scan the remaining on-lookers, saw them staring at him, wearing expressions of dare and irritation. "We got all we need," he muttered. He narrowed his gaze on Arthur, giving a look that was hard with warning, then turned and walked away in a quick stride.

No one in the crowd moved. They watched the police get into their cars and leave. I could hear muttering among the bystanders and the woman who had made the 911 call – a bank officer as we would learn – stepped to Arthur and handed him her business card. "If you need a witness, let me know," she said.

Arthur did his little bow to her. "Thank you," he said pleasantly. He looked at the card and read her name aloud, "Sharon Day." He looked up at her and added, "It's a strong name."

"Thank you," Sharon Day said. Then: "I despise the way you were treated." There was disgust in her voice.

Arthur reached into the side pocket of his coat and removed a small paper flower made from a red napkin, and he handed it to Sharon Day. "This is for your kindness," he said softly. "Not a Rose of Sharon, I'm afraid, but a rose for Sharon."

If Sharon Day had been given a roomful of orchids by Tom Cruise, she couldn't have been more surprised, or happier.

"Why – thank you," she said. She looked at the flower closely. "It's beautiful. Where did you get it?"

"He made it," I told her.

"You did?" she said to Arthur.

"It's a way of relaxing," he answered.

I watched Sharon Day turn the flower in her fingers and I thought for a moment that she would bring it close to her face and inhale, testing it for a fragrance.

"Please call if you need me," she said to Arthur.

"We will," Arthur promised.

"And thank you again for the flower," she added. "It makes me feel special."

"As you are," Arthur told her.

I have seen few moments such as the one that transpired between Arthur and Sharon Day, where there is something pure and tender spoken in language not made of words, and I thought: What a nice thing for him to do. I had no idea I would see it many times.

By the time Arthur and Leo and I arrived at the hospital by city bus, Gerty had persuaded the doctors to keep Lady overnight for observation, telling them it would be a tragedy if something unexpected happened to her – being elderly as she was. Not being present, I did not know the actual words Gerty delivered, but I was confident she had intoned them in the voice she used when making proclamations. None among us was as bold as Gerty. It was my guess that what she said had left an impression, and I could hear it out of the playback of imagination: "Don't make me go to the state, telling them that a poor, moneyless, honky woman was turned away in her hour of need, having nobody but a poor black woman to care for her. And, Lord, we got enough witnesses to fill up the state capitol."

Carrie reported that doctors were stumbling over one another like people in a three-legged sack race, giving orders for Lady's care.

"Go back to the Castle," Gerty told us. "I'll stay here and keep them on their toes." She paused, took a peek at Lady, who was asleep in her hospital bed, then added, "It ain't over. In the morning, there's going to be people bringing the gloom."

Before we left to return to the Castle, Arthur produced another flower from his pocket and placed it on the table beside Lady's bed. "I wish it were real," he whispered.

"It's as real as we get, honey. Folks like us," Gerty told him.

If any of us ever had doubts about Gerty's powers – and all of us did except Arthur, who had no first-hand experience on the matter – we adopted a different opinion of her the following morning.

At nine-thirty, Gerty's prophecy arrived in the presence of a middle-aged man named Roger Upshaw, up-town dressed, a frowning, scolding look buried deep into his face, having a voice that sounded like an army officer accustomed to causing misery.

He was, he said, from the mayor's office.

"This is simple," he told us, his dark eyes suspiciously scanning the room made of dressing screens. "The city will not bring action against any of you for violating the ordinance about attempting a street crossing against the light, on the condition that you do not pursue the matter any further."

For a moment, none of us spoke.

"Did I make myself clear?" Roger Upshaw barked.

"I think so," Arthur replied easily. "Thank you."

"So we have an agreement?" asked Roger Upshaw.

Carrie turned to Arthur. A puzzled expression lodged in her face.

"We'll certainly talk it over," Arthur answered.

Roger Upshaw's face turned the color of crimson. "Talk what over?" he demanded.

"What you said," I told him, trying to keep my own anger at bay. "The poor lady is still hospitalized. She'll need to have her say about it."

"Don't do anything you'll regret," Roger Upshaw warned. His eyes again swept the room. "You wouldn't want to lose this fine place, would you? You better remember you're just a door away from living on the streets with the rest of your friends."

I saw Leo slither toward him, his fists clenched, his eyes blazing, and I knew he was seeing a prison guard full of arrogance and meanness. I moved between the two men.

"We heard you," I said, giving the words the same kind of icy treatment I had heard more than once from Holly.

A smirk, like a smile curled around a sour taste, made its way over Roger Upshaw's mouth. He lifted his head in the haughty gesture of men who have the love of power, and then he walked away, out of the Castle.

No one spoke for a long moment after the heavy sound of the closing of the door echoed around us, and then Carrie asked, "What are we going to do?"

"Sue the bastards," Leo hissed.

"Us?" Carrie said. "Us?"

"Why not?" Leo replied.

"Maybe because we wouldn't have a snowball's chance in hell, Leo," Carrie said angrily. She looked at Arthur. I could tell she wanted him to agree with her.

"Can any of you think of a reason they're so worried about this?" Arthur asked.

"They don't like Jews," Leo declared. "I told you that, I told you."

"My God, Leo, the mayor's Jewish," Carrie snapped.

Arthur turned to me. "Hamby?"

"I don't know," I said honestly. "We get hassled a lot. All street people do."

"But you're not street people," Arthur said in his calm way.

Leo and Carrie and I exchanged glances, and in the glances and in the pause of the glances, we all silently wondered if Arthur was living in the same world of illusion as Lady.

"Well, that's right," I finally said. "Not technically, I guess you could say, but I'm not sure everybody sees it that way."

Arthur nodded thoughtfully. "Why don't we take the bus to the hospital," he said. "Or maybe walk. The sun's shining. It's a lovely day."

Again, Leo and Carrie and I exchanged glances holding questions.

Lady returned to the Castle shortly after the lunch hour, arriving with Gerty in a taxicab that Arthur insisted on financing from the extra twenty dollars I had again slipped into his hat as he slept. She walked gingerly on crutches gladly provided by the hospital after Gerty's sermon about unfortunates who must trust their bodies and souls to agencies top-heavy with honky bureaucrats. She also insisted she would engage the support of the Rev. Locklear Patterson, first-cousin kin to the Rev. Jesse Jackson, if necessary. The Rev. Locklear Patterson did not exist, yet Gerty used his name like a weapon in any circumstance that threatened her purposes.

We said nothing to Lady about the visit from Roger Upshaw. Instead, we fussed over her, making her comfortable in her chair, offering her a rich, creamy soup Leo had prepared from potatoes he likely had pilfered from a grocery as payback for the treatment we had received from Sergeant Ted Castleberry.

Lady loved the attention. She told us a story about her years as a nurse in New York, caring for indigent workers. It was a bit like listening to a glowing history of Florence Nightingale, and it might have been believable had she had not veered off-track to reveal that, as a young woman, she also had spent a brief time as a club singer in New York, a claim that caused Gerty to mutter, "Oh, good Lord."

Carrie, trying to be kind, asked, "Lady, did you ever sing any of the songs of Johnny Mercer?"

A confused gaze moved in Lady's eyes.

"Johnny Mercer," Carrie said. "He was from Savannah. He's buried here."

Lady's eyes suddenly sparkled. "Johnny Mercer? Oh, yes. Johnny was a dear friend," she cooed. "We had dinner the year I moved here. His place was lovely."

Carrie smiled faintly, as did I. We knew that Lady arrived in Savannah in 1997. Johnny Mercer had died in 1976.

SIX

It was Carrie who could not dismiss the matter of the accident involving Lady, or of the visit from Roger Upshaw. She had dreamed of both, she told us the morning after Lady's return from the hospital – a montage of a dream that had flickered through her mind, leaping about like a grasshopper springing from flashing image to flashing image. We were all in it – Lady, Arthur, Gerty, Leo, me, Roger Upshaw, Johnny Mercer, all playing the kind of nonsense that dreams play. And in the middle of it was the car with the nametag reading LILMAR, speeding away, disappearing.

For Carrie, the dream held meaning. Gerty agreed with her. Jumping-about dreams wanted you to follow them, Gerty vowed. Jumping-about dreams told stories the same way sign language told stories for the deaf. The reading of them was the tricky part.

We were talking about it at a breakfast of oatmeal and coffee, taken while Lady slept from her ordeal and late night. It was Gerty's thinking that Carrie's dream had led her to the car. The car had answers, beginning with the owner's name.

"Let's ask," Arthur suggested.

"Ask who?" Carrie said.

"I would think the police should know," Arthur replied.

"So, you think they're going to tell us anything?" Leo said with anger. "Nothing. Not a thing. You don't know how they are. I do. You'll see."

"You could be right," Arthur said. He sat in his chair, looking off, as though reading the air for answers. Then he added, "But I'm at that age where I like to know about things. It's something I've learned over the past few years – not to be afraid to ask questions, especially when people don't expect it from you."

I believed Arthur was remembering his divorce.

Leo shook his head. "Won't work," he mumbled.

"It's worth a try," Carrie insisted and Leo shrugged his surrender, as he always did when Carrie or Gerty took a firm stand about anything.

I can report with honesty that our primary interest in making an inquiry about the car that struck Lady was one of curiosity, not threat. It was no different than anyone's small escapade being made urgent by too much talk feeding the gluttony of imagination. Gerty had even wondered aloud if the driver of the car had been hired to kill Lady – or all of us, for that matter – and had swerved away from her mission in a moment of panic. It was the way one of her cousins had been killed, she said. Run down by a truck driven by a half-crazy Vietnam veteran being paid to do the killing.

Gloom was in the air, Gerty had asserted. Carrie's dream had been about gloom.

Still, whatever each of us might have been thinking, our visit to the police station was one begun in politeness, with respectful behavior and good temper, a mood cast by Arthur. Leaving Gerty to attend to Lady was the same as leaving gloom behind us.

An officer wearing the nametag Foster Gaines wanted to know our business, and I answered by saying we were interested in how we might trace the ownership of a car from its license tag.

Foster Gaines screwed up his face in a sour look. His small eyes swept the four of us. "Why you want to do that?"

"A friend of ours was involved in a little accident," I said. "She was knocked over by a car that drove off, but we were able to get the tag information, and we were wondering who owned the car."

I do not know what advice or information Foster Gaines would have provided, had he had the chance. He didn't. Before he could speak, Sergeant Ted Castleberry appeared, wearing a stern and annoyed expression.

"What's going on here?" the sergeant demanded.

"These people want to know how to trace a car tag," Foster Gaines told him.

I could see the red tide of anger rising in Ted Castleberry's neck. "You can't," he said. "That's private information. Now, get out of here before I run you in."

If Ted Castleberry had slapped us all at the same time, with the same sweep of his open hand, he could not have caused more riling of anger. The only one of us not showing it was Arthur. Arthur's reaction was a slight smile.

"Run us in?" Carrie snapped. "For what?"

Ted Castleberry leaned close to her. "How about starting with prostitution?" he said. "I know about you." He looked at me and Leo and Arthur. "These your pimps?" he added in a low voice.

I saw Leo's body go into a coil, saw his hands closing into fists, and I reached for him, pulling him away. "Come on," I said. "Let's go." I guided him out of the station, partly to keep him from trouble and partly to bring my temper from boil to simmer. Carrie told me later that Arthur had said to the sergeant, "Sir, that was unkind of you."

Ted Castleberry had replied in a haughty manner, "You getting it, too, old man?"

And Arthur had responded in an even voice, "I believe you've made a regrettable mistake."

What happened next, according to Carrie, was this: Arthur took a red paper flower from his pocket and handed it to the sergeant. He made his little nod-bow with his head and smiled and walked away.

"You should have seen the look on the sergeant's face," Carrie said. "I thought he was going to hit Arthur."

Sometimes, the world – fate, or God, I mean – gives you one on the house. A freebie, it is. Good fortune. Timing as perfect as timing can be.

None of us knew that Doyle Copeland, the crime beat reporter for *The Savannah Enquirer*, was observing the exchange between Arthur and Ted Castleberry from across the station lobby. To Doyle, it had the possibility of a clever sidebar story – a paper flower being presented to a policeman by a man with the look of a street vendor offering a give-away to drum up business – so he followed Arthur and Carrie out of the station to ask his questions.

The gesture was only an act of forgiveness, Arthur told him in his gentle way.

"Forgiveness for what?" Doyle asked casually. He was a young, tall black man, heavy, yet not obese. He had a smile that seemed carved into his face, and the innocence of his smile gave him an appearance of someone who saw only amusement, even in events of dread.

"A little misunderstanding," Arthur said. "I simply wanted the officer to know we didn't harbor any ill feelings toward him."

Doyle wanted to know about the misunderstanding, what it was, and why it had caused Ted Castleberry to stalk away, ripping Arthur's red paper flower apart, scattering it across the floor like drops of blood. The answer, eagerly provided by Carrie, told the story of Lady's close call with the drive-off car having the vanity tag LILMAR, and of Lady's night of agony in the hospital.

"Ummmm," Doyle said, a frown easing into his forehead, crowning his smile. "I must have missed the report on that. Think I'll check it out. LILMAR? That was the tag?"

"Yes," Carrie said.

Doyle wrote in his notepad. I did not see the word, but I was sure it was LILMAR.

"Anything else?" he asked.

"A man from the mayor's office came to see us this morning," I answered.

"Who was that?" asked Doyle.

"His name was Roger Upshaw," Carrie told him.

Doyle's smile widened into a grin that said he knew the man and most likely did not care for him. "What did he want?" he asked.

"He said if we forgot about Lady being hit, the city wouldn't press charges against us for crossing the street against the light," Carrie answered. She added angrily, "The light had changed. It was the car that was in the wrong. You can ask anybody who was there."

"I wouldn't worry much about that," advised Doyle. "He likes to bully people."

"It sounded more like a threat to me," Carrie said.

Doyle nodded agreement. He turned his smile on Arthur. "Where'd you get the flower?"

"He makes them," I said.

Arthur reached into his pocket and pulled out another paper flower – a red one – and presented it to Doyle. "For your lady," he said.

Doyle took the flower, turned it in his fingers. "She'll appreciate it," he said. "She thinks I never give her anything." His smile cut deeper into his face.

That night at the Castle, after a dinner of spaghetti, we had an herb tea Gerty had prepared for Lady, vowing it had properties to heal bruises and calm the jitters, and from Carrie's tale of what had happened at the police station, Gerty determined we all needed something to calm our nerves.

"I told you," she said solemnly. "There's darkness everywhere. I been feeling it for days."

I cannot say that Lady understood what had happened, yet she expressed sympathy for the treatment we had received and she asked me if I had taken proper procedures to arm the security system of the Castle.

Carrie looked at me quizzically.

"I've tended to it," I told Lady.

"That's nice," she said. "We must take care. There are people who want the Castle."

Gerty sighed heavily.

"I visited another castle once," Lady said longingly. "In Austria. It was beautiful. We were told it would take a week to go through every room." She remembered meeting a young man who was also on tour with his family. She could not recall his name, only that he was tall and handsome and had flirted shamelessly with her. It was a story told in her soft, cooing voice, the one she used when making a visit to the Land of Nonsense, as Leo called it.

Gerty sat in her chair, balancing her own cup of tea on the chair arm. Her head bobbed as she listened to Lady, mumbling, "Uh-huh, un-huh." And when Lady paused in her rambling, she said, "I met me a king one time."

"And who was that?" asked Arthur.

"Nat King Cole," Gerty answered, and she laughed.

"Maybe that's who it was that I met," Lady said hopefully.

"You wrong there. Nat King Cole didn't have nothing to do with no honky ladies," Gerty told her.

Lady leaned back in her chair and gazed at the ceiling, as though the ceiling held cue cards to prompt her. Her lips moved, but made no sound.

"Is she all right?" Carrie asked quietly.

"Honey, she's never been all right," Gerty sighed in whisper. "No telling what that woman's been through. I just know we the ones been called to see her along her way, and I know we got some bad days ahead of us."

That night, in bed, listening to the low, rhythmic breathing of Arthur and Leo, I thought of Gerty's warning about bad days ahead. I believed she was right. I could have made the same warning myself. Any of us could have. The only thing new in Gerty's pronouncement was the idea of being called to see Lady along her way. I had never thought of it in such a manner, yet it intrigued me. It had a sense of destiny in it, mysterious and ghostly, and there, in my narrow bed, I realized there was a bothersome something nuzzling against the walls of the Castle, making a noise barely audible, and the sound of it was like the scratching of a cat.

SEVEN

I think if it had not been for Wally Whitmire, the little campaign we had building among us – justice for Lady – would have quickly lost its energy. Beaten-down people are fast to surrender. Eager, even. Wally would make the difference we needed. Wally and Arthur.

My first seeing of Wally Whitmire was this: His elbows were propped on the bar in Frank's Fine Dining, pushing his shoulder blades up, like the wings of a buzzard at rest. His head was impressive – big-eared, thick salt-pepper hair with an uncombed look about it, bushy eyebrows over close-set eyes that seemed strained from too much reading, or imbibing. He was sloppy-dressed and he had the expression of a man who was a paycheck away from being a bum and a fellow resident of the streets.

It was a shock to discover he was a man of learning – Dr. Wallace James Whitmire, retired professor of philosophy from the University of Delaware. His story, often and gladly shared with anyone who would listen, had him visiting Savannah in the year before his retirement. He had found it to his liking, not for the history of the city, but for the quaintness of its citizens, and he had moved south, leaving his past and the burial place of his late wife. Also, there was a frisky and independent daughter who had pledged never to travel south of Baltimore, Maryland. It was her line of demarcation, Wally explained with a snarl. Everything north of that line had attained civilization; everything south remained the Land of Mutants. Wally preferred the mutants.

"I hate the rift between us," he said of his daughter, "but it was time to get on with my life, or what was left of it." The way he intoned his sorrow was like an actor ending a soliloquy.

After weeks of wandering-about research in Savannah, Wally had concluded that customers of Frank's Fine Dining had the quality of mutant quaintness he was seeking. He spent his time talking and listening, though the talking side of it was more prominent. And, as he proudly revealed, when he was not at Frank's, he was at his home playing on his computer, searching cyberspace for some sign of intelligence pinging about the satellites circling Earth. He had yet to find any, he regularly announced.

Wally knew he was smarter than the rest of us, yet he insisted he simply wanted to be thought of as one of the regulars. Call him Wally, he said. The degree that declared his preeminence was in the bottom of a cardboard box still unpacked from his move. "Its rightful place," Wally said.

On all accounts, there was some doubt of his claims among those of us who found amusement in his pronouncements. Listening to him, he did not sound like a professor, his language having a saucy, barroom personality even when he tossed about words none of us had ever heard. He favored boozing with his pontificating, and the more he indulged in both, the merrier the company around him seemed to become. If he had had the music of it in his speaking, I would have sworn he was an Irish import given to genetic exaggeration.

Still, Wally was likeable and more often than not what he had to say would hang around in the thinking of his audience long after he'd said it. Among Wally's repeated observations was one about humanity: All events in the life of a person could be traced metaphorically to the falling of a domino against another domino standing close in line – domino striking domino after domino after domino, leaving a fallen-down pattern with the look of a snake's skeleton. "Once the falling starts, it ends only at the grave," Wally proposed. In one soulful, beer-drenched explaining of it, he even compared the look of a coffin to that of a domino tile, and the way he told it, an attentive person could see the final falling of the final domino-coffin dropping into an endlessly deep hole in the ground.

With each hearing of Wally's Destiny of the Dominoes theory, as he called it, I could close my eyes and see the past slamming down on me – the leaving of my father, the dying of my mother, the losing of my home, the risky environment of the Castle. And the day of Arthur stepping off the Greyhound in Savannah. That, too, was another falling of another domino, the power of it striking like a hurricane off the Atlantic, veering inland on a peaceful day, beginning with a breeze in the leaf-tips of trees and then the darkening of the sky in the east – day becoming night before its hour – and the ocean rising up in anger, beating its chest with foam-tipped fingers, and the winds striking land, howling like demons. And trees and buildings and dominoes falling.

Arthur was a hurricane that came to us in a gentle breeze, silently, yet the domino that fell from it would cause such a great thundering there are echoes of it still trapped in the dome of our history.

Doyle Copeland's story in *The Savannah Enquirer* was the start of it. It had grown from an intended little light-hearted feature about a man, a paper flower and a policeman, to a late-edition, front-page headline that yodeled across the top of the page:

Mayor's Wife in Hit and Run?

It was a report about the wife of Mayor Harry Geiger allegedly being involved in the accident that had sent Lady to the hospital.

To sweeten his brew of words, Doyle also wiggled the plight of the homeless, or near-homeless, into his account, knowing it would strike a nerve at City Hall and leave a heart-tug with his readers. Standing behind the protective shields of Allegedly and Supposedly and Reportedly, he fired missiles with heat-seeking warheads, and waited to hear the explosions.

The mood of the story – the reading beyond the words – suggested shenanigans – allegedly, supposedly, reportedly – going on in the mayor's office during an election year. Why else would Roger Upshaw, representing the mayor, make a visit to an old warehouse on Beale Street to confront the alleged victim of an alleged hit-and-run, the involved car allegedly belonging to the mayor's wife?

According to Doyle's story, the victim – having the street name of Lady and the birth name of Melinda McFadden – reportedly owned the warehouse, and had turned it into living quarters for herself and a few friends who were struggling to maintain dignity under trying circumstances. The implication was obvious: Was Roger Upshaw's alleged visit a matter of making apology on behalf of the mayor's wife, or of alleged political insensitivity in the form of an alleged threat?

As we would later learn from talking with him, the story had developed when Doyle, armed with our report of the vanity tag reading LILMAR, did his own snooping in the sneaky way of reporters, and discovered the tag belonged to the Mercedes of Debra Geiger – LILMAR being clever for Little Mayor, if you made the Lil into Little, the Ma into May, and the R into Or.

The way Doyle wrote it, his account of what had happened was far more compelling than our own about Lady being struck by LILMAR's car. None of us remembered one or two of the quotes attributed to Carrie, yet they were favorable and therefore acceptable. Without editorializing excessively, Doyle questioned the police department for failing to follow up with information that clearly would have identified Debra Geiger's car as the one speeding away from the scene of an accident. Such information could be damaging to Harry Geiger's re-election campaign, he suggested among his allegedlys and supposedlys and reportedlys, especially since the mayor had often issued loud complaints about street people damaging the image of the city.

The passage about Arthur presenting the paper flower to Sergeant Ted Castleberry as a gesture of forgiveness was a short sidebar inset, nudged under the headline of the lead story. The photograph of the flower illustrating his story was the one Arthur had presented to Doyle Copeland. In its color reproduction, it had the look of a perfect bloom snipped from a tranquil garden.

The passage of the giving of the flower and Ted Castleberry's destruction of it, would make Arthur temporarily famous and the mayor's office the target of bitter ridicule – all because of Wally Whitmire's bizarre sense of justice and his restless nature.

Wally was fascinated by the events reported by Doyle Copeland, finding in them a cause worth pursuing, or at least worth bellowing about. To Wally, Arthur's offering of a paper flower to a quarrelsome and haughty public official was an act as profound as Jesus forgiving his crucifiers. In a twisting way I did not wholly understand, it also endorsed Wally's theory about the damnation of politics – that real leaders were those who inspired others, yet were never elected to office because they were too noble for the indignity of the position. Arthur was such a man, Wally declared. Arthur had the making of a fine philosopher – a natural philosopher, not one incubated in a classroom with degrees hanging to his name like the tail of a kite. "I've been looking for this kind of man all my life," Wally asserted with enthusiasm bordering on idolatry. He ordered me to tell him everything I knew about Arthur.

And I did – omitting the clean plucking I had done of Arthur's wallet on our first meeting. I told him of the Castle, of Lady and Leo and Gerty and Carrie, told him of the scary way we got by day-to-day. He asked me about the visit from Roger Upshaw and of his threat to turn us out on the street. "What kind of nonsense is that?" he growled. "The woman owns the place, doesn't she? What's her name again?"

"We call her Lady," I answered. "Her name, as we know it, is Melinda McFadden. She says she's from New York and the property was part of the family estate." I paused. "But with Lady – well, who knows?"

He rubbed his chin with his fingers and made a thinking frown. Then he scribbled Lady's name on a napkin. "It'd have to be in the tax records," he mumbled, the way a man does when addressing himself. "Maybe I can do something there." He turned his attention to me. "But right now, ignore that horseshit about having charges pressed against the lot of you unless you turn a blind eye. You won't hear that again. Too much to risk, now that it's become headlines."

Then he smiled. I could see a light flashing in his eyes, the same sort of light that must have flashed in the eyes of Sir Isaac Newton when he saw an apple falling from its tree, tugged to the ground by gravity.

"Let's have some fun, Hamby," Wally said.

The first *Arthur for Mayor* sign was hand-lettered that day by Wally with a red marker on a large sheet of white poster paper supplied by Holly, and it was taped to the front door window of Frank's Fine Dining with Frank's reluctant permission.

Many who saw it – patrons and passersby – put together the one-plus-one of Doyle Copeland's front-page story and the window sign promoting Arthur as a mayoral candidate, and they hooted with glee, which caused Frank to send Holly for more poster sheets and more markers. Frank was old and mean and hobbled from a life-long fight with diabetes, but he liked a good laugh and he had been around long enough to recognize free publicity when it marched up to him and tapped him on the shoulder.

By mid-afternoon, the *Arthur for Mayor* sign contest – inspired by Wally and endorsed by Frank – was up and running.

The most creative entry would win a dinner for two, including a pitcher of domestic tap beer. Wally, being the mastermind behind the shenanigans, would be sole judge and arbiter of all disputes. All of it so pleased Frank, he called the newspaper to order an ad announcing the competition, declaring Frank's Fine Dining the official headquarters for the *Arthur for Mayor* campaign.

By late afternoon, street-word of the sign-making contest had reached students of the Savannah College for Art and Design – the SCAD crowd – and they arrived in Frank's with their free spirits and off-beat appearance and their sometimes-bizarre talent and the credit cards of their parents, and Frank's Fine Dining was soon littered in signs, most of them decorated with little paintings of red flowers. News of the gaiety spilled out the front door and raced down the street like a happy puppy, and people who normally could not have been pulled into Frank's with a team of horses began to elbow their way inside.

Frank was stunned. A leathery smile flourished over his face. He dispatched me to the Castle to invite Arthur for an on-the-house dinner.

"There's more people than just Arthur to consider," I told him. "Six of us in all."

His smile faded to a frown and I could see him making calculations in his mind. Finally he said, "Bring everybody."

Only Gerty refused to attend. She glared at me in her no-nonsense look and declared, "Too many honkies. Nothing good going to come of that."

A large table was cleared near the back of the dining area and Frank led Arthur and Lady and Leo and Carrie – and me, though grudgingly – to it, along with Wally. We were offered beer, but none of us accepted, knowing Lady would object. She ordered lemonade. We all ordered lemonade, even Wally, leaving me to believe someone had spoken to him of Lady.

"Pick what you want from the menu," Frank said in a voice loud enough to carry over the noise. He added, more quietly, "I'd recommend the hamburger."

I hold the memory of that night dear in the moments of gladness I have lived. It was like a wedding or an anniversary, or a rock concert with tattooed musicians and squealing girls with purple dyed hair. It was a circus without elephants and high wire acts, though it could be argued there were more clowns than necessary for three rings. Those not inebriated from the servings of Frank's bar, were tipsy enough from the fun of it all.

Never in the history of Frank's Fine Dining had so many people gathered at one time. Never had the noise level been as dangerous to health.

Arthur seemed pleasantly enchanted by the fuss made over him. He sat, patiently fashioning paper flowers from a colorful array of napkins, distributing them to the young girls and ladies who stood in line, giggling and yammering in their shrill, excited voices. He autographed campaign signs entered in Frank's competition. He shook hands with men rosy-faced with happiness from empty glasses and the awe of the moment. Lady glowed and I suspected she believed the celebration was for her. When Holly began taking pictures from an inexpensive digital camera she kept in her purse – one I had given her at Christmas, after a sizeable tip from a birthday show – Lady leaned close to Arthur and posed dramatically. Carrie and Leo and I took the only invitation we had: we sat and watched. It was enough.

In the fever pitch of the gaiety, Wally was assisted to stand in a chair and someone with the breath to do so whistled shrilly for attention and the noise of the café subsided.

"Good people, friends, concerned citizens," Wally began in a grave, pretentious voice, "welcome to the beginning of a new era."

He paused, waited for the cheers and applause to die away. "Of course, none of us are deluded enough–" He paused again, did a sweep of the room with his head, steadied his swaying in the chair, then added, " – or wasted enough to believe our new hero, Arthur Benjamin, can legally run for mayor, since he's only been here for a few days, but what does that mean?" His voice rose to a roar. "Nothing. It means nothing at all, not when the will of the people demands to be heard."A cheer erupted. Wally bowed. His face blazed with joy. He shouted, "Therefore, I, Wallace James Whitmire, self-appointed chairman of the Arthur for Mayor committee, consisting of all volunteers presently gathered in this fine establishment, do hereby declare Arthur Benjamin, the flower man, as the citizens' choice for mayor of the city of Savannah."

A voice yelped from the back of the gathering, "Is he a Republican or a Democrat, Wally?"

"He's a Demopublican," Wally answered in a cry. "And you have the honor of being delegates at the first national convention of the Demopublican Party."

Cheers exploded in Frank's Fine Dining. Signs were raised. Arthur was urged from his seat. I saw Lady pull her hands to her throat. She looked about in confusion. I saw her mouth make the words, "Oh, my..."

EIGHT

The event my mother had most enjoyed in Savannah was the annual St. Patrick's Day parade, with its greening of the river and its non-stop merriment, even if the silliness of it made a sham of what it was to be Irish. She was different during those days, girlish and excited, then melancholy and heartsick for the land of her childhood. Watching her spirit ebb and flow in such a manner had been a mystery to me as a small boy, yet as I became older, I understood it. It was a need to break away from the monotony of a scrape-by living and believe again in the thunderous joy of escape, even knowing the escape was temporary.

It was the same with Arthur being named a candidate of the Demopublican Party for mayor of Savannah. Absurdity turned loose, bringing out the good feeling of escape, made more joyful because everyone knew the brouhaha of it irritated those in power.

In the days following Wally Whitmire's proclamation, Doyle Copeland and other members of the media caught the fever that had begun in Frank's Fine Dining and turned it into an epidemic of happy mockery. *Arthur for Mayor* signs appeared on utility poles. Graffiti by SCAD students flourished in public restrooms and in store windows. Frank had a quick-print shop run off 300 bumper stickers, urging takers to apply them to rear bumpers of city vehicles. In three days, every police car and fire truck in Savannah carried the sticker – at least temporarily.

The media loved the circus mood of it, in part because it was fun and in part because it caused a row in City Hall. There were in-the-street television interviews with citizens, comically staged to appear critical and serious. A political cartoon depicted Arthur presenting a bouquet of paper flowers to a swooning lady. The caption line read: *Roses, not Rudeness.* A poll of 100 callers, conducted by a talk radio station, favored Arthur over Mayor

Harry Geiger by a margin of 94 to six. When pressed, the six all admitted they were city employees.

Students at SCAD, being young and spirited and brazen, found in Arthur a heroic figure as grand as any in the libraries of literature or in the nonsense of the reality television shows they watched with exaggerated merriment. They began the website, *Arthurthedemopublican.com*, spinning made-up stories each day of some noble, imaginative act committed by Arthur in saving the city from aliens and vampires and sea monsters and, of course, demonic government officials. Their comic book artwork accompanying the stories showed the promise of gifted artists emerging from the cocoon of childhood.

A homeless street musician known by everyone as Mr. Justin Price, Musician – remembering the mid-sixties and the flower children of the hippies and his one-time life in San Francisco – wrote a ballad called *Return of the Flower Child.* A rapper, performing under the name Mo Penny, wrote a rap song called *Street May-O and the Ho.* It was about Arthur befriending a prostitute, making me wonder if Carrie had an uneasy feeling hearing it because of the rumor about her.

Street talk, plentiful and loud, told tales of the city reacting with outrage, with the mayor spewing venom in civic club meetings about litter and the defacing of official property, all caused by a loudmouth in a sleazy bar – the loudmouth being Wally and the sleazy bar being Frank's Fine Dining. Wally laughed about it, but I knew he was incensed. It was in the flashing of his eyes, in the sharp edges of words he continued to fling in the mayor's direction in the form of letters to the editor, questioning the mayor's actions on everything from crime to historic preservation. He signed each letter:

Wallace James Whitmire, PhD
Professor of Philosophy (Ret.)
University of Delaware

Publicly, though, Wally's mood stayed jolly as he kept the drum beating in his campaign for Arthur – frivolous as it was – and when I would see him at Frank's, he was always scheming his nonsense. I knew it was mostly enjoyment for him, a way to pass time and to study the quaintness of humanity he found in Frank's and on the streets of Savannah, leaving me to wonder if he could be keeping a diary in hopes of turning it into a book, a case study of behavior born of conflict.

Oddly, Arthur's reaction to the fuss about his bogus candidacy for mayor remained one of amusement, or so it seemed. He waved away requests for interviews, which left me anxious. I would have been juggling swords and offering soliloquies in the style of Shakespeare. Still, his appearance on the streets of the city drew friendly crowds easy with their chatter and laughter, quick with their cameras. Everyone wanted one of his paper flowers. To Leo, the flowers had business potential. To Arthur, the flowers were gifts, having only the value of the giving.

"A dollar each," Leo argued. "Think about it."

Arthur smiled at the suggestion. Leo rolled his eyes and muttered suspicion of Arthur's claim that he was Jewish.

The only bother it gave me was how my street friends would take it, being that many of them fashioned flowers out of reeds and sold them to spend-happy tourists. To my surprise, they, too, were caught up in the carnival atmosphere of Arthur and his handouts, and early on they gathered around him to learn the art of turning napkins into blooms. It was as though they had been waiting for him, like a lost and wandering people needing a righteous leader promised by a prophet.

At night, as he slept, I replenished Arthur's hat with the money I had taken from him, having changed the hundreds into smaller denominations. He used it to buy trinkets that pleased Lady, or Gerty, or Carrie, and he also used it to supply materials for his flower-making, never questioning how the sweatband of his hat was such a provider, and I began to believe he was more child than adult, having the child's trust that his hat contained magic, like a leprechaun's crock of gold. Soon, he had Gerty helping him with the flowers, then Carrie, then Leo, then me. Lady's fingers had no memory of what to do, though she tried. We destroyed her failures when she was preoccupied with other fantasies.

Still, Arthur's presence did create business for us. At his urging, I plied my tricks of magic on the stage of sidewalks, leaving my silk top hat for contributions, the same as Mr. Justin Price, Musician, and every other performing beggar in the city. Carrie's storytelling was as magical as my tricks and as popular as Arthur's flowers – maybe more so. Watching the faces of children as they gazed wide-eyed and open-mouthed at Carrie left me with the kind of tenderness I had only in memories of my mother.

Yet, as my mother knew, and as I had learned, the parade always has an ending. The bands go home. The river becomes copper with its rain-mud. The garish green costuming is stored in closets. Sweepers roll over the streets, clearing the party trash of thousands. Life clicks back to monotony.

And I knew the high spirits of Arthur's café appointment would also end, but not so easily. Offending City Hall is a sticky matter. What one person regards as humor, another accepts as ridicule.

While we roamed the streets, being glad-handed, the issue of Debra Geiger's car unlawfully leaving the scene of an accident became a crusade for Doyle Copeland and *The Savannah Enquirer*.

Gossip had it that the mayor's response to Doyle's initial story had been one of fury and denial. His wife, he vowed, had been in Charleston on the day of the accident. Through Roger Upshaw, his spokesman, he accused the newspaper of slanderous reporting schemed to support his opposition in the upcoming mayoral election. For Doyle and the editors of the *Enquirer*, Harry Geiger's claim was a red flag in a bull's face and they ran a short, front-page notice inviting information from anyone who had witnessed the accident involving Lady.

Seven people called to say they had been present and each vowed the car in question did, indeed, make an illegal turn and did bear the vanity tag LILMAR. All said they would be willing to testify in court.

Sharon Day was among the callers.

We had no way of knowing it at the time, but Sharon Day's name caused Harry Geiger to do a turn-about with the story of his wife being in Charleston at the date and time of the accident – the Cover-up Caper, as Wally had loudly titled it.

In a next-day statement released to the media by Roger Upshaw, the mayor recanted, saying upon re-examination of his family calendar he had been mistaken about the dates, and in conference with his wife he had learned it was possible her car was on city streets during the time of the alleged incident, though there was no proof it was the car involved. In the statement, the mayor suggested there were many similar cars in Savannah and that it was possible in the confusion of the moment, people saw his wife's car passing by with its car tag leaving a lasting, but mistaken, impression of being the involved vehicle. He also promised a full investigation, which was the just and fair procedure. He further denied any hush-hush deal had been offered the residents of the so-called Castle, calling Roger Upshaw's visit one of courtesy and concern.

Doyle delivered the news of Harry Geiger's recanting to us before it was printed. It was his first visit to the Castle and he became immediately interested in Lady and her Guests, not as victims but as personalities, and in his smiling manner he made inquiries about our quarters. I could see Gerty's eyes clouding in suspicion. A chill made its itchy crawl down my back.

Lady offered the version of inheriting the building from her father's estate, pattering on about the mansion of her childhood in New York and the army of servants attending her family's every small need. Watching Doyle, I was certain he listened only out of kindness and, perhaps, pity. Clearly, Lady was child-like, content with her delusions.

"I've heard about this old place," Doyle said. "Didn't know it was occupied."

"Oh, yes," Lady cooed. "It's our home. We call it our Castle."

Doyle nodded, let his eyes sweep the room.

"It used to be much worse than it is," Carrie said quickly. "Lady's made it livable."

"Thank you, dear," Lady said. She turned back to Doyle. "We're being rude. Could we offer you a glass of sherry?"

Gerty sighed. We had no sherry, had never had sherry.

"Thank you, no," Doyle told her. "I just wanted to tell you the news about the mayor. I would guess the police will be asking you about pressing charges against his wife, if it can be proven that she's culpable."

"Charges?" Lady asked.

"That would be the next step, I would think," Doyle explained.

"We haven't talked about that," Arthur said. He was sitting near Lady and he leaned toward her, reached to pat her hand. "Perhaps we should leave it as it is, just an accident."

"Oh?" Lady murmured. The look of confusion on her face was the same as the look of confusion on Doyle's face.

"Why would you do that?" he asked.

"Yeah, why?" Leo said suspiciously.

Arthur smiled. "Seems like a big fuss," he replied.

"But if you don't press charges, they win," Doyle said.

"What do they win?" Gerty asked cynically. "All the nothing we got?"

"They get away with it," Doyle replied, more patient than I thought he wanted to be with Gerty.

Arthur nodded thoughtfully, let a pause build before saying, "I suppose that's true." He looked again at Lady. "I've never been comfortable with disagreements."

I thought of Arthur's story of his ex-wife, Reba. If what he had confided about her was true, he had had enough of run-ins.

"I think you're right," I said. Then, to turn off the subject, I added, "What would we do with any money we might get out of it, anyway? Look around us. We live in the Castle."

Gerty moaned.

Leo rolled his eyes.

Doyle let his smile become a soft laugh. "Maybe I should move in down here," he said. "Maybe you've got the answer."

NINE

Of the good things coming my way from having discovered Arthur at the Greyhound station, nothing was as pleasing as Holly's affection, and it was more than the acrobatics of bed-play, though that was enough to exhaust me and leave me with a floating feeling of bliss.

Holly's wandering ways ended. She no longer flirted with customers in Frank's, no longer complained to me of mistreatment, or of foolish dreams turned to nightmares. She no longer berated me for being a no-good with no future. She slipped me fresh cuts of pie, turned orders for hamburger into T-bone steaks, occasionally forgot to leave the bill when it came time to pay. Even Wally Whitmire spotted it. He whispered to me, "She's acting like a newly-wed. Your neck's in the noose, my young friend."

Truth be told, it was enough of a good thing to make me uneasy, and it reminded me of a poem I had once read while waiting out a rainstorm in a bookstore. The poem was called *Fats Blows Horn*. It caught my attention because it was about a girl named Holly, and I had copied it on a sheet of paper and kept it with me, reading it often enough that it finally stayed in memory – all but the writer's name.

Fats blows horn in McHerndon's Bar
While One-Eyed Jake plays bass.
And I drink gin two fingers deep
While Holly takes up space.

Now, Holly tries her best with me.
(Her kisses burn hot and bold.)
But Fats blows horn and Jake plays bass
And music feeds my soul.

Sure, Holly gives me love to touch,
Her skin against my skin,
But nothing makes me feel so good
As Fats and Jake and gin.

So take your love, sweet Holly, dear.
Find yourself another man.
For Fats blows horn and Jake plays bass
And I am who I am.

I half-suspected Holly's behavior had to do with her growing belief in the paper flower Arthur made for her. She had unpinned it from the table lamp beside her bed and had begun wearing it in Frank's Fine Dining, proudly telling everyone it was the first flower Arthur had given to anyone in the city. Occasionally, she would place it on the pillow between us after we had made love and she would coo, "Magic." The tender way she said it, I could see the word forming in the heat of her mouth, and being lost in the glory of her giving, I began to wonder if there was more to magic than trickery of illusion, and it made me edgy. Nothing is more dangerous for a magician than believing in his own magic.

The writer of the poem called *Fats Blows Horn* could have his Fats and Jake and gin. I thought of myself as the other man Holly had found.

It was Holly who gave warning of the troubles waiting for us.

She told me one night that a table of off-duty policemen, including Ted Castleberry, had let it slip that Arthur's days in Savannah were numbered. They had laughed heartily, had clicked beer glasses in celebration. She had heard a name mentioned: Cherokee. The name had caused her to drop a tray. Cherokee Robbins, still a teenager, was well known for his violent temper and trouble-making nature. He had been arrested with regularity for disturbing the peace or for fighting or for threatening tourists. On the streets of Savannah, he was considered a hit man. If someone wanted someone else disfigured over a simmering grudge, Cherokee Robbins – the Cherokee Kid, as he called himself – would gleefully oblige for a few dollars or a bottle of good whiskey.

"You watch after Arthur," Holly told me fearfully. "I know that little son of a bitch."

"As do I," I said. "Last word I had of him, he was in jail."

"They just let him out," Holly revealed. "I heard that much."

Two days after the warning, as I over-slept from a pleasurable night with Holly, Arthur slipped out of the Castle for his customary early morning walk. From the tidbits I managed to cobble together over the next few days, what happened to him was a tale of a horror.

A block into the walk, a stout, tattooed young man wearing over-sized, low-hanging pants, a t-shirt advertising an Elton John concert, and a red headband to hold in a tangle of blond hair, stepped from a cluster of azalea bushes in the still-murky light and said, "Hey, old man, you the one everybody's calling mayor?" He had one hand behind his back.

Arthur smiled at him. He said, "Good day, sir."

The young man moved his hand from its hiding. He was holding a baseball bat. A grin slashed across his face. He snickered. "It's about time you was voted out of office." He raised the bat and took a slow step toward Arthur.

A voice, a growl, came from behind Arthur: "Put that thing down, boy."

Arthur turned to the voice. He saw a slight man, his skin the color of polished ebony, standing in a boxer's crouch, his clenched fists raised in a boxer's pose.

The young man stopped. He peered beyond Arthur, saw the boxer. He laughed easily. "Nigger, you want your head caved in? Get your skinny ass out of here."

"Don't think so," the boxer replied. He moved forward cautiously until he was standing near Arthur. He said in a quiet manner, "Mayor, why don't you just step behind me here."

Arthur obeyed.

The young man laughed again. "You know who I am?"

"You the boy they call Cherokee," the boxer said. "Yeah, I know all about you, but that don't mean nothing to me. You just another punk far as I can see. You put that bat down and walk away so I won't have to knock some sense in you."

A flash of temper colored Cherokee's face. "What's your name, nigger? I want to know who I'm about to kill."

"You looking at Wendell Scott, boy. I'm forty-five years old. I weigh one hundred and fifty-three pounds. I live out here on the street, taking what comes my way, just like you. In my prime, I had me one hundred and seven professional fistfights and won me one hundred and three of them. Knocked out eighty-seven, and they was professionals, not some piece of street trash." He paused. "You still want some of me?"

A roar, like the cry of a lion, came out of Cherokee's chest. He jumped at Wendell, bringing the bat down like a woodcutter wielding an ax against a block of oak. Wendell ducked and stepped aside in a move so quick Arthur did not see it. It was as though Wendell had disappeared in front of him and had reappeared a half-second later, six inches from Cherokee. He hit Cherokee's face five times. The sound of it was the sound of an air hammer. Cherokee fell, unconscious, blood spurting from his nose and mouth.

Wendell stood over him, fists still clenched, breathing hard. He hissed, "I forgot to tell you, boy, they used to call me Lightning." He poked at Cherokee with his foot. "You ain't nothing. Nothing," he added. Then he turned back to Arthur. "You all right, sir?" he asked politely.

Arthur nodded. After a moment, he whispered, "Thank you."

"Just happened to be passing by," Wendell told him. "Saw who you was from the newspaper stories and thought I'd say hello."

"Glad you did," Arthur said weakly.

"Guess we better be traveling on before some policeman shows up," Wendell suggested.

Arthur did not move. He stood gazing at the bleeding Cherokee, and, as Wendell would later describe it, a shadow of pity moved across his face like a cloud floating in front of the sun.

It was pity that appeared at the Castle a half-hour later – Arthur and Wendell helping a still-dazed Cherokee Robbins to a chair. Over her muttering objections, Gerty attended to Cherokee's wounds and gave him coffee to drink. I watched helplessly, feeling shame. I had known of the threat to Arthur and had failed him. Now the weight of guilt pulled at my shoulders and chest. I over-thanked Wendell Scott, offered to pay him for his kindness.

Wendell was insulted. "Can't buy me, boy," he said evenly. "I may not have much, but what I got ain't for sale."

Gerty mumbled, "Amen." She handed Wendell a cup of coffee and a doughnut she had secreted in the pie safe. "Honey," she said to him, "he's a honky. Honkies don't know nothing about what it means to have some self-respect."

None of us knew why Arthur did the things he did. Even when we disagreed or were perplexed, he had a calming way of making everything seem reasonable. Once, in Frank's, I had tried to share my confusion about him with Wally Whitmire and Wally had cocked his head in the way I imagined college professors looked while contemplating great thoughts, and he had said, "I'd think the disciples of Christ felt the same way, wouldn't you?" I had not offered an answer, being Catholic and easily offended by people who dangle the name of Christ in a conversation simply to sound brainy. Yet, later I thought about it and could see Wally's point – dismissing the comparison of Arthur to Christ or those of us who resided in the Castle to disciples. Arthur was not a holy man; he was merely different. He had a forgiving nature, a scrubbed-down innocence that kept things simple, making it hard to go against his goodness.

Yet, what he proposed when the question of how to handle Cherokee Robbins' attack was broached, took all of us by surprise, especially Wendell Scott: teach Cherokee to become a boxer.

At first, Wendell chuckled. He looked hard at Cherokee, still regaining his senses, a humbled boy-man having trouble focusing. Then he stood and paced, his head bobbing in a nod, a frown lodged on his dark face. After a long moment, he turned back to Arthur. "He's mean enough," he said. "But he don't know nothing about boxing."

"You do," Arthur said kindly. He waved his hand to a far end of the Great Room, which had last been used as a warehouse for furniture and was now empty. "With Lady's permission, we could get some rope and build a fighting ring there. Maybe even have more people than this boy taking lessons. Seems to me there are a lot of young men in Savannah needing something to do."

Lady clapped her hands gleefully. "Oh, yes," she said. We all exchanged glances. Lady had no idea what Arthur was suggesting.

We tended to Cherokee for two days. The beating he had taken in five swift blows from Wendell Scott, ex-middleweight boxer, had tamed him. Or so we believed. He had even agreed to the suggestion of training under Wendell's direction. In his quiet moments, a look of sorrow clouded his gray eyes, telling a history of tragedy, and he took on the manner of a child who begs for the smallest gesture of affection.

He and Wendell stayed in the Castle, sleeping on two army cots Arthur purchased from a junk store with cash from the dwindling supply of funds that I tucked into the sweatband of his hat as he slept. The cots were placed in the same place the boxing ring would be built.

In the dark pitch of the third morning – sometime after one o'clock, Wendell would judge it – Cherokee slipped away.

Leo and Carrie and I spent the day walking the city looking for him, while Wendell and Gerty followed Arthur and Lady. We did not ask about Cherokee by name – not directly. We let the talk reel out like a fisherman's line riding the current, hoping a listener would take the bait, and some did, bringing up Cherokee's name as a matter of reference. No one had good feelings for him.

In late afternoon, a bearded, long-haired man with a grimy appearance, a man street-known as Preacher – for that had been his profession before giving in to alcohol – began a rambling, incoherent sermon about agents of Satan and first on his list was Cherokee Robbins. Once, he had been mugged by Cherokee and the memory of it was as vivid as visions he often had about the pain of Christ hanging on his cross of crucifixion while his Roman slayers dallied about, enjoying the sight. He had prayed fervently for God's justice as he was being assailed, he told us, but God had left him to bleed in the street. Now, when he saw Cherokee, he took to hiding, he confessed. "Saw him this morning, about sunrise," he muttered. "He was talking to a policeman close down to the river." He shook his head sorrowfully. "That boy scares me to death, but I feel for him. When I'm praying, I try to put a good word in for him. I guess the Lord knows what he's been through."

The following day, Cherokee's body was found lodged against the bank of the Savannah River, a single bullet hole burrowed in his forehead under the red headband he wore to hold his tangle of blond hair.

News reports – the bare-mention kind – called it the work of professionals, likely a payback for some harm Cherokee had caused in the arrogance of his meanness. A spokesman for the police department, a man named Arnie Luttrell, announced it would be a difficult case to solve, since there were so many known and unknown candidates as suspects. We all understood the meaning: the case was closed. Cherokee Robbins, who had been reared in a sorry home with sorry parents, had met the fate that had waited for him from his first cry of life. And few people cared.

We all attended the funeral for Cherokee. Having no relatives willing to pay for a proper service, he was given a pauper's spot in Laurel Grove Cemetery, the same resting place for my mother. Their gravesites were very near one another, divided by a narrow road that separated the paupers from the paying poor. Each time I made a visit to my mother's grave, I left haunted by the knowing that a strip of land kept her from being a pauper. Standing at the site for Cherokee, I could see her slender gravestone.

I had found Preacher and asked if he would offer some words on Cherokee's behalf, and he did, and I was surprised by the eloquence of them, taking his message from the book of Jeremiah, quoting a single verse of scripture: "I will forgive their iniquity, and I will remember their sin no more."

Preacher said he hoped the Lord kept his promise when dealing with Cherokee's soul. Repeating the story of how he had once been fearful of Cherokee, he told of asking around about the kind of life Cherokee might have had in the few years of his existence, and of finding a good thing: Cherokee had been kind to children, especially those with little to be happy about. "He was always giving things to them, from what I hear. Toys and candy, that kind of stuff," Preacher said. "And he was always playing games with them, like he was one of them even when he was older than they was. If he found somebody picking on one of them, he let it be known how much he didn't like it, and everybody here knows what that meant.

"He was a lost soul on this earth," Preacher concluded, "and that's why I hope the Lord looks on his good side. Now we got to pray for the soul of them that did this thing. Wouldn't be right to ask God to be forgiving one person and not the other."

We could have given Preacher a name to fit into his prayer.

"Ted Castleberry and that group," Holly said to me in a frightened whisper the night of the funeral. "That's who it was. They let Cherokee out of jail to do their dirty work and when he didn't do it, they killed him to keep him from putting the blame on them."

She was right, of course, and I knew it, but I did not make a speech about it. We were cuddled in her bed and I held her close, letting the shivering of her fears cross into my body, and I thought of the line from the poem about Fats and Jake and gin:

Sure, Holly gives me love to touch,

Her skin against my skin . . .

And the love of her skin against my skin slowly calmed her fear and gave rest to my sorrow.

TEN

In my childhood, on a trip to the Greyhound Bus Station to await my mother's playful promise of the delivery of a bicycle, I watched an older couple sitting together, both obese, both shabbily dressed, both carrying the look of exhaustion, the woman gazing dully at nothing, the man napping. And then came the call for the leaving of a bus and the woman pushed herself painfully from her seat. She stood, propping one hand at the small of her back as though holding down its aching, and then she turned to the man. I heard her say, "Come on. We got to get on the bus."

The man did not move. She reached to touch his shoulder. He still did not move. She said, "You dead?"

The man did not reply.

She leaned to him, moved her hand from his shoulder to his face, then she said softly, "He's dead."

She pulled her body erect, inhaled slowly, deeply. A gangly boy holding a guitar case sat near them. She looked at the boy. "I been telling him he was about to die," she said. "And now he done it."

I left the station and went home, forgetting the bicycle that would never arrive. When I told my mother what I had seen and heard, she pulled me to her and held me for a long moment. She whispered, "Hamby, some things can't be helped. Some things happen because they happen, and there's no explaining it." I could hear her weeping and I knew she was remembering things that had happened to her, things having no explanation.

It was one of the few times I saw my mother give in to despair.

The killing of Cherokee Robbins had left all of us with the same despair, and not even the mindless rambling of Lady's repeated stories could take us far from the thought of what his death meant. I had finally spoken of the conversation Holly had overheard in Frank's Fine Dining, and had offered the same conclusion Holly had offered about Ted Castleberry and his fellow officers. No one argued against it, yet no one suggested we should take what we believed, but could not prove, to officials. Without debating it, we all understood the risk of such a thing, and we did what we were good at doing – expert, in fact: we left it alone.

We tried to persuade Arthur to stop his morning walks, or to wait until someone could go with him – preferably Wendell, who had become a Guest in good standing, much to the pleasure of Gerty – yet I knew our begging fell on deaf ears. There were many mornings I awoke to discover Arthur gone from his bed, and Wendell still sleeping. After a time, we dropped the subject. Arthur had his own way of doing things, and we knew we would not change him.

Of all of us, Carrie seemed to be most affected by the death of Cherokee Robbins and the threat to Arthur. A shadow covered the brightness of her spirit. She fell into long spells of silence and she wore the look of sleeplessness. When she did leave the Castle, she returned early, always eager to know if anything out of the ordinary had taken place. If her nights out involved men seeking pleasure, there was no sign of it in her manner.

One night, I encountered her on the street as we both were on our walk back to the Castle.

"And where've you been?" I asked in the merriest voice I could find.

She looked at me suspiciously, as though I had been following her. "With a friend," she finally answered. She added, "A special friend."

"I'm afraid to ask," I said, keeping merry.

She moved close to me, slipped her arm into the crook of my elbow. "Let me tell you about him, Hamby," she whispered.

We sat on a park bench and she talked.

Her friend – she would not give his name – was a policeman. He had encountered her on the street the night after Cherokee's body was pulled from the river. He told her not to be afraid. "You'll understand," he had added. Then he had taken a notepad and opened it and had begun to scribble in it as he talked to her, giving it a look of an interrogation, or an interview. Passers-by had peered curiously at them before hurrying away.

It was a ruse, a set-up for a number of meetings he had had with her over the past week, she told me. He had been feeding her information about the politics of the department and the mayor's office. The fitful way she described it, there was enough corruption in Savannah's city government to make Washington, DC, look like the Land of Oz. None of it surprised me. My mother had said the same in her low moments.

I asked if she had told him of our suspicions about Ted Castleberry's involvement in the murder of Cherokee Robbins.

"I didn't have to," she said. "He asked me about it. Wanted to know if I'd heard anything on the street."

"Did you tell him?"

"No. Not yet. He hasn't mentioned it since."

She became tearful and I put my arm around her shoulders and rocked her gently. "Tell me," I said.

She nodded, looked away, inhaled deeply. "They're trying to find a way to get Arthur out of town – not killing him, but getting rid of him. He's made a big dent in the mayor's popularity, believe it or not. My friend tells me everybody that's against Geiger is sitting back enjoying the show."

"Is there some kind of plan?" I asked, trying to cover my worry.

"No," she answered. "Nothing I know about."

"This friend of yours," I said. "Why is he telling you all these things?"

She smiled in a tender way. "He's not a lover, Hamby, if that's what you're thinking. Believe it or not, he's my cousin. I just found out. He's known it for years and he's watched over me when I didn't know he was there. He decided to tell me after the stories came out about Arthur, and he knew I was involved." She paused. "He knew about everything I'd been through – before, you know. Before you, and Lady, and the Castle, and everything else."

"And was it that bad?" I asked, knowing it was a tender question, one I had always avoided.

"It was," she replied in a small voice.

"Do you want to tell me?" I said.

She hesitated, then nodded.

In bed, I listened to the sleeping sounds of Leo and Arthur and thought of Carrie. I had had an early flirtation with her – arm's length, harmless, a teasing between us to see if the teasing meant anything – and then we had settled into the kind of friendship older brothers have with younger sisters. I had always known she carried scars left from the lashes of secrets, but I did not know she had seen her own mother killed in a jealous rage by her father, who had then killed himself in front of her.

She did not cry as she told the story. She simply told it, leaving me to wonder if she had never talked of it because it had a sound too familiar, like a poorly done soap opera or something screamed about in the headlines of tabloid newspapers at check-out lines in supermarkets – the oft-told tragedy. And in her telling of the aftermath of it – the police inquiries, the disinterest of family – I realized that Carrie's escape from it had been a frantic search for joy, no matter how temporary. She had said to me in her confession, "You may not understand it, Hamby, but I have the same feeling of happiness making love as I do telling stories to children, except the children are sweeter and the memories are better."

Carrie was wrong. I did understand it.

When the choices are few or none, it brings some comfort to find happiness where you can for as long as you can, knowing that all of it can be snatched away without warning. It was a lesson learned from my mother's death.

I drifted into sleep thinking of Carrie. Sometime later, I awoke to a faint noise across the room and I opened my eyes the width of a slit and watched Arthur, or as much as I could see of him in the darkness, slip from his bed. He unlocked his small suitcase and opened it, and then he took an envelope from it and closed and locked it again. He pushed the envelope under his pillow and then wiggled his way back under the sheet. In a few minutes, I heard him sleep-breathing in unison with Leo.

The following morning, early, the police arrived, the police being two city detectives named Stuart Marlow and Cary Wilson, both appearing agitated, as though wishing for trouble. They declined Gerty's invitation to enter the Castle, saying they would prefer to speak to Lady outside, in private. Gerty was wise enough to tell them in a low voice, "You listen to me. She's got to have somebody with her. Otherwise nothing she says will make the first bit of sense."

The detectives reluctantly agreed that Lady could be accompanied by two people – only two people. "It's not a circus," Stuart Marlow said in a warning to Gerty. "It starts to get that way, we can do our talking at the station." Arthur and I were selected.

The detectives explained they were conducting an investigation of the incident allegedly involving Debra Geiger's vehicle, the one supposedly resulting in Lady's injuries – minor, they called them – and were there to inquire if Lady intended to pursue the matter.

"The City Attorney doesn't think there's enough evidence to press charges," Cary Wilson said. "If you decide to do so, it will be your responsibility to follow through."

Lady blinked, smiled. She looked at me and then at Arthur.

"And what have you found in your investigation?" I asked.

Stuart Marlow cleared his throat. "There's enough eyewitness testimony to suspect Mrs. Geiger's car was on the scene," he answered. "The mayor has already addressed that. What is not known is whether or not it was involved in the alleged incident, or even if she was the driver of the car on that occasion."

"What does she say?" I pressed.

A coloring spread across Stuart Marlow's face. He scrubbed his lips together like a man who has chapped them in the sun. "None of your business," he answered curtly. "That's got nothing to do with anything we're asking about."

"Why doesn't it?" I asked, feeling a roiling of my blood.

"She doesn't remember," he answered after a moment used for glaring at me. "She's a very busy lady."

"Her maid often uses the car for errands," Cary Wilson added. "But that's an issue for the court to determine, if it gets that far, not for here. We only need an answer about pressing charges."

For a moment, no one spoke, and the silence of it was heavy. Then, to my surprise, Arthur said, "Yes, she will."

The coloring of Stuart Marlow's face deepened. "She didn't say it," he snapped.

Arthur smiled, turned to Lady. "Lady, would you say yes to these gentlemen?"

Lady touched her hair, lifted her shoulders as though she suddenly and clearly understood everything. "Yes," she said calmly. "Why, of course."

"You're sure?" Cary Wilson asked. "You're not being coerced into this are you?"

"Not at all," Lady replied in a stern voice. "Are you implying I'm not capable to making a decision, young man?"

"No ma'am," Cary Wilson mumbled. He dipped his head. "We'll inform the City Attorney."

"Get a lawyer," Stuart Marlow advised bitterly. "You'll need one."

"Thank you," Arthur told him.

We waited until the two men were well away from the Castle, and then I said, "We can't get a lawyer. We don't have money for that."

"We shouldn't worry," Arthur said. "It'll be fine."

The difference between a born family and a found family is how unexpected issues are handled. A born family will talk it out, snarl and badger, and then, if close-bound, will make enough give-ins to keep peace. A found family takes what it gets without the knockdown of argument. A found family gives in to trust, hoping whatever matter is at risk will work for the best of everyone.

It was that way with Arthur's turn-about in his opinion of pressing charges against Debra Geiger, or Debra Geiger's car. Earlier, he had made a case – a good one, I believed – against pursuing charges, and now he was in favor of it.

None of us questioned him, though all wondered about it. My own guessing was that Arthur had found Detective Stuart Marlow's attitude condescending and offensive to Lady. In my thinking, it was a good enough reason. Many wars have been fought over haughtiness.

Still, his answer settled uncomfortably with me. From Carrie, I knew the mayor had placed Arthur in the cross hairs of his anger, and his finger was on the trigger of vengeance.

Arthur seemed totally unconcerned. Late morning we took our walk – the lot of us – and people gathered around us as always and Arthur handed out his flowers and I plucked pennies from the ears of giggling children and Carrie drew her sprightly caricatures and told a story of a princess who lived in the disguise of a little girl in the house of an artist. Lady and Leo and Wendell looked on, blending with the pausing crowd like hired shills in an audience. The day was splendid.

That evening, we had a dinner of chicken roasted on a grill found by Leo on one of his nightly excursions, and when we had finished the feasting, Lady asked Carrie to repeat the story of the princess. "So lovely," Lady said. "So lovely."

Carrie began the story and Lady smiled warmly, letting herself drift into the words, becoming a little girl who had been stolen away by thieves from a palace in a foreign land, only to be rescued by a poor artist named Tomas when the thieves abandoned her out of fear of the king's soldiers.

In Carrie's story, the king, in his sorrow, began a search throughout the kingdom for an artist gifted enough to paint a portrait of his missing daughter, taken from his memory description of her. "Each artist must first render a painting of a small girl as an example of his ability," the king commanded. "He who best renders the image of such a child will be given the honor of creating a portrait of my missing daughter and will be provided riches beyond his imagination."

Having a need for money to provide for the new child he and his wife had accepted as a deserted foundling, Tomas made the long trip to the king's palace and presented his rendering of a small girl, as required. The king was so startled by the likeness that he was overwhelmed. It had to his daughter. He was certain of it. He asked of Tomas, "Who is the model for this child?" And Tomas told of the foundling, whom he had named Jessica, and the king and his wife, the queen, collapsed into tears, knowing the child to be their princess. A heart-shaped birthmark on her shoulder gave proof of it.

"And they lived happily ever after," Carrie said, ending the story.

Lady applauded gleefully, made an oohing sound in her throat.

Gerty mumbled, "That's a honky story if I ever heard one."
"Where you get all them stories?" Wendell asked.

"Dreams," Carrie told him.

Wendell laughed easily. He looked at Gerty, made a wink. "Couldn't be telling about no dreams that come on to me," he said.

"Wouldn't make no sense," Gerty countered. "Much as you been beat in the head."

"That story was only part of a dream," Carrie said. "The whole dream was about all of us."

I teased her to tell the full dream.

"We were all in a real castle, like the one Lady told us about, the one in Austria," she began. "Arthur was sitting on a king's throne and Lady was sitting beside him, and the rest of us were there, standing in front of them. And then the doors opened and people came running inside – all the people we know from the street – and they were shouting, *'Long live the King! Long live the King!'*"

Carrie paused and smiled, holding to the thought that made the smile. "That's when the dream jumped to the princess, living in the house of an artist," she said. "I woke up then. After that, I just made up the rest of the story."

"That's what we need," Gerty said in a sarcastic voice. "We need us a king. Some honky on a mule, wearing all that tin can underwear, waving around his sword, slicing up folks like they was filet mignon." She paused. "That's what we need," she said again, "Uh-huh. All we need. That's it."

Lady's face seemed to glow. She had not heard the cynicism of Gerty's declaration. "Why, yes, of course," she said gaily. "We should have a king. Wouldn't it be fun? And I could be the queen."

"I thought you already was," Gerty mumbled in a hushed tone, turning away from Lady.

It was then that the Castle earned its name, with Carrie's grand foolishness of declaring Arthur the King of the Paper Flowers, using a turned-over green bread basket taken by Leo from Frank's Fine Dining as a crown, and making equal fuss over Lady being the Queen. She and Gerty were ladies in waiting, though Gerty was not pleased with the title and Carrie improved it by naming her the Royal Seamstress. I was a knight, as were Leo and Wendell. "So what's my name?" Leo asked playfully. "Sir Yiddish?"

The room became festive with game playing, with the bowing and scraping of it. We let ourselves be bossed around by Carrie, who had been transformed into a girl-child on a playground of dreams, and we laughed at the shenanigans, each of us letting off the nervous uncertainty of going to court to face the wife of the most powerful man in Savannah.

Lady glowed. Carrie might have been on a playground, but Lady was in her world.

I did not leave the Castle to see Holly. It was her night off from Frank's and she had an appointment to have her hair trimmed at a school for beauticians needing volunteer customers, and I was glad for it. If I had been with Holly, I would have missed the coronation of King Arthur.

In bed, I thought of the foolishness of our blithering about kings and queens and ladies-in-waiting and knights of the court. It was the same as children making pretend over some wandering thought that flittered around in their imagination like butterflies circling a flower. We had often engaged in such dreamy and light-headed make-believe – though not so childish – and I had always celebrated the joy of it, knowing the reason we did it was more for escape than for wish-making. Yet, there was something almost hopeful in Arthur, King of the Paper Flowers. It was as though the table knife he had used to knight us, following Carrie's gushing instructions, was as real and as sharp and as mystic as Excalibur.

I thought of Holly. Holly had said there was something supernatural in the flower Arthur had presented to her, and I had believed it, the way she had gone about her lovemaking.

In bed, in the dark of the transformed working manager's office, I smiled and gave permission for my mind to say the name: "Sir Hamby." It had a good echo.

ELEVEN

In one of her stories of Ireland, my mother told of an excursion she had taken as a young bride from her home in Youghal to Dublin. It was a trip my father had arranged after hearing rumors of jobs being available with the railway – a position far grander than the one he had in Youghal as pub keeper for a stingy owner by the name of Penn, whose ballyhooed claim that he was a relative of William Penn offered higher regard than the man deserved.

For my mother, the trip was as romantic as any she would ever take. For a week, staying in a cheap room a few minutes walk from Grafton Street and St. Stephens Green Park, she had lived the dizzy life of a girlish wish – seeing wonders heard about from strangers, and being in love with a man who had been generous with his attention and happy in his living. One of her treasures was the preserved rose he had given her in Dublin, earning it from a flower vendor with a trick involving a rubber band. Among the things I discovered following her death was that rose, or one like it, pressed flat in a book meant as a diary – a book without any words. Still, the rose told the life story of my mother as eloquently and as poignantly as any poem ever written.

There was a glow in her face, a shining in her eyes, when she spoke of those days in Dublin. None of the hard times she would endure later ever dimmed the memory, and I was sure she retreated often to that week, calling it back to hear good-time laughter and to linger in the promises my father must have made – promises too grand to imagine, promises never kept.

Yet, it was a week of deception. There were no jobs with the railway and while she and my father were lost in the headiness of Dublin, Penn, the pub owner, sold his pub in Youghal and the new owner had his own pub keeper.

"We went home to nothing," my mother would say sadly. "It's when we made our plans to come to America."

She would look at me with her soft gaze, the one holding bewilderment, and she would say, "Hamby, there's always something going on somewhere that'll have a bearing on you. Be ready for it. Always be ready for it."

I have learned the hard way the truth of my mother's advice.

While we were crowning Arthur as King of the Paper Flowers and accepting imaginary titles for ourselves, Roger Upshaw and three lawyers were meeting with Mayor Harry Geiger in his locked office at City Hall. A strategy session, Carrie's cousin reported to her the following afternoon in Colonial Park Cemetery, where they had begun to meet.

The lawyers included Ned Doubleday, who was the City Attorney, Shawn Grogan and Fred Seabrook. All were well known in Savannah. Ned Doubleday had political ambitions and considered himself a protégé of the mayor and successor to the office. Shawn Grogan and Fred Seabrook had financial ties to companies doing services for the city, and each had been recruited by Harry Geiger to influence decisions among aldermen in city council meetings. *Quid pro quo* arrangements. So many fingers scratching so many backs, it could have been a remedy for a poison ivy epidemic.

The session had been about the inhabitants of the Castle, Arthur in particular.

"It's turned serious," Carrie's cousin had confided.

But it was not a cut-and-dried, run-of-the-mill deliberation, though there were plenty of little-known, nit-picking city ordinances to bring the lot of us in and to lock us away on charges ranging from loitering to conducting business without a license. There was still a pitfall – a serious one. With Arthur's popularity, the howl of the media would have been deafening if the mayor had ordered a pickup of any of us.

What Harry Geiger wanted to do was turn the tide back to his favor before his wife went to trial, if the question of her hit-and-run went that far.

Ned Doubleday supposedly informed him that a trial could not be avoided if Lady decided to press the issue, especially since hit-and-run charges went to state court.

"Then you need to find a way to take the run out of it, don't you?" the mayor supposedly had said.

And Ned Doubleday had replied weakly, "I'll do my best."

Carrie's cousin did not know who had gathered the information, but Roger Upshaw had a brief report on each of us, and each had been talked over like suspects in a terrorist organization.

They knew about Leo's jail time, about Gerty's history as a seamstress in Atlanta, about Carrie's suspected prostitution, about Wendell's boxing record, about my haphazard lifestyle – knew even of my relationship with Holly Ellis. Arthur was a mystery. He had only been in Savannah for a short time and had violated no laws of consequence, even with the popularity that had been heaped upon him. They discussed drug use among us, but had no proof of any such behavior. Shawn Grogan even doubted it. "The word I get is the old woman makes them toe the line," he had grumbled.

It was the old woman – Lady – who seemed most baffling to them. In an update on the Beale Street property, they had discovered that tax payments were received annually from a trust fund administered by a Delaware corporation called A.N. Whitehead Properties, a subsidiary of McFadden Enterprises out of New York. It was guessed by Ned Doubleday that Lady's claim of ownership of the Castle – Melinda McFadden's claim – was legitimate. However, using it as a residence could well be an issue, he proposed.

The suggestion had inspired Fred Seabrook. "There's your answer," he had said to the mayor. "Eviction. Have Ned check it out, see if there's anything we can use to get them out of there. Break up the commune, you break up their base of power."

It was a strategy that had intrigued Harry Geiger, yet one that concerned him. The media had roasted him many times on his public stance against the homeless, or near homeless. Putting the inhabitants of the Castle on the street would only increase the yelping. "Not now," he had said. "If it becomes necessary, maybe, but not now."

Roger Upshaw had had his own recommendation: arrest Arthur for causing public disturbances with his crowd-gathering antics.

The mayor had called Roger an idiot, had raged at him. "Have you ever seen him out there? He looks like the goddamn Pied Piper of River Street. If he wasn't Jewish, they'd make him the honorary Pope. I'm surprised those limp dicks over at the Chamber haven't put him on the payroll, for God's sake. And in case it slipped your attention, there was a snippy little story in today's fish-wrapper about making those ridiculous paper flowers he hands out the official city flower. And you want me to put handcuffs on him? They wouldn't wait for the election to run me out of office."

The meeting had ended in frustration and one important decision: keep watch on us.

Carrie's cousin had left her with a warning: "Be careful. Don't do anything foolish."

"How did he know about the meeting?" I asked.

"I have no idea," Carrie answered. "All I know is he told me he had some tricks up his sleeve in case things got out of hand."

"I think we need to tell the others," I said.

"No," she said sharply. "Not yet."

I did not push the suggestion. It was Carrie's cousin and Carrie's call and I trusted her.

"All we can do is wait and see," she said. "At least we know Lady does own the Castle."

I nodded – in a weak way, I suppose, remembering Wally's mischievous story about Lady's ownership being on the books and knowing Wally's love of game-playing.

In the tiresome act of waiting and of watching for trouble in the days that followed, Carrie and I saw an army of policemen, some in uniform, some in such identifying suits they could have had the city name stitched on the back of their jackets in neon orange threading. We said nothing to the rest of our group, yet I think they all knew intuitively something was in the air – all but Arthur, who, to our knowledge, had no experience in such matters, and, of course, Lady, who would have had no understanding of it if she had been in the mayor's meeting as guest of honor. I could see the others looking about warily, could see by their posture that they, too, were on edge.

But we were careful. When I did magic, I did not put out the silk top hat for contributions. When Carrie told her stories, she insisted that parents remain with their children. When we crossed streets, we waited well off the curb for the changing of the light. Once, knowing I was being watched by Stuart Marlow, wearing sunglasses, I gave a dollar to Hobbler Bob. He stared suspiciously at me, and then at the dollar, wondering which was counterfeit, before scurrying away in his crippling walk.

Arthur handed out flowers that Leo carried in a box advertising Jim Beam whiskey, a box I had taken from the throwaway at Frank's Fine Dining. The ladies smiled glad smiles to have one of the flowers. Teenage girls blushed and snickered, small girls gazed in wonder, men thanked him profusely, telling him the flowers were meant for their wives or girlfriends or office companions. I suspected many of them meant their lovers. A popular pose for picture-takers was one of Arthur gently pushing the pipe-stem stalk of a flower into a smiling lady's hair.

And always there was Lady – Lady watching the goings-on as though she were at a garden party, and Gerty watching Lady to keep her from wandering away, Gerty complaining about the heat and the silliness of people. It was all honky business, she declared, yet she was wrong. There were many blacks and Asians and Hispanics who stood in line for the gift of the flower.

In all of it, I imagined Mayor Harry Geiger standing at the window of his City Hall office, looking out at the fawning over Arthur Benjamin, the man who made paper flowers and became a king because of them. Harry Geiger seething in anger, his blood pressure at the sizzle.

It was a pleasant vision. Knowing Harry Geiger was irritated over our presence was worth having the police keep watch, waiting to post a grievance against us.

I never asked Carrie how she knew when her cousin wanted to meet with her, yet I was certain the two had arranged some signal, something unseen by any but the two of them. I knew only she would disappear, usually during my magic act, and later, she would motion me aside and we would pretend we were going for a leisurely stroll and she would tell me what she had learned. I worried only that she was being followed, a worry she brushed off, telling me she knew who was assigned to her and she knew how to distract him. He was, she assured me, stick-dumb. When I learned that it was Billy Pottier, I stopped worrying. Mean as he was, Billy would have lost his own shadow on a sun-bright day.

But there came an afternoon when I saw a look of panic in her face as she gave me her head-wag, and I followed her to Factors Walk, among the tangle and noise of tourists where overhearing would be impossible. She told me her cousin had left a note for her in a book about whales in the back of an antique shop. The note had left her trembling.

"They've bugged the Castle," she said in a whisper.

I was stunned. "When?" I asked.

"This morning, when were out," she told me. "They put it in the Mozart bust."

"Holy Father," I moaned. "If nothing else, they could run us in for being insane."

"I think they're looking for more than that," Carrie said impatiently. She paused, looked out at the river where a cargo boat made its slow crawl upstream. "They're also going to try to bribe us."

"Your cousin told you that?" I asked.

She nodded, keeping her eyes on the cargo boat.

I thought of Wally Whitmire's falling dominoes, saw the tumbling of them, and I realized it had been Wally's jesting promotion of Arthur as a candidate for mayor of Savannah that had aggravated the fix we were in. I also believed he was the one who could find a way out of it.

"I'll take care of it," I said to Carrie.

"How?"

"Just trust me," I said.

"What does that mean?"

"It means what I said," I answered. "Trust me."

"My God, Hamby, do you know what you're asking?"

I shrugged. Knowing me as she did, she had a point.

She pushed me to explain my thinking, but I did not, since I had no thinking beyond finding Wally. Still, I promised she would understand soon enough. I asked her to return to the Castle and to make sure the conversations steered away from our troubles or from any references to the police or the mayor or the mayor's wife. I had no great worry about it since we avoided such talk, yet there was always the chance that one of them – Leo or Gerty, especially – would have an unkind thought to share.

She asked where I was going.

"To see a friend," I told her.

I found Wally at Frank's, as I had hoped. Being late afternoon, he was seated alone at a table in the eating area working on a crossword puzzle from a collection published by *The New York Times.* He seemed relieved to see me.

"I have concluded Satan designed the first crossword puzzle," he said wearily. "The evil son of a bitch knew what they would do to a man's brain." He smiled, took a drink from his beer. "You look as though you've been caught with your pecker hanging out, Hamby," he added. "What's up?"

"I need your help, Wally," I told him.

He leaned forward. "The table's in front of you, my friend. Put the cards on it," he said.

"In confidence?" I asked.

He nodded.

And I told him everything, from our suspicions about the death of Cherokee Robbins to the bug in the Castle. The only thing I hedged on was where the information came from, keeping my promise to Carrie. "Just know it's from a good source," I said.

He picked up his beer mug in both hands, held it front of his face for a moment, then sipped from it. His face was furrowed in thought. After a moment, he muttered, "Damn, Hamby. I feel responsible."

"You're not," I said, trying to assure him. "Maybe you've ruffled some feathers, but the fact is we were in trouble the minute Lady got struck down."

Wally leaned back in his chair. I saw a faint shudder roll across his shoulders and his face seemed to age, like a shadow crossing it. He said, "Hamby, I can't stand the high and mighty."

I did not reply, because I knew he had something more to tell me, something painfully private.

And he did.

It was the story of an artist friend who had taken a job in Delaware as a manager of a small non-profit arts organization, not a good fit, not when his yearning was to paint. He held the position for two years, enduring run-ins, always on the verge of being ousted. Finally, it happened.

"The fact that he got fired didn't bother me," Wally explained. "Probably good for him. Probably good for the group. It was the way it was done."

The story Wally told was astonishing. His friend's mother had died in New Mexico, and on the night he was there conferring with funeral directors about her burial, a board meeting – deliberately called for the purpose – was taking place in Delaware to fire him.

"Cowards," said Wally, spitting the word. "Bastards." He paused. The shudder rolled again over his shoulders. "How can you fire a man when he's burying his mother? How do you settle with that in your soul? How? You tell me, Hamby. What kind of people would dishonor a man's mother with such arrogance? Christ. They could have waited a month, two months. They didn't. They were bunched together in a boardroom, two thousand miles away, being brave and noble, patting themselves on the back for taking such a courageous stand. I think about it, and I can hear them spewing their self-righteous bullshit. 'Look at us. Aren't we grand? We just saved the world.' It's the same as –"

His voice broke. He sat, breathing rapidly. He rubbed his hand over his face. I knew he was thinking of his friend and of his friend's mother and of the heaping on of pain by people who took pleasure in their egotistic sense of power. Then he blinked and shook his head. "We need to do something about the mayor," he said. "This is meanness."

"That's why I'm talking to you," I told him.

He settled back in his chair, laced his fingers in his lap. I could tell he was speed-thinking by the way he stared at the beer mug. After a few moments, he said, "We have to turn the tables. We can't fight City Hall; we have to make City Hall fight us." He looked up at me. His eyes were suddenly bright. "Get me some napkins, Hamby," he said.

For the next hour Wally plotted, and I was astounded by what he proposed and by the detail he worked out on paper napkins, making it all seem as clean and as absolute as a mathematical formula. It had the campaign strategy of a covert war fought in river mist, a war of bluff, of strike and retreat, a war of nerves. None of it sounded completely reasonable, or workable, yet I was caught up in the energy of it and quickly gave him pledges of agreement. He studied the napkins and beamed over his work. The man of learning from the University of Delaware had found a contest more complex and more pleasurable than a crossword puzzle.

When he finished his scribbling, Wally stuffed the napkins into the inside pocket of his jacket, promising me a copy when he had it organized to his liking. "Hamby," he said, "I'm a madman when I'm really pissed off. Understand this, my quaint Irish friend: we're not going to roll over. They won't even know who's firing the shots or where they're coming from. All you have to do is believe it, and make everyone else believe it. That's your job."

The only thing about our meeting that left me with some bother was a comment he made behind a devilish smile: "There may be one or two things I do on my own, for my own pleasure."

Then, as I was leaving, he called for me, and I turned back to him. The amusement had disappeared from his face. He said, in a voice too loud, a voice with tremble in it, "You know what the bastards had the gall to do the night they fired my friend, Hamby? They sent a wreath for the funeral."

At the Castle, Carrie gave me an all's-well nod, and I knew nothing had been said to cause storm troops to break down the door, waving warrants and machine guns. I handed her a note I had written at Frank's. It read: *Take Lady outside for a few minutes. Tell her you want to talk to her in private about something*. She gave me a puzzled look.

I have never asked Carrie what she whispered to Lady. I only know that Lady's expression became one of concern and she followed Carrie outside, making a melodramatic fuss about the need to have fresh air.

When the door closed, I turned on Lady's radio and upped the volume and then made a motioning to the others, instructing them not to talk and to follow me into the small manager's office bedroom I shared with Leo and Arthur. The room being crowded, Wendell had chosen to continue sleeping in his own corner of the warehouse space. I had some suspicion it was done also to have some late-night privacy with Gerty.

In the room, I spoke quickly in a whispering voice, waving down the questions I could see forming in their faces and on the tips of their lips. I told them about the bug in the Mozart bust, about the plans targeting Arthur. "And don't ask how I know," I cautioned. "You'll have to be trusting me on it." I told them also that I had met with Wally Whitmire and the plan we were following was his plan.

Finally, I paused and Leo said in a low moan, "They'll get us. They want us, they'll get us."

"Not without a fight," I said firmly.

"What do you propose?" Arthur asked. As always, his voice was calm.

"You're going to disappear tonight," I said to him. "For the time being, you'll be staying with Wally. You'll come back when you're needed, when they least expect it. We're going to let them think they've got us on the run." I paused, realizing the plan devised by Wally was too complicated to explain and I was not sure Arthur would agree with it. Some of it went against his judgment. It was like an illusion that only a Houdini could pull off, an illusion made of mirrors and trap doors and wires too thin to be seen from the distance of a baffled audience. "Just trust me." I said again, not being sure that I trusted myself.

The expression on Arthur's face did not change. He said quietly, "Yes."

"As far as the rest of us know, Arthur simply left in the middle of the night," I explained.

"What about the bug?" Wendell asked.

I smiled proudly. "I like this part," I said. "Arthur takes Mozart with him as a memento of being here. At least that's the story we'll be offering."

"It's still a bug," Wendell said, shaking his head in doubt.

"Not if it gets knocked out of the bust somewhere on the street, and somebody accidentally steps on it," I replied, remembering Wally's instruction.

A smile spread across Wendell's mouth. He wagged his head in admiration.

Gerty had not spoken. She had listened with a look of worry and I knew she needed to respond, for or against. I said, "Gerty? What do you think?"

She turned her eyes to me and I saw the embers of anger in them. "Make it hurt," she said in a growl.

TWELVE

I had worried that Carrie would be upset with me for revealing the information her cousin had provided, but she was not, not after hearing my vow that I had kept the source of it secret, and when I explained to her the plan Wally had devised, she became wide-eyed with excitement, especially knowing she had already played a major role in it by her contact with her cousin. She asked if she should tell him what we were planning.

I agreed reluctantly, knowing it was a risk, knowing her cousin could well be a mole, a pipeline to the mayor, playing her with his sweet story of kinship while leading us into some elaborate trap. Still, we had no choice but to trust him.

As I would learn, it was a good decision.

It was not an easy thing, having Arthur leave us. We sat, mostly in silence, waiting for the hour, listening to classical music from Lady's radio, long after Lady had retired for the night. At midnight, when I finally gave the signal that it was time to leave, Gerty went to the room she shared with Carrie and returned a few moments later carrying a garment. She held it up, letting it fall open. It was a black cape with a high collar like those once popular on Nehru jackets. She crossed to Arthur and placed it over his shoulders, turned him and fastened the collar with eyehooks, and then she leaned to him and whispered, "Now you look like a king."

Arthur took her face in his hands and kissed her tenderly on the cheek. Tears bubbled in Gerty's eyes and in Carrie's. I could feel moisture welling in mine. I do not know about Leo and Wendell. Both of them looked away. We left, Wendell carrying the bust of Mozart. I had Arthur's large suitcase; Arthur had his small one. Outside, I turned back. Carrie and Gerty were at the door, holding one another in an embrace of sadness.

We did not know as we walked the three blocks to meet Wally that Carrie's cousin watched us from the cover of darkness, knowing full well what we were plotting. Carrie had managed to slip away and call him, giving away enough of the plan to get his attention. He had disbanded the surveillance team assigned to us, sending them home with the opinion there was no reason to waste manpower on snoring people. Later, after meeting him, he told me he had laughed aloud when he saw Wendell nudge the bug from inside the bust of Mozart and grind it into the sidewalk with the heel of his shoe – was, in fact, afraid we might have heard him.

Wally was waiting beside his car, enjoying a Cuban cigar, one of the pleasures he had adopted in Savannah. He greeted Arthur quietly, but warmly, saying he looked forward to the companionship, and then he gave me a wink and drove off with Arthur. Arthur was wearing his cape and holding Mozart in his lap.

Wendell and Leo and I stood watching the car disappear.

"Hope you know what you're doing," Leo said softly.

"Me, too," I told him.

"He's a funny little man," Wendell mumbled after a moment. "Don't seem like nothing bothers him."

The next morning, we attempted to explain Arthur's disappearance to Lady, telling her he had left in the night of his own accord. I read a note to her that I had persuaded Arthur to compose on Wally's instruction. It said:

Dear friends,

After thinking about it, I have decided to take my leave of you to prevent further troubles. Thank you for your kindness. I will always think warmly of you.

Even with the note, Lady was confused, unable to fix in her mind that Arthur had left, and it caused me to wonder how many leavings she had known and if the stories she told were cover-ups for those times of loneliness. She sat in her chair throughout the morning, watching the door to the Castle, believing it would open and Arthur would walk inside. Gerty persuaded her to have a light lunch – broth and toast – and then led her into her bedroom for rest.

"We'll be looking for him," Gerty promised in a gentle deception. "Don't you worry about that."

Gerty was wrong only in who was searching; it was the police, not us.

They knew the bug placed inside the bust of Mozart was dead, or gone, and they knew that Arthur was either staying inside the Castle or he, too, was gone.

In late afternoon, one of the officers – on orders, I believed – approached me as I took my walk to Frank's. He said, "Where's the flower boy? Haven't seen him around."

"Arthur?" I asked.

"Yeah, whatever his name is."

"He left," I told him.

A look of surprise shot into his face. "Left? What does that mean?"

"Gone."

"Gone where?"

I shrugged. It was the only pleasure I had ever had talking to a police officer. "I don't know. When we woke up this morning, he wasn't there. Left a note saying he was moving on. Why are you asking?"

The officer frowned. "Just didn't see him, that's all. He's usually out, looking for attention." He paused, glanced around, tugged at the belt holding his handgun. His expression was that of a man reviewing a checklist of procedures in his mind. "Did he take anything?" he asked.

"Besides his belongs? No," I said. Then: "Well, I'm wrong. Yes, he did. But it had no value. It was a little statue – they call it a bust, I think – that he had a fancy for, one of Mozart, I believe it was. We'd joked about it with him, telling him if he ever decided to find other quarters, we'd make him a gift of it. He must have remembered what we said."

The officer stared at me quizzically.

"He was an odd bird, anyway," I added. "Him and his flowers."

"Yeah," the officer said, regaining some of his smugness.

"And all that going on about being the street mayor, it was becoming a bit tiresome," I suggested. "There were times I thought he believed it."

The officer huffed a cynical laugh. "He was beginning to piss some people off, some people in high places," he said.

"I can imagine," I replied. I offered a smile of politeness. "Have a good day."

"Yeah, buddy, you, too," the officer mumbled. He turned and began to stride away. I knew where he was headed.

In Frank's, Wally heard the story of the officer with glee. "It's in motion," he said of his plan. "Tonight, they'll be celebrating in City Hall."

"And you really think this is going to work?" I asked.

Wally smiled. "Only one way to find out, and that's to do it," he said.

"And how is Arthur?" I asked.

"Fine," Wally answered. "He's as fastidious as an old woman, but he plays a good game of chess."

"Does he, now?" I said with surprise. Arthur had never mentioned chess, and I wondered where he had learned the game, wondered if he had played matches against himself to endure time in the icy environment of his wife.

"Took me easily," Wally admitted, "and I'm not bad at it." He leaned forward and added, "To be honest, Hamby, I'm not sure we've seen the real Arthur Benjamin at all. Sometimes I wonder if all of this is just sport to him, a game he's playing to protect the pawns rather than the kings. It interests me."

If I had not been audience to many hours of Wally's observations and theories, his suspicions might have bothered me. Yet, Wally being Wally, I dismissed it, knowing somewhere in the churning of his brain, he was engaging in possibility, the same as chasing after the meaning of a recently discovered sneeze made by Aristotle.

I was more interested in Holly's attentiveness. We had not been together for two nights and she was restless for the touching that had become natural between us. I could sense the heat of her wanting as she leaned across me to place another beer in front of Wally. She whispered, "I hope you're rested."

I knew that I blushed.

That night, in her apartment, Holly did things to me that are done to men only in fantasy, beginning with the lighting of scented candles and ending with the branding of her flesh into my flesh, hot as a welding torch. When it was over, we both lay exhausted in the wrinkled nest of her bed sheets. She reached for Arthur's flower, tucked it under her chin, curled on her side like a child holding the silk edging of a baby blanket, and she drifted into sleep.

THIRTEEN

In summer, Savannah is a place of heat and humidity, coating the skin with the slipperiness of water-heavy air and the weight of it slows the step and dulls the senses. The wealthy have a little joke they exchange: "Let's go the sauna and get out of the humidity."

The word sultry is used by tourists, saying it with mock southern drawls, like an actor auditioning for a Tennessee Williams play.

Still, at night, if a breeze has found the trough up the Savannah River from the Atlantic, misting the air, you could swear there was a faint scent of saltwater in it. It is mostly imagination. The Atlantic is too far away. The scent is the musk of marshes. Yet, Savannah is a city intoxicating in its mix of frivolity and serenity. If you are a wanderer, you can take yourself off Factors Walk – where tourists and conventioneers gather like ants scurrying in and out of tunnels – and you can have a leisurely stroll along the streets of the city. If you have even a smidgen of a soul, it is a walk that burrows deep into your consciousness. It does not matter if you are tethered to it by family history, or if you are a tourist looking to discover it off a map from the Convention Bureau, the city cuddles you. If you're lucky enough to see it in the season of the azaleas, you'll not want to look elsewhere for beauty.

I have always loved the night walks of Savannah, even from my childhood, tagging after my mother. In her make-do living for the two of us, she often worked the kitchens of the well-off on nights of high affairs for high society. She would find a place for me at such homes – usually outside, out of sight – and she would wave her hand over me and in a whispery voice, she would instruct me to be invisible, saying, "Where's Hamby? Oh, he's invisible and invisible he'll be until the good queen makes him seen again."

I thought of it then as a game played with a blithe, spirit-happy mother. I know now that what she did was as painful as anything she could ever experience. She took her child and trained him as a dog is trained in obedience school. Sit. Don't move. Stay.

And I obeyed. I would sit, being invisible, pretending to be a ghost listening to laughing voices and the clinking sound of glasses and dinnerware and, sometimes, the drifting, happy beat of music from a piano or a harpsichord accompanied by the kind of boisterous singing I would later hear in pubs. The sweet scents of meats and bread wafted across the night air.

Afterward – after the fading sound of partiers leaving for their own palatial homes and after the cleanup – my mother would reward me with an éclair or a slice of cake she had wrapped in a paper napkin. And then we would return to our home, taking detours through the squares that General James Oglethorpe had envisioned in 1733 when he drew out the plan for Savannah. Not a single building from that period remained, yet many of the squares were still there, like restful pauses in the connect-the-dot history of the city.

I loved those night walks with my mother, stopping in the squares to sit on a bench and to have our éclairs or cake, listening to her tell stories of the finery of the evening, or of remembered evenings in Ireland, in the town of Youghal, when she was known as Molly Fitzgerald, but teased as being Molly Malone. Often we took the long way home by wandering to Forsyth Park, which reminded my mother of St. Stephens Green in Dublin.

I still take the walks and still sit in the squares with my mother – or my memory of her, the memory often being strong enough to see her sitting beside me. In Lafayette Square, across the street from the Cathedral of St. John the Baptist, I have sensed her presence as surely as if she had been waiting patiently for me, ready to fold me into her embrace or to scold me in her gentle manner for being tardy, or unkempt or in ill-temper. There, nearby the one edifice she loved more than all others – a building of such majesty and beauty, it caused visitors and worshippers to shudder in awe – she seemed to find peace. It is a great hurt of my life that I did not beg for her funeral service to be held there.

In Lafayette Square, I think of the teasing she had of being Molly Malone, and I remember the song and the line from it that says, *She died of a fever, there was no one could save her . . .* It was exactly the way my mother had died.

At night in the squares of Savannah, I still spend time gazing at trees with Spanish moss draped over limbs like the long beards of old dead men, their ghost faces hiding in the green leaves of oaks. They have been there since Oglethorpe and Tomochichi of the Yamacraws, since the war of Revolution and all the other wars that have called the souls of her people to rest in trees.

On such nights, with the imagined scent of salt air from the Atlantic seeping down streets that Oglethorpe created in his pen strokes, Savannah – the city of my birth, my childhood, my memory – is my Ireland, and it is as grand as any place on Earth.

I took such a walk after my night with Holly, after our long sleep of exhaustion from the lovemaking. It was still dark, though in the east there was a hint of morning and in a tree in Johnson Square, a mockingbird suffering insomnia was up early and in a cheerful mood.

I paused to listen. From nearby, a voice carried to me: "Loud, ain't he?"

It was Preacher. He was sitting on a bench, smoking a cigarette. He had an opened Bible in his lap and an unopened bottle of vodka on the bench beside him.

"You gave me a start," I said to him.

Preacher nodded understanding. He drew from his cigarette, then leaned forward and rubbed out the burning tip of it on the ground and folded the warm nub of it into his shirt pocket.

"You're up early," I added.

"Not been to sleep yet," he said. "Just been sitting here reading my Lord's words. Been at it all night."

I sat beside him. When not drinking, Preacher was a gentle man, a good man to talk with, though I tried to avoid discussions of religion, me being Catholic and him being something he called Primitive Baptist. God takes on a different look when people start pulling Him apart with what's been crammed into their thinking.

Preacher helped me, without knowing it.

"Want you to know again how much I liked your service for Cherokee," I told him. "Everybody did."

Preacher nodded, dismissing the compliment. "I been reading about a man and his wife," he said solemnly. He held up his Bible, squinting under the dim lighting of the street lamp. "Listen to this." He read: "Let thy fountain be blessed, and rejoice with the wife of thy youth. Let her be as the loving hind and pleasant roe; let her breasts satisfy thee at all times; and be thou ravished always with her love."

He closed his Bible, keeping his thumb in it as a bookmark.

"Proverbs," he announced quietly.

"Lovely passage," I said, trying to be accommodating.

Preacher sat for a moment, gazing across the park, peaceful in its silence except for the mockingbird.

"I had me a wife one time," he finally said. "Guess I still do since we didn't do no divorce. She was a man's woman, if ever they was one. Only problem was, I was the wrong man. She found another one. I could tell she had some caring for him without her ever saying a word. It just roosted there on her face. Never left me, but she might as well have. Guess maybe she had some bad feelings over it, but she didn't do nothing about making it right. Just pulled back from having anything to do with me, telling me she needed some time to think things out and I give it to her. Went on for a lot of years. After a while, I got to where it didn't matter. A woman that don't want you touching her leaves a man feeling kind of worthless. Once in a while I call her when I'm sober enough to do it. She don't say much, other than she's making do with the help of the church. Says she's praying for me, but I been around her long enough to know she's praying I'll stay where I am." He paused, pulled his thumb from his Bible, closing shut the Book of Proverbs. "Still got him roosted on her face, I'd guess. Or maybe she's roosting with him. I wouldn't know. She don't talk about what she does."

He fingered the rubbed-out cigarette from his shirt pocket and re-lit it and sucked the smoke deep into his lungs.

"I didn't know about that," I told him in a voice as gentle as I could offer. "I'm sorry."

He made a little shrug and a soft smile moved in his face. "I was some kind of preacher, Hamby. In my time, I was. I had them dancing in the aisles, holding hands with the angels, kicking up sawdust." He nodded in keeping with his memory. "You being Catholic, you wouldn't know nothing about the spirit in a canvas tent, but it was something. It surely was."

I sat back against the bench without speaking, not knowing what to say to him.

"The mayor wanted me to go home and try to start over," he added as an after-thought.

"Who?" I asked.

"The mayor," he replied. "Fellow you call Arthur. That one."

I sat up. "You know Arthur, other than being at the funeral?"

"Good man," Preacher said. "Never had much to do with a Jew, but I got nothing against them. Our Lord was half-Jew, you know, his mama being Jewish and his daddy being God. I never talked to the mayor about that, expecting he'd disagree, but he's a good man."

A shiver struck me in the chest. "When did you see him?" I asked.

"He showed up one morning after the funeral for the boy," he told me. "Used to sit right here and have a talk with him. Just me and him. He'd be out taking a walk. Sometimes, he'd bring me a doughnut and some coffee if it was early enough for the shop to be open." He drew from his cigarette, taking the burn down to the filter. "Give me some money not long ago to make the trip back home, to try and make things right," he added weakly, almost tearfully. He shook his head. "Lord, Jesus, I was tempted to take it and drown myself. Got me two bottles of vodka with part of it. Drank one already, but I been keeping this one closed, waiting to the time I could give him back the rest of his money, but he's not been around the last few days. I'm getting worried about somebody knowing I got it and knocking me on the head to take it."

I remembered watching Arthur remove the envelope from his suitcase when he thought Leo and I were sleeping. I had wondered about it, but had not questioned him. Keeping some privacy is another lesson from the streets.

"He's gone," I finally said to Preacher.

He turned to look at me – a puzzled look. "Where'd he go?"

"I don't know," I lied.

He sighed, dropped his cigarette on the ground, rolled his Bible in his hands. "What he give me was two hundred dollars," he said. "What I supposed to do with what's left over?"

A car approached on St. Julian Street, its lights dipping and rising on the uneven pavement. It made its slow crawl around the square, then disappeared. I remembered the words Wally had once offered: *"To be honest, Hamby, I'm not sure we've seen the real Arthur Benjamin at all."*

I had dismissed Wally's suggestion. Now I was certain he had been right about Arthur, and I wondered what else we did not know.

"Maybe I'll send it home to the wife," Preacher mumbled. "Maybe it'll make her think kindly of me."

I left Preacher after a few minutes. He was holding his Bible in one hand and his bottle of vodka in the other, like a man trying to make a balance with scales. He told me if I heard from Arthur to pass along a message: "I still got the money."

It was the thought of the money that followed me on my walk to the Castle – that and the mockingbird, with its chirping and its tree-hopping, leaving me with an eerie sensation of being laughed at.

Arthur had money I did not know about. Had it in his suitcase. No way of knowing how much, or if he had any left. He had seemed not to care about it at all, and I imagined he had enjoyed my little game of stuffing bills into the sweatband of his hat, never letting on that he knew about it. And maybe he did not know. Maybe he believed it had been left there by some sprite as generous as the Tooth Fairy. Maybe his mind was as innocent, or as muddled, as Lady's.

And maybe I was letting my imagination get ahead of my thinking. I was never good at keeping up with money. Even with the considerable sum I had taken from Arthur, I could not make sense of the balance of it. There were times when I was certain I should have had less than the count I remembered, and I wondered if Arthur had been pulling the same kindly trick on me that I had been pulling on him – slipping money into my wallet as I slept. The thought of it caused a smile. Arthur sneaking across the room to make a deposit, and me giving it back the next night.

I considered asking him about it, or of laying a trap to find the truth if we got back to our old living arrangement, but decided I would do neither. The matter of Arthur's fortune – little or great – was private, and there was no reason to pry into it. If he wanted to stuff a few dollars of it into my wallet, or to pass it out on the streets of Savannah to alcoholic preachers, it was his right.

FOURTEEN

In our planning, Wally had predicted we would hear from city officials on the day following Arthur's disappearance, and we did.

Mid-morning, Roger Upshaw appeared. He was in a frisky, self-righteous mood, the same as a man who has been given a secret that holds a warning.

Carrie and Leo and Wendell and I met with him outside the Castle, explaining that Lady was not well and was being cared for in her room by Gerty. It was half-true. Gerty was keeping her occupied.

I could see him juggling irritation and decision in the spotlight of his brain, weighing the importance of having Lady present. He decided not to waste his visit.

He wanted to inform us – on behalf of the mayor, he said – that Debra Geiger's car had been identified as the one making an improper turn, which may, or may not, have resulted in injuries to Lady.

"Mind you, there's still a question of who was operating the vehicle and, in addition, there's lack of evidence that the vehicle struck Miss McFadden at all," he said. "In the opinion of our investigators, she could have taken a fall due to any number of causes."

He smiled at the startled reaction we gave him – not in words, but in looks.

Finally, I said, "There were witnesses."

His smile curled into a sneer. "Of the ones we've interviewed, no one actually saw the car strike anyone," he replied. "They saw the car, yes, and can identify it, and they saw the lady on the sidewalk, but they'd didn't see what you claim to have happened."

I thought of Sharon Day.

"You haven't interviewed everyone, then?" I said.

The sneer faded and the expression that replaced it was one of having misspoke and the embarrassment that goes with it. "Not everyone," he admitted.

"I see," I said. "And what about us? No one's interviewed us. We were there. We saw it."

Roger Upshaw made a little wiggle of his shoulders. He looked at me with contempt. "We have your statements from that day. I think we know your position. And wouldn't that have been a waste of manpower at this time?" He let his gaze slide toward the front door of the Castle. "However, the reason I'm here is more unofficial than anything," he added. "I'm here with a personal message from the mayor and his wife."

"And what would that be?" I asked.

"In order to prevent embarrassment for all involved and to keep from burdening the court with a frivolous contest, the mayor is willing to provide Miss McFadden with a check for one thousand dollars to dispense with the matter," he answered, and the smugness came back in his voice.

Carrie laughed. "Oh, my God," she said. "He wants to buy us off."

Once I had heard a saying by a man saddened over a family dispute: *You don't need matches; you can light a dynamite fuse with words*. It had stayed with me. And now I was watching it happen.

Roger Upshaw's face turned crimson in anger. "That, young lady, is defamation," he snapped.

Carrie stepped close to him, thrust her face near his face. "You slimy bastard," she hissed. "This is harassment. Now get out of here."

Roger Upshaw wheeled and started to march away. I waited until he was five steps away from us and then I called for him: "Wait a minute."

He turned back to me.

"Tell the mayor we're willing to compromise," I said, adding a little dramatic tremble to my voice.

The crimson seeped out of Roger Upshaw's face. "What did you say?" he asked.

"I said we're willing to compromise," I repeated. "Arthur Benjamin's gone. He was the one that wanted charges to be pressed."

"That's the only sensible thing to do," he said. He cut his eyes to Carrie.

"But we don't want the money," I added. "Carrie's right. The money's an insult. We may be one step away from sleeping on the street, but we've got some pride, same as you, same as the mayor, same as everybody. What we want is something else."

"What's that?" he asked.

"Two things," I said. "First, you've got an officer on the force who seems to take some pleasure in causing trouble for us. His name is Ted Castleberry. If he's involved with us in any way, the agreement is off."

Roger Upshaw did not respond immediately, leaving me to wonder if he knew about Ted Castleberry's behavior and was calculating an argument for his answer. If so, he put it aside. "What else?" he demanded.

"There's a rumor going about that the mayor's talking of evicting Lady," I said.

A look of shock flashed in his face.

"We want that stopped," I added.

He made a little flicking gesture with his head, the same as a man tossing off an annoyance, then he said, "I've not heard that, but we can't bend the law to favor somebody's whim. This administration believes in fairness for all people."

"That's our offer," I said bluntly. "Tell the mayor to keep his money, and if he wants to keep his wife out of court and out of the newspapers, then he's got a way to do it."

"I'll give him the message," Roger Upshaw replied. "But I'm not making any promises."

"Understood," I told him. I stepped close to him. "But I've got one other thing to say."

He glared at me, waited.

"Carrie was right," I added. "You really are a slimy bunch, all of you. If you'd had any sense at all, you'd have given Arthur a medal for bringing a little merriment to the good citizens of the city."

I thought he would strike me, his temper flared so quickly. He opened his mouth to speak, but Wendell stopped the words. Wendell said, "Don't go making no trouble. No sir, don't go doing that." His voice was hard in its warning.

Roger Upshaw turned and left the Castle, rushing away in near-sprint.

"He bought it," Carrie whispered in relief.

"We're dead," Leo said heavily. His eyes carried harsh memories.

"I'd say we're more alive than we've ever been," I told him.

"What makes you think that?" he groused.

"They're following human nature," I said.

"What's next?" asked Wendell. There was a faint smile of delight on his face.

"Now we wait," I replied.

Wally was elated with the news of our exchange with Roger Upshaw, but warned that the predicted period of our waiting would wear on our nerves. "Stay busy," he advised. "And stay outside, near City Hall, where they can see you. Be as visible as you can be, and as noisy. In short, Hamby, be obnoxious. Buy some balloons and give them away. Do all that ridiculous magic stuff you do, have Carrie do her drawings and tell her stories." He paused in thought, and then added with a laugh, "Have Lady throw a tea party at the Castle." Wally had never seen the Castle, but I had described it to him and the image of it intrigued him. "I might even come myself," he said. And he gave me one hundred dollars for expenses, though I objected, still having some of Arthur's money. "Call it my buy-in," he insisted.

If the rest of us had moments of doubt about what we were doing, Wally did not. For Wally, it was the same as watching some zany production from a rag-tag company of actors, but with consequences of importance. The difference between Lady and her Guests and the characters from the pen of Shakespeare was only in language, he proclaimed. "To do or not to do," he uttered dramatically. "To kick ass or have ass kicked," he amended.

The day following our confrontation with Roger Upshaw, we began doing as Wally suggested, doing it in Emmet Park, in full view of City Hall, doing it with enough noise to cause passers-by to slow their pace or to stop altogether to take in the antics, leaving them to wonder about the reason for the goings-on. The only thing we did not have was a calliope and a pitch man singing, "Yowsir, yowsir, yowsir…"

We also distributed hand-written cards in shops and businesses, inviting guests to the Castle for an upcoming afternoon tea with Lady Melinda McFadden, formerly of New York City, making sure some of the cards found their way inside City Hall.

We called it Lady's Hour.

And it was that.

It was also madness.

Energized by the thought of a party carrying her name, Lady spent days making a fuss over the planning of it, sending Gerty out for party treats, as she called them. "Little cakes, Gerty, little cakes," she cooed. "And the best tea you can find. And some of those lacy little napkins they sell in the good stores. Have Leo find some flowers."

"Who's going to be paying for all this stuff?" Gerty asked me irritably. I gave her the hundred dollars from Wally, adding ten to it from my own reserves. Later, Gerty would give me back forty, saying she had not needed it, saying cookies from the dollar store were good enough for a honky tea party, and, as for the tea, it would be of her own brewing.

I did not ask Leo where he got the flowers, but from the looks of them, from the way they were bunched together, I had a vision of cemeteries suddenly gone gray and I made a little prayer that no one attending the party would recognize any of the arrangements. Leo was proud of both the quality and abundance of his provisions.

Truth is, the Castle looked as quaintly inviting as some of those reproduction buildings you would find in Williamsburg, Virginia, or in theme parks making a bid for the nostalgic vacationer's dollar. Wendell and Leo and I spent time tidying up the outside, trimming hedges with clippers Holly had borrowed from Frank, and gathering up paper trash that had blown in from the streets. And while we were at work on the outside, Carrie and Gerty cleaned the inside. Holly helped them and I was glad for her visit. I had been nervous about Holly and Carrie, having seen the way women can be when put-off by another woman. It was needless worry. They hit it off like sorority sisters who have not seen one another for years, the giggly way they went about their business, with Gerty mumbling under her breath over the silliness of honky girls, but enjoying it all the same.

I had not shared with Holly the whole of what was happening, for I knew she had a habit of speaking before thinking. She believed Arthur had left of his own accord, and her weeping over his absence was painful to hear. I knew also that when she learned the truth of the matter, she would be furious with me for not trusting her. As for the tea party, I had explained we were doing it to lift Lady's spirits, and Holly, having liked Lady from the first meeting of her, had volunteered to help with the preparations.

"She's such a sweet old lady," Holly had said. "She reminds me of my grandmother just before she lost all her senses." A film of moisture had bubbled in her eyes. "I sure hope she doesn't start thinking she's an angel, like Granny did. Seeing her like that, thinking she had wings, was scary. I still dream about it sometimes."

We did not know if anyone would take the cards of invitation seriously, the guessing among us ranging from none (Leo) to dozens (Lady).

Lady was closer in her estimate.

The invitation had announced Lady's Hour being from four o'clock to five o'clock.

At five-thirty there were still more than twenty people wandering around the inside of the Castle, sipping Gerty's tea from Lady's dainty little teacups and nibbling on cookies from the dollar store, cookies that had twice been replenished by Leo. I did not know what ingredients Gerty used for her tea, but feared it had some narcotic in it judging by the requests for re-fills and by the silliness of the ladies and the students from SCAD, and by the observation that the more they drank the happier they appeared. I knew also that Gerty was secretly rejoicing. I could see it in her smile and in the evil sparkle of her eyes as she boiled pot after pot of water on the gas stovetop. Once I heard her whisper, "Honkies," and then she laughed, making me wonder if she had been sipping her own brew.

But there was a melancholy about all of it, also.

It was not a real tea party with close friends, as Lady believed it to be. It had the off-beat mood of celebration for an off-beat occasion, and it reminded me of a party the parents of a childhood friend had given for his birthday, a family of little means and little to offer. News of the party had got out among the rich kids and they had arrived full of mischief and put-downs. They had eaten the cake and scooped up the ice cream and had made snide remarks about my friend and his home, and then they had left in a chorus of laughter, taking with them some of the gifts meant for my friend.

I had the sense that Lady's Hour was like that – that the revelers were enjoying the oddity of their environment as much as Gerty's tea, and there was some evidence I was right. Later, when we took stock of it, six of Lady's teacups and saucers were missing.

Yet, Lady's Hour and the balloons and the magic tricks and the storytelling had served the intended purpose, as we would learn from Carrie's cousin: Mayor Harry Geiger snapped.

The following morning, in a quick-called meeting with Roger Upshaw and Ned Doubleday, he had ordered the preparation of a summons for a hearing against residents of the Castle, citing a violation of zoning laws that Ned Doubleday had discovered: the property could be used for commercial purposes, but not for occupancy.

To Harry Geiger, the discovery was all he needed.

"He didn't like what was going on," Carrie's cousin reported to her. "Giving him demands and calling him names and then putting on a show in front of him, was more than he could take. He didn't give it a second thought: he was going to strike back."

It was not a surprise to us. Wally had predicted it, having zeroed in on Harry Geiger's reputation for arrogance. Arrogance was his blind spot, his Achilles heel. He had the politician's need to be right, to have his way, and it did not matter if he left decapitated bodies in the wake of his rage. He was the same as many I had seen in my life – people made insane with power. Nothing meant as much to them. Nothing.

Carrie's cousin told her the mayor's meeting had been loud enough and vile enough to be heard outside his office, causing his assistant to shoo people away. He had bellowed threats, saying we would be lucky to find a cardboard box to live in after he was finished with us, saying we were no better than a nest of rats, saying he would find someone to burn the Castle if it became necessary, saying he knew a lot of people who would do it for a bottle of whiskey and a carton of cigarettes.

Ned Doubleday had tried to caution him against making harsh remarks or a hasty decision, reminding him of unrest already bubbling up over the upcoming election. It was not a warning that pleased Harry Geiger. He roared back that he did not give a damn, that when he got rid of us there would be a horde of people coming out of the woodwork to support him. He had also reminded Ned that Arthur Benjamin – the man everyone was fawning over – was gone. In two weeks, Arthur would be completely forgotten, like a cult movie star who had caused people to tittle-tattle mindlessly before finding something else to talk about.

But the thing that had most inspired Harry Geiger to shake the building with his rage, was Roger Upshaw's questioning of the hit-and-run case against his wife. Harry yelled about us first saying we wouldn't press charges, and then saying we would, and then offering a compromise with strings attached. He was, he said, finished with the dilly-dallying, and he issued an order to find a way to dismiss the threat.

Ned Doubleday had cautioned him again that a hit-and-run charge went to state court, and there was nothing any of them could do about it.

According to our hearsay of it, the mayor had snapped, "You don't understand me, do you? Find a way to dismiss it."

"What about Ted Castleberry?" Roger Upshaw had asked.

For a moment, the mayor had remained quiet, and then he had replied, "Have Castleberry deliver the summons."

Carrie's cousin said the mayor's answer produced the only laugh out of the meeting. It had come from Roger Upshaw, and it was evil.

FIFTEEN

God was the reason Leo Rosten had been freed from prison after serving six years of a twenty-year sentence on an embezzlement conviction.

God spoke to Compton Dunn and told him to set things right, and Compton obeyed. He was on his deathbed, God was in the room with him, or so he believed. God and a host of angels.

Compton Dunn's confession of framing Leo was a shock to his family, as was his conversion and his tender begging for baptism, yet none of it was a complete shock. He had been a hard, unfeeling man with the conceit of a third-world dictator, a man obsessed with wealth and the spotlight of notoriety to go with it. As president of Oxford National Bank in Atlanta, he was known for his ability to bluff, to cajole, to stare adversity in the eye and never blink. Looking into the eye of Death, he blinked and when he did, God moved in with his host of angels.

Leo had never talked to me in detail about the legal traps that took him from behind his desk at Oxford National Bank to stand trial over a missing half-million dollars. When he did speak of those times, he tended to ramble and to become angry and fragile. His time in prison had cost him a good life. He was a CPA with a respected job at a respected bank. On the day he was arrested, he was one month away from marriage. Two years after being incarcerated, his bride-to-be married a rabbi who had become her counselor.

With Compton Dunn's confession of culpability – and the uncovered proof of it, freely offered – Leo was released from prison with an apology from the state and from the prosecutor who had dehumanized him in trial. He received some money for time served and for the insult of the experience, but none of us ever knew what he did with it. It was my guess that he gave it to charity, wanting to start his life over from scratch, and from scratch, for Leo, would have meant from nothing.

If I had not known him well, I would have thought of Leo as a funny little man with the bug-eyed look of a character actor in an old gangster movie comedy, a tough-acting fumbler with a gentle soul.

And, in many ways, that was who he was. Even when he disguised it with his grumbling, Leo had a good and gentle soul.

Yet, he also had fury, the kind of fury a volcano has with its gurgling, unseen lava. Psychologists would call it a disorder of social behavior, I suppose, but it was more than that. The heat of Leo's fury came from the heat of tears. It was why he had refused to see his family after attaining his freedom. They had never visited him in prison, had never written to him, choosing to believe the slander that Compton Dunn had stacked against him and, out of shame, choosing to deny their kinship of him. Yet, when it was over, when the media carried stories of his release, his siblings posed happily for photographers and television cameras, wiping tears from their eyes, proclaiming their never-wavering belief in his innocence, saying with glad voices how eager they were for him to return home, and to prove it, they had arranged a grand party in an expensive restaurant to celebrate his freedom.

Leo had left them waiting. Like Arthur, he had boarded a Greyhound bus for Savannah, and he had never again communicated with any of them.

In Savannah, we had become his family, those of us who resided in the Castle. Lady – addled as she was at times – was the one person who knew how to calm Leo. She did it by being helpless. Leo needed to be useful.

His only warning to me during our encounter with the forces of City Hall was, "Don't do anything to hurt that old woman. Anybody that does, he'll have to deal with me, and I can tell you I learned a thing or two in prison – a thing or two you don't want to know about."

The way he said it left a chill in my chest.

And on the evening he went with me to meet with Wally, I would learn why.

Arthur for Mayor signs were still displayed in the windows of Frank's Fine Dining, gaudy reminders of the festivities we had enjoyed, but being mid-afternoon, only a few of the regulars were there, sitting at the bar toying with their beers, annoying Frank with niggling complaints meant for humor. Old as he was, Frank had seen the likes of them from as far back as the good days – as he called them – before the tourist and convention crowd changed the character of the city, making it brochure copy. He had heard all they could offer in their parrots' re-telling of jokes and legends. Watching him wipe down the bar with his damp cloth – done in hard, rapid circles – always gave me the thought that he was wiping away the jabbering, the same as he would wipe away spilled bourbon.

Wally was in the back, at a table with a woman he introduced as Melody Comstock. He proudly shared the information that she was a 47-year-old student at the Savannah College of Art and Design, a late-life artist who had kicked the shackles of her boring life and had found excitement in canvas and paint. Something in memory teased me about her, and Wally gave the answer: Melody Comstock had been at Frank's on the night of the *Arthur for Mayor* foolishness. Her submission in the poster contest had been judged by Wally as the finest of the lot, earning her Frank's announced prize of a dinner and a free pitcher of beer for two. She had chosen Wally as her companion and the two had struck up a relationship that gave off the heat of simmering passion.

Melody Comstock was not beautiful, but she had sensuous green eyes and full lips and a slender, well-toned body that made promises of pleasure. She was also laugh-and-touch friendly, giving her the kind of personality that seemed a good fit for Wally's new lifestyle.

"Melody works in watercolor," he explained. "She's really quite accomplished. We were just discussing a commission I'm thinking of giving her."

"He can't afford me," Melody said.

"I'm a rich man," Wally countered. "But frugal. You have to prove your worth before you get the order."

Melody blinked seductively, purposely, a blink so obvious it caused Leo and me to blush. Both of us, in unison. "Oh," she said, "I thought I'd already done that."

Wally grinned, winked at her. "No, my dear, I've only seen your portfolio. I'm waiting for the exhibition."

For another thirty minutes, the shameless and silly flirting between Wally and Melody continued, with little effort to invite either Leo or me into the talk that played between them, and so we sat, Leo and I, drinking beer Wally had ordered for us, and waited for the sexual tension of the table to subside. It was not easy for me. My mind was on Holly, thinking it was good she was not yet at work.

When Melody left for a late-afternoon class, Wally settled back in his chair, making a pleasing sigh, and watched her disappear. He shook his head in wonder. "Gentlemen," he said happily, "there goes a miracle, an absolute miracle. Worse artist I've ever seen with a brush in her hand, but when she walks away from the canvas and slips between the sheets, she's a bloody Michelangelo."

Leo pushed his beer glass away. He glanced at his watch, and I knew he did not like Wally's talk, or Wally.

"Tell us about Arthur," I said.

"He's fine," Wally replied. He turned to look again in the direction Melody Comstock had taken in her leaving, and he wagged his head comically. Then he turned back to us. His transformation was immediate and startling. "Catch me up," he said seriously, a furrow buried in the bridge over his nose, between his eyes, leaving lines that had the look of the Roman numeral III. "What's going on?"

I told him about the mayor's orders to find a way to evict us, and the news pleased him.

"So they learned Lady was the rightful owner?" he said.

"That's what we understand," I replied.

Wally glanced toward the front of Frank's, where the early regulars were laughing over the re-telling of an ancient joke. "I thought they would," he said. "Now they have to make the next move." He leaned his body closer to us. "You'll be getting a summons to appear in court – municipal, I'd guess – to answer charges of violating zoning codes. When you get there, the judge will give you a date to evict."

"And you're sure that's the way it works?" I asked.

"Hamby, trust me," he said. "My field of philosophy is based on logic. It's how I paid my way through college. I know I don't look the part, but I was a pool hustler because I knew something very few people I played understood: Every pool shot you see is a triumph of logic. I don't just sit on my ass hanging out in sleazy bars, my friend. Sometimes I do some good in the world."

Leo carried a look of worry. Wally saw it. "Look," he said earnestly, "you've got things working the way we talked, but if you're having second thoughts, now's the time to say it. Once that summons is served, there'll be no backing off."

Leo looked away. He rubbed his hands together.

"We've come this far," I said. "We're going to see it through."

"All right," Wally replied, and then he let his smile return. "Hey, Leo, this could turn out to be the most fun you've ever had."

Leo shrugged. A bead of perspiration had formed over his top lip.

"Think of it as a game," Wally said. "Or games. We've still got some games to play, some things I've been thinking about."

"What things?" I asked suspiciously.

Wally looked across the room. A man was sitting alone, reading a newspaper. A half-finished beer and a near-empty plate of onion rings were on his table. "You know why that man reads the newspaper?" he said.

I frowned confusion.

"For the comic strips," he said. "I've watched him. He's here every day. Has his beer and onion rings – same thing every day – but he never finishes the rings. He reads the comic strips. That's all he's interested in. I like that about him, because I like the comics, too. They're a hell of a lot more profound than the editorial page. I still read them. Always have. And here's what I like, Hamby: I like those made-up heroes. Dick Tracy. Batman and Robin. The Phantom. Damn, the Phantom's good. When he leaves the skull mark on something, it puckers butts all over the place." He laughed easily. "Always wanted to be the Phantom," he confessed.

"What things, Wally?" I said again.

He ignored the question. "Anything you want me to tell Arthur?" he asked.

I knew there was no reason to insist on an answer. Whatever it was that Dr. Wally Whitmire, pool hustler, professor of philosophy, had working in his mind, it was best to keep private. "Tell him he missed a great party," I said.

Leo and I stayed at the table until Wally left the café, giving him time to pause up front among the regulars, taking and giving in the rowdiness that men exchange. The separate leaving was Wally's suggestion. If we were still being watched, it might be worth a few gallons of city gasoline to follow him, he offered. "No reason to give them any crumbs to follow."

I was on a seesaw of wanting to leave with Leo, knowing his mood, and wanting to wait at Frank's until Holly made her appearance for work. Leo won out. He had become increasingly antsy during our meeting with Wally, and I worried that he might go on a shoplifting spree to calm his nerves.

The timing of our leaving could not have been worse.

As we pushed open the front door to Frank's, we encountered Ted Castleberry, dressed in his civilians. Two men of considerable size were with him and I guessed they, too, were officers about to have an off-duty beer.

"Son of a bitch," Ted Castleberry said. He made a show of putting a grin on his face for the benefit of the men with him. "Look who we've got here, boys."

The two men glared at us.

Leo stepped back, lowered his head, crossed his arms over his chest, and I knew immediately that it was his prison gesture, his surrender.

Ted Castleberry laughed, and a surge went through me, the kind of electric shock that makes a person suddenly bold and straightforward.

"Were you looking for us?" I asked.

A puzzled expression wandered across his face. "What for?" he said.

"I wouldn't know," I replied. "Maybe to apologize."

Ted Castleberry stepped close to me, his face only inches from my face. "Maybe I should take you and your Jew friend off for a long ride on a short pier," he hissed.

I do not know why I said it – anger most likely, the sudden surge still throbbing – but the words slipped from my mouth before I thought about them: "Like Cherokee Robbins?"

Ted Castleberry's face turned pale. He glanced at one of the men with him and the man moved to me. He had small, dark eyes.

"What do you mean by that?" the man growled.

"Nothing," I answered.

"Bullshit," the man said. He caught my belt at the buckle and yanked on it, bringing me to him. "I asked you a question, asshole. Answer it."

I swallowed to keep my temper in check and to make time for thinking. The stupidity was done; now I had to cover it. "You mean you haven't heard?" I said, putting on a voice of astonishment.

"Heard what?" the man demanded.

"It's on the street about his dying," I told him. "About the police trying to rid the city of him by giving him a ride to the city limits, and how somebody picked him up while he was hitchhiking, somebody who had a grudge to settle."

The man released my belt. I could see his eyes making a picture of what I had said. "Where'd that come from?" he asked.

"Who knows?" I said. "It's the word."

The man stepped back, yet his eyes stayed on me, cold as ice.

"We don't know what you're talking about," Ted Castleberry said. "Sounds like bullshit to me." He turned to Leo. "You the one saying all that bullshit?"

Leo did not answer. He ducked his head and looked away. I could see a twitch fluttering under his left eye.

Ted Castleberry laughed. "I hate Jews," he said. He pushed against me, forcing me to step back, and then he went into Frank's. The two men with him followed, leaving the coldness of their eyes on me.

When the door to Frank's closed behind them, Leo whispered, "Somebody needs to kill him."

"Well, it won't be us," I insisted.

"Who said anything about us?" he said in a hard way. He inhaled sharply, deeply, and then added, "I don't need you." He began to walk away in such a stride it forced me to quickstep to stay with him.

SIXTEEN

We did not know until the following day, but on the night of the confrontation with Ted Castleberry and his partners in front of Frank's, Wally became the Phantom, or a version of him.

He drove into Savannah from his home in Pooler and found Mayor Harry Geiger's car – a Mercedes twin to the one driven by his wife, but bearing the tag MRMAR. It was parked on the street outside the Visitors Center and Historical Museum off Martin Luther King, Jr. Boulevard, where the mayor was attending a reception for a benefactor named Martin Van Welks.

Wally knew of the reception because notice of it had been posted on the city website.

He left one of Arthur's paper flowers – yellow in color – wedged under the driver's side windshield of the car.

Then he drove to the mayor's residence and dropped a row of flowers in different colors on the walkway leading from the street to the front door.

There was no purpose in it for him other than revenge over being called a loudmouth, and the pleasure of knowing the mayor would become enraged to the point of hysterical madness.

When we heard of it the next day – a report from Carrie's cousin, saying the mayor had ordered around-the-clock security from the police department – I knew immediately the leaving of the flowers was one of the games Wally had promised, and it left me skittish. Wally was flirting with danger and we had danger enough without teasing for more of it.

I called him at his home from Frank's place. He chuckled over my complaint. "Those flowers could have been from anybody," he said, faking innocence. "Arthur's given out a lot of them from what you tell me. They're easy to make. He's even got me doing it, but that's not a confession."

I cautioned him about taking risks and I could hear an impatient sigh in his voice as he agreed to behave.

"You're taking the fun out if," he griped.

"I don't see it as fun," I told him. "And I don't find any logic in it."

He sighed again. "You're right." He asked if we had been served with a summons.

"Not yet," I said.

"Soon," he guessed. "It'll be there soon."

"No more surprises," I said, trying to be forceful.

"No more," he promised.

Wally stayed true to his word. The surprises that were to come would not be of his doing.

The surprises would come from Arthur.

Wally's report on Arthur had always been the same: he was doing well, his behavior remaining gentlemanly, his mood calm. His day passed in reading or in making his flowers – so many of them, the guest bedroom he occupied had the look of a florist. Occasionally, he watched television with the expression of a man playing tug-of-war against boredom. Occasionally, he played chess against a software program Wally had installed on his computer. And occasionally he surprised Wally by cooking a simple, but superb, dinner taken from one of the cookbooks Wally had acquired in his learning curve of living alone.

But it was his quiet way that intrigued Wally. At night, in the seclusion of a fenced-in backyard, they sometimes talked, and as the days of his visit passed, Wally became more fascinated by what Arthur said – or didn't say – about human nature.

"You have to listen carefully," Wally told me. "Sometimes he says something so simple, it's as though he's talking in riddles. You hear him and you think you're just hearing words, but if you listen carefully you know you're hearing something that makes so much sense it'll cause the hair on your neck to stand up."

When asked for examples, Wally fumbled to find them, leaving him with the eerie sensation of having had a vivid sleep-dream, but forgetting the details of it when awake.

"He's spooky," Wally offered.

As it turned out, Arthur was also resourceful.

On nights when left alone while Wally made his visits to Frank's, or escorted Melody Comstock to art shows, Arthur spent time on the computer doing research. His subject was law. When it later came to light, we were only mildly surprised, especially Wally. The way Wally would choose to interpret it, Arthur thought of law in the same way he thought of chess: to know the strength of a move, you had to know the weakness of it. To Wally, Arthur's dreamy, preoccupied mind was radar-equipped to pick up signs of weakness.

Knowing the summons was coming, we did our best to keep our anxieties in check, and I suppose we overdid it at times. We urged Lady to shop, yet also urged her not to purchase any items. The shopping was a way of getting out for all of us, taking walks instead of staying put in the Castle, worry-pacing in circles. In antique shops and flea markets we let our attention gather around items that had some interest strong enough to call up stories – typewriters, kerosene lamps, flat irons, sewing machines of the vintage owned by Gerty. The stories were as old and as used as the items that inspired them.

For me, there was also the matter of keeping watch on Leo. After our run-in with Ted Castleberry, the look of hatred he wore was more than the moodiness of his personality. It was darker. There was danger lurking in it. He sat, arms crossed over his chest, gazing solemnly into the space around him, lost, I believed, in thoughts of punishing a man who was a blight on humanity.

His was the face of someone who had spent a lifetime being pushed into corners and had decided it was time to strike back. I knew if he did, he would spend the rest of his years in prison, and I knew he would find a way to make those years short.

As it happened, Fate also had an eye on Leo, and Fate, having much the same sentiment about Leo as I had, decided to do something to detract his attention from Ted Castleberry.

Fate took Lady by the hand one afternoon and led her away from the Castle while the rest of us were preoccupied with our own doings.

It was Gerty who discovered Lady was missing, and the wailing she let out could be heard for two blocks. "Lord, Jesus, watch over her," Gerty begged in her anxiety. "She's not got enough sense to do it herself."

The search we made for Lady was hastily put together – Leo and me going to the shops she loved, Gerty, Wendell and Carrie covering the areas she favored in her walking. If Leo and I did not find her in the shops, we were to check with hospitals. None of us mentioned the police, but I had it fixed in my mind that if it came to such a need, we would send Gerty to do it.

It was hard keeping pace with Leo on our tour of the shops. His walking was more of a jerky jog than a walk, and the way he dipped in and out of door fronts, making his quick surveys, put me in mind of an animal seeking a place to hide. The look of bitterness had been wiped from his face, replaced by one of worry and fear.

We covered our route in a short time and then I called local hospitals from Frank's Fine Dining, inquiring if they had treated an older lady who might have seemed disoriented. None of them had.

"She can't be far," Leo said. "Let's go look for the others."

We found Carrie on Price Street near Crawford Square. She told us Gerty was going to Forsyth Park and Wendell was searching in Colonial Park Cemetery.

"We need a taxi," Leo said. He turned to me. "How much money have you got?"

I thought of the money Arthur must have left in my wallet in our night game of sneaky exchange. Though I had been careful in my spending, it still had dwindled down during his absence, leaving me with a guessed-at sixty or seventy dollars. Spending it on a taxi had the sound of foolishness, yet there was such a look of despair in Leo's face, I told him, "We can spare forty."

"Good," he said. "You wait here." He walked away in his jerky-jog steps, headed toward Bay Street.

"You've got money for a cab?" Carrie asked suspiciously.

"It's not mine," I answered. "I'm just holding it."

"Who for?"

I hesitated. "Arthur," I said.

She kept her gaze on me and I could feel the shame of having the money closing on me. Finally she said in an icy voice, "Did you steal it, Hamby?"

I decided to lie – or half-lie – not wanting to confuse Carrie or to have her walk away in anger: "No. I'm holding it. He gets it back a little at a time."

"Why haven't you told me?"

"It's a private matter," I said.

"Is that how we've been able to buy all the stuff we've bought?" she asked.

"It is," I answered.

She blinked tears and turned away from me. "I miss him," she whispered.

The taxi Leo hailed on Bay Street was driven by a man identified on his name display as Roberto Gonzalez. He was short and pudgy-faced, having a dark mustache and matching-color sideburns. His nose was flat, like the nose of a boxer who never learned the art of ducking and weaving, and an image flashed of Wendell and Roberto in a boxing ring, with Wendell raining blows against Roberto's flat nose. But he had a happy, nodding disposition as he drove, his hands holding to the steering wheel in a vise grip, his head bobbing on his shoulders as he talked, yet what Carrie and I saw when we slipped into the back seat of his car was one of Arthur's flowers dangling from the rearview mirror.

"Where did you get the flower?" Carrie asked, leaning forward behind the front seat.

In his pieced-together English – said merrily – Roberto explained the flower had been given to him by his eight-year-old daughter, who had gotten it from a man in a park where his daughter and some of her friends had watched a magic show and had had their picture drawn, making them look funny. He called it his lucky flower.

"We know that man," Carrie told him eagerly. "We were there, the three of us. I did the drawing and my friend here did the magic."

Roberto bobbed his head vigorously. "Si, si," he said, as though he recognized us.

"I told him what we wanted was for him to drive around, but to go slow, since we were looking for somebody," Leo said. He turned to glance at me. "You watch the meter."

"What about Gerty and Wendell?" Carrie asked.

"We don't have time to find them," Leo insisted and the force of his answer was stern enough to cause Carrie to sit back and hold the argument I knew she wanted to make.

I do not know how many miles we rode – enough to cover the distance Lady could have walked, regardless of the direction she might have taken from the Castle, and enough to stop the search at forty dollars. Roberto dropped us in front of the Old

Cotton Exchange Building. It was late afternoon. Leo was agitated, and afraid. He told us he wanted to go again to the shops Lady favored.

"All right," Carrie said quietly. I could tell she, too, was fearful.

On Factor's Walk, we found Gerty and Wendell and told them of our search in Roberto's taxi. They had explored the area around the Civic Center and the bus station.

"No telling where she's gone to," Gerty said heavily. She wiped at her eyes with the heel of her hand. "Crazy old honky woman, somebody'll knock her over the head."

"They better be on their way out of town if they do," Wendell told her.

Gerty turned to me. "What we supposed to do now?"

"Go to the police, I guess," I answered.

Gerty looked as though I had slapped her. "What for?" she demanded. "You think they'll be doing something for us?"

"Gerty, maybe that's where she is," I said carefully. "Maybe they picked her up for some reason."

It was a thought Gerty had not entertained. An expression of fury flew into her face. "They better not," she snapped. She wheeled and started striding in the direction of the police station; her body leaned forward like a soldier going into war. We followed in quickstep.

The officer on desk-duty was an older black man with a bored look about him. The name on his chest tag was Gaston Ryles. I explained the reason we were there and asked if they had any reports about an older woman wandering the streets, looking lost.

"When did she go missing?" he asked.

"This afternoon, around three, maybe earlier," I answered.

He gave a little shrug with his shoulders. "That wasn't long ago," he said. "You been looking for her?"

"We've looked," I told him. "We've been everywhere we can think she might be."

"I don't know what you want us to do," Gaston Ryles said. There was a tone of dismissal in his voice.

Gerty nudged me aside. "We want you to help us," she growled.

Gaston Ryles repeated his shrug. "We're busy," he replied. "Why don't you keeping trying on your own?"

Gerty thrust her face across his desk. "Listen to me, brother," she said in a threatening voice, "we need some help here. You understand me?"

Gaston Ryles glared at her. "Well, come back in a couple of hours if you can't find her."

"You got a telephone?" Gerty snapped.

"What for?" Gaston Ryles asked.

"Because I'm about to make two calls," Gerty told him. "The first one is to the ACLU, telling them about the do-nothing treatment some poor people needing help are getting down at the police station in Savannah, Georgia. The second one is to a good friend of mine, the Reverend Locklear Patterson."

"Who's that?" Gaston Ryles said.

"You don't know him?" Gerty asked in her haughty voice.

"Never heard of him."

"You ever heard of the Reverend Jesse Jackson?" Gerty shot back. "They're cousins, and whatever the Reverend Locklear Patterson gets worked up about, so does the Reverend Jesse Jackson."

Gaston Ryles blinked in surprise. He pushed back from his desk. "Okay. Give me the woman's name and description and I'll put the word out about her."

Gerty inhaled, sniffed. "That's more like it," she said.

I was sure that taking the information about Lady was for show, yet if it was, Gaston Ryles made a convincing performance of it, even telling Gerty, "Seems to me I've seen that old woman out on the street, and that name sounds familiar, but I live across the river, so I don't keep up with what's going on like I ought to." For a moment, I thought Gerty would tell him about the run-ins we'd already had over Lady. She did not, and I could tell by the expression on her face that she understood the lucky break we'd had with Gaston Ryles – dealing with a man who didn't read newspapers or pay any real attention to reports from radio and television, or even to the gossip that echoed about the police station.

It is a feeling of despair and helplessness, not knowing the whereabouts of someone dear to you, especially if that someone is a child or child-like. Once, as a small boy, I had slipped away from my mother in a grocery, following some butterfly fancy of my imagination out the door and down the street. When she finally found me, an hour later, she was in hysterics, catching me up in her arms and holding me tight enough to make me struggle for breath. It was as though she wanted to fuse me to her.

Looking for Lady, I understood what my mother had experienced.

Lady was one of the child-like people, almost certainly caught in the sticky web of Alzheimer's. All of us knew it, but none of us wanted to say the word or to make an issue of it. It was easier to think of Lady simply as being Lady, given to her peculiarities. Still, I believe all of us – especially those who had been around her for a good length of time – had noticed changes in her behavior, like the dimming of light in a burned-down candle. Forgetting our names at times was one of them. She would be talking gaily about something concocted from a speck or dot of her memory and she would pause and look at one of us and say, "There I go again, forgetting your name." She would give a little giggle-laugh and add, "I've never been good at names. I used to confuse my beaus, and that never set well with any of them." And the one of us she was addressing would say, "Don't you worry about it, Lady. I'm . . ." and we would fill the blank with our name and Lady would wave her hand as if to say, "I know that," and she would giggle-laugh again and add, "Now, what was I saying?"

I suspect only Gerty knew how to read the signs with any understanding. Her own mother had died from Alzheimer's, wasted away because she had forgot how to eat and the drippings of the liquids ordered by doctors were not enough to nourish a sparrow. Gerty's description of it had been as poetically sad as anything I had ever heard: "I was praying she wouldn't know Death when he showed up, but when she saw the face of Jesus everything would come back just like it always was, and she'd know she was where she was supposed to be."

When we left the police station, we stood for a few moments on the sidewalk forcing talk, though none of us had the feeling for words. I suggested we separate and continue looking until dark, all except Gerty. I knew she was exhausted from the worry she carried on her. "Why don't you go back to the Castle," I said to her. "Maybe she's there, wondering where we are."

Gerty agreed with a nod. The hope of finding Lady at the Castle shivered across her shoulders.

"Arthur should know what's happened," Carrie said.

"I'll go over to Frank's," I told her. "If Wally's not there, I'll try calling his home."

"Don't waste time," Carrie said. She sounded like an older sister issuing orders.

"I won't," I promised. I asked where she would be looking.

"Around," she replied. Then: "I need to make a call." I knew she was thinking of her cousin.

Wally was not in Frank's. Holly told me he had been there earlier with Melody Comstock and the two had left for a late afternoon movie. When I gave her the story of Lady's disappearance, she became tearful and volunteered to leave work to help me look. It was a sweet and tempting offer, but I knew she would become more anxious with each step we took, with each failure we encountered, and I persuaded her to stay at Frank's in case Wally re-appeared. "If he does, tell him what's happened and tell him he should get in touch with us." She embraced me tenderly, whispered something that caught me off-guard: "I love you, Hamby." Shamefully, I thought of Fats and Jake and gin.

I left Frank's and wandered again to the squares – Orleans, Chippewa, Telfair, Wright, Oglethorpe, so many of them I confused their names. In the walking and the looking, a part of me simmered with irritation over Wally. I had allowed myself to fold eagerly into his scheme for avenging the indignities against Lady – against all of us – and now, when he was needed, he was off cavorting with a pleasure-seeking woman, and to make matters worse, I thought of calling Wally's home and leaving a message on his answering machine, a message that Arthur would surely hear, but decided against it – at least for the time being. Wally had insisted that Arthur was not to answer the telephone, a tactic I had thought unnecessary, guessing it was Wally's way of playing James Bond. Yet, I knew if Arthur heard a message about Lady being missing, he would call a cab to join us in our search and all the deliberating we were doing with the city would be in danger of exposure. I reasoned that it would be best to hold off on the call for a night, and make prayers that Lady was safe.

Darkness fell on me in Warren Square.

I do not remember that any of us took food that night. We sat in the square of the folding-screen walls – the room within the room – and waited for whatever would happen. There was a drowsiness about us, a numbness broken only by an occasional, quick sob from Gerty or a whimper from Carrie. Leo leaned back in his chair, staring at the ceiling, having the expression of a man who has surrendered to hypnotism. Wendell sat close to Gerty, patting her hand with each sob, mumbling softly to her, "She'll be fine, she'll be fine." It was like being in the waiting room of a hospital, where people gather for a dying, knowing that soon there would be an appearance of a grave-faced doctor delivering his two-line benediction, "I'm sorry."

We were all dozing, still in the places where we had settled, when a knocking came at the front door. I believe we all leapt to our feet in unison, but it was Carrie who was first to the door.

Roberto Gonzalez was standing there, a splendid smile on his face. Lady stood beside him.

Carrie screamed and flung herself through the door to embrace Lady. And then Gerty. And then Leo. And then me. Wendell stayed back, watching, smiling.

Roberto had found Lady walking along Pennsylvania Avenue, many miles from the Castle. He was driving a double-shift he told us – or that is how we took it, not being sure of Roberto's interpretation of English – when he saw a woman strolling casually along the road. He said he knew who she was from the way we had talked about her, and he stopped, telling her he had been sent to bring her home. Lady had been pleased at such service.

"How did you know where we lived?" Carrie asked.

"She tell me," Roberto said, and his answer informed us that Lady had regained some sense of who she was.

I tried to pay Roberto, but he refused. He had Arthur's flower and the memory of his daughter's happiness over Carrie's drawing and over my magic, and that was payment enough. He bowed graciously to Lady and left.

Lady's response was Lady as we knew her: "Such a nice man. We had a lovely ride. It reminded me of taking drives with my father's chauffeur when I was a budding young lady. Have I told you about him? He was Hungarian, I believe. My father had to terminate him because he was infatuated with me."

We did not ask Lady about her day of wandering, or how she had managed to travel so far, or what she might have done. The questions would have been useless. She did not appear injured or even overly fatigued, no more so than a person cooling down after a bracing workout in a fitness center. If she knew we had been searching for her, she did not acknowledge it. She sat in her chair, fanning her face with her ivory-handled fan, telling a long-winded story about a trip she had once taken with her father to Boston, driven there by the Hungarian chauffeur, and how the chauffeur had purchased a cheap trinket at a service station to show his affection for her. The trinket, Lady said, was a bracelet made of false beads. She had kept it for years in a jewelry box of memorabilia. "I lost it in the fire," she added with a touch of sadness. "All those pretty things I had, each one of them being a chapter in my book of life. Burned. Just burned."

As with many of her stories, the revelation of a burned home was new to us, catching us by surprise, the same as her story of her late husband had been a surprise. Yet she told of the fire with such conviction, it sounded possible.

"When did that happen, Lady?" asked Carrie.

"The fire?" Lady said.

"Yes," Carrie replied.

"Oh, before I came here," Lady answered brightly. "I had everything packed for my move. My trunk was on the lawn, waiting for the limousine – everything in it, except for my little box of secrets." She smiled behind her fan, as though hiding a thought too mischievous to share. "Silly me, I left my secrets in the house."

"How did the fire start?" I asked, wanting her to believe we had an interest in her story of secrets.

She looked at me. Her expression was one of gladness. "I did it," she answered.

"The fire?" I said in disbelief. "You started the fire?"

"Oh, yes. Yes, I did."

"And why did you do that?" I asked.

She peered around her as if looking for eavesdroppers. "I never liked that old house," she answered quietly and with a touch of acrimony. "There was always something awful going on in it."

We sat gazing at Lady, all astonished.

She nuzzled her body into the back of her chair. A speck of memory was cradled in her smile. A little hum came from her throat.

Carrie leaned forward, opened her mouth to speak, but Gerty stopped her with a lifted finger and a shake of her head.

In a few minutes, Lady was sleeping peacefully. Gerty found a thin blanket and covered her, then moved one of the circulating fans near her and aimed its breeze on her face.

The last thing Gerty said before retiring to her room was, "We didn't hear nothing about no fire. Nothing."

The story Gerty said we did not hear would stay with each of us, as firmly fixed in our minds as if we had watched the burning in person, and it would be told again when we least expected it.

SEVENTEEN

The summons for Lady to appear in municipal court to answer charges of violating city ordinances regulating zoning arrived on Monday of the following week, delivered, as we expected, by Ted Castleberry. He was accompanied by the same two men who had been with him at Frank's. They were in uniform and they were happy enough with their task to be smiling about it.

Lady had no idea what the summons meant, only that it came from the city government. To her, it might have been an invitation to attend a ball. She thanked Ted Castleberry, telling him she would consult her calendar. The smirk on Ted Castleberry's face was one of triumph. As he was leaving, he motioned me to follow him. Outside, he said, "Tell your little whore if she wants to talk trade for a place to stay when we yank your asses out of here, she can give me a call." He leaned to me and whispered, "You pissed off the wrong people, boy."

I was glad Leo was not at the Castle.

The summons was for Thursday morning, ten o'clock, before Judge Renee Morgan of the municipal court, a woman of high regard and admiration, even among the attorneys who had felt the sting of her judgments. The city was to be represented by Ned Doubleday. It was expected to be a quick hearing with a quick order issued by Judge Morgan for all of us to vacate the Castle.

Routine, we believed. Case opened, case closed.

It was not to be so easy.

At eight o'clock on the morning of the hearing, Arthur and Wally arrived at the Castle, bearing the gift of a full breakfast for all of us – a sausage-egg casserole, muffins, fruit, orange juice. The surprise of seeing them had squeals of delight about it, taking away the gloom of the morning. Arthur was wrapped in embraces from Carrie and Gerty and even Lady, though it was dignified, and he was glad-handed by Leo and Wendell and me.

Wally watched the greetings with a pleased smile.

I asked why they were there.

"Because it's time," Wally said.

I chose not to push him on the matter.

We had a noisy, festive breakfast, with Carrie and Gerty badgering Arthur, wanting to know how he had managed to live without them. His answers were gracious in praise of Wally's hospitality. Wally took the compliments and heaped them back on Arthur, saying he had been the perfect guest. The mood of it was that of a party on holiday, carefree and happy.

When we finished breakfast, Arthur asked Lady if he might spend a few minutes with her outside, and the way he said it all of us understood it was meant for privacy.

"I would enjoy that," Lady said to him.

The thing – the something – that tickles suspicion told me the time between Arthur and Lady had been carefully orchestrated by Arthur and Wally, and it left me with a sense of apprehension, knowing Wally as I did.

While Arthur and Lady talked outside, we gave Wally a tour of the Castle. He was impressed, he said earnestly. It was a fine building, the sort of construction that had promise for anything from a restaurant to a mini-mall of shops. Could even be divided into apartments bringing high rent, he mused. I knew there was more than idle chatter to his observations and wanted to ask him about it, but there was no time for it. Arthur and Lady re-entered the Castle. A pleased, relaxed expression rested in Lady's face.

At nine-twenty we left for City Hall.

The only hint of things to come was from a single whispered comment by Wally as we made our parade down the street. He said to me, "I want you to know that what's about to happen is all Arthur's doing. I have no hand in it."

I had not thought of the hearing attracting attention, but I was wrong. The small courtroom designated for it was packed with people, leaving the impression that it might have been the judging a high profile murder case might have drawn. Holly and Frank and a number of regulars from Frank's occupied one side of the room. Holly blew a kiss that landed as a blush on my face. I saw Doyle Copeland and other members of the media. Doyle gave us a little nod as we entered.

I also saw Sharon Day. She was sitting on a back row with a group of ladies. When I glanced at her, she lifted Arthur's paper flower in a signal of support. The ladies with her also lifted flowers.

A small, serious-faced woman wearing a police uniform instructed us to sit in reserved seats on a front row, asking in a low voice if we had representation. Wally replied that we were not legally represented, but he identified himself and Arthur as the companions who would sit with Lady, if permitted. The small, serious-faced police lady frowned – as did I, being unaware of such a plan – and then she led Lady and Wally and Arthur to a long, narrow defendant's table in front of the audience railing.

Ned Doubleday entered, carrying a large briefcase, looking cocky, a look that turned to shock when he saw Arthur and Wally sitting with Lady. He settled at the matching plaintiff's table across from us, opened his briefcase and removed a stack of papers that he spread out before him. His eyes kept cutting toward Arthur and Wally. His expression was one of annoyance.

And then Judge Renee Morgan, a petite, well-groomed lady with black, short-cropped hair and a serious countenance, entered the courtroom, and we stood in unison on command of the bailiff and sat in unison on command of the judge's nod.

Ned Doubleday immediately demanded to know the purpose of Arthur and Wally sitting with Lady.

"I have the same question, Mr. Doubleday," Renee Morgan said. She directed her attention to Wally and Arthur. "Gentlemen, please identify yourselves."

"My name is Dr. Wallace Whitmire," Wally said with pride. "I am a retired professor of philosophy from the University of Delaware, recently relocated to Savannah."

The judge acknowledged him with a nod and then looked to Arthur.

"I am Arthur Benjamin," Arthur said softly. "I am friends with Miss McFadden and those accompanying her today."

"Arthur Benjamin," the judge said. "I thought I recognized you. You may the only man in American history to be promoted as a mayoral candidate in the first few days of his arrival in a city."

"Merely a harmless prank, Your Honor," Arthur said. "Done without my encouragement, I assure you."

"From what I can tell, it's provided some levity," the judge said.

"As was intended," Wally remarked.

A soft rumble of laughter rolled across the courtroom, bringing a flare of irritation to Ned Doubleday's face. "Unless they meet the requirements of the court by qualification, they may not position themselves to represent the defendant," he said indignantly.

Judge Morgan shot an angry glance at Ned Doubleday. "I do believe I have a rudimentary understanding of the protocol, Mr. Doubleday," she said evenly. She glanced at a thin stack of papers on the desk before her, read quickly from one of the sheets, then pushed the papers aside. She looked again at Wally and Arthur.

"Gentlemen, you are not qualified to legally represent a position in this manner, are you?" she asked.

"That is correct," Wally answered. "We are merely asking the court's indulgence to permit our presence as a matter of comfort to the defendant."

The judge wrinkled her brow. She again studied the papers in front of her for a few moments, and then she said, "Mr. Doubleday, a brief conference please."

From where I was sitting, I could see Ned Doubleday frown. He stood and approached the judge's bench and leaned toward her. No one could hear what Renee Morgan said to him, though later I would learn she shared a medical report she had among her papers regarding Lady's mental fragility, a report none of us were aware of. Presumably, it was from a county health facility describing a brief hospitalization before Lady began to invite her Guests to the Castle.

When the judge finished her explanation, Ned Doubleday nodded weakly and returned to the prosecutor's table.

"I am aware of some extenuating conditions that could possibly affect the issue before the court," Renee Morgan said, "and though it is highly irregular, I am going to allow Dr. Whitmire and Mr. Benjamin to sit with the defendant – keeping in mind this is not a trial; it is only a hearing to examine evidence and to make recommendations accordingly." She turned her face back to Wally. "I trust you understand you are not to make a mockery of this decision and begin to assume the role of an attorney. The first objection you make, or the first hint of advice you offer directly to the defendant, you will be removed from the defendant's table and from the courtroom."

"Of course," Wally said.

She looked at Ned Doubleday. "Are you satisfied, Mr. Doubleday?"

"Yes, Your Honor," Ned Doubleday mumbled.

The judge again shuffled the papers in front of her. "Now," she began, "I understand this is a matter of the city pursuing a violation of zoning ordinances as it relates to a certain property on Beale Street. Am I correct, Mr. Doubleday?"

"Yes, Your Honor."

"In the documents you've prepared, you maintain that said property is zoned specifically for commercial use, prohibiting residential occupancy, and that a certain Melinda McFadden, with others, is in violation of that ordinance. Is that correct?"

"It is, Your Honor."

Judge Renee Morgan leaned back in her chair and leveled her gaze on Ned Doubleday. "Let's cut to the chase, Mr. Doubleday," she said. "You want these people to vacate the property." She paused, glanced at the documents. "I believe Ms. McFadden calls it the Castle."

"Yes, Your Honor."

"And the City of Savannah feels this alleged violation is of such importance, it merits a hearing?"

"Yes, Your Honor."

The judge shook her head. "So, it boils down to this," she said. "The City of Savannah would prefer that six people – and I think I'm correct in the number, unless we now again include Mr. Benjamin – should be required to vacate their lodging and possibly be forced to live on the street, rather than try to reach a reasonable compromise?"

The look on Ned Doubleday's face was one of confusion. He had not expected the judge to ask such questions. "Begging Your Honor's pardon, but that makes it sound overly harsh," he said. "There's also concern for their safety."

The judge again shuffled through her papers, glancing at them. "Safety? Are you saying the facility is unsafe, Mr. Doubleday? If so, I'm curious as to why that concern is not addressed in your preparation for this hearing. Has the city inspected it?"

Ned Doubleday fidgeted at his desk. He cleared his throat. "Not officially," he admitted. "Yet, reports we've received provide a good indication that it could be a danger."

"Reports? Whose reports?" the judge asked.

"Ah – the police, among others," Ned Doubleday replied nervously.

"Others? Name them," the judge said.

"Well, Your Honor, the major's personal assistant, Mr. Roger Upshaw, has visited the premises, and he has expressed his concern over conditions."

The judge smiled slightly, yet enough to signal her dislike of Roger Upshaw. She turned to Wally and Arthur. "Gentlemen, are you familiar with these concerns?"

"We are familiar only with the fact that the police and Mr. Upshaw have visited the Castle," Wally said forcefully, sounding the way a professor would sound in making an argument. "Though I have not been present during those visits, Your Honor, it is my understanding that no one has ever broached the subject of safety with Miss McFadden or any of the other occupants. I'm sure they would be happy to verify that understanding."

The judge turned to face us. "Is Dr. Whitmire correct? Has anyone from the City of Savannah expressed any concern to any of you, collectively or individually, about potential danger in the place you call the Castle?"

We all muttered, "No."

The judge nodded and made a notation on a notepad. Then she turned her gaze again on Ned Doubleday. "Mr. Doubleday, in reading your filing I was troubled by what is at best a hazy ownership history of the facility in question. Are you satisfied that Miss McFadden is the proper owner?"

Ned Doubleday swallowed hard. He reached to touch the knot in his tie. His face was the tint of red painted by blood pressure. "We are, Your Honor, and I want to go on record as saying you are correct in calling it a hazy history. The facility in question was constructed in eighteen eighty-one, originally as a warehouse for cotton exports. Since that time, it has changed ownership a number of times for a number of purposes and the recording of deeds in some of those transactions is vague at best, particularly in the period of the nineteen thirties. It's our opinion that the facility was unaccounted for during a number of years, resulting from clerical error. Our current research shows that taxes due on the facility have been paid by A.N. Whitehead Properties out of Delaware, functioning as a subsidiary of McFadden Industries of New York, which seems to make Miss McFadden's claim of ownership legitimate." He paused, inhaled, licked at his lips. "However, Your Honor, we are not here to prove or disprove ownership of the property in question. The city is comfortable with accepting Miss McFadden's claim in that matter. We are here only to seek enforcement of an important city code."

The judge held her gaze on Ned Doubleday for a moment, then leaned her head against the cushioned headrest of her chair and looked toward the ceiling as if deep thought. It was a gesture, I believed, done for theatrics, done to make Ned Doubleday uncomfortable, and it worked. Ned Doubleday bowed his head, then took a sip of water from a water glass on the table.

In the courtroom, someone coughed. I glanced at Doyle Copeland. His smile was a held-back laugh.

Finally, the judge leaned forward and looked at Lady. She said, "Miss McFadden, do you own the facility in question on Beale Street?"

Lady answered the question with a vacant smile.

Arthur raised his hand. "May I, Your Honor?"

"Of course, Mr. Benjamin," the judge said.

Arthur stood at the defendant's table. "In a manner of speaking, Miss McFadden does not presently own the facility," he said calmly.

Renee Morgan blinked surprised. "She doesn't?" she asked. "Then who does?"

"I do, Your Honor," Arthur answered. He added again, "In a manner of speaking."

I suppose if an atomic bomb had exploded in the courtroom, it would have caught us more off-guard than Arthur's reply. Or, perhaps not. The only person who did not gasp over the announcement, or show shock, was Wally. Wally smiled and looked at me and gave a little shrug.

"Mr. Benjamin, it's obvious you've just caused something of a stir," the judge said. "I'm sure Mr. Doubleday and the rest of us would appreciate a fuller explanation."

Ned Doubleday stood. "I certainly would," he mumbled. His face had gone from red to ashen.

"Of course, Your Honor," Arthur said. "I purchased it about an hour ago."

"From Miss McFadden?" the judge asked.

"That is correct, Your Honor."

"Do you have papers verifying the sale, Mr. Benjamin?"

Arthur pulled a sheet of paper from his inside coat pocket and held it up. "I have an agreement in principal," he answered. "We hope to conclude the sale in the following few days."

"Then you don't, at the moment, have full title?" the judge said.

"No, Your Honor," Arthur replied quietly. "And I apologize if I've misled the court. We have the agreement. I simply wanted the court to know the proceedings are underway."

For a moment, the judge did not speak. She sat gazing at Arthur with the kind of expression that carried pondering. Finally, she said, "May I ask a question, Mr. Benjamin?"

"Of course, Your Honor."

"How much did you offer for the facility?"

A smile, barely made, grew on Arthur's lips. "The sum of my hat," he said.

If his answer irritated Renee Morgan, she did not show it. She, in fact, finished Arthur's smile for him. "Your hat, Mr. Benjamin?"

"I keep some money in it, in the sweatband. It's an old habit," he said.

The judge bit at a laugh. "And how much was in it at the time of the offer?"

"I believe it was eleven dollars," Arthur answered.

A snicker rippled throughout the courtroom.

"And Miss McFadden accepted?" the judge asked.

"She did," Arthur replied. "She's a very reasonable lady."

I could tell Renee Morgan was both amused and perplexed. She glanced at Ned Doubleday, who took her look as a signal to speak.

"Your Honor, this is clearly a case of extortion against a citizen who, obviously, is incapable of making critical decisions," he said, sounding righteous. "On behalf of the city, I – "

The judge's eyebrows arched. She raised her hand to interrupt him. "Really, Mr. Doubleday? Is this the same person you were eager to have vacate her living quarters a few minutes ago? The same lady who should have been cognizant enough to realize she was deliberately violating a city ordinance?"

Ned Doubleday's opened mouth stayed open.

The judge shook her head and sighed. She looked at Arthur. "Mr. Benjamin, the right of Miss McFadden to sell her property – at any price negotiated – is not at issue in this hearing. However, I am going to remain interested as a personal matter, and as an officer of the court, in the particulars of the sale to assure that Miss McFadden is, first, fully aware of her actions, and, second, that she has not been unfairly treated." She paused, cocked her head slightly to one side, and then added, "May I also ask, Mr. Benjamin, what are your plans for the property?"

Arthur turned to look at Lady. "My plans, Your Honor, are to hold it in trust for the care of Miss McFadden."

"Do you plan to sell it?" the judge asked gently.

"I haven't thought about that," Arthur replied. "I'd rather have ownership of it before any action is taken. However, if I did sell it, the first consideration would be to offer it back to Miss McFadden."

"And what price would you ask, Mr. Benjamin?"

"I believe twelve dollars would be fair," Arthur answered.

The giggle of the courtroom turned into laughter. Even the judge chuckled. She did a shrug, shook her head. "I don't think I want to inquire further, Mr. Benjamin."

Arthur did his little head bow and sat again in his chair.

The judge picked up some of the papers before her. "Still," she said, "Mr. Doubleday is correct: the issue before us today is less about ownership than it is the violation of a city ordinance. After careful review of the documents provided me, I have concluded the complaint is legally justified, and, frankly, I was surprised. In many cases, a commercially zoned district permits some occupancy. However, the zoning ordinance relating to this property – and other properties of that vicinity – lists it as commercial only. Therefore, the complaint registered by the city stands the test of legitimacy." She paused again, looked apologetically at Lady and Arthur and Wally. "Regrettably, it is my duty to issue an order to vacate the premises by August six, one week from tomorrow. If this order is ignored, the owner – and I hope that question will be settled by that date – will face contempt of court charges."

I saw a smirk rise up in Ned Doubleday's face. He said, "I presume you mean all occupants would be in contempt, Your Honor."

"No, Mr. Doubleday, I do not," the judge said bluntly. "I would only hold the owner – whoever that might be – in contempt. I see no reason in having the police deploy SWAT teams to arrest the horde of citizens I can envision being there in protest of an unpopular action."

Ned Doubleday sniffed haughtily. He did not reply.

"Do you understand the order I am issuing, Mr. Benjamin, Dr. Whitmire?" the judge asked.

"We do, Your Honor," Wally answered brightly.

"Miss McFadden, do you also understand?" the judge said in a kind manner.

Lady lifted her face majestically and all of us knew immediately that she was alert and suddenly free of the disease of confusion that haunted her. We knew also it would be a momentary miracle. She often paused for reality in unexpected, surprising moments, then, finding reality painful, floated back into her dream world of castles and mansions and suitors and royalty.

"Miss McFadden?" the judge repeated. "Are you clear on my order?"

"I am," Lady answered with dignity. "I'm not insane. I know perfectly well what I'm doing."

"I pray you do," the judge replied. She scanned the court. "From the attendance at this hearing, I am certain the decision made here today will be a topic of considerable controversy," she added. "I want everyone to know that I personally find the order an unfortunate necessity. As a public official concerned with the well-being of all citizens of the city, I am impressed that Miss McFadden has used her property as a safe harbor for those unfortunate enough to have lives of uncertainty, and it disturbs me that city officials have made no apparent attempt to settle this matter amicably."

She looked at Lady, and then added, "I hope you accept the seriousness of this order. I would not like to see any of you returned to this or any other court." She paused, and then added, "Though I fear I will."

EIGHTEEN

If Renee Morgan had put out a sign advertising services as *Madam Morgan, Reader of the Future,* she could not have been more accurate in her prediction of considerable controversy over her order for us to vacate the Castle.

Throughout the day, the story of it sang over the airwaves of radio and television and the following morning it made its way to *The Savannah Herald* in a screaming headline – *Judge Sides with City* – and the mix of it caused the uproar Wally had pinpointed in his paper-napkin treatise in Frank's Fine Dining when we were planning our strategy.

It was Doyle Copeland's account that would be most quoted and talked about, for Doyle knew it from the beginning, from the overheard quarrel that had occurred in our appearance at the police station. His story of the courtroom proceedings could have been turned into a three-act opera of villainy, performed by an ensemble of street people and dissident wheeler-dealers full-throated enough to be heard as far away as Charleston.

It would be a story surging in passion, beginning with a description of Lady and the Castle, and of Lady's guests, all living in harmony in a kind of no-rent Brigadoon, where civility reigned on the fringes of a lifestyle made of chaos. It would tell of the impending sale of the Castle to Arthur Benjamin for the sum of eleven dollars, pulled by Arthur from the sweatband of his hat.

Doyle would describe it as Arthur taking a bullet for Lady, and he was right.

And then the story would pivot on a single word, clean as a ballet dancer doing a pirouette: *However . . .*

Behind the *However* would be a building story of conflict, beginning with the run-down of Lady – admittedly, an exaggeration, since it was more a brush-down than anything – and ending with alleged threats and alleged bribery attempts by Roger Upshaw, speaking on behalf of the mayor.

At the center of it would be the protagonist Arthur Benjamin, who would be described by Doyle as a gentle man, soft in speech, forgiving in nature, a man who made paper flowers from colored napkins and passed them out as ornaments that celebrated the soul, a man strong in his belief of the meaning of innocence. He was not unlike Don Quixote de la Mancha, Miguel de Cervantes' romantic hero of classic literature, Doyle would suggest, and he would give a little word chase to make his point: Arthur's purchase of the Castle seemed directed to one purpose – to prevent Lady from suffering the indignity of possibly being arrested. If there needed to be a jousting with the windmills of City Hall, it would be Arthur holding the lance, risking life and limb.

An uninterested reader of Doyle's story might have found humor in its hyperbole, in its imagery of Arthur on a sway-back horse charging Mayor Harry Geiger driving a Mercedes bearing a vanity license tag, yet Doyle's words would make it matter, as time would reveal. Arthur had, indeed, purchased the Castle to keep Lady out of jail, and to provide for her care.

And with caring readers, that was worth celebration.

As we left the courthouse to return to the Castle, a cluster of supporters trailed after us – Frank and Holly and the regulars of Frank's, and Sharon Day and the ladies with her, and people on the street who had heard the news from the fluttering tongues of those who had been in the courtroom with us. I was pleased to see Dale Stewart among them. I had not seen her since vacating the apartment my mother and I had occupied. She waved and I made my way to her, folding her in an embrace that was warm and healing. She said, "I'm proud of you Hamby. Your mother would have been, too. I think of her all the time."

As we walked, the crowd multiplied. It was a crowd with the look of an old, Grade-B western movie where a trembling, good-hearted sheriff begins an ambling, lonely walk down a muddy street to face a gunslinger in front of the saloon, the gunslinger thinking he has the town cowering from his reputation and from his evil gaze and the black teeth behind his evil smile. And then, store-by-store, the townspeople step out, carrying rifles and shotguns and six-shooters and pitch forks and knitting needles, and the crowd grows until there is an army of people marching on the gunslinger, many wearing the aprons of storekeepers, showing innocence. Music swells, coming from clouds and from tumbleweeds. A close-up of the gunslinger shows a twitch on his face before he mounts his horse and gallops away in a cowardly attempt to escape, only to be brought down by a single rifle shot fired by some put-upon woman from the upstairs window of a bordello.

It was how I felt, walking between Holly and Wally, following Lady and Arthur – Arthur of the Paper Flowers, or maybe it was Don Quixote we followed. If more Don Quixote than Arthur, it was a toss-up as to who would be Sancho – me or Wally.

"My God, Hamby, did you ever see anything like this?" Wally asked happily.

"It's impressive," I admitted, "but I still don't understand what happened in there."

"Where?" Wally said.

"The courtroom. What Arthur did."

"He just put himself in jeopardy," Wally replied. "I tried to talk him out of it, but he wouldn't listen. He's a strange man, my friend. A strange man."

Having Wally tell me of Arthur's strangeness was much the same as having an automobile mechanic tell a brain surgeon about a lobotomy. I was the man who had robbed the poor fellow, who still carried the weight of a few dollars from that shameful moment – Judas with his pieces of silver.

"Does Lady really own the place?" I asked in a voice only strong enough to carry from my mouth to Wally's ear.

He smiled, but did not answer.

"I don't like this," I protested.

"It's an adventure, Hamby," Wally said. "An adventure. Take it in. It's one you're not going to forget."

Behind us, as we walked, a chorus of voices chanted, *"Arthur, Arthur, Arthur . . .* "

In late afternoon, after the well wishers had left us with their pledges of support, we huddled as a group – Wally included – and talked about what had happened, and what could happen, and what we might do about it.

Wally had tugged along a flip chart he once used in seminars during his career as a professor and traveling lecturer, and as we talked, he made notes for what he called *The Arthur Stratagem.* To Wally, we were at war and we needed to arm ourselves with courage, beginning with the vow that we would ignore the court order to vacate the Castle.

The way he said it, having the fervor of a general commanding a rag-tag troop of guerrillas, if we planned it with care and flair, we would be countering every move Harry Geiger made, before he thought to make it.

"Like dominoes," he said with pride. "Push the first, the rest will follow."

By refusing to move from the Castle, Arthur, being the owner, would be summoned again to court to face a contempt charge, Wally speculated.

He would refuse to appear.

First domino to fall.

"That's when it becomes a war of nerves," was Wally's way of describing it. "If Arthur fails to show, that would force the judge to issue an arrest warrant. But they won't jail him. Too risky. Bad publicity. They'll bring him in to face the judge and she'll find him in contempt and impose a daily fine of some piddling amount until he agrees to vacate."

"Fine him?" asked Leo. "And where do we get the money for that?" There was anger in his voice.

Wally smiled. "It's covered," he replied.

"Covered?" said Leo.

"Covered," Wally replied. He smiled, and I knew there was no reason to interrogate him. Wally had tricks up his sleeve and likely had a bank account to support them. He capped the black marker he had used to make his notes. "And that's how the dominoes fall," he added.

A hush – silence made from the air that swept through the Castle – surrounded us.

I think all of us were realizing the same thing – all but Lady, who had taken on an expression of a pleasant dream: the arrest of Arthur. The way Wally had framed his war plan; the arrest was key in the scheme of things. He was rolling the dice – or maybe the dominoes – that there would be such a public outcry it would cause the city to fold like an accordion at rest, its air gone from its billows, its music muted, and there would be a negotiation – initiated by the city – to rezone the Castle, making it dual-purpose for business and occupancy. The way Wally saw it, the city's zoning board would cover itself in ink in its haste to approve the request.

On paper, the plan had the look of good reasoning about it, yet the only weapon we had in the battle was faith – faith that the public would rise up in protest, and that the hammering attack of their words of anger would riddle the mayor's office like sniper fire. Wally's War was a war of nerves, of pressure. It was no different than what Harry Geiger and Ned Davenport and all the others were doing, he proclaimed. They were using the pressure of their positions. Government against the governed. History was rife with noble examples of the governed rising up to level the playing field, Wally preached.

"We can beat them at their own game," he urged, "if they don't know we're playing it."

Leo did not like the plan, nor did Carrie or Gerty or Wendell. None of us knew about Lady. Lady remained in the comfort of her dreamy, distant thought.

"You keep saying he won't go to jail," Leo argued. "How do you know this? Have you talked to the judge?"

"I've talked to some lawyers I know, here and in Delaware," Wally told him. "They don't think the city would want him in jail, and they also think the judge wouldn't want it – gambling that it would be Judge Morgan."

"But there's a chance he could go to jail?" Leo asked irritably.

Wally gave me a look showing wear on his patience. "Of course, there's a chance, but it's remote."

"I'm not concerned about it," Arthur said quietly.

Leo turned to look at Arthur. "So, I ask you, what do you know about jail? Let me tell you: Nothing. You know nothing. Somebody goes to jail, it should be me. I know a thing or two."

"I'll be fine, Leo," Arthur told him.

"It's possible he won't even be arrested," Wally suggested with too much confidence. "There's a chance the city will find a sudden need to make compromises before the deadline to vacate."

"And how do you know these things?" Leo snapped. "You ever deal with these people? I have. They don't break. They bend, but they don't break."

"That's the truth," Wendell mumbled.

I was inclined to agree with Leo and Wendell. Wally had spent too much time in a classroom making off-the-cuff judgments that always worked the way he wanted them to work because he was dealing with nothing more than history and hypothesis. On the street, history and hypothesis were as laughable as a bawdy joke.

Wally carefully tore the sheet from the easel and folded it and put it into a briefcase he had with him. We watched him in silence, and then Gerty began to weep softly in a look-away fashion, dabbing at her eyes with her fingers. Carrie joined her.

"If I thought he was going to jail, I'd be happy to change places with him, " Wally offered sincerely, and I knew it was said truthfully, not as a way of placating Gerty and Carrie. For Wally, being in prison for a cause he considered righteous would represent the crowning of his life, placing him in the company of Gandhi and Martin Luther King, Jr. and Sister Teresa and Nelson Mandela and all the other martyrs who had put their shoulders to change and nudged it forward with the strength of their will.

"It wouldn't be the same," Arthur said softly, almost absently.

It was the closest statement to boasting any of us would ever hear from Arthur, yet we knew he was right. Wally in jail would have meant nothing to the citizens of Savannah. He could have rotted behind bars, writing books of outrage, and other than Melody Comstock and residents of the Castle and Frank of Frank's Fine Dining, no one would have raised an eyebrow.

The same would have been true with any of us, other than Lady. If Lady had been jailed, the outcry would have echoed around the globe.

"So, we just wait, is that it?" Carrie asked.

"Unless we decide to give in," I replied.

"No," Arthur said. He smiled. "We won't do that. We'll be fine."

Holly was sweet to me that night, knowing I carried more than a little sense of regret for having taken our troubles to Wally, permitting him to place Arthur at such risk. She pampered me with a full-body massage using an oil she had purchased from a co-worker named Mandy, who vowed the oil contained aphrodisiac powers taken from the essence of herbs grown only in China. After forty minutes of being kneaded – gentle to vigorous – I was a believer. The love-making that followed made me wonder if my body would take flame from the friction.

Afterward, we talked quietly and late into the night. Holly purred about how her life had changed since meeting Arthur and it was more than the imagined magic of a flower made from a paper napkin. She had changed, she told me, because I had changed.

"You're not a fool, like you used to be," she said. "You used to drive me crazy, being a fool. All that Irish nonsense, those little tongue-twisting lies you told, making it sound like the words of some poem, and I'd fall for it and you'd screw it up and then I'd stay mad for a week. You haven't done that at all since that first night you showed up with Arthur."

I confessed that being in Arthur's presence had made me more aware of my responsibilities. Hearing myself say it, I wondered if it wasn't another of the tongue-twisting lies, the truth resting with the fact that following Arthur around, carrying the guilt of having stolen from him, had become an occupation and like every occupation, it required work and work had taken the edge off my foolishness.

"I don't know what it is," Holly whispered, nuzzling her mouth against my neck, the hot tip of her tongue darting out to leave a burn-mark. "I just know it makes me love you." She paused as though listening to her own words. "I do love you, Hamby. I do. I wish to God I didn't, not as much as I do, but I can't help it. Of all the men I've ever known, you may be the most irritating, but I want to be with you. The only thing I'm afraid of is that one day I'll wake up and you'll be gone."

It was in that moment, in the child-like honesty of her fear, that I knew I felt the same for her. I could feel it fluttering through me like a shock of electricity. Holly could feel it too. She said, "Are you all right, Hamby?"

"Yes," I told her.

"What just happened?" she asked.

I thought of my mother, remembering her promise in the tender hours before her death, a promise that happiness would come to me in its own time, in its own way. Not on a Greyhound bus, she had said with a weak, knowing smile, but out the blue of sky, out of the quickness of surprise. "It's true magic, Hamby," she had said. "True magic."

"Hamby? What happened?" Holly asked again. There was a sound of fret in her voice. She moved her body against mine. Skin against skin. "What was it?" she whispered.

I did not know the words to answer. The quickness of surprise had struck me dumb.

NINETEEN

Carrie's cousin would tell her the mayor had held another private meeting with his brain trust – Roger Upshaw, Ned Doubleday, Shawn Grogan and Fred Seabrook – on the morning following Judge Renee Morgan's order, the morning that Doyle Copeland's story in *The Savannah Enquirer* caused a yelping of outrage in homes and business establishments throughout the city.

It was a meeting prompted by a telephone call from Dr. Clyde Webster, the alderman from District Five and a member of the City Council, a mild-mannered, principled man with a private dislike for the antics of Harry Geiger. I had known of him for years, had seen him on the streets, behaving in the gentlemanly way of his reputation. A psychiatrist with the kind of clientele who hid behind put-on smiles at country club functions, Clyde Webster could be a formidable foe when riled, and the matter of enforcing an ancient zoning ordinance against Lady, or Arthur, or whoever actually owned the Castle, had riled him. To him, the public reaction to Judge Morgan's ruling made the city of Savannah seem like the Gestapo with dehumanizing tactics, no matter how clean the legality of it was.

Supposedly, Clyde Webster had urged the mayor to get a handle on the controversy, telling him of dissatisfaction among the council and of phone calls from business leaders – a half-dozen before nine o'clock that morning – threatening a recall petition. He also spoke bluntly of the shaky position the mayor was already in because of the hullabaloo about his wife possibly being involved in a hit-and-run accident. To Clyde Webster, the city was wearing a black eye that had the rest of the world pointing fingers and railing about mistreatment of unfortunates.

The way it came to me from Carrie – quotes and all – Harry Geiger did not like the threat, but he also knew Clyde Webster was serious. The meeting with his brain trust was intended to achieve two things: first, to calm the council and, second, to tighten the screws on Arthur Benjamin.

Shawn Grogan and Fred Seabrook had volunteered to handle the council by going one-on-one with them, excluding Clyde Webster.

"We know enough about every one of them to keep them in line," Shawn Grogan reportedly had boasted. "If anybody's up for a recall, it'll be Webster, the pompous son of a bitch."

Tightening the screws on Arthur was another matter. It had been Fred Seabrook's suggestion that no one should question the sale of the Castle to Arthur. "Let the old man have the place," he had urged. "They're playing the sympathy game, that's all. They're not about to honor that order, for Christ's sake. Even Renee knew that when she issued it. All they're doing is throwing the gauntlet at your feet, daring you pick it up. Put him in jail for a couple of days, and you'll hear a different tune. But he did do us one big favor: he put himself on the line, instead of the old woman. My God, we'd have a blue-haired parade that'd reach from here to Atlanta if she were the one we'd have to take in."

Harry Geiger had agreed.

"You're going to take some heat, Harry," Roger Upshaw had advised.

"I know that," Harry had growled in reply. "This job comes with heat. You take it; you'd better have an asbestos ass. You think I'm afraid of that? "

"Of course not," Roger had replied meekly.

"We do have some good news," Ned Doubleday had said. "We've managed to get the state off our backs about Debra. She's going to get a citation for failing to come to a complete stop at a signal light, and she'll have a fine to pay, but that's it."

"What if the old woman decides to pursue it?" the mayor had asked.

"She won't," Ned Doubleday had answered confidently. "We'll have Benjamin. She'll not want anything to happen to him. None of them will."

The report from Carrie's cousin did not surprise her, or me, yet it did make both of us fearful for Arthur. I thought of his story about his wife and knew he had some experience with cruelty, but it was not the same cruelty he would find in jail, if that became his fate. In jail, his kindness would be seen as weakness. No one wanted paper flowers in jail.

"I wish to God we hadn't started all of this," Carrie complained bitterly, and I knew her anger was directed to me, as it should have been. Still, I believed Arthur would have done something on his own to protect Lady and the rest of us, if we had not become involved. It was in his nature, the same as the real, or imagined, King Arthur. Right was right, and it was worth the fight to keep from being rolled over by all the wrongs that existed.

I asked Carrie if she would appeal to her cousin to keep Arthur safe if he landed in jail.

She looked at me with disbelief, as though I had insulted her. "Do you think I haven't?" she snapped.

"And what did he say?" I said gently.

"He said he'd do what he could," she answered. The moisture of tears came back to her eyes. "Damn it, Hamby. Why couldn't you leave it alone?"

It was a question that caused pain. A good question. One I should have considered. I had the experience for it.

After the death of my mother, I got it in mind to somehow notify my father of her passing and I wrote to my father's brother, an uncle I had never seen, still living in Ireland, in Youghal. His name was Sean. I informed him of my mother's death and inquired if he knew the whereabouts of my father. The letter I received back was brief: He had not heard from my father in years, but if there were an inheritance in the consideration, he would accept the bother of holding it for my father. Not a word of his letter expressed sadness over my mother's death. Not a word asked of my own welfare.

It was another thing I should have left alone, another weight of sorrow to carry around.

I apologized to Carrie for my actions and she made the sigh she always made when coming down from a flash of temper.

"It's not your fault, Hamby," she said quietly. "You were trying to do the right thing. I'm scared, that's all."

"I know," I told her. "So am I."

I had called Wally, saying Carrie and I wanted to see him, and we were sitting in Frank's, waiting his arrival. Between taking and delivering her food orders, Holly darted about us like a hummingbird, shamelessly leaning to me for quick kisses. The silliness of it charmed Carrie. "You really should marry that girl," she said to me in whisper.

"And maybe I will," I said. "Someday."

"And maybe she'll get tired of waiting and find somebody else," Carrie retorted. She added, "Somebody with a bank account and enough ambition to keep it filled."

I took her jest with a smile, and with a thought: When the matter of the Castle was settled, I would go job seeking. Holly had already dropped hints about moving in with her, telling me I needed a place to settle. I was grateful her hints were gently offered. Fragile as I was about everything around me, a demand would have sent me scurrying.

"You know we're all going to have to go our own way," Carrie added, as though reading my mind.

I nodded.

"My cousin has already invited me to stay with him and his wife," she told me. "They want me to go to college to study art."

She paused, toyed with the slice of coconut cream pie Holly had put before her as a gift. "I'm thinking about it."

"Good," I told her. "It's where you should be."

"I don't want to be a burden," she said.

"I said the same thing to my mother once," I replied. "She gave me a great answer. She said you can't be a burden to someone who wants you."

Carrie's smile was tender. "I would have liked your mother."

"You would have loved her, Carrie," I said.

Wally arrived in good spirits. He was carrying a folded-up copy of *The Savannah Enquirer* under his armpit and a large box of Arthur's flowers in his hands. The flowers were leftover makings from Arthur's time with him, he told us. "You need to pass them out on the street," he said. "After the story this morning, there'll be a demand for them, and that gave me an idea: if Arthur goes to jail, we should use the flowers to show support. Maybe get that talk-show fellow at the radio station to promote it, or have the kids at SCAD put it on the website. Wear a flower for Arthur, that sort of thing. Melody tells me those kids think he's the greatest thing to happen in America since Starbucks sold its first latte."

I could sense Carrie's irritation over Wally's blustery manner.

"We'll think about it," I said, and Wally picked up on the uneasy mood still suspended over our table.

"Just a thought," he said. He added in a kindly voice, "And maybe not a good one at all. Sometimes my imagination gets away from me."

Carrie wanted to agree, but did not.

"So, tell me about things," Wally added. "Where's Arthur?"

"On the street when we left him," Carrie answered. "He was with Lady and Leo and Gerty and Wendell."

Wally wanted to know about the reaction people were offering.

"A little scary," I told him. "They're still up in arms. A lot of people are wanting to start a fund to hire a lawyer."

Wally could not stop his smile. "So, why did you want to see me?" he asked.

I looked at Carrie. There was a warning in her eyes. Tell him, the warning said.

"We want to know the truth about Lady's ownership of the Castle," I said quietly, aware of the reader of comic strips sitting across the room at his familiar table. "When I've asked about it, you've avoided giving me an answer. Now we want one."

"All right," Wally replied after a moment. "The truth is, I don't know. I've done some research – more than the city, I promise you – and what I've learned is a little vague and a little disturbing."

The story that Wally told confirmed the Castle was likely owned by the McFadden estate, won in a poker game on St. Simons Island by Chester McFadden, as Lady had claimed in one of her stories. What was not clear was the matter of the deed. Supposedly, it had been sent to McFadden, but was lost in a house fire that also killed him. The loser of the poker game had never inquired about it, either showing some honor for holding a bad hand, or not caring enough about the property to squabble over it.

Carrie gasped when she heard of the fire.

"What is it?" Wally asked.

"She told us about a fire a few days ago," Carrie answered. "She said she started it."

Wally cocked his head thoughtfully, but did not speak.

"She killed her father," Carrie whispered. "My God."

"I doubt if it was planned that way," Wally offered. "Not from what I understand."

In his snooping, Wally had talked to an attorney in New York who had handled the will of Chester McFadden, and the attorney had spoken of an investigation concerning the fire, one that had pinpointed Lady, but one lacking in conclusive evidence. There was also some doubt that investigators were seriously bothered about the details of Chester McFadden's death. He had steamrolled enough people in his life to earn the reputation of being overbearing and cantankerous. Further, there was the question even then of Lady's mental stability.

Wally knew only that shortly after the fire, Lady had left New York for Savannah. What was left of the estate was little more than a name on a sheet of paper. "When they added it all up, the Castle was the last piece of property the old man owned – if he even had it," Wally said. "He was broke. The house had been sold to pay creditors a month before the fire. Everything else was written off."

"But why did Lady burn it?" Carrie asked.

"I'd guess it she had an argument with the old man over the Castle," Wally suggested. "From what I was told, he had one will giving her his properties, and another one cutting her out of any inheritance. I'd say that's why she came here. A little subconscious act of triumph." He leaned back in his chair, pulled one of his Cuban cigars from his shirt pocket and rolled in between his fingers. I could tell his thoughts were on a chase. "If I were a betting man, I'd put my life on the line that it went back to her marriage."

Carrie's face blinked in astonishment. "What did you say?" she asked. "Lady really was married?"

"If you could call it that," Wally replied. "It only lasted for a day – less than a day, really."

"A day?" Carrie said incredulously.

"The old man had it annulled," Wally replied.

The story he told was like the finding of an out-of-place thread in a garment of rainbow colors. Chester McFadden had been obsessed with control and he would not permit his daughter, his only child, to date, or if she did, he had ways of ending the relationships before they became serious. Lady's mother was of no help; she, too, was a victim of the control.

In her late 30s, Lady had begun to date a young man, a teacher, without her parents' knowledge, and after a few months, they eloped. Chester McFadden learned of the deception within hours. The couple was found in a hotel in New Jersey and Lady was forcibly removed, with her husband vowing to fight for her in the courts. The annulment was enforced the next day. Afterward, Lady's disdain for her father was the hurricane eye of family storms, turbulent enough to cause her mother's death. Her husband of a few hours was never heard from again – a payoff, Wally guessed.

"The attorney I talked to suggested her marriage and annulment led to Lady's breakdown," he added. "If she did spark the fire, I don't much blame her. When a person has a reservation in hell – as her father must have had – it's an appropriate send-off, wouldn't you say?"

Carrie was amazed by the story. "She was right," she said. "The night she met Arthur and said he reminded her of her late husband, she was right. But why did she call him her late husband, if it was just an annulment and she never heard from him again?"

"Maybe that's the way she thought of it," Wally suggested.

Carrie slumped back in her chair, her face still holding a look of shock.

"So where does that leave the property?" I asked. "And what about this Delaware company paying the taxes?"

Wally leaned in at the table, rolled the cigar in his fingers. He said, "That's the irony of all of it, Hamby. I knew nothing about the poker game or the fire, or anything else, when I – well, played around with the city's tax records."

"Jesus, Wally," I whispered, "I don't like the sound of this. What are you talking about?"

Wally's smile grew across his face. "I'm good with computers, Hamby."

"You're scaring me," I told him.

He laughed easily. "All right, I'll tell you all of it, but you'll have to swear secrecy on this one, both of you."

We gave him our oath.

"The name of that Delaware company is A.N. Whitehead Properties," Wally said smugly. "Do you know who A.N. Whitehead was?"

We did not, we told him.

"Alfred North Whitehead was a prominent mathematician and philosopher of the twentieth century," he explained. "A brilliant mind. I've always considered myself a disciple of his work. The address given on the information is as bogus as a promise of assistance from the Internal Revenue Service, but every lawyer on Earth genuflects when they read the words, A Delaware Corporation."

I could see the look of shock and fright on Carrie's face as she realized what Wally had done. "My God," she whispered, "you hacked into city records. You've committed a felony."

"My dear, what I've committed is an assault against arrogance," Wally said patiently. "But I'm not concerned about it. Even if they bring in a Sherlock Holmes of computer investigation, they'll never trace it to me. I used one at – well, another facility."

Carrie and I sat for a moment, looking in astonishment at one another as the dots of Wally's doing connected with thick, dark lines of recognition.

"So, who does own the place?" I finally asked Wally. "Truly, I mean."

He made a little shoulder-roll shrug. "I wish I knew, Hamby. Best I can tell, no one knows for certain. If the deed exists, it's Lady's free and clear. But who knows? If it burned, there'd be an argument. Maybe Lady knows the answer, but I doubt if she could remember it."

TWENTY

Because there was a promise of rain in the thickening of clouds, Carrie and I left the box of Arthur's flowers at Frank's, giving Holly permission to distribute them. Wally offered to drive us to the Castle, but we refused, knowing he was waiting for Melody Comstock.

Outside, drizzle turned into a downpour, and we stopped in a coffee shop on Bull Street to wait it out. We were surprised to find Leo there, huddled over a cup of coffee at a table, writing on a sheet of paper that he slipped quickly under the table and onto his lap when he saw us. I knew instantly what he was doing, and I did not want to embarrass him.

As we made our way back to his table, I signaled to a waiter to prepare two go-cups of coffee, saying the order loud enough for Leo's hearing.

"What're you doing?" I said cheerfully to Leo. "Ducking the rain?"

He nodded his swift, nervous nod. "Yeah, yeah," he mumbled. He kept his eyes from us.

"Feels good," I said. "Carrie and I were going for a walk in it, but we wanted a coffee to take with us."

"I love the rain, especially in summer," Carrie said too quickly and I knew she, too, had seen Leo hide the paper he had been writing on.

"Yeah, yeah," Leo repeated.

I asked if he had been with Lady and Arthur. He had, he replied. Earlier. The last he saw of them they were on their way back to the Castle with Wendell and Gerty. He drummed the table nervously with his fingers. His body rocked.

"Any problems with them?" I asked.

Leo shook his head. "None I know of."

We stood for a moment in the fidgety awkwardness of a pause. I could tell Leo wanted us to leave. "Okay," I said, "we'll see you later."

He nodded.

"Later," Carrie added.

We took our coffee and left. Outside, in the rain, Carrie asked, "What was that about?"

"You saw, didn't you?" I asked.

"The paper he was hiding? How could I miss it?" she answered. "But what was it?"

"Probably filling out an application for a job," I answered. "At least I think that's what it was."

"Oh, my God," she said, looking up at me in astonishment, the rain streaming down her face. "They'll never hire Leo. Never."

"Probably not," I replied, "but it's a sign."

"Of what?" Carrie asked in her demanding way.

"Of change," I said. "Sometimes you just have to move on."

We talked as we walked, the rain pelting us. What I had said about change gnawed at Carrie. She lamented that, to her, change was like being at the top of a slide on a playground, sitting comfortable, and having someone, or something, give you an unwanted shove, sending you squealing down the slick tin. "It happens that fast," she sighed, adding, "and that's what's happening to us, Hamby. All of us. We've got another week together, and that's it."

We walked a few steps in silence, and then she added, "I lied to Leo."

"How?" I asked.

"I hate walking in the rain," she grumbled.

With Leo still out, the dinner we had in the Castle was one of soup and grilled cheese sandwiches – the soup from Gerty, the sandwiches from Wendell. All of us wore faces that belonged to performers masked in drawn-on smiles. We tried to make merry with merry-sounding stories, not realizing – as I did later – that the stories were all taken from the nostalgia of our time together. Arthur seemed comfortable, pleased to be among us again. When we decided to play a board game of checkers, winners taking on challengers, he waved off the chance to participate, saying he was not good at it. I laughed and I think Arthur knew why, the way he smiled.

Leo did not return to the Castle until after nine o'clock. He was in a gloomy mood. Gerty told him she had held back some soup and a sandwich for him, but he refused it, claiming he was not hungry. He went into our room and went to bed.

"Is he all right?" Carrie asked quietly.

"He will be," I told her.

"Oh, Gerty, tell us about the first dress you made," Lady enthused. "I love that story."

Gerty closed her eyes and shook her head. "Lord, Jesus," she whispered, and then she leaned back in her chair. "I was eight years old," she began in a monotone, "and my mama put me down at the sewing machine and said she was about to give me a life. She tore apart a flour sack and cut it with the scissors and then she made me stitch it together, and that's the story and that's been my life."

"Was it pretty?" Lady asked.

"Looked like a gown a movie star would wear," Gerty answered in a tired voice, waiting for the exchange she knew would follow.

Lady: "What color was it?"

Gerty: "Yellow."

Lady: "Oh, I thought it was red."

Gerty: "They didn't make no red flour sacks."

Lady: "I wonder why."

Gerty: "Turned the flour red."

Lady: "Oh, my. I didn't know that."

Gerty: "Well, it's the truth."

Carrie giggled. She loved the exchange, loved the sound of boredom in Gerty's voice and the way Gerty's face took on a smile without wanting the smile to be there.

"I'd love to have a dress like that," Lady sighed. "Someday, Gerty, you must make one for me."

"Honey, if you can find me a yellow flour sack in the city of Savannah, Georgia, I'll do it," Gerty said.

It was that kind of night. Clustered in the Castle, holding on to fragments of what had been, quiet-talking, quiet laughing, knowing we were sitting atop a slide of change, waiting for the shove that would send us off in different directions.

I wondered if, in years before us, whether we would remember such nights as the one that closed around us, and if we did, would the melancholy of it leave us feeling warm.

TWENTY-ONE

We awoke to a day of such loveliness it made me wonder if the Holy Father was practicing the making of another world. The rain of the day before had the greenery of summer reaching in a stretch for the sun, and a soft breeze coming off the river cooled the air like a return of spring. Birds were fine-tuning their throats for a concert.

Even Leo seemed revived. On a mission with Arthur and me to find the makings of breakfast, he cheerfully told us of a holiday he had taken with his parents and his two younger sisters and brother at a Jewish resort in the Catskill Mountains of New York – the Borscht Belt – and how the summer weather had shocked them with its cold nights and warm days. He called it the best of his memories, and there was a smile to prove it. Hearing him, I had a sense of the happier times in his life – the bright young man that he was, gifted with numbers, causing his parents to beam with pride and to boast of his accomplishments. It was one of the lessons I had learned from Jewish friends: pride. Pride was not sin. Pride was celebration.

"I've thought of going back there," he admitted in his tale of the Catskills. "But from everything I hear, it's changed so much I wouldn't recognize it."

To my surprise, Arthur also gave an account of a trip to the Catskills. His former wife's family had owned a summer home near Monticello, and once he had accompanied his father-in-law there to prepare it for the season. "He needed a little inexpensive labor," Arthur said without resentment. "I enjoyed the time, even if it was mostly work."

I asked if he had ever returned to the home for vacation.

"It was sold the following year," he replied. "I never went back."

"Maybe we should both go," Leo said with a rare hint of humor. "Catch the Greyhound and have a vacation." He looked at Arthur. "Two Jews going to the Promised Land."

Arthur smiled, nodded. "Perhaps we should," he replied. "Perhaps we should go there and find a little hotel that's been closed by time, and re-open it." He paused, walked a few steps. "All of us," he added. "We could call it Lady's Castle Number Two."

"You can count me out on opening a hotel," Leo told him. "I know what that would mean. I'd be the cook, and we'd all be sued for food poisoning."

He laughed when he said it, but I suspected there was more to what he suggested than the words that said them. I suspected the application Leo had made in the coffee shop had been for a short-order cook's position and it had been rejected. Making fun of his skills – or lack of them – was an easy out for him. I had seen him go through the same depression and the same recovery after other applications for other jobs – a dark mood followed by a carefree spirit.

Still, I could see Leo and Arthur together on a Greyhound bus, making a quest for the Promised Land. A man in his mid-forties and a man in his mid-sixties, closer in spirit and in experience than in age. I could see them operating an inn having charm and comfort. I could see them finding work for wanderers needing a handout. I could see them having pride in themselves.

I could also see Lady sitting in a rocker on the porch of the inn, having no memory of an annulled marriage or of a killing fire, no memory even of a warehouse in Savannah or of the people she had called her Guests.

In the coffee shop, we ordered pastries and bagels with cream cheese, and when we pooled together our money to pay the check, the owner, whose name was Moody, refused to accept it. "On the house," he said with emotion. "I read about what happened down at the courthouse. The sons of bitches."

"It's kind of you," Arthur said, "but we can pay."

"I know you can," Moody replied in his rough way of speaking. "I see you got the money, but I want to do something." He paused, inhaled hard, the way a man does who is fighting temper. "A lot of people do," he added.

We would learn that Moody knew more about the mood of the people of Savannah than we did.

The crowds that surrounded the lot of us when we went for a walk after our breakfast, were agitated and boisterous, putting me in mind of a football game I had attended in Athens at the University of Georgia in the company of a man named Ollie Evans, a beer distributor with an itch to become an importer of goods from Ireland. It was Ollie's thinking that I would become an agent for him, and the trip to Athens was part of his scheme to get me at a low wage. The game was madness. Dog-woofing loud enough to damage eardrums. Bellowing that had the sound of an army making a charge with bayonets fixed. I remembered nothing of the game played against Auburn University, but I could feel the energy of the occasion clinging to my skin for a week, and the dreams I had were of people clothed in red, their heads thrown back, woofing at the skies like pagans calling for some god sitting on a throne of clouds.

The same energy churned among the people who surrounded us. They gave loud, passionate speeches of shock and anger over what was considered a callous court order, and they vowed to make known their dissatisfaction with letters and telephone calls and by affixing their names to the recall petition that a religious group called *Faith in our Fellow Beings* had begun circulating. They offered financial support for our welfare, an offer Arthur waved off, saying we were managing well.

Some among them had fashioned new signs: *Arthur for President*. The signs made him smile. Others – those who lived on the streets – stayed back, watching, some dour-faced, some wearing grins. Preacher was among the grinners and I wondered if he had spoken to Arthur, or if he still had the unopened bottle of vodka he had purchased with some of the money Arthur had given him. From the expression on his face, I suspected the bottle was as empty as his life had become.

Cars slowed on the street to gawk at the crowd. A voice from one of the cars bellowed, "We're with you, Mayor." Arthur lifted his hat and waved it in the direction of the voice.

We stood as a group, with Arthur and Lady up front, a confused, yet pleased smile adorning Lady's face. Arthur wore the cape Gerty had made for him, and I wondered if he did so to claim some imagined place of importance, or if it was done simply to compliment Gerty. Whatever the reason, it created a mild stir: people were reaching out to touch it, as people had reached to touch the hem of the garment worn by Christ, and, being Catholic, it gave me an uneasy feeling.

"What are they doing?" I said to Carrie.

"Who?" she asked.

"Those women," I replied in a whispery but quarrelsome voice. "Grabbing at his cape."

She watched the women for a moment. "I don't think they're groping him, if that's what's bothering you. It looks like they're just admiring Gerty's work. Nothing more than that."

I suppose there was some truth in what Carrie said. The cape did have a stylish, debonair look about it, something that might have been worn by gentlemen of another era, and women, curious about how things are stitched together, might well have been doing nothing more than satisfying their curiosity. My view of it was more base: when the women touched it, it gave them a jolt of some romantic thrill, especially for those who made oohs over it. It also gave them closer contact with Arthur, and in the devilish way the mind plays tag with images; I lost my troubled thought of Arthur being treated as Christ and saw him as a sex symbol.

"You'd like all that pawing, wouldn't you?" Carrie said to me. She snickered. "But you would look good in it, too. Maybe Gerty will make one for you."

"I'd look like an idiot," I told her. "I just hope nobody's laughing at him."

I was never so wrong.

In *The Savannah Enquirer*, the following morning, there would be a front-page photograph of Arthur, wearing his cape, presenting one of his paper flowers to a pretty young Asian girl, whose face wore the happy expression of awe. The caption under the photograph would refer to the cape as a fashion statement, a look of dignity befitting a man of dignity, and from that day the cape would be as much a part of Arthur as his arms or his legs.

And it would cause Gerty to take on the proud look of the royal seamstress Carrie had appointed her to be.

The only dark moment of our stroll-about was when Ted Castleberry came riding by in a patrol car. He slowed the car to a crawl and glared strong enough to cause us to stop our walk. I saw Leo ease forward toward the street, and I saw Ted Castleberry make a fist pistol of his hand, aiming his forefinger at Leo. His thumb curled in a motion of cocking a hammer and he made a gun-firing sound with his mouth. He smiled, winked, and then sped away.

The color of Leo's face was the color of blood.

In late afternoon, after we had returned to the Castle, three men paid a visit. They identified themselves as Fuller Bishop, Mason Reinhart and Damon Ayers of the law firm, Bishop, Reinhart and Ayers. All well dressed. All having the look of actors in some serialized drama about high-profile lawyers. They told us they wanted to volunteer to represent Arthur in the deliberation that would certainly come about if Arthur decided not to obey the court order. *Pro bono*, they said. Done for nothing more than the pleasure of taking on Ned Doubleday and the city government.

"They're nervous," Damon Ayers said. "They did a poor job in their preparation and they know it. All they've got to stand on is a questionable designation in a zoning matter. They don't even know the rightful owner of the property during that transaction."

We listened with interest, but without question, knowing the decision on accepting their service was Arthur's to make. From the expression he carried, I did not believe he would agree to the representation.

I was right. After hearing them out, he thanked the men, but told them he did not wish to create a furor over a matter so trivial. I could see shock on the faces of Fuller Bishop and Mason Reinhart and Damon Ayers.

"Do you understand that you could be sentenced to serve time in jail?" Fuller Bishop asked.

"I'm sure it won't be that," Arthur told him. "A small fine, perhaps, and, perhaps, a short probation."

"Mr. Benjamin," Fuller Bishop said patiently, "I must tell you that this trivial matter, as you call it, has created more turmoil in the city of Savannah than anything I remember in years, and I don't really disagree with you about its importance. Placed against other matters, it is trivial. The truth is, the question of this place – He did a sweeping look at the inside of the Castle. " – has almost nothing to do with what has happened, or what will happen. This, sir, is about you."

"And how is that?" asked Arthur.

Fuller Bishop glanced at Mason Reinhart and Damon Ayers and a faint, puzzled frown crossed over his face.

"Well, sir, like it or not, you have become an icon," Fuller Bishop answered with sincerity. "You may believe that you only represent the people gathered here, but it's more than that. You represent the average person everywhere, the working class, the people who believe in the possibility of fairness and goodness. Surely, you understand that, sir. On the street, you see them everyday. I've watched them crowding around you. You're their hero. People need heroes. They may have them on television, but they need them on the street."

Mason Reinhart and Damon Ayers nodded in unison, their serious faces holding on Arthur.

Arthur smiled and I wondered if he was amused over being called a celebrity or by the soft-voiced plea of Fuller Bishop, a plea that had the sound of a defense attorney giving his begging summary to a jury, hoping for tears and an acquittal wrung from the cloth of passion.

"I don't know about any of that," Arthur said after a moment. "I'm just a person who's grateful for the friendships I've made since I've been here. I consider them my family since I am the last of my biological family. All I want to do is show my appreciation."

Fuller Bishop, to his credit, did not try to further persuade Arthur to accept the offer of representation. He said only, "Would you object to having one of us sit with you in the event you need consultation on matters of law?"

"I would be honored," Arthur told him.

"Is there anything else we can do?" Fuller Bishop asked.

"One thing, perhaps," Arthur answered. "Could you guide us through the sale of the property?"

"I'm familiar with such matters," Mason Reinhart replied. "I'll be happy to take care of it."

And then Arthur surprised us. "I have the deed," he said.

I glanced at Carrie and Leo and Gerty. The expression they wore was one of astonishment.

"Where did you get it?" I said.

"Why, dear, it was in my trunk," Lady answered patiently. "It's always been there."

I wanted to ask about it, how it came to be in her possession, but thought it the wrong time with lawyers sitting among us. Knowing Lady, she would have gladly, cheerfully recounted the setting of the fire that burned her family home and her father with it. Still, in the quick flashing of imagination, I could see her in a fit of anger stealing the deed from her father's belongings and tucking it into her trunk, the thought giving some merit to Wally's guess about an argument over the Castle.

"Certainly, that's the key to what we need," Fuller Bishop said.

Arthur reached into the inside pocket of his coat and removed the deed, and handed it to Mason Reinhart. "I believe it's the only copy," he said.

"We'll be careful with it," Mason Reinhart promised. "I'll have some copies made."

Arthur thanked him, and the three men took their leave. We sat for a few moments without speaking, still stunned by the news of the deed, wanting to talk about it, but shying away from the subject.

It was Leo who broke the silence. "One Jew to another, are you a *meshuggener*?" he said to Arthur. "You just turned down three big-shot lawyers working for free. You know how much they cost, these big-shot lawyers?"

The comment, and Leo's way of saying it, made Arthur smile. "Everything will be fine, Leo," he said.

"You don't know these things," Leo argued. "I do. You need the big-shot lawyers. You don't want to go to jail, I can tell you. Not here. Not with these men having it out for us."

"That's right," Wendell said firmly, leaving me to wonder if he too had spent time behind bars, and guessing he had, the kind of hard-luck life he'd known.

I never asked about the particulars of how Mason Reinhart transferred ownership of the Castle to Arthur for the sum of eleven dollars. I know only that it was done by Wednesday, two days before the deadline to vacate the premises, and I know that Arthur was pleased and that Lady, if she understood what had happened, was also pleased. She wanted to have a party to celebrate, and so we did, Wally included. We gathered at Frank's Fine Dining for dinner, and at Lady's insistence, we even had party hats and little noise makers, like revelers on New Year's Eve, and Frank – sensing a bump in his night's profits – hired an accordion player named Dutch Arnold, who had wavy orange-blonde hair and wore his shirt open at the chest, exposing a skinny body dyed brown by liquid sunshine.

The party was sponsored by an anonymous donor; Frank told me when I confided that we might be forced to go on the books with him. I did not pressure him for information, for I believed the donor was Wally, making a pitch to assuage his guilt over putting Arthur in harm's way. And the way Wally was behaving – wearing his gleaming red party hat and tooting his noisemaker, being the loudmouth he could be in moments of gaiety – I was certain my guess was a good one.

Holly was there, waiting the table, though she forced me to help her pass out food and to bus dishes. The way she bossed me about, calling me Love and other such terms, caused jesting and the kind of snickering that leaves a blush of embarrassment. Carrie said it was the language of a wife still antsy from the honeymoon, and Gerty said it was honky-talk. Wendell said the only chance I had was to walk out the door and keep walking. "She's got you down for the count, boy," he chuckled. Arthur watched with approval.

If there was any distress over Lady's sale of the Castle to Arthur, it was with Leo, though his mood was hard to read. He was never comfortable in large gatherings, a holdover from prison,

I assumed. He had taken a chair nearest the wall, under a shadowed spot, and he sat, pushed back, watching the turmoil around him with the wary look of a caged bird. He crossed and uncrossed his arms in his habit of fidgeting. The party hat on his head – a green one, selected by Lady – gave him the appearance of a befuddled senior citizen forced to suffer the bubbly enthusiasm of a fellow resident's birthday in the recreation hall of an assisted living home. The way his eyes darted over Wally, I believed he was wondering if Wally's plan was a way of stealing the Castle. The only time I saw a flash of joy in his eyes was when he palmed a saltshaker and slipped it into his pocket.

After the dinner, Wally tapped against his glass with a knife and we all stopped our yammering and Dutch stopped his accordion playing.

"I propose a toast," Wally said, lifting his glass of lemonade and standing. He turned toward Lady. "To Lady McFadden, who brought together."

We toasted, giving our approvals with little cheers. Lady stood and bowed graciously; then she sat again.

"And I think we should toast the Castle, Lady's place and home to some of the finest people I have ever had the pleasure of knowing," Wally added.

We applauded – not in a raucous way, but politely. A little empty, to be honest. All of us had accepted on our own terms that if we left the Castle, most likely we would not return.

And then the oddest thing happened: Lady began to sing *When Irish Eyes are Smiling* in a clear, sweet voice, causing us to turn attention to her. She had the palms of her hands pressed against one another, held under her chin as in prayer. Her eyes were closed, her head tilted back. Everyone at the tables around us stopped their talking and their eating, and Dutch Arnold began to play the tune tenderly on his accordion.

"Well, bless Jesus," Gerty whispered in awe.

Carrie leaned close to me. "Hamby?" she said in shock.

I hushed her with a wave. We sat, listening, amazed, and then I began to quietly sing with her in the tenor that God gave the Irish, and, one by one, everyone at the table joined in, as well as those at the tables around us.

And for a moment – brief, chilling – I could sense my mother standing near me, could hear her voice soaring in the music.

TWENTY-TWO

I did not stay with Holly after the party, telling her I thought it would be best if I returned to the Castle, what with Lady acting more peculiar than usual and Leo becoming so skittish I was having to stay close by him. She put on a bit of a pout, but it was mainly for show since she had the late shift and, being tourist season, expected to be on the run until closing time.

"You never told me Lady could sing," she said to me as I was leaving.

"I didn't know she could," I said. "None of us did."

"She's so sweet," Holly gushed. "I hope I'm that sweet when I'm that old, but I also hope I've got a few more marbles to play with."

It was the missing of the marbles that had all of us worried about Lady. Little things had been different in her behavior since our date before Judge Renee Morgan. More rouge than usual on her cheeks. The afternoon Gerty found her watering a display of Arthur's paper flowers. Sitting before her dresser mirror for hours at a time, changing expressions of her face, like a person rehearsing for a role in a play. Holding a newspaper upside down, pretending to read it. Little things. At least, that is how we saw it. Under normal circumstances, I suppose such antics would have caused great alarm, but having become accustomed to the off-center nature of Lady's personality, we kept our peace. Lady was Lady.

Still, the singing in Frank's had startled us, being so sudden and done in a voice so fine and loving. The only time we had ever heard her mention singing was the night she claimed to have been a club singer in New York, and none of us had believed her. We had laughed about it among ourselves, saying the story was as outlandish as her tales of being a champion skeet shooter or of winning dance contests with a man from a Greek dance company on tour of America.

Without speaking it, all of us had the same queasy sense about Lady: she was either breaking down or she was adding to her repertoire of bizarre memories. It depended on how many marbles she still had.

On the walk back to the Castle, Gerty stayed close to Arthur and Lady, holding Lady by her arm, talking to her in a mumbling way, and I could tell that she was close to having a vision of doom. It would be a long and nervous night, I believed.

Leo and Wendell trailed behind Lady and Gerty and Arthur. Carrie walked beside me, slowing our pace until we were several yards behind the others, far enough back to keep words between us. I was certain she wanted to talk about Lady, but she didn't. Instead, she talked of her cousin.

"He was there," she said.

"Where?" I asked.

"At Frank's," she answered. "Up front, in the bar, but hidden in the crowd."

"What was he doing?"

"I'm not sure," she told me. "He gave me a signal to call him."

I tried to bring back a picture of the bar and of the people who had been in it, wanting to find him among them, but saw only bodies and the blur of faces, some of them as familiar to Frank's as the neon lights advertising brands of beer.

"I wonder what's happened," I said.

"I don't know, but I'm going to slip away and call," she replied. "I'll be in later. If anybody wants to know where I am, tell them I forgot something at Frank's – my lipstick."

She turned and walked away in a rush.

In front of me, Lady strolled happily, surrounded by her Guests, her entourage. She had the look of an elegant woman who had just dined in a fancy Paris restaurant and was taking in the sights of the Champs Elysées with the nobility of France.

I waited up for Carrie to return to the Castle, playing cards with Leo and Wendell – the same Joker's Wild poker game that had won the Castle for Lady's father. The luck, being the Joker, was with Leo. If we had been betting real money, he would have been a millionaire by game's end. Our money was from a stack of plastic chips that Leo had acquired on one of his marauding trips through a junk store. With plastic it is easy to play a high-stakes game.

Arthur and Gerty and Lady had watched the playing for a time and then each had wandered off for bed. Lady's demeanor had calmed on the walk back from Frank's, and she seemed pleasantly exhausted, saying she wanted to shop the following day for teacups. Arthur had agreed to accompany her. Gerty had turned away, hiding tears.

At midnight, we put away the cards and went to bed. No one mentioned Carrie, and I had a nagging fear her cousin had caught her in a trap that he'd baited with tales of kinship, a traitor's trap. He was, after all, a member of the police department. I only hoped she was safe, that whatever had called her away into the night would not be harmful.

I have read many stories about dreams – what causes them, what they mean, how they whisper to us like psychics who read the rainbow colors of our auras and see us as we are when our guards are down. No one understands dreaming. No one. People make a fuss over it and do their studies and write their books and talk on talk shows, but all of it is guesswork. To have dreams, floating through us free as a cloud, is as fine a mystery as the mind can conceive, and the ones that keep returning, night after night, year after year, are the most puzzling. To me, dreams are connectors, the fine wiring attaching what is real to what is wished for, or to what is happening at the time of the dream.

There is a dream I have had since childhood. I am in a bed, a narrow one that has been placed across the room from where my mother sleeps. A light – ghostly in its silver color – steals in from the window, falling across my mother's bed. I am awakened by a movement in the room, and I open my eyes to watch my father gently pull back the covering over my mother. He slips his body onto the bed beside her, cuddles her to him, pulls the cover over both of them. I hear my mother sigh softly, gladly.

It was the dream I was having in the Castle when I awoke to a sound near me. I turned my head to see Lady trying to ease her way onto Arthur's cot. She was dressed in a white bed gown. Her hair was loose around her shoulders. I saw Arthur rise up from sleep, heard him say quietly, "Do you need something?"

Lady leaned down and kissed him tenderly on the lips. She said, "He won't find us here. We're safe here."

I rolled from my bed and stood. Arthur raised his hand toward me, motioning me to be still. Across the room, Leo slept soundly.

"No, my dear, he won't find us here," Arthur whispered. He pulled back the covers and offered his hand to her and she lay down beside him. "Sleep now," he said. "Sleep."

The light from the window was the ghostly color of silver.

Lady slept peacefully beside Arthur for an hour before he and I led her back to her room. She moved as if in a daze, and I was certain she did not know what was happening to her. Surprisingly, no one awoke and Arthur whispered to me, "Why don't we keep this to ourselves? It might disturb the others."

I agreed with a nod and we both returned to our beds. I did not sleep, and I do not think Arthur did, either. I could not hear the rhythm of sleep in his breathing.

Thinking about what had happened left me with an eerie sensation. Since his arrival in Savannah, the presence of Arthur Benjamin had brought about changes none of us could have expected, and nothing about him was more perplexing than the regard Lady had for him. On the first meeting, she had spoken of his resemblance to her husband – her late husband, as she called him – and none of us had thought anything about the comment, other than the humor it offered. Yet, Wally had discovered there was possible truth in the story, and from what I had seen and heard – *"He won't find us here. We're safe here."* – I knew her mind had taken flight back to a hotel room in New Jersey, where her father would find her in her runaway, hiding out with a man who would be too weak to stand up for her. It was hard to believe Chester McFadden had diseased his child with a madness so filled with anger that it would cause her to light a match and burn away her history, leaving her brain too brittle for reality. The only protection she had from such madness were her dreams and the pretend world she had fashioned in an abandoned warehouse she had named the Castle. It was the right name, I thought. The Castle. To Lady, the Castle was the center of a kingdom existing only in her fancy, and she had settled in, waiting to be rescued heroically by a man still keen in her memory, a man promising to return to her.

I wondered if she saw Arthur as the rescuer, a reincarnation of her husband – her late husband.

And, in the tricky way the mind works, I wondered if, in fact, Arthur was that reincarnated man, wondered if his tale about being a furniture salesman and a tormented husband to a woman named Rita was nothing more than a convenience. I wondered if his purchase of the Castle and his promise to return it to Lady was a belated wedding present.

It's the Irish in me, I suppose – the tales of spirits – that left me uncertain: Was Arthur a real man, or was he a spirit of the Other World, given flesh for the temporary duty he was performing?

Carrie returned by morning light and I rushed her away to buy bagels, eager for whatever news she might have. She told me her cousin had shared a tale of humor. Harry Geiger had developed a skin rash from his aggravation over Arthur and Lady and the den of misfits, as he called us. It covered his arms and chest and legs and throat, like the creeping of poison ivy, and not even the shots injected into him by his doctor had eased the discomfort.

Worse, he had been confined to his bed, where he had to endure constant harping from his wife, Debra, over what she had termed an obsession. It was his wife's opinion that he should call off the dogs that were nipping at our heels. There was nothing serious in the charges against her – a fine, and the obligatory lecture about safe driving. The case was over.

She accused him of being egotistically arrogant, telling him he had permitted a harmless old man strolling the streets of the city to back him into a corner. And what gain was in it? Nothing. But there could be loss, with the backlash of public opinion going against him daily from the war camps of the media.

Unless he backed off, Debra warned, unless he found a way to make an apology to Arthur and Lady and to the rest of us, he would be ushered out of office and out of Savannah society by the ballot box. Debra did not care about her husband's office; she cared about Savannah society.

Carrie's cousin believed the ranting of Harry's wife had only made him more determined to stand his ground, taking the political high road of righteousness about making tough decisions. He would posture as a defender of the law, citing the promise he had made during his campaign for mayor.

"He's not going to back down," Carrie said.

"I didn't think he would," I told her. "It's what Wally expected."

We were sitting outside the Castle on the stone bench left by the furniture maker. It was mid-morning. Lady had slept late, had awakened refreshed, remembering her wish to shop for tea cups, and Arthur and Leo and Gerty and Wendell had accompanied her. If she had any memory of sleeping with Arthur on his cot, she did not show it, and Arthur did not speak of it. Nor did I.

"You were late coming in," I said to Carrie. "You had me worried."

She smiled and looked away. "My cousin took me to his home, to meet his wife," she said.

"And how was that?" I asked.

"I enjoyed it," she answered after a pause. "She's nice. Really nice. Really beautiful."

"Will you like being there?" I said.

She looked back at me. "Yes."

"And when will that be?" I asked.

"Not until it's safe for him," she told me. "A while."

"And what'll you do until then?"

"If we leave here, I'll find a rooming house," she said. "My cousin's going to loan me the money for it." She looked at me. "What about you? Will you move in with Holly?"

"I suppose so," I answered. "She wants me to."

"She's got you, Hamby. I hope you know that," she said.

TWENTY-THREE

We did not vacate the Castle on Friday, August 6, the date ordered by Judge Renee Morgan. We spent the day as usual, taking our walks and entertaining those who gathered about us – some of them becoming as regular as patrons at Frank's Fine Dining. We knew we were being watched by the police, knew they were photographing us as we went in and out of the Castle. They made no secret of it. We knew also that the media were watching, eager for a confrontation, yet satisfied with their nipping reports about the stand-off, knowing their reports would chafe Harry Geiger.

It was all a part of Wally's master plan: pressure.

And over the weekend, it seemed to be working.

In *The Savannah Enquirer*, an editorial appeared on Sunday under the headline:

No Laughing Matter for the Mayor

It read:

> And so it continues, this tug-of-war, pitting the muscle of the city government of Savannah against seven near-homeless people living in an abandoned warehouse on Beale Street, known by its occupants as the Castle.
>
> It's a shame, especially since the bickering seems to have more to do with the bruised ego of Mayor Harry Geiger than it does with whether or not a city ordinance has been violated.
>
> The fuss, according to Roger Upshaw, assistant to Mayor Geiger, is over illegal occupancy of a facility that is zoned for commercial use, yet has been abandoned for that purpose for longer than anyone can remember.
>
> On July 29, Judge Renee Morgan ordered the premises vacated by August 6. Residents of the Castle have ignored that

order and are certain to be served with a summons to answer contempt of court charges.

All because the mayor can't take a joke about the upcoming mayoral race.

A news bulletin, Your Honor: The man in the center of your blind spot – Arthur Benjamin – cannot run for mayor. He's not eligible. He's barely been in Savannah long enough to qualify as a tourist. It's a joke, Your Honor. All those *Arthur for Mayor* signs. A joke. Fun. A good time. Arthur Benjamin is simply a pleasant fellow – a retiree from Atlanta who chose to live in Savannah. He gives away paper flowers made from napkins. He is guilty of nothing, unless being pleasant is now a crime. If you had laughed about the goings-on, you'd be a shoo-in for re-election. If you had invited him to City Hall and commissioned him to do a bouquet as a centerpiece for your office, you might be in a position to run for governor.

Ah, but you didn't laugh, did you? And you didn't invite him to City Hall for coffee and a pat on the back. There was a little traffic matter possibly involving your wife and the inhabitants of the Castle, and you got your dander up, didn't you? Word is, you even tried to pay your way out of that one, but the offer was refused. *Refused*, Your Honor. Refused by people who could surely have used the cash. The last we heard, the issue was settled by a little slap-on-the-wrist fine for your wife. And, by the way, the residents of the Castle could have insisted on a court hearing, but they didn't. Seems to us, you got off pretty easy.

Now, we're left with this *Us vs. Them* squabble – Us being you, dragging the city into the fray with you, and Them being, well, *them*, which now includes everyone who finds the city's stand heavy-handed.

Gossip around the water cooler tells us that a number of high profile people, such as Dr. Clyde Webster of the City Council, are among the *them*.

Is that the applause for a recall petition we hear?

> Face it, Your Honor, this is a silly position you're taking. Instead of looking to evict people from make-do housing arrangements, maybe you should be studying how to use other such facilities for those who are in need of housing. We've got a lot of empty space, as you know, and a lot of people needing shelter.
>
> As to Arthur Benjamin, he doesn't need to run for mayor. He already holds the office where it really matters – on the streets. Some people seem to be suited for that high regard, even when they aren't seeking it. There's a poem by the great writer, Robert Frost, called *How Hard Is It to Keep from Being King When It's in You and in the Situation.* It's a catchy title – perhaps more interesting than the poem itself – but the title does seem to fit here. It's hard for Arthur Benjamin to keep from being who he is (Mayor? King?) when he's in the situation he's in.
>
> Makes us want to vote Demopublician.

Wally was ecstatic over the editorial. He appeared early at the Castle, bearing five copies of the paper. The editorial – unsigned, but believed by all to be written by Doyle Copeland – was the straw the city camel could not carry, Wally insisted. "They'll back off now. They don't have a choice. It's my guess they'll show up Monday morning with a proposition to reconsider the whole issue."

Leo was not as enthusiastic. "You know what that story's going to do?" he argued. "It's going to make him meaner than he already is. You don't listen to me; these are not people to push around. They don't back off. They roll over you."

It was not Leo's reaction that bothered me. He had seen things none of us had seen, and it had left him fearful. His pessimism was understandable.

What bothered me was Gerty.

Gerty had heard the whispering of voices.

"There's sorrow coming," she predicted in a moaning voice.

Wally tried to console her. "What's coming is victory."

Wally was wrong.

That night, the heavy timbered door of the Castle was struck with three bullets fired in rapid order, then, after a pause, two more shots rang out, sending two more warnings of lead into it.

The attack was after midnight. I awoke to the gunshots and to the burrowing sound of the bullets. I rolled from my bed and slipped quickly into my trousers and rushed into the Great Room, terror drumming in my chest, and I saw Leo standing near the door, holding a small handgun I had never seen. I called to him and he whirled to me, the handgun raised. He growled, "Get back," and then he opened the front door and stepped outside. I saw Wendell moving forward from the back of the Castle. He was holding a lead pipe.

I do not know why Lady slept through the commotion, but she did. An overdose of Gerty's tea, perhaps. The rest of us were awake, seized by a fit of fear and anger. Leo had only seen a lone figure running away, but could not identify him. His guess was that of Ted Castleberry, and I did not try to argue away his suspicion. I was too grateful he had not been shot, or that he had not shot anyone. I did not ask him about the handgun he had. If anyone else had seen him with it, they kept quiet. Truth is, we were all caught up in listening to the low moans of Gerty, saying over and over, "The doom's coming, the doom's coming..."

My only disagreement had to do with timing. The doom wasn't coming. The doom was already there.

It took Arthur to calm our jitters. "Tomorrow, this won't seem so bad," he counseled. "Why don't we wait and see what tomorrow brings."

The next day, a Monday, brought Doyle Copeland to our bullet-scarred door, though he said nothing of the damage if he noticed it, and by agreement, we did not tell him of it. It would do no good to call in the police or to make a complaint in the media. As Leo asserted, bullets one night, bombs the next. We did not want to make such an invitation by running our mouths.

Doyle wanted to know if we had received any communication from the city. We told him we had not, leaving him with a worried expression.

"I went by City Hall this morning," he told us. "No one would talk to me, but one of the security guards let it slip that Geiger had been in early with some of his staff, and none of them were in a good mood."

"Maybe they're working things out," I said.

"And maybe they're checking their ammunition," Leo mumbled, causing a puzzled look on Doyle's face.

"We'll let you know if we hear anything," I added.

"Thanks," Doyle said. "And I'll do the same." He started to leave, but turned back. "I hope the editorial in the paper yesterday doesn't cause any problems."

We all looked to Arthur. After a moment, he said, "Not at all. It was nice. Thank you."

Doyle smiled. "They weren't so happy about it at City Hall," he said.

Monday afternoon, Sergeant Ted Castleberry delivered the summons for the hearing on a contempt of court charge. He was alone, sporting a smile as he handed the summons to Arthur. His only words were, "Be there, old man."

The summons was for Wednesday morning, again at ten o'clock.

On Tuesday, the news of the summons flooded Savannah. Carrie's cousin told her the mayor had stayed secluded in his office, taking no calls and receiving only one visitor – Ned Doubleday. He did not know what the conference was about, only that it lasted for three hours.

On the streets, the mood was both excited and angry, the fidgety way it gets before ugliness takes over. Along Factor's Walk, shopkeepers displayed a new set of signs made by SCAD students: *Get Geiger* and *Keep the Castle a Castle*. Arthur was surrounded by well-wishers, some vile in their put-downs of Harry Geiger. I was worried the police would begin making arrests on charges of disorderly conduct.

Arthur's response was his smile.

Tuesday night, we had a dinner provided by Frank Jeanetta, and it was an occasion of historical import. There had never been a catered meal prepared in the kitchen of Frank's Fine Dining. Never. It had been a standing rule with Frank's father and then with Frank: If you can't come to my place to eat, then you don't need to eat.

Yet, the catering had been necessary. Arthur had politely declined an invitation from Frank for another dinner at the café, saying he preferred to stay at the Castle – "Home," was his word for it. It was my thinking that he didn't want to stir things up more than they were.

"You won't come to me, then I'll come to you," Frank had declared in an outburst of near-tearful emotion. "I owe you that."

When he and Holly appeared in late afternoon, bearing boxes, I expected hamburgers and fries and, perhaps, a pie or cobbler. Instead, we had steak and roasted potatoes and steamed asparagus and fresh-sliced tomatoes and cucumbers. And two cobblers: one peach, one blackberry.

"I owe you," Frank said again to Arthur.

The shock of it to me was two-fold: first, that Frank's kitchen could prepare such a meal and, second, that such a meal from Frank's kitchen could be so superb.

I told him he could improve his menu by offering the same in Frank's Fine Dining.

"Too much trouble," he said. "People start complaining when you serve steak; they don't say nothing about a hamburger or fried chicken. If they do, I kick their sorry asses out the front door. A man that'll raise a fuss over a hamburger ain't worth living."

We insisted that Frank and Holly join us for dinner, and they did after a mild protest of being intruders. Wally was also there, but not in the company of Melody Comstock. His explanation was simple: "My God, Hamby, she's a nut."

It was a good night, a night of feasting and good company, the kind of night made of friendships strong at the core. We did not talk about what would happen the next morning, or the days following the next morning. Such talk would be held until the last minute, like the putting off of dread. All of us knew that, even then, the words would be few.

When the dinner and the visiting were finished, dying down like embers of a small fire, I walked Holly to her apartment. She stood at her door and held me for a long time, not speaking, her face resting comfortably on my shoulder.

"Are you going to invite me in?" I finally asked in whisper.

"No," she answered. I could hear the held-back sadness of her voice. "No," she said again. "Go back to the Castle. They're going to need you." She pulled her face from my shoulder and looked at me. "If we're going to have any time together, it's ahead of us, Hamby. Their time is now."

"Do me a favor," I said.

"What's that?"

"Stay away tomorrow. I don't know what's going to happen."

"All right," she said.

Leo was sitting outside when I returned to the Castle, smoking a cigar Wally had given him. I suspected it was a peace offering of sorts, Wally knowing Leo was wary of his offbeat ways. I had never seen him smoke and said in a jesting way, "That'll stunt your growth." He drew from the cigar, made a shrug, a tilt, with his head.

"Everybody in bed?" I asked.

"Where they were headed," he answered.

I sat beside him on the stone bench. The thick smoke from his cigar waved in the night air, leaving a rich scent that belonged to history. I said, "Have you got the gun, Leo?"

He patted his pocket.

"Where'd you get it?" I asked.

He answered with another shrug, and I knew that would be his only offered explanation.

"For God's sake, Leo, don't kill anybody," I said.

"Don't plan to, unless they make me," he replied calmly.

"You know you're making it hard on me, don't you?" I told him. "If I had any sense, I'd make you give it to me and then I'd throw it in the river."

For a moment he did not speak, and then he said in a quiet, gentle voice, "Don't ask me that, Hamby. I think too much of you."

I knew it was useless to argue the point with him, so I said, "You got any plans if they move us out?"

He took another draw from the cigar and let the smoke stream from his mouth. "Watch after Lady," he finally replied. "Wherever she goes. That's my job."

"She thinks she's going to stay here," I told him.

"Then I'll be here, too," he said.

"They're going to move us out," I warned.

Leo's body rocked. He looked away, toward the lights of the city. "Wally said we could stay with him if they do," he said. "Until we find something on our own."

The announcement caught me by surprise. In all our planning, Wally had never made such an offer, and I wondered if Leo had heard something not said, or something said in such a roundabout way he took the wrong meaning of it. Or maybe it was like the cigar, a peace offering.

"Hope we don't have to do that," he added. "I don't much like the man."

I stood. "Well, we'll be facing it when we have to," I said.

Leo looked up at me. "Hamby, you've been a good friend," he mumbled. "I just want you to know I appreciate it. No matter what happens, I won't forget all you've done."

"Same goes for me, Leo," I said.

I left him sitting, smoking his cigar, guarding the Castle, and went inside. No one was in the small square of the room-within-the-room we had constructed of dressing screens and junk furniture, but on the coffee table was a setting of seven teacups, neatly arranged.

TWENTY-FOUR

On Wednesday, we stayed in the Castle, ignoring the summons, though there was no relaxing to be had. Tension was as thick as the humidity that gathered in the high ceiling of the Great Room. It was a waiting game we were playing, and we all knew it, but we did not speak of it. Truth be told, our silence was as heavy as the humidity, and nothing is as dreary or as tiresome as moping-about silence.

Our waiting ended in mid-afternoon. Ted Castleberry reappeared, his smile gone, his mood dangerous.

"This is a warning from the judge," he told Arthur. "You've got until tomorrow morning to turn yourself in, or we'll come and get you." He thrust his face close to Arthur's face. "She's kissing your ass, but I hope to God you stay put," he whispered. "I love coming after people." Then he turned to Leo. "Especially Jews," he added. He turned and stalked away. Leo's hand touched his pocket holding his pistol.

We stayed put on Thursday and the silence stayed with us, clammy and heavy, eerie and raw against our nerves.

In late afternoon, we received a printed note in a plain envelope, revealing that Judge Renee Morgan had issued an arrest warrant for Arthur, to be executed Friday morning. The note, unsigned, was delivered by a young man riding a bicycle, wearing a racing outfit of red spandex and sporting a matching swept-back helmet. He did not speak. He simply knocked on the door, handed the envelope to Wendell, and then turned away. After reading it, I believed the note was from the judge, giving the gift of a warning.

When Gerty heard about it, she quickly left the Castle, saying she needed to be alone. I knew she wanted to try to divert the gloom making its way toward us, set to arrive on Friday – Friday, the 13th.

I do not know how word got out about the pending arrest of Arthur, but it did. Gerty maybe, saying it to one person, who said it to another, who passed it along, mouth to ear, until it ran through the city like an epidemic. Still, it was astonishing that the arrest would create such a furor, calling people to assemble at the Castle on Friday morning like a church bell calling congregants for worship on Sunday.

The first people to arrive were from the street – Preacher and Hobbler Bob and a dozen others I recognized, and a few I knew more by peculiarity than by name.

It was sunrise. I saw them when I went outside to wait for Wally, who had insisted on being present when the police arrived. They sat huddled, drinking coffee, smoking, all holding flowers, some made of paper, some made of reeds.

I asked why they were there.

"Nice day. Seemed like a good place to be," Preacher answered soberly.

"There could be trouble," I said.

"Son, you ought to read your Bible," Preacher continued, his voice even and strong. "They's trouble all through it, mostly about how people treat other people. You read it right, you'll be seeing how shaky everybody gets when trouble comes around, how they turn tail and run. Well, sir, you won't see none of us running. No sir. Let the cock crow all it wants to, we'll be right here. Crow the feathers right off his tail, it won't matter. They want to haul us off, that's all right. We been there. We here because it's where we ought to be."

I thanked them – all of them – and turned and went back into the Castle. I had to. I did not want them to see me weeping.

By nine o'clock, there were more than a hundred people gathered outside the Castle. They came from the hidden places of the homeless, from classrooms, from business establishments, from homes of splendor tucked away in suburban neighborhoods. Young and middle-aged and old, white, black, Hispanic, Asian. Their dress ranged from pinstripe suits to walking shorts to rags. The only thing common about them was their expression: intense frowning, the seething look of anger.

The media were there too. Television trucks parked along the street, their reporters antsy, their cameramen holding cameras at ready, like soldiers hefting rifles. Doyle Copeland stood with a knot of reporters from newspapers and radio stations. He seemed pleased to be the center of attention, the insider, the acknowledged source of information about the goings-on between the city and the residents of the Castle. From a low window near the front door, I could see him making conversation, answering questions.

Inside, we waited. There was little talk among us, and what was said carried more nonsense than anything. Gerty sat with her face buried in her hands, making mumbling sounds. Leo stared at the front door. He was wearing a faded seersucker suit I had never seen, one a size too large, and I guessed it was selected to hide his firearm. I made a prayer that he would not try to use it, and that he would have the good sense to leave it behind when we went to court.

Only Wally tried to bring some lightness to the mood, pattering about the nature of people being attracted to violence, remembering a story of confrontation in some ancient time, telling it as though we all knew the particulars of it and how those particulars had changed mankind. No one listened to him.

Arthur sat calmly in the lounge chair that had become his place, his slight, restful smile fixed on his face. He did not appear at all fearful, or worried, or regretful. He was dressed in his brown suit, neatly pressed by Gerty. His cape was folded in his lap. Lady sat near him, wearing her finest outfit, a long beige dress with long sleeves and high collar. An imitation pearl necklace of three strands dangled from her neck, having earrings to match. Carrie had brushed and swirled her hair in the bun she preferred, and had applied her makeup with care, keeping it subdued, giving her the look of someone awaiting the arrival of a renowned portrait artist eager to paint her likeness for a grand museum in a grand city.

Wendell and I kept watch at the window. Wendell was tense. He shifted about constantly, foot to foot, his hands swinging loose by his sides, his head bobbing, and I knew the fighter in him was waiting for the roar of a crowd and the sharp, hammer-struck sound of a ringside bell.

At nine-thirty, the crowd roared; the bell sounded.

Six police cars – five marked, one unmarked – pulled to a stop in front of the Castle and the occupants quickly emerged: eleven uniformed officers and one in a suit. The one in a suit was Detective Cary Wilson.

From the window, I could see the crowd begin to make agitated movements toward the officers – not a stampeding, but a leaning forward, like people do when they are caught in a loud argument. I heard a voice cry out, "You bastards." And then a chorus of shouts rose up, making words so jammed together they had no sense to them. Old men and old women shook their fists, and the students around them cheered.

The police did not shout back or retaliate. They formed a line, a corridor, leading to the Castle, and Cary Wilson walked between them to the front door and knocked.

I opened it.

"Is Mr. Benjamin in?" Cary Wilson asked courteously.

"He is," I answered.

"May I speak to him?"

"Come in," I said.

We crossed to where Arthur and Lady and the others were waiting in the Great Room. Arthur stood as we approached, draping his cape over his arm.

"Mr. Benjamin," Cary Wilson said, nodding in a gentlemanly way. He looked at the others, added, "Everyone."

"Good morning, sir," Arthur replied. "We've been expecting you."

"It seems that way," Cary Wilson said, and there was a little smile on his face, but it was not made of arrogance. He reached into his inside coat pocket and removed his identification and displayed it to Arthur. "I'm Detective Cary Wilson with the Savannah-Chatham County Metropolitan Police Department," he added. He closed the leather wallet holding his credentials and slipped it back inside his coat. "My purpose is to inform you that you are in violation of an order issued by Judge Renee Morgan of Municipal Court. You are aware of that order, are you not, sir?"

Arthur nodded. "Yes," he answered.

"And you are aware that the conditions of that order directed you to appear for a hearing regarding contempt of court?"

"I am," Arthur replied.

"Then it is my duty to place you under arrest for failing to adhere to that order," Cary Wilson said.

"You don't have to handcuff him, do you?" Carrie said suddenly, tearfully.

Cary Wilson swallowed hard. He shook his head. "I'm sorry," he answered. "It's procedure, but I can wait until we leave. I don't think there's much risk in doing that."

"None at all," Arthur said. He turned to Gerty and handed her the cape, and Gerty placed it on his shoulders. Her eyes were streaming with tears. "May I have a moment with my friends?" he added.

Cary Wilson nodded. "Please make it brief. You're scheduled for an appearance before Judge Morgan at eleven o'clock." He turned and walked away, stopping to wait at the front door.

"I don't want you to worry about me," Arthur said to us in a low voice. "This won't be anything serious." He reached inside his coat and removed an envelope. "It may be that I will be detained for a sort time, and if I am, and if they insist on removing you, I want you to follow the instructions I have here, but don't open it unless it's necessary." He smiled. "I have poor penmanship." He handed the envelope to me. "I'll ask you to hold it, Hamby. And I'll ask you to care for my belongings."

I could not answer in words, only a nod.

Arthur turned to Lady, still sitting, face lifted, regal in her bearing. "And I'll ask each of you to take care of our dear Lady," he said softly. He leaned to her and gave her a kiss on her forehead, then turned and walked away, toward Cary Wilson.

None of us moved. None of us could move. We watched as Arthur extended his hands to Cary Wilson, watched as Cary Wilson snapped the handcuffs over his wrists. Watched as Cary Wilson opened the door and guided Arthur through it. A loud bellowing erupted from outside, rushed in through the opened door, and then went mute as the door closed behind them.

Television reports of the arrest of Arthur would tell a story of high drama, giving the appearance of a mob scene ready to storm City Hall like rebel soldiers caught up in the frenzy of a coup. There were close-ups of the street people – Preacher and Hobbler Bob and the others – looking proud and defiant, and of students noisily ragging the police – as much for the attention of the camera as for the passion of their support for Arthur – and of businessmen and shopkeepers and housewives, holding paper flowers and wearing faces of weeping and aching as Arthur passed among them, walking with Detective Cary Wilson to his unmarked police car. The voice-overs riding the surf of the images would have the grave sound of war correspondents under assault. It was the same on radio, where sound bites would be spit from tape recorders like steel-tipped bullets, and talk-show hosts would take on the tone of auctioneers seized in such a frenzy of yapping they began selling themselves to whichever bidder listened to them. The story they were telling was the same story as Jesus being led to Golgotha for his crucifixion.

Only Doyle Copeland, in the following morning's edition of the *Enquirer*, would provide a version closer to truth: Arthur's arrest had been met with the kind of hisses and boos people have over an unpopular act, but, for the most part, it had been handled with sensitivity and without the threat of violence. Cary Wilson was given credit. It would have been different, Doyle would suggest, if other officers had been assigned the duty. I was sure he was thinking of the likes of Ted Castleberry or Billy Pottier.

Yet, it was not the arrest that became the heat of stories fanned by the media. The arrest was a prelude, a set-up. It was Arthur's appearance before Judge Renee Morgan that caused the uproar.

At eleven o'clock, Arthur was ushered by Cary Wilson into the courtroom – again crowded with on-lookers, so many they spilled into the hallways and out the doorway, knotting together on the street. He was led to the assigned table for defendants, where Fuller Bishop waited, and his handcuffs were removed. Cary Wilson leaned to him and whispered something we could not hear. Arthur nodded. He slipped his cape from his shoulders and carefully folded it and placed it on the table before him and then he sat beside Fuller Bishop. Cary Wilson left to stand with two uniformed officers at one side of the courtroom.

People sitting nearby, behind the railing, were speaking his name quietly, but he did not turn to the voices. From where I was sitting, I could see his face in profile. He was calm, serene, and I knew what was about to happen would be not be forgot.

Ned Doubleday had the same irritated expression over Fuller Bishop's appearance with Arthur as he had offered on the day Arthur and Wally appeared with Lady, and when Judge Renee Morgan gaveled the session to order, he demanded to know Fuller's role in the proceeding.

Renee Morgan did not speak. She merely nodded to Fuller.

Fuller stood. He said, "If it pleases the court, I am here, Your Honor, merely to counsel Mr. Benjamin on points of law. I have not been afforded the privilege of representing him." He made a head motion toward Ned Doubleday and then sat.

The judge frowned noticeably. "This feels a little like déjà vu," she said after a moment. "I understand Mr. Doubleday's position, for I, too, have a lot of discomfort with testing the system to the degree you are testing it, Mr. Bishop, but I'm going to allow your presence at the defendant's table, with the stipulation that you are limited only to explanation on points of law. I draw the line at offering legal advice." She looked at Ned Doubleday. "Mr. Doubleday, since you know Mr. Bishop's qualifications, I assume you have no objection."

Ned Doubleday shook his head in surrender. "No, Your Honor," he mumbled.

Renee Morgan turned to look at Arthur. "I'm sorry to see you before me, Mr. Benjamin," she said. "I hope you understand you left me no choice in the matter."

"I do," Arthur replied.

"Let me dispense with the formalities," the judge said. "You are here, Mr. Benjamin, because you failed to obey a court order to vacate the premises on Beale Street that is now under your ownership, as I understand it."

"Yes, Your Honor. I legally own the property," Arthur told her.

"Good. We won't have to worry about that matter, then," the judge replied. She leaned back in her high, cushioned chair and laced her fingers. She inhaled slowly, deeply. A sadness rested in her eyes. "Mr. Benjamin, I warned you about being in contempt of court if you disregarded my earlier order to vacate the premises, did I not?"

"You did, Your Honor."

"And, yet, you deliberately disobeyed that order."

"I did, yes."

"Is there a reason?"

"I did not believe in it," Arthur answered calmly.

"I'm sure a lot of people don't believe in judgments made by the courts, Mr. Benjamin, especially if those judgments have an adverse effect on them," Renee Morgan said. "Yet, we cannot simply choose to obey laws we approve of and disobey laws that don't suit us. That would create anarchy, and no civilization can long exist under such conditions." She unlaced her fingers and leaned forward, her arms resting on her desk. "I hope you understand, Mr. Benjamin, that I am bound by oath to uphold the laws that govern us, and I have before me a legal petition to find you guilty of contempt of court, as filed by the city attorney. By your actions and your own admission, I must comply with that petition."

She paused, looked at Ned Doubleday, sitting stoically, yet smugly, at the plaintiff's table. He had not had to make a single statement in his case against Arthur.

"I do have, however, some discretion in the sentencing," the judge continued. "Therefore, I am going to release you on your own recognizance and, retroactive to the date that I first established in the order for you to vacate the property in question,

I am going to impose a fine of ten dollars for each day you remain in defiance of that order."

A murmur swept across the courtroom. Ned Doubleday sprang from his seat. "Your Honor," he exploded, "that's ludicrous. Ten dollars a day? My God, that in itself is contempt of court."

Renee Morgan slapped the flat of her hand on her desk, making a sharp, rifle-shot sound. "Mr. Doubleday, must I remind you where you are?" she snapped.

Ned Doubleday stood, trembling, his flushed face contorting in anger.

"I will not tolerate such outbursts in my courtroom," the judge continued. "If you wish to question my authority, or my judgment, in this matter, you know the procedures to do so. But in this courtroom, you will behave with civility, or there will be a second contempt citation and it will stun you in its severity. Do you understand me?"

Ned Doubleday nodded. He bit at his lips. "Yes, Your Honor," he said quietly.

The judge turned to Arthur. "Do you understand the sentence you have just received, Mr. Benjamin?"

"I do," Arthur answered.

"Good," the judge said.

"May I address the court?" Arthur asked.

The judge blinked surprise. "You may," she said.

Arthur stood slowly. "If I do not pay the fine, what will happen?" he asked.

I saw Fuller Bishop lean toward Arthur, a look of worry making a walk across his face.

"Then you would force me to sentence you to jail, Mr. Benjamin, until you do comply," the judge said.

Arthur let his head bob in a single nod, keeping his gaze on the judge. And then he said, "I would prefer you do that now."

I saw Wally's face freeze in shock, saw the coloring in it disappear, leaving him ghostly. For a moment, like the holding of breath, no one in the courtroom moved or made even the smallest of sounds, and then there was a single gasp from Carrie, sharp and painful. Around us, I could hear whispering, the not-quite-audible sounds of disbelief.

"Mr. Benjamin, do you know what you're requesting?" the judge said.

"I do, Your Honor."

"Mr. Bishop, though it tests the boundaries of my earlier directive, I'm going to be lenient for a moment. Do you wish to confer with Mr. Benjamin to explain the consequence he's facing?" the judge asked, her voice carrying a plea. "But you are not to provide advice. I would simply ask you to clarify the circumstance he is imposing on the court."

"Yes, Your Honor," Fuller said quickly. He tugged Arthur back to his seat and then leaned to him and whispered. Later, he would tell us he informed Arthur that the judge had just given him the freedom to carry on his crusade against the city, and he could not do that in jail. Arthur sat, listening. After a moment, he said something back to Fuller, and Fuller nodded and turned to look at the judge. It was an expression of bewilderment.

"Mr. Benjamin, what is your wish?" the judge asked.

"I would prefer to go to jail," he answered quietly.

"I don't understand, Mr. Benjamin," the judge said.

"I think it's best," Arthur told her.

"But, why, sir?"

"Because I think it's better to stand for something, rather than make compromises that amount to little," he said.

The sentence received by Arthur was one offering escape: He would remain incarcerated until he either agreed to the imposed daily fine, or until a settlement could be reached with the city.

In an argument raised by Ned Doubleday, Judge Morgan denied the city's request to forcefully evict the rest of us from the Castle, and I could see a look of pleasure on Arthur's face, the same as a man would have from winning a wager, or sending a pawn to make a killing move against an enemy knight.

"I will not issue such an order," the judge said sternly. "I am going to permit those people presently residing in the facility to remain there as a safe haven until this issue is settled. But I will direct the city attorney to begin a dialogue with Mr. Benjamin's representatives to seek a sensible resolution to this question before it results in irreparable harm to this city or to its citizens. Further, I will instruct that those representatives include someone with legal expertise, such as Mr. Bishop."

The judge sat for a moment, holding her gaze on Arthur, and then she added, "Mr. Benjamin, I hope you know what you're doing. You do not impress me as a man lacking intelligence, but sir, I have to admit that you baffle me. It's not often a defendant actually asks to be incarcerated, and it's not often that I admire people I send to jail. You are an exception. I do wish you well."

She made a nod to the two officers standing with Cary Wilson and we watched as they moved to Arthur. They instructed him to stand, and then snapped handcuffs on his wrists, in front of his body. One of them picked up his cape from the table and handed it to him before leading him away.

Arthur did not look back at us, and it was good that he didn't. If he had, I believe Carrie would have collapsed. I was also glad that Gerty had refused to accompany us to the courtroom. There was no reason, she had said. She knew what was going to happen. Gerty's wail would have been as shrill as the siren of doom she was forever hearing.

As it was, the only sound in the room was of quiet sobbing, the same as heard in funeral parlors when death is realized and mourning rises up from the chest of the grieving.

I did not doubt what Arthur would do. He had made his decision before his arrest, plotting it carefully. I remembered again what Wally had said about him: "*To be honest, Hamby, I'm not sure we've seen the real Arthur Benjamin at all. Sometimes I wonder if all of this is just a human chess game to him, one that he's playing to protect the pawns rather than the kings. It interests me.*"

In his fanciful reasoning, Wally had been right. What Arthur was doing was the same as manipulating a game of chess, and he had chosen his next move.

TWENTY-FIVE

None of us truly blamed Wally for the jail sentence Renee Morgan imposed on Arthur. The plan he had sketched out on barroom napkins and later refined in pages of detail as *The Arthur Stratagem* had been near flawless, allowing for the complexity of it. Or so it appeared to us. Wally always seemed to have an escape clause in his thinking.

Still, he was crestfallen over the proceedings. The philosopher's nagging question of *Why?* tormented him. Arthur's decision did not fit his logic. It was, in fact, anti-logic to Wally. What did it gain Arthur to be locked behind the steel bars of jail? Was it inspiration from Martin Luther King, Jr., or Nelson Mandela, or the hundreds of Freedom Marchers from the Civil Rights movement? If so, it was senseless. He could have been on the streets, his presence building support for the pressure needed to bring Harry Geiger to his knees. Martyrdom was noble, but only if it made sense.

"I need to think," Wally told us after the sentencing. He went away, shaking his head, mumbling to himself, giving me some worry that his next move could be as brash as planning a jail-break for Arthur.

I would be close the truth, as it turned out.

In the Castle, we sat in silence for most of the afternoon, numbed by what had happened. I had the envelope of instruction Arthur left for us in my pocket, and wondered about its content, wondered if it gave some explanation of his actions. Yet, Arthur had requested us not to open it unless we were forced to leave the Castle. I was bound by that request. Having robbed him once, I could not rob him again.

We were mostly worried about Lady. She had a smile applied to her face like a paint-on, but there was a dazed look in her eyes. She asked repeatedly the whereabouts of Arthur, and when we tried to explain it, she would move her head to each of us with the kind of almost-nod people have when making a silent count. She would say, "Oh, yes," and then settle back in her chair, and after a moment she would again ask the question, "We're missing Arthur, aren't we?"

Carrie and Gerty tried to console her with tea and with talk of parties and dresses. Leo sat, his arms folded over his chest, holding in pain, his face having an old and tired expression, and I knew he was thinking of Arthur being in jail. Wendell paced, tried to make himself useful with the tea-making. He seemed caged and I wondered if he had thoughts of leaving us and returning to his scrape-by ways, living with his memories of glory as he stood over the fallen bodies of eighty-seven men.

We tried to take stock of where we were, hoping some glimmer of understanding would come about when we separated the knowing from the not knowing.

When we made a talking list of the knowing, it offered more comfort than we realized.

We knew, first, that we had been given a reprieve for leaving the Castle.

We knew Renee Morgan had directed Ned Doubleday to negotiate for a solution to the question of using the Castle for occupancy.

We knew Fuller Bishop had pledged support of his firm on our behalf, telling us he had some ideas he wanted to discuss with his partners, and that he would contact us later with recommendations. The way he said it – determined, like a man eager for fight – I believed he was on the verge of being enraged, and I wondered if there was something personal between him and Ned Doubleday.

We knew also that we had backing from those who followed us away from the courtroom. They brought noise and tension to the fray, and the sight of the crowd caused the police to step back and let us pass without incident.

Mostly, we knew that our cause – if that was the right word for it – was not what it appeared to be. It was not a quarrel over the Castle, as Ned Doubleday had asserted in court. Our cause was Arthur, as Fuller Bishop had defined it and as Doyle Copeland's editorial in the *Enquirer* had emphasized – Arthur, the flower-maker, vs. Harry Geiger, the mayor. The Castle meant nothing to Harry Geiger. It was an old building, an eyesore, having no value to him or to the city. The thorn in Harry Geiger's side was Arthur. Harry Geiger could not abide the presence of Arthur because Arthur had a power Harry Geiger did not understand: Arthur was a good man who had only one agenda – to care for his friends.

It was that simple, and the more I thought of it, the more startling it was to me. My mother had always taught that nothing mattered more than caring for someone, that if you cared enough, cared until the pleasure of it turned to a joyful aching, and then you had been blessed beyond the heaping-up of riches.

Arthur cared.

Cared enough to shame the rest of us.

That afternoon, I had a lesson in it. When I opened my wallet in search of money for our dinner groceries, I found three one hundred dollar bills tucked inside it. Money from Arthur. Money placed there as I slept, and I knew my suspicions about our late-night swapping – wallet to sweatband, suitcase to wallet – had been true.

I have a scrapbook put together by Holly of the news stories that would come roaring from the media after the sentencing of Arthur – Doyle Copeland's articles from the *Enquirer*, print-outs from websites of talk show hosts, written with spear tips of exclamation points, reports from the Associated Press traveling with electronic swiftness to small dailies and weeklies in close-by towns such as Statesboro, Hinesville, Jesup, and in cities farther away, such as Augusta, Brunswick, Macon, Atlanta.

They all spewed outrage, tempered only by admiration for a man who was willing to sacrifice his freedom for his belief. And they all made a target of Mayor Harry Geiger. There were demands for his resignation, for a recall petition, for an investigation by the state Attorney General's office. Lawyers from the American Civil Liberties Union were interviewed, and the answers given warned of civil disobedience and lawsuits.

We, too, were part of it – Lady and her Guests – and the heat of the spotlight made us curtail our daily walks, our mingling. When any of us ventured outside the Castle we had cameras aimed at our faces and microphones poked toward our mouths. We quickly learned to dodge the questions, saying we had been advised to hold our tongues. And it was true. Fuller Bishop and Mason Reinhart and Damon Ayers had visited on the day after Arthur's sentencing, giving the advice and telling us they were close to confirming some damaging evidence against the city in the matter of the zoning restriction. The three of them were edgy with excitement. "It'll take a little time to confirm everything," Damon Ayers told us, "but we're on the right track."

None of us cared about the evidence – whatever it was. We cared only about the treatment Arthur was receiving in jail, and about visitation rights.

Our worrying about Arthur was wasted energy, as Carrie would learn from her cousin. We had feared he would be tormented behind bars for the foolishness of his act – a certainty, Leo believed – yet the opposite had happened: Arthur was thought of as being heroic. The cheering for him in jail was stronger than the cheering on the street, and the inmate leaders, those with muscle matching meanness, had put out word that anyone bringing harm to Arthur Benjamin would pay dearly.

"They can't believe he did what he did," Carrie's cousin told her. "The way they see it, it took guts, and that's the only thing they respect. He'll be fine, maybe better than being on the streets."

"When can we see him?" I asked.

"Tomorrow," she answered. "But we'll have to have a car."

"I'll call Wally," I said.

"I'm surprised he hasn't been around," Carrie replied, her voice having a hint of cynicism. "The way he was acting, I thought sure he'd have the answers by now."

I ignored her pitch for a quarrel. "Did your cousin say anything about the mayor?" I asked.

It was a question that made her smile. According to her cousin, Harry Geiger had been as stunned as everyone by Arthur's request for jail, and had demanded a meeting with Ned Doubleday in the privacy of his home. No one knew what happened in the meeting, only that the mayor had appeared later in a foul humor at a dinner party for a retiring banker, aware of the grief the media would certainly pour on him.

"Nothing's working the way he thought it would," she guessed.

"I wonder if he's going to go along with the judge's order to deal with us," I said.

"I hope not," she replied.

"Why?"

"I'd like to see what the judge would do if he doesn't," she said. "Maybe he'll wind up in jail with Arthur."

A jar once holding pickled eggs had been placed on the bar in Frank's Fine Dining, having a note taped to its side: *Arthur's Defense Fund*. It was crammed full of bills. In the lounge, there was no talk of loose women or politics or sports, only of Arthur. Bully talk. The kind of loud complaining done by men urged on by the alcohol content of whatever drink was wrapped in the curl of their fists. Even the few who thought Arthur unwise for his choice of jail over a ten-dollar-a-day fine agreed it was a nervy move. In their noisy ranting, they tried and judged and convicted Harry Geiger for the crime of being Harry Geiger. The kindest thing said about him was that he was "...an arrogant son of a bitch."

I had gone there in search of Wally, to ask if he would drive us to the jail to visit Arthur, but he was not there. Frank, too, was mystified, saying he had not seen Wally since the afternoon of the sentencing. "He came by for an hour or so," Frank told me. "Took a beer to his table and just sat there, staring off in space. Then he got up and left. Didn't touch the beer. Looked like he was in a hurry to get somewhere. My guess was he'd forgot about meeting that woman he's seeing, but she came in later looking for him. You want to call him, use the phone in my office."

Wally did not answer the call. I left a message on his voice mail, explaining we were in need of a ride to the jail, and asked him to call Frank's if he got the message before midnight.

He did not call.

I had gone to Frank's with a touch of dread, knowing Holly's fondness for Arthur, but not knowing the mood she would be wearing. It was my guess she would be grieving in her melancholy way of feeling helpless, the way I had found her dozens of times. I was wrong. She was angry, angrier that she had ever been with me, angrier than any of the men yapping their bravado in the lounge. She called the men gutless for doing nothing more than talking. She wanted to have a protest march on City Hall, wanted to roll Harry Geiger's home in toilet paper, wanted to bomb his cars with eggs, or real bombs. She was in such a bother, Frank asked me to talk to her.

And I did, being gentle about it. I asked, "Do you think Arthur would approve of any of that?"

Her anger dissolved as the question settled in her. "No," she said pitifully. A bubble of moisture formed in her eyes. "He'd just smile."

That night she lay close to me in her bed, cuddled like a child needing to be held, and it was how I drifted off to sleep. When I awoke, she was in her kitchen, baking a lemon pound cake to be delivered to Arthur.

"I don't think they'll let him have it," I told her in a cautious manner.

"I don't care," she said. "I had to cook it."

Mid-morning, I tried again to call Wally and, again, there was no answer.

"What are you going to do?" Holly asked. "You can't walk to the jail. It's too far."

I thought of Doyle Copeland. He had offered to help us if we needed him and I called the home number he had given me and told him of our need for transportation. He promised to be at the Castle at eleven o'clock.

Holly wanted to go with us, but I persuaded her to stay in her apartment, citing the number of people cramming into Doyle's car and the fact that I had not registered her for the visitors' list. "I'll add your name and we'll go together, just the two of us," I promised.

She made me take the cake. "If they won't let him have it, give it to Lady," she instructed.

And then she said something that swept over me in a chill of memory. She said, "Hamby, you'll always have me with you."

Holly's words were exactly those my mother had whispered in the last minute of her life – her last words.

I returned to the Castle early enough to avoid anyone stopping me on the street, though I did see Preacher ambling toward Factor's Walk. I offered a wave, but he did not return it. He seemed lost and I knew he had spent the night with his Bible and his bottle – verse for swallow. I doubted if he still had any of the money Arthur had provided him.

From the east, the dark pink-purple of morning colored the underbelly of clouds having the look of storms. The air was crisp, autumn-like. In Frank's the night before, there had been mention of a tropical storm gathering speed north of Cuba, and weather-trackers had given warnings of its twisting, meandering path skimming the coastline of Florida and Georgia and the Carolinas. Savannah was a possibility for a dip-in. If nothing more, there would be rain and wind making a blustery howl. A pirate wind, my mother had called it in my childhood, leaving me with visions of peg-legged, eye-patch pirates raiding the city with sabers and flint-fired pistols, bellowing like elephants. In a pirate wind, my mother would pull me into the one closet we had and she would wrap a quilt around us and she would sing softly until the pirates had traveled on. Each time, she would say, "They didn't find us, did they?"

The greeting I got from Carrie in the Castle was a scolding for being away all night. She called me irresponsible, hissed at me about keeping my hormones under control.

It took the explanation of Holly's cake and the news of Doyle's agreement to drive us to visit Arthur to calm her and to cause her to apologize. She admitted she was edgy and tired, telling me that after I left for Frank's, Lady had become more confused and more incoherent, and it had taken a strong dosage of

Gerty's tea to settle her. She was still sleeping, as was Gerty. Leo and Wendell had left earlier, saying they wanted to walk off their anger, but I suspected it was Wendell keeping an eye on Leo.

"Lady kept talking about the fire," Carrie said.

"What was she saying?" I asked.

"The same thing – how she had her belongings on the lawn, how she started the fire by burning curtains in the library, and how she watched it burn. The only thing different was something about a fireman who begged to call on her."

I wanted to smile, but held it. Lady's mind was full of suitors, all competing with the memory of a day-long husband.

Carrie wanted to know what had happened to Wally, and I told her of trying to call him, but not getting an answer.

"He's probably got a caller ID," she groused. "He's ashamed, as he should be, and he's washed his hands of us, and if you want to know how I feel about it, we're better off."

I reminded her that it was Arthur who had chosen jail, not Wally.

"I know it," she said irritably. "I just need to be mad at somebody."

TWENTY-SIX

It was an act of kindness on Doyle Copeland's part, driving us to the jail. There was nothing he would gain from it since his name was not on the list of approved visitors for Arthur. But he did not seem to mind. There would be time and opportunity for him to get his story.

Thankfully, his vehicle was a Nissan van, large enough for all of us – Lady sitting up front with Doyle, Leo and Wendell and Gerty in the middle seats, Carrie and me in the back. The trip to the jail was not a long drive, yet Doyle took it at a creeping pace, playing his reporter's trick of making casual conversation, hoping for something revealing from one of us. It was a lost effort; none of us had anything revealing to say – other than Lady. Lady remembered a trip taken with her mother and father to Staten Island to celebrate her sixteenth birthday. There was a man in it, as everyone knew there would be – everyone except Doyle. The man had kidded Lady about having the look of the movie star Veronica Lake. It was the way she wore her hair in those days, letting it flow over her face, covering one eye. "I liked that style," she said wistfully. "I wonder if I could wear it again." Doyle glanced at us through the rearview mirror, asking the question of sanity. We answered it with look-aways, with tight-lipped smiles.

As I had expected, we were not allowed to take Holly's cake into the jail.

And as I had further expected, Leo became weak with the memory of his time in prison. He tried to go with us behind the locked security to the visitor's area but could not. His legs and his heart would not carry him, and Wendell volunteered to stay with him and Doyle in the reception room.

"Tell Arthur I'm sorry," Leo whispered.

"We will," Carrie promised. She hugged him, rubbed the back of his neck with her hand.

I think all of us had a fear of seeing Arthur, worried that he would be depressed or that he would wear the look of the defeated, and his words to us would be hollow and confused. There was no reason for such worry, knowing the report from Carrie's cousin, yet it was there, ghost-like and terrifying. Most likely it was carryover from being around Leo, I thought, or maybe it was the working of imagination inspired by old movies, showing gaunt men wearing the bruises of beatings from prison guards or fellow inmates having a fondness for the sadistic. Whatever it was, it left us anxious – all but Lady. Lady hardly noticed the surroundings. In her mind, there were tidbits of the story of her trip to Staten Island she had omitted and she talked blithely of them. As far as Lady was concerned, we could have been touring the Louvre in Paris, or Disney World in Florida.

When Arthur appeared, the concerns we had – kept private, except for telltale expressions on our faces – vanished in surprise. The man we saw had the look of a doctor making rounds, pleased with his work. His inmate clothing was the color of green worn in operating rooms. On Arthur, the dress had a look of distinction, and the smile crossing his face was one of gladness, the same as a person would have greeting friends at a holiday party. The only awkwardness of it – sadness, really – was the heavy glass separating us. It is a cold touch, putting palm to palm against a sheet of glass.

We took our turns talking to him over the phone hookup, each of us trying to be light-hearted and clever – little jokes about his fashion and about the healthy glow he had acquired from jailhouse food. He told us not to worry about him, saying he had been treated well and had made friends, and from his description of two of them, they could have been missionaries jailed for their kindness. Later, when Carrie asked her cousin about them – providing names – she learned they were awaiting trial for murder.

We did not stay long. There was no reason to do so. Lady, being the first to talk to Arthur, became fascinated by the glass partition separating him from us, and by the need to use a telephone. She stayed close to the window, peering at him, trying to read his lips, and when she could, she would call out what he had said.

My words with Arthur were made in a kind of code, yet we both understood them. "You're a good man," I said, speaking of the money left in my wallet.

He understood and he nodded and he made his smile. I wanted to ask if there was more of the money and if he had left it in my care without telling me, but I did not. Somehow, I knew the answer.

"Have you talked to Fuller Bishop?" I asked.

"I will today," he told me. "This afternoon, I think, or tomorrow."

"They're hard at work on it," I said, without telling of the report from Damon Ayers about finding something questionable in the zoning matter of the Castle.

"They've been helpful," he replied.

We spoke of Leo and Wendell, and of Doyle Copeland's willingness to transport us. He wanted Leo to know that he was well. And then he asked about Wally.

"I tried to call him, but he didn't answer," I said. "No one's seen him at Frank's for a couple of days, not since we were in court. I don't know what's happened to him."

A little frown wiggled over Arthur's forehead, and then disappeared. "I'm sure he's fine," he said, "but if you see him, give him my regards."

We left the room quickly, not looking back at Arthur, who was still sitting behind the glass partition. None of us spoke until we were again in the reception area, and then we began to tell Leo and Wendell and Doyle of the visit, our words tangling together. Leo was relieved. I could see it in his eyes and in the way his body rocked. Still, he wanted to leave. The weather, he said. It was about to storm. No reason to be caught in it. I knew the weather was only an available excuse. Leo wanted to be away from steel bars.

The storm struck an hour after returning to the Castle. It came with a howl – the pirates of my mother's stories swinging on wind-ropes from the decks of pirate ships, roaring threats of plunder – and the darkness of it was like midnight blown up from the Day of Judgment. The lights flickered and went off, and we sat in our home of dressing screens and junk furniture and listened to the howl and to the lashing of rain, brutal enough to believe the Atlantic had lifted its waves over the sandbars and over the inlands and had dropped them against the city of Savannah. A single candle burned from a candleholder Carrie had placed on the coffee table. The slight stirring of air inside the Castle made the candlelight wave nervously.

I thought of my mother, thought of our closet for hiding in the days of storm, thought of the warmth of her as she nestled against me under the heavy quilt, thought of her voice, soft against my face as she sang in a whispery voice of Ireland.

Outside, wind pirates battered at the walls, looted trees of limbs and billboards of advertisements, split roofs with their broadswords, sent debris sailing in wind funnels having the look of miniature tornadoes. And the city ducked from the siege, kneeled in surrender, having only one wish: to be spared. If the storm was not a full hurricane, it was God being in an ill mood.

Carrie cuddled in an armchair, her knees drawn to her chest, her arms wrapped around her legs, her chin resting on her kneecaps. Gerty had draped a thin blanket over Lady and had taken one for herself, and the two sat motionless in their chairs, staring at the dancing flame of the candle. Wendell and Leo tried to play a game of checkers, not caring about winning.

Something slapped hard against the door, making a sound of metal on wood. A lid of a trashcan, I guessed. I could tell from the furrowed look on Leo's face that he thought it might be another gunshot.

"It was raining on my wedding night," Lady said suddenly, pulling her blanket under her chin. She had a memory-smile on her face, the kind that begins across the mouth and brightens in the eyes.

"It was?" said Carrie. She looked at me, made a little ripple of her eyebrows to signal curiosity.

"Oh, yes," Lady answered. "I remember saying, 'Rain, rain, go away. You can't rain on my wedding day'." She laughed a silly laugh. "My husband said rain on a wedding day was a sign of good luck."

"What was his name, Lady?" Carrie asked. "I don't remember if you ever told us." There was some caution in her voice.

"His name?" Lady said. "Oh, I thought you knew. His name was William. William Lancaster. He was of the Pennsylvania Lancasters, a very fine family. Farmers – cows, I think – but educated. William went to Princeton." She paused.

"He was a teacher wasn't he?" Carrie asked.

Lady turned her face to Carrie, offering a puzzled look. "Did I say that?"

"Yes, I think you did," Carrie replied.

"Well, I must have. That's what he did. A high school teacher. A principal. He was very popular."

"He must have been a nice man," Carrie said gently.

Lady smiled again. "He was beautiful. Gerty, you've seen his photograph. Wasn't he beautiful?"

Gerty frowned, made a look-away to cover the rolling of her eyes, the same look she always gave when placating Lady.

"Handsome," she answered. "That's the word, I'd use. Sure is. Handsome as handsome can be. I thought he was Cary Grant."

For a moment, Lady said nothing. Then: "He died in the rain that night."

Carrie gave me a puzzled look, and then turned back to Lady. "He did?" she said. "I didn't know that."

"Oh, yes," Lady replied. "The rain swept him away." She lifted her face, listened to the storm. "It was like it is now," she added. She closed her eyes. A shiver of pain waved across her face.

"Honey, you need some more of Gerty's tea," Gerty said quietly. "It'll help you sleep."

None of us spoke as Gerty moved from her chair and poured another cup of tea and carried it to Lady. I knew Carrie was having the same thoughts I was having – that Lady's confusion had made a death of William Lancaster, if that had been his name. Yet, in her mind she had remembered his promise to return for her.

The rain and the wind did not subside until late afternoon, just before day's end. A left-over coloring of gray in the aftermath of the storm gave enough light outside to see the damage – tree limbs and trash blown about, curled roofing tin from a nearby building lodged against the door, water running in the flooding of little rivers across the ground. The sound of sirens came from nearby streets, telling wailing stories of need.

Carrie announced she was going to the police station to check on the condition of the jail, and, of course, on Arthur's well being, vowing she would be insistent enough to be arrested herself if the police did not cooperate. She gave an impressive speech about it, yet I was certain she was going in search of her cousin, knowing her cousin would check on Arthur in enough of a business-like manner as not to cause a disturbance.

It was decided that Leo and I would go in search of food for dinner – if we could find a place open for business. Pizza, maybe, since pizza, covered in pepperoni and cheese, was an odd favorite of Lady's. Wendell volunteered to stay behind and clean up some of the rubble, saying he needed the exercise to keep his muscles loose. I got the feeling he wanted to stay near Gerty.

On Bay Street, we watched people who had been held hostage by the storm emerging from buildings, first peering out of doors and windows, taking a measure of conditions, and then stepping outside, wearing looks of awe or shock. They talked in rushed conversations with neighbors and strangers over what had happened to them or to someone they knew about. It was the same as with any great storm I have ever seen – the need to take inventory of the leavings and to make declarations about God's power when people got too big for their britches and needed a reminder about the pecking order of things. God could make his point with a little huffing and puffing.

In Wright Square, we encountered Preacher and a beefy, sad-eyed woman we all called Mazie sitting on a bench. From somewhere, they had found a sheet of tarpaulin and had wrapped it around themselves during the storm, huddling on the ground against a hedge of shrubbery. They both were trembling from the terror of the wind and from the soaking of rain that ran off the tarpaulin, both smoking cigarettes to calm their shakes, both bemoaning the fact that the storm had flooded out their camp, leaving them with more of the nothing that had become the sum of their living.

"We got nowhere to go now," Mazie whimpered.

Preacher told us he had seen a man named Zeke, and Zeke had told of the rumor that Hobbler Bob had been struck with a limb snapped from an oak and was near death with a caved-in skull. It was most likely true, Preacher said, Hobbler Bob not being able to move about quick enough to dodge a falling limb.

"It were close to being Armageddon," Preacher said of the storm. "Me and Mazie was waiting to be drowned."

I asked if he had any money for food, and he said he did not, giving me a guilty look that said I had been right in my doubt: he had spent all the money from Arthur.

I gave him five dollars, telling him I trusted him to use it for food, not drink.

"God bless you, boy," Preacher said. "We got to stick together in times like this. We don't, we'll be struck down like Hobbler Bob."

Leo and I turned to walk away, but Leo stopped and turned back, narrowing his eyes on Preacher. I could see a thought forming over his head, like words in the balloon of a cartoon character.

"What is it?" I asked.

He pulled me a few feet away from Preacher and Mazie and put his face close to mine. "Know what we should do?" he said.

"No. What?" I replied.

"Take them to the Castle," he said in whisper.

"Why?" I asked, also in whisper.

A smile danced across Leo's face. "You want to get to this mayor, or not? You tell me."

"I do, yes," I answered. "In the worse kind of way."

"Fill the Castle," he said eagerly.

It is in my nature, and in my genes, to be easily taken by notions that have the sound of genius, and Leo's thought struck me as being near brilliant, much in the way Wally's plotting had been until Arthur took his stand for jail. As Leo explained it in a rush of words – pushed around by the waving of his hands and illuminated by the shine of excitement in his eyes – the thought was taken from a prison memory of inmates who had refused to leave the exercise yard until officials heard them out over an inmate who had been put in isolation on a trumped-up charge from a guard. Not wanting a full-scale riot, or the publicity that would follow, the warden had held a conference with them and had found the truth: the Inmate in isolation was an older man slow of thought and near deaf, and did not understand what the guard wanted of him. The inmate was released from isolation; the guard reassigned.

Leo had remembered it as a lesson of power in numbers.

"So, what about it?" he asked. "We bring everybody to the Castle, then see what the mayor says."

"It's a thought," I conceded, "but there's Lady to consider."

"Lady? To her, it's a party," he argued. "What did Preacher say? We stick together. It's what the Jews have always done. How do you think we got out of Egypt? By taxi?"

I wanted to mention the name of Moses and of his handling a cantankerous mob of doubters with a shepherd's crook, but resisted. "All right," I said after a moment. "God knows they need to be some place, but we'll have to control it, and if Lady objects, they're gone. Out the door and down the street, and, Leo, I'll be stubborn about that."

Leo's agreement was a grin, and I knew what he was thinking: Lady would want to serve them sherry and cucumber sandwiches, and to tell them of her childhood in a New York mansion.

TWENTY-SEVEN

The news Carrie shared about Arthur was upbeat. The storm had struck the jail with fury, but the jail's thick cement-and-steel construction was almost hurricane proof, and there had not been any damage of serious concern to the facility. Most important, all inmates were safe and accounted for.

Also, Carrie announced that someone would carry word to Arthur that all of us were unharmed and the Castle was still standing, a little waterlogged, but otherwise in fine shape.

Wendell doubted the promise, saying he knew the police too well.

"I trust this one," Carrie told him.

I knew she had found her cousin.

I had expected bedlam in opening of the Castle to street people of Savannah, guessing the rush to get inside would be the same as looters descending on a broken-in shop during a riot. I was mistaken. The dozen or so who appeared – mainly chosen by Preacher and Mazie in the short time we had before the fall of night – were as quiet and orderly as visitors in a cathedral. Knowing most of them by name or by reputation, I supposed that Leo had delivered a stern and threatening lecture about Lady's high expectations, and I knew that Preacher and Mazie had exercised some quality control by weeding out anyone they considered undesirable. I was glad to see Hobbler Bob among them, and to learn the speculation of his injury was false; the limb that had struck him was barely larger than a twig.

And Leo had been right about Lady: She did consider the occasion a party, becoming elated over the attention, and she did insist on offering refreshments – sandwiches made by me and Leo and Wendell and Carrie and Gerty, the supplies for them coming from a portion of the money Arthur had left in my wallet. Of the lot of us, I had worried that Gerty would object loudest over the invasion, and, again, I was wrong, though she did express concern regarding the hygiene of a few in need of a soap-bath and a change of clothing. She would tell us later that she had always believed the Castle should have been a place of respite for those as needy as we had been before being appointed Guests by Lady, but had always been afraid of speaking out about it. "Didn't want to be kicked out," was her way of explaining her silence. As bold as Gerty appeared, she was also skittish, the lingering fear of being rejected that had haunted her from childhood.

In the memory I have of the night, it was the same as watching an improvised play by a traveling troupe of actors, the play being the story of civilized people suddenly forced to make-do with throw-away clothing and soup-line food – the way photographs tell tales of the Great Depression. Still, it was more than performance; it was also the going back to better days, to remembered decorum of times having some comfort and happiness. I did not see a single demonstration of abrasiveness or of complaint, behavior that was common on the street. It was as though some transformation had taken place as they passed through the bullet-marked door of the Castle, and whatever transgressions they had committed were set aside, like shoes left on the doorstep.

"Doesn't take much to make people happy, does it?" Carrie said to me privately. I knew she was both sad and proud.

I did not stay in the Castle long after the feeding of sandwiches, telling Carrie that I wanted to check on Holly's safety and to report on our visit with Arthur. She understood. "Don't worry about things here," she said. "We'll handle it."

I knew she was telling me it was all right if I wanted to stay the night with Holly, a make-up for the anger she had had from the night before.

I learned something new about Holly that night: unlike my mother, she loved storms. For her, storms were sensuous. Storms made her touches flicker like lightning and formed flash floods of passion. Storms blew hot winds across her body and the pattering of rain on window glass played to the rhythms of her movement.

There is no reason to waste words attempting to describe that which I cannot. I will only say the new thing I learned about Holly left me in praise of hurricanes, especially those with fury, and my only regret was not being with her when the storm actually struck; if the rainy aftermath of it worked such wonders, I do not think I could have survived the eye of the storm.

She also delivered a message: Wally had called her at Frank's earlier, wanting to know if she expected to see me. He had some news, he told her, but it would have to wait until the next day. The wind had taken out a tree in his yard and he had to remove it before he could get his car from his garage. "Tell him I'll see him at the Castle in the morning," he had said.

I asked if he had given any hint of what the news was about.

"Nothing," she said. "But he sounded serious, maybe a little worried."

I wanted to slip out of bed and call him, but knew it would not go well with Holly, not with the snuggled way her body fit against mine. I kissed her on her shoulder, felt her body shiver, heard her moan softly.

I did not stay the full night with Holly and she was understanding about it, especially after I told her of taking in Preacher and Mazie and the other street people. It was, to Holly, a tender act. Shamefully I took more credit for it than I should have, being that it was Leo's idea, and it left me haunted with the thought that another God-mark had been checked against my name in the Book of Sins kept by the angel Gabriel.

"I think I'd better be there, in case something goes wrong," I said.

She agreed, then asked me about the cake.

"Lady loved it," I told her. It was a shading of truth, but not a serious violation of it. Lady had not tasted the cake, only admired the look of it. Yet, I was sure it had been consumed, cut in slivers of serving pieces, passed out among the new, temporary residents of the Castle.

"I'll make one for Arthur when he gets out of jail," Holly said. She added wistfully, "I hope that's soon."

"It will be," I assured her. "The lawyers have a trick or two up their sleeves."

By the time I returned to the Castle, electricity had been restored and there was some merriment underway – not raucous, but spirited. It came from the guitar playing of Mr. Justin Price, Musician, composer of *Return of the Flower Child,* his tribute to Arthur. On Riverfront Plaza, Mr. Justin Price, Musician, was a favorite for both his music and his friendly bantering about the beauty of women and the ugliness of men. If you could name a tune, he could play it, or play something close enough to fool your memory.

I knew immediately that our visitors had settled comfortably in the Castle, making their places for sleep in the far end of the cavernous space of the Great Room. I suspected some of them had showered and changed into clothing collected by Leo on his nightly scavenger hunts and stored away for the giant yard sale he dreamed of having. At least, that was the sense I had from them. Being in a festive mood, it was hard to tell if the freshness they seemed to have came from water and soap or from the gladness of having a dry place to stay.

"Word gets out about this, we'll have a hundred of them tomorrow," Gerty sighed in the makeshift kitchen she and Wendell and Carrie had fashioned. "Lord, what we gonna do?"

It was a good question. I was down to less than two hundred dollars of the money Arthur had provided. There was no way to provide food for the masses bound to coming knocking.

"Well, the word will be out in the morning," Carrie said.

I asked what she meant.

"Doyle Copeland came by after you left, just to check on us," she told me. "He said he wanted to do a story on how we'd opened the Castle to people left without a place to go after the storm." She gave me one of her mischievous smiles. "The mayor's going to have a fit."

Near us, Mr. Justin Price, Musician, played *Amazing Grace*, as requested by Preacher. Preacher began singing with him: "*... how sweet the sound that saved a wretch like me...*" And then Lady joined, and then Mazie, and then the rest of us. The echoing sound of it was like a choir giving a concert in the church of St. John the Baptist.

"*...was blind, but now I see...*"

At sunrise, only five of our visitors were still in the Castle, causing Carrie to wonder if we had somehow insulted them.

"You been here too long," Wendell told her. "You forgot how it is out there. Reason they left was because they don't want to take just to be taking. There's some that'd do that, and steal what you didn't give them, but them's not the kind we let in last night. Ones that were here, they out to find some food, without having us do it. They got their pride. Most of them, at least. They'll be back."

Preacher and Mazie were among the five remaining, but they would not take our offered breakfast, both claiming to be out of the habit for morning food. The other three – two scrawny men known as Reed and Tattoo, and an aging woman who called herself Old Girl – ate sparingly, saying they would work at cleanup to pay for what they took. I saw Gerty turn away, saw her body shudder with pity, and I knew she had remembered something harsh from her own history of survival, perhaps the same trade-off of menial work for food.

Wally arrived at eight o'clock, bringing a dozen bagels with little cups of cream cheese. He was shocked to find the extra people in the Castle, yet when I told him what we had done, a brightness came to his eyes. He muttered, "That's good, that's good. A good move." Then he said to me, "Come on, let's go get some more bagels and maybe some doughnuts."

It was his way of getting me away from the Castle.

In his car, he said, "Hamby, we've got more of a problem than I thought we had."

"And what's that?" I asked.

"Arthur."

"Arthur?"

He nodded. "Yeah. I couldn't imagine why he wanted to go to jail, so I went to Atlanta to check him out."

"And?" I said.

"And he's everything he said is. He just didn't tell us the details."

Wally had gathered the left-out facts by making a visit to the furniture business – Solomon's, by name – of Arthur's former father-in-law. He went pretending to be a repeat customer, saying he had been assisted in years past by a pleasant gentleman named Arthur, and in the exchange that followed with a saleslady, he had learned something from the small print of Arthur's divorce and leaving. According to Wally, the saleslady, named Floyce, was an older woman with a taste for gossip and a lingering fond memory for Arthur, and she had confided, "From what I understand, he was well paid to disappear, but I doubt if he kept a penny of it. He was always giving away what he had, and that was the big problem for Reba, his wife – well, ex-wife. She's engaged to be married again."

"It's what he told me, for the most part," I said to Wally. "Except for giving away the money, though I have no doubt of that part of the story. None, whatsoever." Wally gave me a puzzled look, but I did not offer to explain myself.

"It makes sense to me, too, from what we talked about it when he was staying with me," Wally suggested. He added, "But the fact is, he didn't reveal a lot about himself. It just seemed that way."

"So, what's the news?" I asked.

Wally wagged his head slowly, as a man will do when the words he is about to speak are heavy on his tongue. "It's his health," he said. "He's got a seriously bad heart."

The words fell across me like a slap to my face. I stared at Wally in confusion.

"It's true," he said.

"She told you that?" I asked in astonishment.

He nodded. "She felt sorry for him, even if she did think him odd. She said he'd been hospitalized a few times with it, even had a pig valve replacement."

"What does that mean?" I said. "A lot of people have that surgery."

"Did you ever see him take any medication?" he asked.

"No," I answered.

"I didn't see it, either, when he was with me," he said. "From what I learned, he was supposed to be on heavy dosages of something. I don't know what, but something."

We rode for a few moments without speaking, and then Wally added, "We need to get him out of jail, Hamby. Get him to a doctor."

"You're right," I said. "But how?"

He rolled his hand over the top of the steering wheel of his car. "It doesn't matter, does it? I was thinking about playing with the computer, sending a release for him." He paused. "Judge's orders."

"Not that," I protested. "Mother of Christ, no. It won't work. They'd never believe that, not with all the publicity that's been had."

"Then you tell me," he said. He sounded disappointed.

I suggested we talk to Fuller Bishop and his partners, hoping there would be an answer in the news they would give us.

"But let's keep this thing about Arthur between us for the time being," I added, being firm with Wally. "If he's not said anything about it, I don't think it's fair to spread the story around, and I promise you it'll bother everybody who knows him."

To my surprise, Wally agreed. "I just hope nothing happens to him in jail," he said in a worried manner.

Shortly before noon, Wally and I went to the law offices of Bishop, Reinhart and Ayers, as we had been instructed after placing a call to Fuller Bishop. The three men were waiting for us in a conference room having a long mahogany desk and soft leather armchairs. Papers were neatly arranged on the desk. We were greeted with smug smiles holding back a secret that begged to be told.

"We've got the answer," Fuller told us.

"The bastards pulled a fast one," Damon Ayers added.

As Damon had suspected, the zoning description of the Castle had been manipulated.

"I remembered something about that property from my study at Savannah Country Day school when I was a teenager," Damon explained. "It was a history project, working in teams. We did a cataloging of potential historic sites when that craze began in the city, and the Castle was one of them. I was on the team that studied it from its groundbreaking to its business purpose and, eventually, to zoning." He paused and looked at his partners. They were all smiling.

"What you have to keep in mind is that zoning, as we have it today, did not exist when the Castle was built," Fuller Bishop added. "That came about in the fifties. Until that time, it was mostly an issue of political give and take, and a lot of backroom trading of favor went on."

Damon picked up a sheet of paper and held it for us to see. "We took photographs of those transactions to pad the report," he added. "Every one of them. As luck would have it, it was still in a box my mother has – her little keepsakes of my life." He slid the sheet of paper he was holding across to the table to Wally and me. "That's the one in question, the one Ned Doubleday used for his argument."

If a revelation rested in the words of the paper, I could not see it. Nor could Wally. "Okay, what are we looking for?" he asked.

The smile on Damon's face grew. He slipped a second sheet of paper across the desk to us. "This is the first zoning of the property, a copy of the one my mother saved," he said. "I've highlighted the important language. It shows that the Castle and two other facilities – both long ago demolished – were grandfathered by the zoning authorities of that time. Though the area was identified as commercial, those specific properties had a variance. They were commercial, but occupancy was allowed."

Wally and I stared at the highlighted language of the second sheet and compared it to the document Ned Davenport had used in court. It was plainly different. The language of the variance was missing in Ned Davenport's documents.

"I'll be damned," Wally whispered. "He edited it out. Son of a bitch."

"I like the story – or the gossip – behind it," Mason Reinhart said. "Seems a few public officials used it to provide housing for a lady or two, and had to make provisions for their comfort."

Wally chuckled. "It was a whore house?"

"With public officials, it's never a whore house," Mason replied. "It's a gentleman's club."

"And what do you do with this?" Wally asked.

"What every good lawyer would do, Dr. Whitmire," Damon replied calmly, yet with the kind of smile that holds the joy of mischief. "We're going to use it for negotiation. In the meantime, let's keep it private."

TWENTY-EIGHT

It is a wonder to me that I can juggle tennis balls while walking at a brisk pace, or roll coins across my fingers, or play the shell game with such skill people gasp in disbelief. The truth is, I am easily confused when more than one thing crowds my attention, and I become antsy. I have always blamed this condition on my father, carrying his walk-away blood as I do.

My only defense is this: I seldom walk away.

I often wish I could.

Yet, I also carry my mother's blood.

After the meeting with Bishop, Reinhart and Ayers, my father's blood teased me to catch a Greyhound bus to some distant place, taking on the lie and the life of another person as I had done before on occasions of needing to be someone nobler than the person I was at the moment.

My mother's blood told me to stay.

Before the day was over, I would question my mother's tolerance.

Doyle Copeland's story in the *Enquirer* about the Castle taking in street people after the storm was placed prominently across the bottom of the front page, carrying the headline:

Finding Room in the Castle

It was Doyle at his word-playing best, a tender tale of have-nots sticking together despite the on-going dispute with Harry Geiger and the city of Savannah over use of the Castle. The way Doyle twisted it, not even Harry Geiger would be foolish enough to raise an objection – or so we thought.

The story also acted as an invitation, and by mid-afternoon a crowd of street-dwellers began to assemble, taking on the look of conventioneers waiting in line for a reception – forgiving their questionable dress and skittish manner. They were not unruly, yet it was clear they were eager to have their share of whatever the Castle could offer them.

For Leo, watching the gathering from the front window temporarily diverted his attention from his gun-carrying protection of the Castle and his lookout for Ted Castleberry. For Leo, the gathering was a triumph. "I told you," he sneered. "Didn't I say it?"

Gerty, standing beside him, a look of worry clouding her eyes, was stunned. "Lord, Jesus," she moaned. "Where we gonna put them?"

"We can't," Carrie said. "Not everybody."

"Well, honey, you better find some good honky way of saying who gets in and who don't," Gerty told her.

Thankfully, Wendell and Leo volunteered to make the selections. I would learn later the process was based on handout numbers and then a bogus drawing from my top hat, numbers to match numbers. It had the trickery of street magic and the smoothness of a con game. Human nature being what it is, if Wendell or Leo disliked someone, that person could have stayed around as long as Methuselah and would never have stepped through the door.

By nightfall, there were forty additional visitors in the Castle, not counting those from the night before.

They were fed soup, prepared by Leo with help from Wendell. The soup was concocted from a case of tall cans purchased at random from a dollar store by Leo, soup of all kinds –lentil and tomato and potato and mushroom and split pea and carrot and celery, and some varieties I had never tasted nor knew existed. Leo simply poured all of it together in a commercial-sized aluminum cook pot he drug from his closet, a throw-out by some restaurant, but one still having use. Can after can of it, with equal amounts of water, seasoned with salt and pepper taken from a collection of party shakers he had pilfered over time. He added a small jar of chicken bouillon cubes, and as an afterthought, threw in two large bunches of carrots and celery, washed and chopped, four quartered onions, and a dozen ears of corn, shucked, silked and cut in halves. For body, Wendell poured two large packages of rice into the pot, stirred it, covered it and stepped back. "It needs to simmer," he pronounced.

I asked Leo what he called it.

"Queen Louisa," he answered profoundly. "It's Jewish."

The dinner of Queen Louisa soup and crackers required thirty-seven dollars of the money Arthur had given to me. I knew we had run the course of our generosity, and a little voice inside me prayed for Harry Geiger to send his troops to close the Castle. I was not prepared to become a surrogate father to the likes of myself.

I did not partake of the soup, though I later heard praise of it and Leo vowed he had been asked to reveal his recipe by a number of the lucky diners. It was not that I refused to eat it; I simply wasn't present when the simmering was finished and the rice had thickened the mix.

In late afternoon, Detective Cary Wilson appeared at the Castle to tell us of a meeting that had been arranged between Ned Doubleday and Fuller Bishop, and following Judge Renee Morgan's order we were invited to participate. The way Cary Wilson said it, I had the sense he had found humor in his duty of delivering the message. "No more than two of you," he said, looking around at the crowd assembled in the Castle.

"Where's the meeting?" I asked.

It would be in the council's conference room at City Hall, he replied. "Seven o'clock. And I was told to encourage you to keep this private. No media."

He turned to leave, then turned back. "By the way," he said, "I think you need to read the fire code." He paused, again scanned the crowd with a shake of his head. "Just a suggestion," he added. He nodded to us, then left.

"I wonder what he meant by that?" I said.

"Maybe he's trying to tell us something," Carrie answered.

It was determined that Carrie and I would go to the meeting, leaving Gerty and Leo and Wendell to handle Lady and the gathered masses. The way Lady was behaving – wandering among the people, chatting breezily about some party at the mayor's residence in New York – I believed we had the less taxing duty.

I had suggested our makeup of the meeting, knowing I would have to tell whoever went with me about the manipulation of the zoning matter that Damon Ayers and his partners had uncovered. I knew Carrie would accept the news of it in a more reasonable manner than Leo or Gerty or Wendell, and would permit Fuller Bishop to play it out without interruption in the meeting. With Leo or Gerty or Wendell, an uproar would have been possible.

Carrie's response was as I thought it would be: "We've got them, Hamby. We've got them." She clapped her hands like a delighted child.

At City Hall, we were greeted warmly by Fuller, who was in a cheerful mood as I knew he would be. He had with him his briefcase and in his briefcase, he had proof of the shenanigans played by Ned Doubleday, or one of his minions. Ned Doubleday was not so gracious in his acknowledgement of us. He nodded, looked us over with disgust, his eyes disapproving of our dress, then he told us where to sit.

The first words of the meeting were from Ned Doubleday: "To prevent any future misunderstanding of what transpires here today, I am going to record this session." He looked at Fuller. "I assume you have no problem with that."

"None at all," Fuller said.

Ned Doubleday placed a tape recorder on the conference table and pressed the record button. He began by giving the date, the time, and the place of the meeting, adding that those in attendance were Fuller Bishop of Bishop, Reinhart and Ayers, himself, and two representatives of the residents of the property known as the Castle. He did not offer our names, or ask us to identify ourselves, an omission Fuller corrected.

"For the record," Fuller said evenly, "the names of those representatives of the property known as the Castle, are Carrie Singletary and Hamby Cahill, and I would ask you, Mr. Doubleday, to refer to them by name, or we will assume that you, as a representative of the city of Savannah, regard them as less than worthy of proper respect."

Ned Doubleday's face colored red. He glared at Fuller. After a moment, he mumbled, "Ms. Singletary and Mr. Cahill. I wasn't aware of their names."

"Now you are," Fuller said.

A pause lingered in the room. I could hear the faint scraping of the tape running in the tape recorder. And then Ned Doubleday said, "This meeting is being conducted on instruction from Judge Renee Morgan to seek a reasonable solution to the illegal habitation of the property in question on Beale Street. I've spent considerable time with the mayor over this issue, and, frankly, Mr. Bishop – " He paused, turned his eyes to Carrie and me. "Mr. Cahill, Ms. Singletary, we're perplexed over your position."

"How so?" Fuller asked.

"You're expecting privileges the law doesn't allow," Ned Doubleday answered in a rough voice. "And you're using the media to try and gain those privileges. The mayor sympathizes with the plight of those in need of shelter, as do I, but you cannot hold the city hostage. If you want the city of Savannah to work for a proper resolution of this issue, you are going to have to demonstrate your willingness to conform to the court order to vacate this place you call the Castle. After that, the mayor and the city council will establish a committee to study the merits of using such properties for homeless shelters, property approved and supervised by established agencies."

Fuller nodded thoughtfully, his brow furrowed. He reached inside his coat pocket and removed a pen and rolled it in his fingers, gazing at it. A little show-off move, I thought.

"Let me tell you how we see it, Mr. Doubleday," Fuller finally replied. "We have a place, a building, housing citizens of Savannah who would be homeless without that building. Granted, it's not an apartment complex, or even a dormitory. Some people would say it's ugly. For some time now, seven people have called it home, a reference you and I might find laughable – compared to our standards of what a home should be. I doubt if there's a piece of furniture in it worth a hundred dollars, and if some of our better citizens took a tour of it, they might be surprised to find something that once belonged to them before being left on the street to be carried away by trash collectors. A lamp, a table, a footstool. Not a single person you and I know would accept a single item as a gift." He paused, offered a faint smile. "But, my God, it means a lot to those seven people who have been living there. One of them is in jail because of it, and, granted, it was his option to be there. You might think he's simply showing off, or you might think he's found better living quarters, but you would be wrong, Mr. Doubleday. He's there because he believes the position the city is taking is wrong." He paused again, leaned forward at the conference desk. "Privilege? Is that the word you used? Privilege? What a strange word."

"It applies, Mr. Bishop," Ned Doubleday said in a growl.

"All right, let me tell you what we want," Fuller replied. "We want the mayor to issue a statement saying the city, in reviewing the matter, has discovered an oversight that does, indeed, allow for occupancy in the Castle. We further want you, as the city attorney, to draft a petition to present to Judge Morgan, requesting that she dismiss the contempt of court finding against Arthur Benjamin and that he be released from jail immediately."

Ned Doubleday sat, his gaze fixed on Fuller, a half-smile curled across his mouth. The silence of the room was eerie. I glanced at Carrie. She looked apprehensive.

"Mr. Bishop," Ned Doubleday finally said, "you are not going to get any of those requests. What you are going to get, if you persist with such demands, is the full effect of the law as it applies to the occupancy of the place you call the Castle."

"That sounds very much like a threat," Fuller said.

"Consider it as you will, sir," Ned Doubleday shot back.

Fuller pushed back in his chair, and stood. His movement was so unexpected, so quick, I thought at first he wanted to leap across the desk and strike Ned Doubleday, and I think Ned Doubleday thought the same, the way his body flinched.

Fuller reached for his briefcase and opened it and pulled an envelope from it, sliding it across the desk to Ned Doubleday.

"This meeting is over," Fuller said bluntly, "but I'm going to leave you some reading material. I would suggest you share it with the mayor. You have twenty-four hours to respond to our request." He turned to Carrie and me. "Let's go," he said.

Outside, Carrie threw her arms around Fuller and laughed. "Did you see the look on his face?"

"It's the look on the mayor's face I'd like to see," Fuller told her.

"What do you think they'll do?" I asked.

Fuller looked back at the front of City Hall. "To be honest, I don't know," he said after a moment. "Harry Geiger's a hard man to figure. He hates losing." The tone of his voice was not as sure as it had been, and the expression of his face caused a shiver in my chest. He made a little smile to cover whatever thought he was keeping private. "I don't think we'll have to wait long to find out."

He was right.

At nine o'clock that night, there was a banging on the door of the Castle, strong enough to quiet the goings-on inside from those who had met the new standards of the Castle. The talking and laughing stopped, the games of cards and checkers, the guitar playing of Mr. Justin Price, Musician. All of it stopped abruptly, in the kind of freeze a photograph makes at the click of the shutter. The banging at the door echoed.

Leo gave me a look of apprehension and I knew what he was thinking: Ted Castleberry and his troops making a raid, or some drunk, put off by not being invited to stay in the Castle, come back to make trouble.

"I'll check on it," I said. The only voice I heard as I crossed to the door was from Lady. Lady was talking to someone – or to no one – about a hat she had favored as a young girl. Her voice was as happy as music.

When I opened the door, I knew the answer to our meeting with Ned Doubleday.

A half-dozen policemen stood behind a man dressed in a suit. His face blazed with authority and when he spoke his voice was low and mean. He said his name was Lon Marcus, fire marshal of the city of Savannah. He announced that he was there to evict everyone found harbored in or around the building, an action made necessary because of the violation of numerous fire safety codes, including failure to have an inspection, accessibility of egress, lack of fire alarms and fire extinguishers.

He did not ask for explanation. He said we had forty-five minutes to vacate the property, or we would be forcibly removed. "Starting now," he growled, taking a look at his watch.

Standing among the police was Sergeant Ted Castleberry, bearing a wide grin, and Billy Pottier, looking cocky. Ted Castleberry again lifted his hand and made a gun barrel of his index finger and pointed it at me, cocked an imaginary hammer with his thumb and made a little popping sound with his lips. He then turned to Leo and repeated the gesture. I saw Leo's hand reach for his pocket, but I caught his arm and stopped him. Leo glared at me. I whispered to him, "Let's go."

And then Leo did a strange thing. He took one step toward Ted Castleberry, lifted his own hand, made a pistol of his fist and forefinger, fanned an imaginary hammer with his thumb, pulled an imaginary trigger, and made a sharp cluck with his mouth. Ted Castleberry's face burned red in anger.

I pulled Leo away.

The exodus was made with grumbling and hissing from our homeless visitors, with curses, with voodoo spells cast on the city of Savannah from the simmering anger of men and women being hurried into the night, having no place to go. The policemen only smirked.

We were the last to leave – Lady and her Guests. It was confusing for Lady, as I knew it would be. Gerty and Carrie outfitted her prettily and put her broad-brimmed hat on her head and led her to her chair and persuaded her to sit while they gathered what they could carry – thought-of valuables and keepsakes. For myself, I had three suitcases, one of my own, hastily stuffed with belongings, and the two belonging to Arthur.

Dragging them to the front door, I remembered the envelope Arthur had given me, saying, "If they insist on removing you, I want you to follow the instructions I have here, but don't open it unless it's necessary."

I went into the bathroom on pretense of gathering my shaving razor and toothbrush and I opened the envelope. In it was a single sheet of paper folded around four one hundred dollar bills. On the sheet of paper, Arthur had written, *Take this money and go to the Glendale Hotel. Rooms have been reserved for each of you in my name for as long as they are needed, charged to an account I have with them. Please do not inquire about the arrangement. I will explain all of it in due time. Tell no one where you are going.*

The note was signed *Arthur* and below his signature was a postscript giving a name and a telephone number. It was a taxi service.

He can be trusted, Arthur wrote of the contact.

I did not say anything of the note or of the money to the others. Instead, I asked – as politely as my nature would allow – if Lon Marcus would allow one or two of the police cars to drive us to the bus station, planting the thought with him that we were likely plotting a getaway on a Greyhound.

To my surprise, he agreed, adding a snarl to his lecture that we should remember his kindness. Still, he agreed. The snarl did not matter. What mattered was covering our tracks, allowing no trace of our whereabouts.

It is not easy to leave a place that has been home, and it does not matter if the home is a palace or a shanty, or even a warehouse. Memories, warm and harsh, reside in homes. Leaving those memories is the same as sudden death, and having lost our homes of the past, all of us knew the heaviness of the moment. We did not speak of it to one another, yet as we rushed about gathering what belongings we could – with Lon Marcus counting off the time – I could sense the sorrow of it from Carrie and Gerty and Leo and Wendell and Lady. In each of them – and in me –

there was a need to weep until the weeping made a pool deep enough for drowning.

We carried the goods we were able to assemble to the street, the last trip being made by Wendell and Leo to remove Lady's trunk.

Two police cars, voluntarily driven by Ted Castleberry and Billy Pottier, escorted us, and our belongings, to the bus station. Neither man said anything. It was not necessary. Their happy faces and barely suppressed laughter made speeches for them. I could see Leo cringing in the back seat of the car we occupied, the one driven by Ted Castleberry. He seemed to be in a daze.

I waited until we were alone in the bus station before I made the call to the number Arthur had left in his note. The man who answered put me on hold. A few seconds later I heard another voice. He identified himself as Joab. When I mentioned Arthur's name, he asked: "Where are you?"

"The bus station," I told him.

"How many?" he said.

"Six," I answered.

"Stay there," he instructed. "Look for two cars."

Everyone except Lady was watching as I came away from the telephone. Lady was gazing curiously at a soldier who was sleeping in a chair. The soldier was holding a white stuffed rabbit, one with long, bent ears, and I thought of my years of pretend in the station. In the years of my pretend, I would have made him a hero of a foreign war, on his way home to a son he had never seen.

It was Carrie who pressed me. She took my arm and led me outside, not concerned by what the others might be wondering. "What are we doing?" she asked forcefully. "What was that call about?"

It was then that I handed her the note Arthur had left. When she read it, tears glazed her eyes. She handed the note back to me. "What do we do now?" she whimpered.

"In a few minutes a couple of cars will be here to take us to the Glendale," I told her. "In the morning, call your cousin. Let him know what's happened."

She nodded rapidly, touched at her eyes with her fingers.

"Let's keep this to ourselves until we get settled," I said. "I'll tell everyone about it tomorrow morning."

She nodded again, then turned and went back inside the bus station. I watched as she went to Lady and sat beside her. She reached for Lady's hand, pulled it to her. Lady broke her gaze from the sleeping soldier. She turned her face to Carrie. Her smile was that of a helpless person who did not know she was helpless.

In ten minutes, the man named Joab arrived, followed by a second car driven by a heavy, dark-haired woman. Joab said, as he loaded our belongings, "Just so you know, we didn't do this."

His meaning was clear.

TWENTY-NINE

The Glendale was a small motel on the outskirts of Savannah, one catering to weekly rentals for men working construction jobs or making sales calls. It was old, but well kept, having large rooms and a dining area overlooking a swimming pool. The color scheme was forest green and yellow, faded by age and sunlight.

Arriving shortly after ten o'clock was not as risky as I thought it might be. The motel owner, a lady named Olga Marchman, was in the lobby, engrossed in the watching of a television show about a group of nearly nude women collected in a hot tub, contesting for the affections of a handsome man with a handsome bank account. It must have been a moment of high drama, for when I interrupted Olga Marchman's preoccupation with the goings-on, she scowled. Yet, when I mentioned Arthur, her face took on a glow and I knew she had been expecting us.

"You're lucky," she said. "It's been a slow week. How many rooms do you need?"

"I think we can get by with three," I replied.

"You've got more than three people with you," she said, peering over my shoulder to look through the front window.

"We can share," I told her.

She shook her head. "Arthur said to give each of you a room."

The way she said Arthur – familiar, friendly – made me ask, "How did you meet him?"

She told me he had arrived one afternoon in a taxi and had spent a couple of hours discussing his wishes with her. From her dating of it, I realized the meeting had taken place during the time Arthur had stayed with Wally, a sneak-away on a day Wally was off, most likely courting Melody Comstock.

"Of course, I knew who he was from the stories I'd been reading in the paper," she added. "He gave me one of his flowers."

"And what did he tell you?"

"He said it was possible that some of his friends would be needing rooms, and he wanted me to take care of them," she said. She added, "He also said you might show up late at night." She glanced toward the television, then turned her look back to me. "He was right, wasn't he?"

I did not ask about the arrangement Arthur had made with Olga Marchman, though my curiosity wanted to know, and I believe Olga could see the question in my face. "Everything's to go on his account," she explained. "Rooms, meals, whatever you need. But if anybody needs to know, everything's on me." She paused, kept her gaze on me. "He was very emphatic about that, about keeping his name out of it. All of you need to remember that."

When I think of that night, I remember how each of us – except Lady – described it the following morning: too strange for sleep. And it was not the strangeness of another place, another bed, or of different scents and sounds; it was the strangeness of being alone in a room. Lady was accustomed to such privacy. For her, the only disturbing thing was being in a room not having teacups.

At breakfast, in the dining room, I finally told everyone of the message in Arthur's envelope, and of the money he had left for our needs, and of Arthur's instruction to Olga Marchman about keeping private his agreement with her, and of the arrangement with the taxi driver, Joab, who had driven away quickly, before I could offer fare for the ride. I could tell they had questions, as did I, of Arthur's wealth, but out of respect, no one asked them. The only comment was from Gerty. "God bless him, he's the strangest honky I ever knew," she said, shaking her head.

"So what's next?" asked Leo.

"I'm going to make some calls this morning," I said. I looked at Carrie. She blinked her understanding: she, too, had a call to make.

Fuller Bishop said he had read of the eviction in the *Enquirer*, and had been waiting to hear from me. His voice carried frustration.

"I made a couple of calls to some people I know at City Hall," he told me. "The mayor's going to have a press conference tomorrow."

"About what?" I asked.

"About closing the Castle," he said. "He'll claim it was done for the sake of safety, and he'll say he's going to put together a citizen's committee – mainly clergy, I'd guess – to review the problem of the homeless."

"What about the papers you left with Ned Doubleday yesterday?" I said.

"I'd say he's rolling the dice," Fuller replied. "He'll probably acknowledge them, but will find a way of refuting our finding."

"How?" I asked, hearing the frustration in my own voice.

"We've talked about it," Fuller said. "Playing the game, we're guessing he'll blame it on clerical error, saying the note about the variance was simply dropped by whoever translated the material into the city's computer files. And it does happen, but he won't make much of it. That's a slippery slope."

"Wouldn't he have to prove it?" I asked.

"Hamby, he's a politician," Fuller said. "Politicians don't prove; they talk. The burden of proof will be on us. It's why he's waiting a day to hold his press conference. He knows what the media will do with the eviction last night, and he can't let it appear that he's having a knee-jerk reaction. Tomorrow will give him time to report they've done their investigation."

I asked if he would attend the press conference.

"Not me," he said. "Mason's going, maybe Damon. Since I delivered the papers, I would be a direct target. No reason to cause a problem we don't need."

His answer sounded cowardly to me, yet it also made sense.

"I don't want you there, either," he added. "None of you. In fact, I'd prefer you didn't tell anyone where you are, but if you do, make sure they keep it to themselves. We'll talk later. Don't worry, we're not rolling over. I'm going out to see Arthur this morning. He needs to know what to expect."

"Tell him we're okay," I said.

"I will," Fuller replied.

"One other thing," I said.

"What's that?"

"We need to get him out of jail," I said. "I don't care how you do it, he needs to be out."

"Is there something you're holding back?" Fuller asked.

I wanted to tell him of Arthur's medical condition, but I did not. It was a private matter with Arthur, one we knew about only by the gossip of a woman who had been charmed by Wally, and I did not want to violate the trust he had in me.

"No," I answered. "Nothing I know for sure. It's just a feeling. We'd be more comfortable if we had him with us."

"Maybe we can do something now that the city's padlocked the Castle," Fuller reasoned. "There's really no reason to keep him there." He paused. "I'll talk to the judge about it."

I made two other calls – one to Wally, one to Holly.

Wally had spent his morning reading internet copies of Delaware newspapers and did not know of our eviction. His response to it was blunt: "Son of a bitch. Stay where you are. I'll be there in an hour or so." I could almost hear the humming of his mind.

Holly was relieved to talk to me, but was also angry over the lateness of the call. The news of the fire marshal's padlocking of the Castle had made it into Frank's before midnight – delivered by Doyle Copeland, who was looking for me – and not having any idea where we had gone, she had spent a sleepless night of worry. I could only apologize and cower behind the excuse of being busy with the move to the Glendale.

"You could have stayed with me," she said. "You still can."

I told her we would talk about it later, promising to see her at Frank's if I could, though I had some doubts about it. "We're trying to stay out of sight until we know what's going to happen. It's best no one knows where we are." She pouted, but only mildly, finally saying she understood. "They're depending on you," was the way she put it, and I liked the sound of it. My mother had been the only other person ever to suggest that I was worthy of such praise.

Carrie's call to her cousin verified what Fuller Bishop had told me. The fire marshal's appearance was a strike against the threat Fuller had made to Ned Doubleday. The word pre-emptive was used, giving it the sound of combat. Harry Geiger was willing to bet his political life that he could turn the tables on us in a press conference. All he had to do was leave the impression we were not as innocent as the public might have believed. We would be called blackmailers, con artists, traitors of trust. He would play an edited version of the meeting with Ned Doubleday, using it to charge that our actions were detrimental to the real street people of Savannah – the ones who had been left in the cold – and, as Fuller Bishop had predicted, he would blame a clerical error in the misreading of the variance for the Castle.

"He's good at pulling off those tricks," Carrie's cousin had admitted.

I asked if he had any suggestions for us.

"He said he wanted to think about something," Carrie replied. "He's going to call me later."

"He sounds worried," I suggested.

"I don't think so," she said.

We were sitting in folding chairs at an umbrella-covered table in the swimming pool area of the Glendale, watching the noisy frolicking of two children – a boy and a girl – in the shallow water as their pudgy mother sunbathed in a pink bikini that fit her only in a memory of earlier years. The morning sun, high and hot, shimmered on the water, its light dancing across splashes make by the children. I wondered where their father was. Off on a business call, I guessed, making a mix of work and leisure, likely charging everything to his company expense account.

I asked Carrie if she thought Lady was faring well enough.

"Gerty told her we were on vacation," she said. "I think she believes we're on the Riviera, but she's enjoying it and that's all that matters. She's watching television. I think she'd forgot about it. Every show that's got theme music is a spectacle to her."

"And Leo?" I said.

She smiled. "I think he's missing being downtown. Not edgy enough for him out here."

"And you?" I asked.

She reached for my hand and held it. The way she looked at me, her hazel eyes soft, her smile gentle, I thought again of the moments of flirtation we had had, moments of teasing and blood-rush, our bodies doing the dance-about of animals in heat. Still, I was glad we had backed away and that we were as we were – closer than the lovers we might have become.

"I'm fine, Hamby," she said quietly. "Really. I had a dream last night. I was with my mother on a shopping trip. We had lunch in a restaurant – a good one – and she was in a happy mood. Talking, laughing." She paused, swallowed, blinked. "I didn't see her happy very often, and I don't ever remember going shopping with her. I know it was just a dream, but it was as though she was actually there, like she used to be when I was little, coming to my bed, thinking I was asleep. I remember her whispering to me."

She looked away as one of the children belly-flopped into the water, squealing in delight. "It was a good dream," she added.

We were still at the pool when Wally arrived, wearing his serious professorial countenance and carrying a notebook. He made a glance at the sunbathing mother in her pink bikini, his eyes blinking in shock, and then he took at seat in a chair at the table and opened his notebook.

"I've got an idea," he said.

I saw Carrie's face wince in dread.

Wally called his plan an addendum to *The Arthur Stratagem*. The outline of it had been hastily penned in his scrawling manner, leaving the impression that it was the work of sudden inspiration. It was, instead, a display of nonsense with a single concept: protest. Yet, the way Wally talked about it, he had created something akin to the Declaration of Independence.

"We take to the streets," he said, spilling energy. "Get out a story about the press conference. They're pre-empting us, we pre-empt them. Get a crowd to show up at City Hall. Talk to the guy down at the newspaper – Doyle What's-His-Name. If we've got time, we could take out a full-page ad, one of those with signatures from everyone we know. And we need to call those guys at the radio stations. They'd snap this up in an eye blink. Maybe the two of you could do an interview with one of them, talk about how it felt to be rousted out of your home at night, like the Gestapo herding up the Jews, or maybe Leo should do that. And I was thinking I could get Melody and some of her classmates to make placards like we did before. Have them reading *Free Arthur* or *Storm the Castle* – something along those lines."

His words rained on us. They came from his mouth and his eyes, from the rolling of his shoulders. His hands conducted the harsh music of their sound, *pianissimo* to *crescendo*. Within the invisible walls of the table, his words charged the air like electricity running on conduits of syllables.

When he finally paused, proudly tapping his notebook with the tip of his finger, I said, "I don't know, Wally. It could help, but we might not need it."

"Why's that?" he asked, his face showing impatience.

"I promised the lawyers we wouldn't do anything until we talked to them later today," I replied. "They're working on something." It was half-lie, half-truth, yet it caused Wally to sit back and to furrow his brow in thought.

After a moment, he said, "All right, but as soon as you know what's taking place, give me a call at home or at Frank's, and don't worry, I'm not going to broadcast where you are. When we get ready to make our move, we need to be the ones controlling it." He stood, reached into his pocket and withdrew a domino tile and placed it upright on the table. "When that one falls, we go to work," he added dramatically. He turned, glanced again at the woman in the bikini. He whispered, "Good God," and then he left in a strong, confident stride.

We stared after him until he disappeared from sight, and then Carrie turned to me, an incredulous expression lodged in her face.

"Did you hear that?" she said. "He's turning this into a circus. My God, I'm surprised he didn't mention selling cotton candy or peanuts."

"He means well," I replied weakly.

"Hamby, he's nuttier than Lady," she said. "And a lot more dangerous." She reached across the table and pushed the domino over.

Fuller Bishop did not call until late afternoon, and the waiting had left me wondering if something unexpected had happened – a run-in at the jail for Arthur, news of Harry Geiger's people discovering Wally's doctoring of city records about the A. N. Whitehead Corporation, a fire at the Castle. Anything was possible and I knew it.

Thankfully, the report was more tempered than my fear of it. Arthur had not been surprised by our eviction from the Castle, and was pleased we were safe at the Glendale. Still, he declined Fuller's arrangement to have him released from jail.

"I talked to the judge before I went to see him," Fuller told me. "She was willing to order a release for him since the Castle was no longer occupied, provided he pay the fine for the few days he ignored the order before his contempt of court hearing. He wouldn't do it. I couldn't believe it. At ten dollars a day, he owes seventy or eighty dollars."

"He needs to be out of jail," I said. I thought of the money – Arthur's money – left in the envelope of instructions. "I'll pay the fine," I said.

"So would I," Fuller replied. "I offered. He just smiled and thanked me, but said he was where he wanted to be."

"The way things are going, what's the gain in it for him?" I asked.

Fuller paused before he answered. "I don't know. Pride, maybe. I don't know. It's still a rallying point, and that's the only advantage I see in it. It's a lot like the civil rights movement, when going to jail was a badge of honor."

I could hear a sigh coming from Fuller, the same as I was feeling. Dealing with a man standing on principle was not easy. It was like free-climbing the surface of a rock mountain having no crevices for finger or toe grips.

"And how did he look?" I asked.

"Fine," Fuller told me. "A little tired maybe, but all right. Probably all that sitting around and the food he's getting." He laughed softly. "One thing was amusing. He had his cape with him – not wearing it, but holding it. I asked a guard about it when I left, and he told me the inmates had raised hell about taking it away from him, so they gave it back. First time I've ever known them to do anything like that out there."

"I'll tell Gerty," I said. "She'll be happy."

We made no plans other than to wait for the press conference and the fall-out of it. I promised that none of us would attend. Fuller suggested a meeting at the Glendale after it was over. To review things, he said. To develop a strategy. In my mind, I made a note not to mention the meeting to Wally. Fuller's strategy and Wally's stratagem were not birds of the same flock.

"If anything comes up, call me," Fuller said. "No matter how late it is, call me. In the meantime, I want all of you to stay where you are. If we're lucky, no one will find you for another day or so. There's no reason to fan the flame."

THIRTY

It was not easy staying away from Frank's and from Holly, yet I knew there was wisdom in being out of sight. The media furor over the eviction of the Castle had roared in a loud, collective voice, and from the report called in to us by Wally – his voice low and secretive – we knew the people gathering in Frank's and in every other lounge and shop in Savannah were ready to throw themselves into the fray. The homeless who had found a brief refuge with us in the Castle, had taken to the street like sidewalk evangelists, telling stories of horror over their mistreatment in the furor of the eviction. In their striking out at the city, they had concocted a scary tale of our disappearance, saying they knew only that we had been driven away in two police cars and, in all likelihood, had been removed from the city on orders from Harry Geiger. One rumor had us in the Savannah River, floating face-down toward the ocean.

A more reasonable report told of being deposited at the Greyhound Bus Station by the police, who believed we were leaving Savannah. Yet, there was no record of ticket sales to fit our descriptions. We simply had left, and no one remembered how or when. It was a tale that inspired the investigative instinct of the media. Eager reporters went on safari for us, grilling every cab driver in the city. What they discovered was that no one knew anything beyond the misinformation of gossip. When the search turned to motels within a fifty-mile radius, Olga Marchman lied. Her prattle was: "Wish they were here. I could use the money."

"We need to take advantage of this," Wally urged. "We could have so many people at City Hall in the morning, they'd have to call out the National Guard."

"Not yet," I told him. "The lawyers want to know what's going to go on in the press conference. They think it could help us even more."

I could hear him sigh. In the background there was a babble of voices and the sound of glass against glass, and I knew he was at the bar in Frank's Fine Dining.

"What we need, Hamby, is for you to pull off one of those tricks you laughingly call magic," he said. "The one where you make somebody disappear. Harry Geiger, if you want a name. But if you can't do it, I'm in the company of a bunch of drunks who are willing to take on the task."

"I'll work on it," I told him.

I had no idea when talking to Wally that there was a person who would do exactly what he had suggested in his grumbling – someone who would make Harry Geiger disappear.

Not a magician.

Not a drunk.

It was Sharon Day.

As I have pieced it together over time, using a mix of hearsay and fact, this is what happened, or the gist of it: At nine o'clock on the morning of the ten o'clock press conference, Sharon Day entered City Hall and asked to see the mayor.

She was told he was unavailable.

"Call him," Sharon said forcibly to the security guard. "Tell him Sharon Day is here."

The guard did as instructed. Something in Sharon's voice caused a shiver in him.

Upstairs at her desk, Harry Geiger's secretary, a lady named Jenny Bloom, took the call and informed the mayor, "Some woman named Sharon Day wants to see you."

Harry Geiger turned pale, his eyes widened, his mouth opened in shock.

"Do you want me to send her away?" Jenny asked.

"No, no," he stammered after a moment. "Have her come up." Then he added, "You stay."

"Why?" asked Jenny.

"Just do it," he snapped.

The entire meeting with Harry Geiger took less than a minute.

In that less-than-a-minute time, Sharon reached into her purse and pulled out an envelope and dropped it on Harry Geiger's desk. She said to him, "The press conference you have this morning will be an apology to all those people you had evicted at the place they call the Castle, and the city will make it safe for them to return to it. You will also promise to establish a committee to work on housing for the homeless, and I will be a member of that committee. And you will order Arthur Benjamin's release from jail. Today. This morning. If you don't do these things, I will litter this city with copies of the contents of that envelope, beginning in your wife's dressing room, and it will become the confetti of your last parade."

She turned and walked out of his office.

The announced press conference was delayed by thirty minutes. Harry Geiger did not appear. Roger Upshaw released a hastily prepared statement from the mayor, saying he had spent the evening reviewing the matter of the Castle, and had concluded the city acted prematurely in its eviction of the inhabitants, though there were legitimate concerns for fire safety. He further stated he would instruct the fire marshal to remedy the most serious of the violations immediately, at city expense. As to the zoning dispute involving the property known as the Castle, he would seek agreement with the court for continued occupancy until an acceptable resolution could be reached between the city and concerned parties. Further, he would ask the city council to establish a committee of involved citizens and business leaders to do a detailed study of the city's homeless population, with a mission of offering care and rehabilitation and job assistance. Last, he would request the immediate release of Arthur Benjamin from the Savannah-Chatham County jail.

"This is an open administration," Roger Upshaw said on behalf of the mayor. "We have been made aware of an honest misinterpretation of the status of the facility known as the Castle, a misinterpretation caused by clerical error, and we are doing all in our power to correct that error. It is our sincere wish to right any perceived wrong inadvertently created by well-intended actions."

The announcement was met with a yelping from the media, a muddle of laughter and cursing, driving Roger Upshaw into the safety of his office.

Harry Geiger and his wife left in the afternoon for a long vacation to Asheville, North Carolina, dodging the questions being hurled his way, hoping the words *not available* would keep the media wolves at bay long enough to lose their hunger for his flesh.

Eventually, that is what happened.

I know the story of Sharon Day because she told me, and though there have been many rumors of her early-morning meeting with Harry Geiger, the truth of it has been kept between us since the night we met in her office, two days after she was named chairlady of the Committee for the Study of Indigent Citizens.

She had asked for the meeting under the pretense of talking to me about our return to the Castle, where we had found all of Lady's teacups smashed and the furniture we had collected broken into splinters. An investigation had revealed nothing, though the police report suggested it had been the work of the homeless who were rejected by Leo and Wendell's selection system. Preacher vowed that after we had been driven away, he had seen police enter the Castle carrying baseball bats and clubs. The investigators dismissed his version of what had happened, saying he was a drunk and a rabble-rouser.

"It's not over," Sharon told me, explaining that certain civic leaders with clout had requested a covert inquiry by the Georgia Bureau of Investigation. "They're getting close to the truth," she said, "but all of that's private. You're not to repeat it to anyone."

Intuitively knowing she was one of those with clout, I gave her my promise of secrecy.

And then she said, "I think it's time to share something with you."

"About what?" I asked.

"Harry Geiger," she answered.

That is when I heard the story.

She had been on a retreat to Amelia Island a year earlier, one sponsored by the Chamber of Commerce for city officials and business leaders. After a rowdy reception one evening, Harry had made a brazen pass at her and then had written her a note in a drunken flourish of passion.

She handed it to me. "I want you to read it," she said.

It was a silly note – childish, vulgar, unguarded, the kind of writing found in the graffiti of bathroom walls in bars and service stations. In it, Harry confessed he had fantasized having sex with Sharon in a hotel suite on a bed with silk coverings. He wrote of licking champagne from her body, of using sex toys, of promising her jewelry and cars and exotic trips to exotic places. And in a line that made me smile, he wrote, "You've never had a man like me."

For Harry Geiger, it might as well have been a suicide note.

"He forced his way into my room, making a fool of himself, trying to pull my clothing off," she said when I handed the note back to her. "I finally got him to leave, and to be honest, I was prepared to forget about it. I've been to too many conferences to be naïve about powerful men when they're away from home. Then he slipped this note under my door, and that was more than I was willing to tolerate. I told him I was thinking of charging him with sexual harassment, and that's when he started begging me to forgive him. He promised to stay away, so I let him off the hook."

"But you kept the note," I said.

She smiled. "Yes. I'm glad I did."

"And that's why the press conference turned out like it did?" I asked.

"Let's say it had some merits of persuasion," she answered. "At least it got Arthur out of jail."

"We're thankful for that," I told her.

The office Sharon Day occupied was large and had the look and feel of authority, from wall decorations to its furniture. The only thing about it that seemed at all dainty was a vase placed on the desk. The vase held Arthur's flower.

"Let me explain something," she said. "I don't totally trust anyone. Not even my lawyer." She pulled open a drawer and took out an envelope and held it up. "As a safe-guard, I want you to have a copy of the note Harry wrote. I've also prepared a letter to you certifying the authenticity of it, and I've had it notarized by a very close friend in Charleston. As you may expect, I will ask that you keep this discussion private, and to assure that someone doesn't accidentally find it, I've reserved a safety deposit box for you here at the bank. Tomorrow, I want you to come back during business hours and we'll complete that transaction. In the meantime, I'll keep this copy of the note and my letter."

I sat, numbed, gazing at Sharon Day.

"You wonder why I'm doing this, don't you?" she asked.

"I do, yes," I answered.

She leaned back in her chair. Her eyes stayed on my face in a soft gaze, and then she said, "When I first read the stories about Arthur and the accident that put Lady in the hospital, I saw your name, and there was something about it that bothered me. On the day we were in court when the judge issued her order to vacate the Castle, I realized why it meant something." She paused and looked at me in a way that made me wonder what I might hear. "Your mother used to work for us," she said after a moment. "When we had parties. I remember her vividly because of her Irish accent and because of her patience with me. I was not a very agreeable young girl, I'm afraid. I liked attention. One night I saw her wrapping some cake in a napkin and putting it in her purse, and when she left the house, I followed her. She went to a small boy, not much younger than I was, who was hiding behind some shrubbery and the two of them left. I was curious, so I kept following them. They went to one of the squares – Lafayette, I think it was – and sat on a bench and she took the cake from her purse and gave it to the boy." She paused, inhaled slowly. "I cried that night, Hamby. Cried because it was the first time I had ever seen poverty. There has never been a moment in my life as significant as that one."

She paused again, leaned forward and folded her hands in her lap. "Of course, you were that boy. My mother's still alive. I asked her if she remembered the name of the Irish woman who used to work for us, and she did. Mary Cahill. I checked on her and found that she had died. I found also that she had a son named Hamby. You."

I looked away, unable to speak.

"That's why I'm doing this," she said softly. "I owe you and your mother more than money could ever provide. What I saw that night gave my life direction."

I often think of the meeting with Sharon Day, and of the days of jubilation following the quick negotiations that released

Arthur from jail and cleared the way for our return to the Castle. All of it so sudden and so pleasing, it became a blur of happenings – the cleaning up of the destruction of our furniture, the anonymous gifts of replacements that were far superior to what we had had, the good wishes we encountered on the streets as we made our daily walk – Arthur giving out his flowers, me doing a little magic, Carrie making funny faces with her caricatures.

There were many offerings of financial help, all refused at Arthur's insistence. We never spoke of the money he had given to me, or of the money he surely had in his suitcase. Such talk would have been insulting to him and it would have spoiled the quiet game he and I continued to play at night – Arthur slipping cash into my wallet, me filling the sweatband of his hat. It is a wonder we did not plow into one another in the back-and-forth crawling we did in the dark of the room.

The only great change in our routine was the need for one of us to always be with Lady. Her mind became more fragile by the day, like an unseen cancer devouring a body from the inside, and I wondered if our stand against the city – the presence of the police, the days in court, the eviction – had mangled her thinking and set about her deterioration. Or maybe it was only a single, bothering thing, a horror, a click of memory holding a scream. Her teacups maybe – gone when she returned to the Castle. I remember it was a worry for all of us, knowing we could not replace so many of them. Instead, we settled on five cheap sets, and displayed them prominently. On the day of our return, I watched her closely as we escorted her into her room, telling her she had new furnishings. I saw her eyes sweep the shelves, saw her blink once, and then saw a smile grow on her face as she went to the new sets we had purchased, taking them in her hands, making her to-do over them, telling us she once had a collection of teacups in her home in New York, gifts from her mother, and had always wanted more of them. The way she meandered in her story, it did not seem she remembered the cups that had been smashed, yet I have wondered if she faked the forgetting of them to cover the hurt.

Arthur did not sell the Castle back to Lady, as he had considered. Fuller Bishop advised against it, given Lady's condition. Instead, he designated it for Lady's care, authorizing any future use or sale of it to go for her needs during her lifetime. After her death, it would be sold and the proceeds of the sale would be divided equally among us.

Wally and I did speak to Arthur about his health. Not straight on, but in a roundabout way, pretending we were concerned about Lady, saying she needed a physical and would likely submit to one if Arthur set the example. His answer was a look-away and a smile. Wally took it as agreement. "We should do it soon," he said, and Arthur replied, "In a few days."

There were visitors to the Castle – Holly and Frank, Wally, Preacher, Mazie, Mr. Justin Price, Musician, Olga Marchman, the partners of Bishop, Reinhart and Ayers, even Renee Morgan and Sharon Day. They came by invitation and unannounced, knowing there was a welcome for them, knowing they were walking into a fairy tale, a theme for an on-going party to celebrate the luck of living.

It would not last.

One morning, in the chill of winter, in the week before Christmas, I awoke to find Leo sitting on the side of Arthur's bed. He was holding a pillow in his arms, hugging it.

A shiver flew over me. I sat up quickly.

"Leo?" I said.

Leo looked at me. "He's dead, Hamby," he whispered. A damp map of tears flowed in twin rivers from his eyes.

THIRTY-ONE

By his wish – expressed to Fuller Bishop in the making of a will none of us knew about – Arthur was cremated and his ashes were taken to Laurel Grove Cemetery and buried in a sealed urn at the pauper's gravesite of Cherokee Robbins, a dispensation Fuller had arranged in some undisclosed manner. The cremation bothered Leo. "Jews don't do that," he said. Then he added, "But Arthur was Arthur before he was Jewish or anything else. So be it."

The notice of his death, written by Doyle Copeland, appeared on the front page of *The Savannah Enquirer*, a simple accounting of a good man who, for a fleeting time, had managed to brighten the spirits of those he met by offering the gift of a handmade paper flower and the grace of a smile. There was no mention of his stand against the city.

The day of the gravesite service was bright, yet having enough of a December chill for over-jackets or heavy sweaters. We were driven to the cemetery by Wally and Doyle. Carrie and Gerty had groomed Lady as royalty would be attended, yet the expression of her face was one of sadness and bewilderment. She had not spoken the entire morning. It was a silence that would rest with her for two days.

We were surprised to find a large gathering of students from SCAD at the entry to the cemetery. They had with them boxes of paper flowers they had spent the night constructing – flowers of bold, bright colors, like paint samples in a paint store – and they were passing them out to those who came to mourn, or to celebrate, Arthur – at first, only a few, then dozens. Before it was over, there would be more than five hundred people making their slow walk to circle the gravesite.

Someone had leaned a cardboard sign against a flowerpot sunk into the sand where the urn holding Arthur's ashes was buried. Hand-lettered in thick black marker were the words, *How Hard It Is to Keep From Being King When It's in You and in the Situation.* I looked at Doyle. He shook his head. No. No, the sign was not of his making. I thought: Wally. Yet, when I asked about it later, he denied being involved. I believe he lied.

There was no formal service, no eulogies of praise, no mourner's Kaddish. Arthur had not wanted them. Still, Preacher was moved to utter a short prayer in a loud voice: "Lord God, maker of us all, we bring one of your miracles to rest today. We thank you for knowing him." He raised the flower he held – red, the look of a carnation, or as he would tell me later, the color of the blood of Jesus – and he dropped it at the head of the urn.

And, then the crowd began to disperse, moving slowly, quietly, in an unfolding circle around the gravesite, and as they moved, they dropped the paper flowers given to them by the students of SCAD. The flowers grew in a heap, a kaleidoscope crown of color covering the ground.

The only sound among the mourners was the sound of weeping.

The following morning, needing time at the gravesite without the crowds, we returned to the cemetery – Lady and her Guests. The wind had swirled up from the river during the night and had scattered the flowers across the pauper and poor sections of Laurel Grove, leaving the ground dotted with splotches of color, putting me in mind of a field of Easter eggs set out for easy seeing by small children carrying baskets and squeals. Across the divide, one had nestled on my mother's grave against a blade of grass. The way the wind had lodged it, it had the look of growing from the soil, a solitary yellow carnation. My mother would have seen beauty in it, would have kneeled to touch it.

Something else was also there, something strangely odd and sadly inappropriate. On a metal stand beside the grave was a large wreath of cut flowers from the city of Savannah. A wide ribbon stretching across the chest of the wreath read, *In Memory of the 'Mayor'*.

I thought of Wally, of the death of his friend's mother, and of the hypocritical offering of flowers by the people who had fired her son on the day of his grief.

"My God," Carrie whispered, staring at the wreath. "That's asinine."

"Politics," I said.

"It's too late for that," she replied.

"What does that mean?" I asked.

She turned to look at me. "I think it's time you met my cousin," she said.

That evening, Carrie and I walked to Bay Street and hailed a taxi and Carrie gave the driver an address that led southwest of Savannah, off Skidaway Road. We stopped at a large, ranch-style brick house on a cul-de-sac, one with an island of trees in a manicured front yard.

"This is it," Carrie said with excitement. She turned to me. "Promise you'll behave."

"Why shouldn't I?" I asked.

"I think you'll be surprised," she replied.

We walked up the driveway to the house and Carrie pushed the button to the doorbell. I could hear it chiming inside.

In a moment the door opened and a grinning Cary Wilson said, "Welcome."

Thinking about it later, I was amazed that I had failed to put Carrie and Cary Wilson together in all the hours I had spent wondering about the identity of her cousin. Ironically, both had been named for their grandfather, and standing side-by-side, they shared a surprising physical similarity. When I thought about it later, I should have known it was more than coincidence, or assignment, that had Cary making the arrest of Arthur. He had volunteered as a means of protecting Carrie and to make certain the arrest was handled without insult.

Carrie had promised I would like her cousin and his wife, whose name was Rachel, and she was right. They were gracious hosts and glad to come out from the hiding of their secret, though Carrie insisted it was still necessary to keep quiet about the relationship. "There's too much to jeopardize," she said. "Cary wants to tell you about some of it."

It was an evening for putting together the pieces of a puzzle, and at the preparation of dinner – a steak grill-out on the patio of his backyard – Cary willingly answered every question I had. The reason he knew of the goings-on of Harry Geiger was because he had bugged Harry's office as part of a covert investigation conducted in conjunction with the Georgia Bureau of Investigation. There had been stories from informants linking a suspected drug operation to members of the Savannah police department. One of the rumors gave hints of Harry Geiger benefiting from the transactions. It had proved to be a false lead, and Cary was glad of it. The mayor was guilty of nothing more than arrogance and of being a politician, and though he was on the take for small gifts in exchange for small favors, he was honest in his public disdain for drug-pushers.

Yet, the investigation, which had been concluded in late November, would send Ted Castleberry and a half-dozen other officers to federal prison. It would be a highly publicized case and Leo and I would be in the courtroom daily during the trial, Leo cheering in his heart as the prosecutor brought Ted Castleberry and his cronies – including Billy Pottier and the two men who had been with him on the night of indignity in front of Frank's – to their knees. Each day of the trial, Leo cocked his fist pistol at Ted Castleberry and fired a cluck and a smile into his soul. I have never seen a man so jubilant over payback. To Leo, prison was a more fitting punishment than the death he had wished -- or perhaps plotted – for Ted Castleberry.

Cary had destroyed the tapes he made in the mayor's office, but only after he was sure that things had worked out well for us. With them, he had some leverage, but admitted he was relieved not to use them.

"Here's what's funny about all of that," he said. "On the morning of the press conference, I had copies of all the tapes in a box, ready to drop off at his office. I got delayed by a meeting with a federal drug agency over Ted Castleberry." He wagged his head the way a person does when having disbelief. "Talk about timing, that was close." He paused, turned a steak on the grill. "Someone else beat me to it." The way he said it, glancing at me, I was certain he knew about Sharon Day. From his bug, no doubt.

He also told of bugging the Castle – on orders from Roger Upshaw – and how the operation had amused him. He called it television-show police work, the meddling of a political lightweight trying to become a heavyweight.

I asked about Stuart Marlowe, who had been with him on his first trip to the Castle.

"Some people have no manners," he said. He looked at Carrie and winked. "I didn't like what he was saying about some of you, so we found other people for him to push around. I didn't have very much control over Ted, but I could handle Stuart."

"Tell him the best part," Carrie urged gleefully.

"You think it would interest him?" There was tease in his voice.

"Stop it, Cary," Rachel said. "Tell him."

"All right," he conceded. He looked at me. "Harry's days as mayor are limited."

"What do you mean?" I asked.

"He's decided not to run for re-election."

"Why?"

"He knows he can't win against a ghost."

Carrie and I were driven back to the Castle by Rachel Wilson, who filled the time of the trip with stories of the excitement she and her husband had had in being with Carrie, and of their eagerness to have her live with them and to attend college. "We couldn't have children," Rachel said in her chatty way, "and I know it's not the same, but both of us can't wait for Carrie to move in with us. I love my husband, but having someone else in the house just seems to brighten it up, like fresh flowers or new furniture. The only thing I'm worried about is driving her insane with all my blithering."

Rachel Wilson was a stunningly beautiful woman – dark-eyed, a quick smile, a bright aura of wonder clinging to her presence. I believed her blithering – as she demeaned herself – would be a healing for Carrie.

We got out of the car on a side street not far from the Castle – a cautionary move to keep spying eyes from becoming fluttering tongues – and I watched as Rachel pulled Carrie to her in a quick embrace across the front seat of the car. The shine of gladness from Rachel's eyes was like the light of a new star, and I knew that Carrie's life was in safe hands.

We watched as the car pulled away.

"I love her," Carrie whispered.

"I think the feeling's mutual," I said. Then: "I'm glad I know who they are."

"They've always liked you," she told me. "If Rachel had her wish, you and I would move in as a couple." She turned to look up at me. "I think that's funny, don't you? They must know I'm too old to sleep with my brother." She leaned to me and kissed me on the corner of my mouth. "Are you going to Frank's?" she asked.

"I think I'll just take a walk," I told her.

She nodded and began to stroll toward the Castle. There was a little girl's happiness in her step.

The walk I took was a journey into memory, having no map. It was the same as riding in one of the horse-drawn tourist carriages leaving out of City Market, but without a driver to guide the horse and to tell me of sights along the way. The imaginary horse pulling me wandered aimlessly in a slow pace, along streets decorated for Christmas in blinking lights and glittering stars hanging from the eaves of porches. It carried me to the home of my childhood, to Laurel Grove Cemetery, to the Cathedral of St. John the Baptist, to the squares dreamed of by James Oglethorpe, to Forsyth Park, to River Street. And at every place, there was a conversation to be had with someone not there.

My father was one of those people.

His presence was at Laurel Grove Cemetery, standing beside the grave of my mother.

"I'm sorry, son," he said to me.

"It's all right," I told him. "We had a good life."

"I wanted to come back, but I couldn't," he lamented. "The shame of the leaving was too heavy on me."

"You're here now," I said.

"It's where I've always been," he whispered. "Your mother wouldn't let go of me, no matter how much begging I did."

I wanted to yell at him, to swing my fists through the apparition of my seeing, yet I did not. Near me, the imaginary horse taking me place to place pawed restlessly at the ground, and I turned and walked away.

In Telfair Square, I saw Preacher. He was slumped forward

on a bench, smoking a cigarette. The scent of cheap bourbon was on him. He looked up when I spoke to him and a grin wormed its way across his face.

"I'll be damned," he said. "What're you doing?"

"Just walking," I replied.

He bobbed his head, took a drag from his cigarette. "Cold out," he mumbled.

"A little chilly," I acknowledged.

"Sure wish I was in that place you got," he said.

"They won't let us have anybody until they work out some things," I told him. "Truth is, it's more of a fire-trap than we thought it was."

He laughed wearily. "Life's hell, ain't it?"

"Sometimes, it is," I admitted.

He dropped his cigarette, moved his foot to crush the burning tip, coughed.

"I sure miss that old boy," he said, and I knew he was speaking of Arthur.

"Me, too," I replied.

"Makes you wonder, don't it?"

"About what, Preacher?"

"Why would God take a good man like that, and leave trash like us here?"

"I don't know," I answered.

He reached into his pocket and pulled out an empty cigarette package. "Makes you wonder, don't it?" he repeated, crushing the empty package in his fist.

I took my wallet from my pocket and fished ten dollars from it and gave it to him, saying it was a little Christmas present.

He nodded his appreciation and his eyes welled up in tears.

"Nights like this, I miss my wife," he said softly. "Nights like this, curling up beside her was about as good as it ever got. Cold outside, warm inside. Used to be, when we was young, she couldn't go to sleep until she'd touched me and said she loved me. Night she stopped doing that was the night everything changed. Since that time, I just been getting by." He rolled the cigarette in his fingers, gazing at it. "Just getting by don't leave much time for nothing else," he added.

In the Castle, Carrie and Gerty and Wendell were decorating a tall Christmas tree, a spruce. Lady sat in her chair, watching, her eyes wandering in bewilderment over the dangling ornaments and the tangle of white lights weaving across limbs. A scent of hot cider, spiced with cloves and cinnamon sticks, was strong in the room. Christmas music played from the radio – spirited, catchy tunes made for sing-alongs or humming.

As it had been for the two previous Christmases we spent together, Leo was being ragged about refusing to help with the tree decorations. He protested, as he always did, that he was Jewish and Jews did not kill the forests of the world to celebrate the madness of going in debt for gifts that were mostly worthless after the opening of them. Yet it had always been Leo who appeared with the tree, vowing it had been thrust on him by vendors trying to rid themselves of their overstock. I suspected different. I suspected Leo could not resist lifting a prize so obvious when the vendor had his back turned.

After the final decoration had been placed, we sat and had spiced tea and made rambling talk, trying to avoid the mention of Arthur.

It was impossible.

Gerty was the first to break. She said, without using his name, "I wish he was here with us." The room became silent, except for the music, which had been turned low by Carrie.

"Maybe we'd better not talk about it," I suggested.

"We've got to sometime," Leo said. He pulled himself from his chair. "I'll be back in a minute," he added, and he crossed the floor of the warehouse to his closet of collections. We watched as he unlocked the door and reached inside and removed a large, black garbage bag. He closed and locked the door, then crossed back to us.

"I was supposed to wait for Christmas, but now's the right time, far as I'm concerned," he said. He opened the bag and began to take wrapped boxes from it. "These are from Arthur. He had me hide them, and before you wonder about it, we agreed not to do gifts for one another, being Jewish. It's your holiday, not ours."

He passed out boxes to everyone except me.

"Go on and open them," he said.

I looked at Carrie and Gerty. Both were weeping shamelessly.

I remember each gift.

For Wendell, it was a pocket watch, inscribed with the word, *Champ*.

For Gerty, it was a necklace of white gold with a black onyx setting. Its inscription read, *Beauty*.

For Carrie, it was a silver drawing pen, having the word *Gifted* on its stem.

For Lady, it was a butterfly mounted on a stand of cut glass. The butterfly's wings were made of yellow stained glass, outlined in silver. Cut into the glass stand were the words, *Flight of Joy*.

And when the opening of the boxes was finished, the gifts found and cried over, Leo said to me, "Hamby, Arthur was going to hand your gift to you." He paused, swallowed hard. "He can't, so I will." He reached into the bag and took out Arthur's brown felt hat and presented it to me.

A chill rushed through me and I swallowed to hold back the tears that I could feel pooling in my throat. I turned the hat upside down in my hands. Inside the crown, in the sweatband, was a twenty-dollar bill. I laughed – the kind of a laugh a man makes when sorrow is unbearable. Hard. Sharp. Painful. And then I began to sob. And no one knew why.

EPILOGUE

I wish I could say we all lived happily ever after, as they do in nighttime stories for children, and that the presence of Arthur – Maker of Paper Flowers, King of the Situation – was as lasting and as magical as that of the legendary Arthur of the Round Table.

I would like to boast that Savannah became Camelot, but it did not. It did not lose its beauty and the awe of its grandness, but it was a city built of steel and brick, wood and plastic, not one puffed up by gods of imagination.

Truth is, the only thing that the reigns of the two Arthurs had in common was a line from the *Camelot* musical: "*...for one brief shining moment...*"

That is what it was with us – a brief, shining moment too quickly put aside.

It was like the parades on St. Patrick's Day that my mother had loved, but knew was only pretend merriment. Ump-pah-pah, ump-pah-pah, and then silence.

But silence is filled with echoes of memory.

Arthur wandered into our lives those many years ago, and managed to charm us and to baffle us and to rally us, and then he was gone and things became as they had always been for the likes of us, or the likes of what we had once been. The muggers and the drug-pushers and the hookers took to the streets again, and though some went about things in a gentler way because of their memory of Arthur, many of them continued to find their pleasure in meanness, not much caring who got hurt in the goings-on.

One of them killed Preacher. Slit his throat, then propped his body against a tree, with his legs spread out to keep him from toppling. He was holding his Bible in his lap, his forefinger stuck as a bookmark in the Gospel according to Saint Matthew. A braided crown of briars had been jammed down over his forehead in mockery. A policeman described Preacher's corpse as having the look of a diseased Jesus, and it seemed to me an apt description. Thinking about it, it must have been the way Preacher felt in those weak, mournful moments that racked his soul.

The politics of the city did improve for a short, deceiving time, yet none of us truly believed that what had happened would bring about a new civilization. Those of us who had been street people knew something about promises, and we knew the politicians of old would gradually return, dressed in different outfits and calling themselves by different names, and sooner or later, they would taste the sweet, intoxicating nectar of greed, and they would drink their fill of it until another voice of reason came whispering, or bellowing, for change. History is written in the blood-ink of promises.

Yet, those of us who were known as Lady's Guests have enjoyed life found only in sentimental soap operas – compared to what we had known in the time of the Castle, I mean.

As for me, I have learned to take things as they are, though I still spend more than a reasonable amount of time in the escape of dreams. I'm Irish. I cannot wholly exorcise the melancholy. There are times, when I am alone, that I remove Arthur's cape from my closet and drape it across my shoulders, and then I take the brown felt hat and fit it on my head, and I stand in front of the mirror and look for Arthur in the image. He is never there, of course. There is no magic in any of it, nothing to call him back, just as there was no magic in an oak twig magician's wand to call back my father from his wandering ways.

Still, I am proud to wear the cape and the hat, even in private.

The cape was given to me in Arthur's will, a thank-you as he described it to Fuller Bishop during the dictation of how his goods were to be dispersed. If I had not met him at the Greyhound station on the day of his arrival, he would never have known us, he told Fuller. That act of fate had given him the joy he always wanted.

He also left the contents of his suitcase and the deed to the Castle in my caring, with instructions to use both for the benefit of Lady's needs. When the suitcase was opened in the presence of Fuller and Lady and Leo and Carrie and Gerty and Wendell, we were stunned to find more than four hundred thousand dollars in it, divided in envelopes containing bills in the denominations of twenties and fifties and hundreds. A short note gave credit for the money to a settlement for his ten percent ownership in Solomon's Furniture, where he had spent a career in the monotony of an arranged life.

I did with it as Arthur wished – after agreement with the others on Lady's select Guest list. I used a portion of the money to buy antiques from England and Ireland and to open a shop in the Castle that we call Lady's Tea Room. It is a joint venture Leo and I manage for all of us, and with Leo's financial wizardry keeping us from foolishness, it has been profitable enough to provide for Lady's care in an assisted living home and to afford Leo and me daily employment with a decent income. Carrie occasionally brings Lady to visit with us, but she has no strong memory of living in the Castle, no memory of our names or faces. Still, her favorite place is her old room, now set aside for displays of teacups.

Though we have joint ownership of the Castle, none of us live in it. The zoning board corrected the variance that provided a place of pleasure for those in high places in that long-ago time. It is now officially a commercial facility.

I am with Holly in a larger apartment, married now for two years. She no longer works in Frank's Fine Dining, but is in training to become a paralegal. I am not sure I will survive the righteousness of her resolve.

Leo has a small apartment near the Castle. Gerty and Wendell did move to Charleston and Wendell became a boxing coach for young men needing someone to keep them on track. He has twice been honored for his work. They visit often, or we will drive to Charleston to have the kind of happy reunion close families have. Wendell still wants to marry Gerty. Gerty still refuses. Living together is good enough for her. She knows about the sorry nature of men, she vows. If you can't walk out on them, sooner or later, they'll walk out on you.

Carrie was with Cary and Rachel Wilson until completing her study in art at SCAD, moving from caricatures to oil paintings. Her first major canvas, a shadowy rendering of Arthur in his cape – Arthur holding a bright red flower – hangs in Frank's Fine Dining. Frank tells tales of awed customers offering thousands of dollars for it. It is a lie, but one of such sweetness we all repeat it. All has worked well for Carrie. She now has her own apartment and is engaged to an artist who teaches sculpture at SCAD. She tells us she will not marry him until he agrees to create the likeness of Arthur in bronze, a full-size rendering, a cape over his shoulders, and offer it as a gift to the city. There is a rumor that it is near finished.

I do not know about Wally. A few weeks after Arthur's death, he moved back to Delaware to be with his frisky, independent daughter, who had given birth to twins and, as a single mother, needed her father. In the few calls he made to us, he seemed content enough, though he did admit it had been a trying adjustment not having us, or Frank's Fine Dining, or Melody, to occupy his time. He also said he had been working on a paper about Arthur. The title he had for it was *The Last Domino*. It is my guess that the title is all he has written, or will ever write. For people like Wally, it is faster and easier to say words than to write them.

Still, the thought of Wally sticks with me. I learned a lot from him. Confidence, for one thing. Certainly, I learned confidence, for he was as confident as any person I have known. I also learned the power of bravery and the willingness to stand and be counted. And I learned that laughter was good and that curiosity was as intoxicating as strong drink.

Yet, the most lasting and important thing taken from Wally's presence was the passion of his anger over mistreatment of people who simply got caught in the camouflaged traps of living.

It was why those of us in the Castle mattered to him, and it was why he could not temper his great aching for his once-upon-a-time artist friend, the one callously fired on the night he was arranging the burial of his mother. It has stayed with me that Wally's bitterness had nothing to do with his friend's termination. It was about the disregard for the life of his friend's mother, and when I think of it – which is often – I have a tugging to be at the burial spot of my own mother. People who do not ache for the dying of mothers, who do not pause in honor of them when they leave this world, do not deserve to be cared for. It is a rage that feeds the insatiable hunger I have for justice – or, perhaps, it's more revenge than justice, the two being close enough kin to keep the quarrel over them at high pitch. Whichever it is, I am pleased to know that it's in me.

Holly tells me I have changed since Arthur's death, that I have matured into a reasonable imitation of a sensible man. It is both a compliment and a complaint. She hounds me not to become as boring as the stuffed shirts who habitually slipped into Frank's Fine Dining looking for a few moments of reprieve, yet she wants me to be regarded as a man with purpose. It means I am to keep my gaze on the now and the morrow, and to put aside my meandering ways. She warns that she will not tolerate a man with an itch for wandering.

Still, the wandering is part of me, and there are days when the sweet-sad melancholy of my soul beckons me back to the bus station, and I stand watching travelers in their arriving and leaving, letting my imagination give them the adventure of temporary names and lives. They do not know I have made of them Olympic athletes and movie stars, giants of industry and music celebrities, Nobel Prize scientists and artists as grand as Cezanne and Da Vinci. If I told them, they would laugh at me.

Yet, I could tell them of a man who once arrived in Savannah on a Greyhound bus, wearing a wrinkled brown suit and a brown felt hat, looking lost, a man who spent his first two minutes in the city being bullied about and burgled, only to become the defender of a Castle.

If they would ask me how this came to be, I would tell them the truth as I believe it: Arthur Benjamin was meant to change the world, if not in whole, then in some small space of it, and if not forever, then in some remembered moment that made a difference for those of us who stood in his presence.

It is why I go again to the bus station on days made of wonder and wishes.

For I have seen a king step from a Greyhound.